Saturdays at Noon

RACHEL MARKS

PENGUIN BOOKS

PENGUIN BOOKS

UK | USA | Canada | Ireland | Australia
India | New Zealand | South Africa

Penguin Books is part of the Penguin Random House group of companies
whose addresses can be found at global.penguinrandomhouse.com.

First published 2020
001

Copyright © Rachel Marks, 2020

The moral right of the author has been asserted

Set in 12.5/14.75 pt Garamond MT Std
Typeset by Jouve (UK), Milton Keynes
Printed and bound in Great Britain by Clays Ltd, Elcograf S.p.A.

A CIP catalogue record for this book is available from the British Library

ISBN: 978–1–405–94007–8

For Jacob, so you always know how magic you are

Alfie

I hope none of the grown-ups out there find me. I used my invisible spell to sneak under the table but I'm scared it might wear off. Sometimes, if I don't make my spells very well, they don't last very long. I still have to be really quiet because, even when you're invisible, people can hear you. Mrs Young says, 'Be quiet as a mouse,' but when there was a mouse in Mummy and Daddy's bedroom they said it was so noisy, scratching and running around, that they couldn't sleep, so I don't think mice are very quiet really. I'm going to be quieter than a mouse and try really hard not to move. But sometimes my arms and legs just move on their own without me telling them to. Mummy and Daddy get cross faces when they do that, but I don't know how to make them stop.

It's really dark under here, like when I go to bed. I hate going to bed because I have to stop what I'm doing and I'm scared when it's dark a robber will break in and steal me. When I'm busy with my Lego or my puzzles or my games, they fill up my head, but when Daddy makes me stop and go to bed, the worries come back because there's more space. If I had my pebble light, it would be better. I like watching the colours – they go round and round, and I don't feel so terrified. My pebble lamp goes red, purple, blue, green, yellow, orange then back to red and it does the same pattern every time, which is good because then you know which colour is coming next. I like knowing which one's coming next.

Emily

To tell you the truth, it's not quite what I'd expected. I had visions of hung heads, clenched fists, swear words muttered through gritted teeth. Instead, there's an elderly man tackling a crossword, a woman crocheting what looks to be a mobile-phone cosy and a pair of middle-aged men chatting away merrily about the amazing bread peacock they saw on this week's *Bake Off*. I re-check the venue details on the letter scrunched up in my coat pocket. Anger management? It feels more like games afternoon at a dingy social club.

The irony is I probably look exactly like I belong in anger management: newly shaved head, hoody, chewing gum like an insolent teenager. It's like I've come in character. But I shouldn't be here. It's a joke. I didn't do anything wrong.

To avoid having to engage in small talk with a bunch of people I've never met, I head over to the canteen-style table in the corner. There's a dent in the wall behind it and I wonder, with a flicker of anticipation, whether it was caused by an irate fist or a hurled mug. Perhaps things are going to get a little more exciting after all.

I make a coffee, piling in the sugar, and loosen the lid of the biscuit tin. It's a meagre selection. A few digestives, an abundance of the blandest biscuit in the world – the Rich Tea – and two chocolate Bourbons. It's not really a choice. I take out a Bourbon, dunk it in my coffee and, great, lose most of it as it disintegrates and sinks to the bottom of the cup. What I really need is a bacon butty, something substantial enough to soak up some of the excess alcohol currently circulating through my veins, but beggars can't be choosers, I guess.

As I look down to check that my jeans aren't embarrassingly hoicked up over my socks, I notice two small shoes sticking out from under the table. They're bright blue with dinosaurs embossed on the side. Crouching down, I lift the tablecloth to be met by the eyes of a little boy, his eyebrows comically furrowed.

'Hey, are you OK down there?'

The boy, who must be only about five, studies me as if reading the words on a page but doesn't speak. Then he buries his face in his knees and covers his head with his arms. I'm only being nice. Surely my face isn't that off-putting? I scan the room to see if he belongs to anyone but, unless they've simply forgotten that their child exists, there are no obvious claimants so I try again.

'Shall we go and find your mum or dad?'

Tentatively, the boy uncovers one eye and peers out at me, then shakes his head, so, using the only strategy I know to successfully communicate with children, I reach up on to the table, locate the biscuit tin and hold it out to him.

'Want one?'

The boy eyes me suspiciously, then examines the selection before taking out the last Bourbon.

'Good choice. Go on, take another one, if you want.'

He looks at me as if he suspects it might be a trick, then slowly picks out a digestive. I can't exactly leave him sitting on his own and I'm in no hurry to join the adults in the room, so I squeeze under the table and position myself next to him. The cramped dark spot turns out to be strangely appealing, like returning to the womb. Perhaps no one would notice if I spent the whole session down here.

For a short time, we both tuck into our sugary snacks, the little boy looking over at me occasionally but still not saying a word. I'm not really sure what kids like to talk about anyway, so I'm happy to adopt the silence. Then, suddenly, there's the sound of the door slamming shut and a man's voice, breathless and panicked.

'Alfie? Alfie, are you in here? Anyone seen a little boy?'

I slither out from underneath the table and stand up. 'He's here.'

A man and a woman run over, looking like they've just escaped from the pages of *Tatler*, him in his woollen pea-coat and her in her Burberry mac. They *definitely* don't look like they belong here.

'Where is he?' The man looks at me accusingly, like he thinks I'm just pretending to have found his son as some kind of sick prank.

'He's under the table.'

Clearly devoid of manners (I guess money can't buy you everything), he practically pushes me out of the way before he bends down, grabs the boy's hand and pulls him out from under the table. The woman looks on expressionless, evidently not surprised to see her husband being so obnoxious.

'What were you thinking, running off like that? We were so worried about you. Do you understand that, Alfie? We were terrified. Anything could've happened to you.'

The man glances at me as if his son being found by

4

someone who looks like me is near the top of his list of feared outcomes.

The little boy crosses his arms and turns his head away from his dad. 'You and Mummy were shouting.'

'We were not shouting. Anyway, that's no excuse. You know you should never go where we can't see you.'

Alfie glares at his dad and then lifts the digestive to his mouth in an unmistakable act of rebellion.

'Give me that.' The man grabs the remains of the boy's biscuit out of his hand and, in what turns out to be an extremely unwise decision, throws it in the bin at the end of the table.

Well, it's like a switch being flipped. The once silent boy starts screaming, at an incomprehensible volume given his small stature, and pummels his dad's thigh like it's a punching bag.

The dad holds his son's arms by his sides. 'Alfie, be quiet. You can't scream in here.'

'Come on, Jake. Let's just take him out,' the woman says in a hushed voice. 'Everyone's staring.'

The man surveys the circle of chairs, then looks at me before finally turning to his wife. 'And that's my fault, is it?'

The boy refuses to walk of his own accord so his dad pulls him along with his feet dragging on the floor and bundles him out the door while the woman hurries behind, her eyes glued to her expensive leather boots.

As they exit, a man strolls in carrying a folder. From his authoritative presence, I guess he's the group leader. He has dreadlocks down his back and his clothes look like they belong to someone twice his size. I pick up my coffee, now offensively cold and laced with remnants of Bourbon, and join the circle, locating the final three empty chairs and purposefully sitting on the middle one.

The elderly gentlemen who was doing the crossword puts it aside, leans across the empty seat and holds out his hand. 'My name's Bill. Welcome to the group.' As he speaks, his eyes emit such kindness I can't imagine him ever saying a cross word to anybody.

'Thanks.' I shake his hand. It always feels uncomfortable – a gesture more befitting a bygone era. Then there's a pause during which he doesn't look away – an implied expectation for me to offer more – but I'm not sure what 'more' he's looking for.

'And you are?'

'Oh, sorry. I'm Emily.'

He nods, raising his eyebrows in a playful expression that strips years from his face. 'Ah, my granddaughter's called Emily. I hope you're nothing like her, though. She's a pain in the backside, to be honest with you.' He laughs and I smile awkwardly, looking down in the hope that will end the conversation. 'Well, it's lovely to have you here, Emily.'

When I glance up to acknowledge his comment, I notice someone surveying me from across the room. It's a woman in her forties. Clutching her imitation Prada bag and wearing shiny black patent heels, she brazenly looks down her nose at me. Women like that always do. Unfortunately for her, her low-budget hairdresser has gone for a slightly cheap-looking shade of red and her manicured fingernails are just that bit too long. Try as she might to disguise it, it's obvious she's from the same side of town as me. In fact, she looks a lot like my mum, which just makes me dislike her more.

'Good afternoon, everyone.' The group leader flashes perfectly straight white teeth, contrasting with his short black beard.

'Good afternoon,' the group responds in school-assembly-style unison.

'Before we start today's session, I just want to welcome a couple of new members to the group. They will be joining us until the end of this term, and beyond, of course, if they would like to.'

No, thank you, I'd rather do an Aron Ralston and get my arm trapped by a boulder for 127 hours.

Much to my embarrassment, he gestures towards me and all eyes turn in my direction. Then he looks around, searching for someone else. As he does so, the little boy's dad walks back in, holding up his hands in apology.

'Sorry I'm late,' he whispers, walking through the centre of the circle.

Unfortunately, the only empty spaces are next to me. He removes his posh coat, hangs it on the back of a chair and sits down. I shuffle away from him, my chair betraying me by squeaking against the floor.

'Not a problem, Jake. There's tea and coffee over there if you want to grab one in a minute. There might even be a biscuit if you're lucky and these gannets haven't eaten them all. Anyway, everyone, say hello to Emily and Jake.'

'Hello,' the group choruses.

My face starts to burn and I sink into my chair. It's like my first day at grammar school. Walking into the form room, worrying whether the heels of my shoes were high enough, if my skirt was the right length. Trying to disguise the rip in my second-hand blazer by wrapping my arms around my waist.

I don't say anything but offer a please-stop-staring-at-me twitch of the lips, then look down at my hands; the skin around my nails is dry and sore.

Jake runs his hand through his exceptionally healthy-looking hair. 'Nice to meet you all.'

'Don't worry, I'm not going to ask you to say anything about yourselves just yet, but I wanted to welcome you into the group. My name is Sam, by the way.'

Sam has the perfect smile for someone whose job it is to maintain the calm of inherently pissed-off people. It's warm and uplifting and I wonder if he's developed it over time, practised it in the mirror, or if he's just one of those irritatingly happy people who see the positive in everything. *Lost your job? It's the perfect chance to follow your dream! Car got stolen? Think of the health benefits!* I've never understood it, myself. My counsellor once suggested that my 'life experiences' – what a great term that is – have skewed my view of the world, but I'm not convinced. I'm just a realist. Statistically, most marriages end. Most people work nine-to-five dead-end jobs that they hate, go home to houses that they'll never be able to afford to buy, watch television programmes that don't really interest them and then go to sleep, repeating the process until whatever ailment the Fates decide upon ends it. It's like when my foster mum told me she had terminal cancer. I was heartbroken but, at the same time, there was a familiar inevitability to it. Of course the one adult who'd ever really cared about me was going to be taken away.

It dawns on me, sitting here, that Sam's is the kind of smile that makes me want to make a Sam effigy and stay up at night sticking pins into it.

Maybe I am in the right place after all.

Sam brings out a triangle and taps it. All at once, the group close their eyes, bow their heads and put their hands together in what looks like prayer. I'm not sure if my ears are deceiving me but I'm pretty sure some of them are actually emitting a low hum. They're a few steps away from getting on the floor and launching into the downward bloody dog.

After a few moments, Sam hits the triangle again and they all look up, like they've come out of hypnosis.

'Now that we are all feeling centred and mentally and emotionally open, we shall begin. Please greet the person next to you. For our newbies, we make a declaration. Heather, Sharon, would you care to demonstrate?'

Miss Hoity-Toity, the one who was eyeing me up earlier, sits tall in her chair, clearly revelling in taking centre stage. 'Of course.'

'Thank you, Sharon.'

Her partner, a timid-looking woman with hair like black candyfloss, looks less sure, her head scanning from side to side as if she's hoping there's someone else in the room called Heather. But, with a sinking of the shoulders, she seems to accept there isn't and takes hold of her partner's outstretched hands.

Predictably, Sharon speaks first, announcing her declaration theatrically. 'I promise to listen without judgement and to be honest to myself and to you.'

Heather repeats the line quietly, then they let go of each other's hands.

After that, excruciatingly, we're all expected to do the same. Jake rubs his palms on his jeans, turns to me and holds out his hands. I keep mine tucked firmly under my legs.

'Look,' he says through gritted teeth, 'I don't want to do this either, but we've got no choice. Sam's watching us.'

I glance over at Sam and he looks away, pretending he hasn't clocked my rebellion. Poor guy's got his work cut out with me.

Seeming to accept I'm not going to hold his hands any time this millennium, Jake drops his, then says, loudly enough for Sam to hear, 'I promise to listen without judgement and to be honest to myself and to you.'

I chew the skin around my thumbnail. 'What you said.'

'OK, everyone,' Sam says. 'Great. So the talking point for your pairs today is key triggers. Things that really set off your anger. It doesn't have to be the big stuff – just anything that you know really riles you. Try to make a list, then we'll share with the group. Because remember –' and here the whole group joins in with him – 'it is not until we understand ourselves better that we can heal ourselves.'

Sam sweeps his hands out in front of him like a priest delivering a sermon and the group respond with a uniform bow. It feels like I've accidentally walked into some kind of cult.

'You want to go first?' Jake holds out the pen and paper we've been provided with.

I take it and write, voicing my words aloud. 'My main trigger is being forced to sit in classes that I do not effing belong in, discussing an anger problem that I don't actually have.'

Jake raises his eyebrows. 'You sure you don't have an anger problem?'

He laughs, smugness striding across his lips.

I smile in a way that shows him I'm not amused. 'I'm

sure. You, on the other hand . . .' I stop and leave him to fill in the blanks.

'What?'

'Well, it's pretty clear why you're here.'

'What do you mean by that?'

I bite my tongue. I'm not sure getting into an altercation at the class I've been sent to supposedly to curb such behaviour is in my best interests. 'Nothing. Doesn't matter.'

'No, go on. Tell me why you think I'm here. I'm fascinated.'

Arrogant prick.

'Well, if you really want to know, I saw how rough you were with your little boy. No wonder he ran away. Your wife looked scared shitless too. It doesn't take a genius, does it?'

Jake exhales vociferously out of his nose, chin down, like a bull preparing to charge. 'I was not rough with my son. You think you know everything about me because you witnessed one incident? You haven't got a clue.'

I slip my hands into my pockets. 'You asked.'

'So how about you then, Little Miss Perfect? If you haven't got an anger problem, why are you here? Let me guess, you got lost on the way to teaching your parenting expertise class?'

'Yeah, something like that.'

'Come on. Didn't we just promise to be open and honest?'

I put my foot up on the chair and re-tie the lace of my boot. It's scuffed and dirty so I drop it back to the floor, irrationally feeling that not taking proper care of my footwear weakens my moral standpoint. 'It was either this or a prison sentence.'

I can tell from the way he starts to laugh and then stops

that he's not sure if I'm joking. I'm not going to clarify it for him.

He gestures to the piece of paper in my hand, his face almost pleading. 'Look, shouldn't we get some triggers written down?'

'Why? Scared you might get told off?'

The tinny sound of the triangle echoes around the hall and the group goes quiet.

'OK. Right then. Is there anyone who would like to share what they've got so far?'

A man on the opposite side of the circle raises his hand. He's in his fifties, stocky, and his skin is ruddy and weathered, like he works outside. He has a thin layer of greying stubble and eyelids so heavy-looking I imagine they'd be hard to see out from under.

'Tim, thank you.'

'Well, one of my triggers is my dog,' he says, clasping his hands behind his neck and leaning back. 'He's literally just there all the time. I get back from a hard day at work and he's under my feet, hassling me for attention when I just need time to breathe, and it drives me crazy.'

I laugh and everyone looks at me like I just let out a whoop of joy at a funeral. I genuinely thought he was joking, that he was one of those people who hide their true inner turmoil behind a veneer of tomfoolery. But witnessing the nodding heads and murmurs of agreement, I clearly misjudged the situation.

'My cat's exactly the same,' a tattoo-covered guy pipes up. 'As soon as I sit down to relax, he's crawling all over me, padding me, licking my face. It makes me want to launch him through the window.'

'Why have a pet then?' I say it under my breath but it's like they've all got supersonic hearing because, again, all eyes turn on me.

'Just because he winds me up doesn't mean I don't love the thing,' the cat-launcher retorts. 'My kids do my head in sometimes, but I'm still glad I've got them.'

His anger towards me seems to reflect the mood of the group. The session has not started well. Sam gives me a reassuring smile, underpinned with pity, and redirects the conversation to different triggers. There's an incredible variety. The misleading photographs on Tinder, people who ride horses on the road . . . the self-service checkouts at supermarkets get a particularly severe battering.

'It's my fucking neighbours,' Bill shouts, and I nearly jump out of my chair at the profanity being expelled with such venom from the mouth of this outwardly mild-mannered man. 'I'm not sure whether they're blind or just stupid. If the bin has 'fifty-five' written on it, it's mine, so stop filling it up with your stinking nappies. If they're not careful, they're going to find them scattered around their front garden when they wake up one morning.'

Well, I guess looks can be deceiving.

I glance up at the clock and, as it finally strikes one, I'm like a kid when the bell rings for playtime, automatically reaching for my bag underneath the chair.

Sam raises his hand. 'Just before you go, we do a quick breathing exercise. We have a list of calming phrases up on the board there to help you, but feel free to use any of your own. So, we all make sure we're sitting upright . . .'

The group sit up straight in their chairs. Already conditioned, Jake follows suit.

'We breathe deeply – from the diaphragm, not the chest. And then we slowly repeat our chosen phrase. Just keep repeating it while you breathe deeply for two minutes.'

Everyone else begins. I look up at the list of phrases on the board. *I'm in charge of my stress response. In every moment, peace is a choice. Stop and smell the roses.* I feel like either I'm losing the plot or Ashton Kutcher is about to jump out, flash his winning smile and shout 'Punk'd!'

I mutter, 'Only thirteen sessions to go, only thirteen sessions to go,' under my breath and wait for the two minutes to be up. It's like the hands of time have momentarily paused. Then there's the reverberation of the triangle, like angel song straight from heaven, and everyone gathers their belongings and goes on their way.

I swing my rucksack on to my shoulder and start to leave, but Jake holds out his hand as a barrier.

'I don't hit my son. Or my wife, for that matter.' He rocks from one foot to the other.

'It's really none of my business.'

'But I don't. I know it didn't look great, me grabbing my son like that, but it's complicated. He's . . .' He pauses like he's struggling to remember the word. 'Challenging. I get stressed out sometimes and it's "driving my wife away". Her words. So I agreed to give this a go.'

'OK. Well, I hope it works out for you.'

I'm not sure why he's being so insistent. Doth he protest too much? I don't really care. I just want to leave.

'Well, I'll see you next week,' I say.

Jake's head drops. 'Yeah, see you.'

Then I run out of there as fast as I can and don't look back.

Jake

I take a deep breath in and try to mentally locate a calming phrase, while Alfie lies at my feet screaming, bang in the middle of the self-service tills in Waitrose.

'I'm going to count to three and if you don't get yourself up off the floor and follow me out the door, I'm going to use your baseball bat to smash up each and every one of your Lego models.'

I crouch down and say it under my breath so that, hopefully, the people nearby won't hear me reaching this new parenting low.

Alfie doesn't even acknowledge what I've said. 'I want the cake with the red Smartie on it.'

'Well, it's yellow. Get over it. You're very lucky to have a cake at all.'

Spoilt brat.

'I want the red one. I want the red one.'

I place my card on the reader and pick up my shopping. Thanks to the fact I'm a stingy bastard and not willing to pay five pence for a plastic bag, I now have two boxes of Coco Pops, a four-pack of beer, a bottle of wine and a loaf of bread precariously tucked under both arms, a six-pint bottle of milk in one hand and a box containing a cake with a sodding yellow Smartie on it in the other. Therefore, my six-year-old son has me cornered. And he knows it. In fact, I'm pretty sure he's taking great pleasure in it.

I try a different approach. 'Please, Alfie. I'll find you a red Smartie at home and we'll swap it.'

Alfie shakes his head and kicks his legs. He knows I haven't got any Smarties at home. He could tell me every treat we have and its exact location in the kitchen.

A man in his sixties glares at Alfie and makes a show of having to step over him. As he does, one of Alfie's flailing legs catches his trailing foot and nearly sends him flying.

'I'm so sorry, mate. Are you OK?'

I want to reach out to him, but I have no free hands. He turns around and shakes his head slowly. His face looks like he's just found me parking in a disabled space.

'I'd have got the belt if I'd behaved like that. You shouldn't be pandering to him. You need to show him who's boss.'

I look at him for a minute, considering my response. The one that comes is not the one I planned. 'And you need to fuck off.'

He steps back, opens his mouth as if to speak and then closes it again. Then he turns and hurries out, with his shopping sensibly packed in a bag for life.

I know everyone is staring at me. I know they're thinking I'm a monster. They might just be right. Sometimes it feels like that's what I've become.

I put the shopping down on the floor next to my screaming son, tuck the beer and the cake box under one arm and pick Alfie up and hold him under the other, like a roll of carpet. Struggling to the car, I shove him in through the back door and slam it, welcoming the muting effect it has on his shrieks. After throwing my two salvaged bits of shopping into the boot, I lean up against it with my head in my hands, unable to face getting in.

'Excuse me.'

'What?' I snap.

I look up to see a young woman with a little girl gripping on to her leg, terrified by the ogre growling at her mummy. The woman holds out a bag of shopping and it takes me a minute to realize what it is.

'My little girl would be lost without her Coco Pops so I thought you might want this. Sorry to have disturbed you.'

I'm not sure if it's because she has a pretty face, or because this is probably the nicest thing anyone has done for me in a very long time, but I have a sudden desire to run off with this woman and never go home. To raise her cute, well-behaved little girl as if she were my own.

'Thanks. And sorry for snapping at you just then. I thought you were just another well-meaning member of the public coming to tell me what a terrible job I'm doing.'

She doesn't commit to a full smile. 'We've all been there. Take care.'

I want to cry, 'But you haven't been there. This isn't just an overtired tantrum. This is every day, about everything.' Instead, I watch her walk across the car park, her daughter skipping along beside her, obediently holding her hand, and then I get into the car with my son, who I know won't stop screaming about that bloody red Smartie for the entire fifteen-minute journey home.

* * *

'Can't you hear he's kicking off in there?'

'Yes, I can. Can you?'

Jemma sighs. 'Please, Jake. I've really got to finish this presentation.'

I'm not actually busy. I'm wasting precious minutes of my life scrolling through the inane stuff on my Facebook feed. How many motivational phrases can one person share in a day? One of my friends, or more accurately one of the people who is classed as my 'friend' on Facebook, must have shared over five riveting quotes every day this week. This morning's corker was: 'Make today count. You'll never get it back.' The irony makes me chuckle. I can just picture Tom sitting at his laptop, googling gems to share, really squeezing the life out of every moment.

I stand up to go and see what minor problem has riled Alfie this time, but not before making sure I have the last word.

'I have work to do too, you know? I've got to clean up all the stuff from the lunch I just cooked, then wash Alfie's uniform for tomorrow, then tidy all the mess he made earlier when I did painting with him, and then prepare something for our tea. People might not appreciate it, but I'm doing a "job" here too.'

I feel my balls shrink as I say it. I'm not quite sure how I got here. But here I am – a househusband. Whining about the dishes while my wife pays the bills. Don't get me wrong. I'm a modern man. I was always comfortable with the fact my wife earned more than me. It didn't threaten my masculinity that she paid more than half towards all our holidays or that quite often *she* would take *me* out for dinner. But now that I have nothing to bring to the table, I can't help but feel inadequate using Jemma's money to pay for a round on the rare occasion I go out with my mates. I hate that the most exciting thing I have to share with her these days is that bio washing liquid is so much more effective at getting off those hard-to-tackle stains than the non-bio stuff she always used. I wish I could still treat her occasionally, surprise her.

Before we have the chance to rehash this daily argument, Alfie comes running in. His eyes are still red from all the tears he cried earlier, but he's calmed down. For now.

'I need help, Daddy. Why aren't you coming?'

Because I'm not your bitch.

'I am, son. I'm coming now.'

Alfie pulls my arm, dragging me into the lounge, and my heart sinks at the minuscule pieces spread out on the floor. I hate jigsaw puzzles. I'll fight with foam swords and shields until the cows come home. I'm happy to read stories. To draw superheroes to be coloured in. But puzzles . . . just looking at them makes me break out in a cold sweat. And Alfie is a puzzle genius. He was completing hundred-piece ones with ease aged four.

'Do we have to do a puzzle?'

'You should be encouraging him,' Jemma calls through from the other room. 'It's better than him playing that rubbish with you on the Xbox.'

Because you're providing him with an abundance of valuable play experiences.

'Yeah, I suppose you're right, darling.'

Alfie quickly and efficiently picks out the edge pieces and starts to construct the sides of the puzzle. Once all four are done, he holds out his hands, as if to say ta-da.

'Good job, Alfie. You're so much better at this than me.'

'Just keep trying, Daddy. You'll get there.'

I smile at one of my many trite pearls of wisdom being reflected back at me. 'Thanks, little man.'

'And you're really good at making up superhero stories. Everyone is good at different things.'

I ruffle Alfie's hair. 'You're getting so wise in your old age.'

Alfie screws up his face. 'I'm only six.'

I laugh. 'You're right. You are. And already wiser than me.'

Alfie powers on, slotting in the middle pieces like a puzzle ninja, while I desperately search the floor for anything that looks vaguely like it might fit. After a minute or so, I spot part of the monster's face and position it in the correct place. I'm pretty chuffed with myself. That is until Alfie explodes, launching the box across the room.

'What's the problem now, Alfie?'

He tries to say something through the mass of tears.

'Calm down. Use your words.'

'You did my bit. I do the monsters.'

'Will you just chill out? I only put one piece of puzzle in. It's not that big a deal.'

Alfie sweeps all the puzzle pieces across the floor.

'Fine.' I stand up and throw the piece I'm holding and it inadvertently hits him. 'Do it your bloody self.'

People used to marvel at my relaxed demeanour. *You're so laid-back you're almost horizontal.* I was the guy who would leave my A-level marking until 9 p.m. the night before the results were due but never sweat about not finishing it in time. I'd pack my stuff for a holiday on the morning of the flight, despite the fact Jemma had started packing hers at least a week before.

But there is something about the utterly illogical behaviour of my son that makes me want to either throw something through a window or jump in my car and drive. To the sea. To the mountains. Anywhere things make sense.

Because my son does not make sense.

Not one bit.

Alfie attaches himself to my ankle to hold me back. 'Please, Daddy. Please don't go.'

I'm so sick of always ending up the bad guy. It feels like whatever I try, I get it wrong. I treat Alfie to a cake – it's got the wrong colour Smartie on it. I help him with his puzzle – I do the wrong bit. I can never win. And failing every day takes its toll. Especially when it feels like I'm doing it all alone.

I pull my leg free and storm into the dining room. 'You fancy helping out at all?'

'Oh, Jake. Give it a rest. I haven't got time to get involved in your silly fights with Alfie. Just do the right pieces of the puzzle next time.'

'Are you serious?'

Jemma breathes out through her nostrils. 'I've got a deadline, Jake. You need to deal with this.'

'I *am* dealing with it. Every fricking day, I'm dealing with it.'

Jemma shakes her head, like talking to me is an inconvenience she could do without, the extra car that pulls out when you're already stuck in traffic. Picking up her laptop, she walks past me to go upstairs. I know that she will now remain in the study until I call her down for tea and it takes immense self-control not to take her a coffee and 'accidentally' spill it over the keys.

When I put my head round the door of the lounge, Alfie has stopped crying. He is kneeling right in front of the television, his face almost touching the screen, watching his favourite episode of *Spider-Man*. He knows it so well that he mouths all the words and laughs before the funny thing has happened. For a moment, I want to pick him up and cradle him like I did when he was a baby, but then I look around to see the room is trashed. All the puzzle pieces are scattered across the floor, beneath the sofa, under the TV unit. The sofa cushions have been catapulted across the room and a drink has been knocked over on the hearth. Jemma would flip her lid if she saw the mess he's made of her pristinely organized living room.

'What have you done, Alfie?'

Alfie looks up at me and covers his ears. 'I'm not your friend, Daddy.'

'Good. I don't want to be your friend. Now, you need to tidy this mess up or no bedtime story tonight.'

As threats go, it's weak, but tiredness does nothing for my ingenuity. He has snot streaming across his face and his eyes are swollen from the earlier onslaught of tears. I know I should feel some kind of sympathy for my son, but at this moment I just want to run and hide.

'And no more TV for a week.' That's better. Hit 'em where it hurts. I pick up the television controller and turn *Spider-Man* off, then, like *I'm* the child in the relationship, stomp up to my bedroom and slam the door, ignoring Alfie's protests.

When we first realized our bedroom door jammed and would only open with an almighty shove, Jemma put fixing it on the list of things for me to do. But now I'm glad nothing on that list ever gets done, because our bedroom has become my sanctuary. I used to find peace out in the ocean, gliding across a wave on my surfboard. Or flying down a mountain surrounded by white powder under intense blue skies. Now I have my bedroom. And a pillow to clasp tightly over my head. I can still hear Alfie on the other side of the door, kicking it and shouting my name, but it's muffled and there's a peace in knowing whatever he does, he can't get in.

I know that soon I will have to come out. I'll apologize to Alfie, help him tidy the lounge and then do his puzzle with him, avoiding any parts of the monster. I will cook the tea, salmon because it's Jemma's favourite. I'll ask her how her presentation is going and be supportive when she responds. I will. Just not yet. I'm not ready yet.

* * *

I'm on the home straight. Alfie is bathed, his pyjamas are on, his story has been read. There's a feeling in my chest and it's best described as elation.

'Can you put my lava lamp on please, Daddy?'

I switch it on.

'And my pebble light.'

'I know, buddy.'

'Don't forget to turn them off when I've fallen asleep.'

Alfie never stops and he notices every infraction. Just being with him exhausts me. What it must be like living in his head twenty-four hours a day, I dread to think.

'I won't.'

'And don't move my Lego figures off the windowsill.'

'I'm not that crazy, Alfie.'

As soon as I say it, I wish I hadn't, because I know it'll spark another long tirade of questions. Alfie doesn't do well with turns of phrase.

'What?'

'Don't worry.'

'What do you mean you're not crazy?'

'Don't worry, little man. I was being silly. I won't touch your Lego figures, I promise.'

'Perhaps I should move them. I think I'll put them in my box.'

Alfie starts to get up.

'It's fine.' I sit beside him. 'No one will touch them.'

'But . . .'

'Alfie, you're tired. Leave them.' I rest my hand on his tummy.

Alfie lies quietly for a minute, but his eyes are darting back and forth so I know there are more questions to come. I'm not over the finish line just yet.

'Daddy, "bloody" is a naughty word, isn't it?'

'Yes, I'm sorry. I just got cross.'

'My teacher told me.'

A wave of panic rushes over me. 'What do you mean, your teacher told you?'

Alfie's cheeks flush. 'I said it to another boy.'

'What?' I don't mean to shout it but, despite my earlier lapse, we are not *that* family.

'I thought it was something you said when you wanted someone to do something. To show them you meant it. I told him it was time to tidy up and that he needed to put the balls away in the shed. He didn't listen, even though I told him lots of times, so I said, "Put the bloody balls away," and he ran off saying, "I'm telling."'

I want to put my little boy in a cocoon and never let him break out.

'So what did the teacher say to you?'

'She said, "Did you say the b-word?" so I said, "What b-word? Bloody or balls?" and she got really cross and told me to stop being so cheeky and that it was not OK to use that language.'

'Oh, Alfie.' I run my hand through my son's hair. I can just picture him, all big brown eyes and serious expression, shifting his weight from one foot to the other, completely unaware of what he was doing wrong. 'Why didn't they talk to me about this?'

'It was the day Mummy got me, so they talked to her.'

I nod slowly, careful not to show Alfie the volcano of irritation bubbling inside me.

'Well, you know now not to use that word, OK? And Daddy will try his very best not to use it too.'

'I wasn't being naughty.'

'I know you weren't.' I kiss him on the forehead. 'Now get some sleep.'

'I'm just going to put my Lego figures in my box.'

I know it will take longer to argue than to just let him do it. 'OK. Quick.'

'I will be, Daddy. By the time you count to ten, I'll be back in bed.'

'Night-night, little man. Love you.'

'Love you too.'

I adopt my nightly position, sitting at the end of his bed with my laptop on my knee, the voice of the health visitor tapping away on the inside of my skull. *They need to learn to settle themselves. Let them cry it out.* Except Alfie doesn't cry it out. He didn't when we tried it at four months, when he was waking every hour and a half and Jemma had begun to look like she belonged in *One Flew Over the Cuckoo's Nest*, or at a year, when it *really was time for him to be sleeping on his own*, or at age three, when he moved into a 'big boy' bed. If you left him to cry it out, he would wail until we were drawing a pension. So, eventually, we gave up and one of us, usually me, sits with him each night until he falls asleep, the resentment slowly eating into my bones.

'Daddy . . .'

'Go to sleep.'

'But, Daddy, it's important.'

'No, it's not. Go to sleep.'

'In the morning, can I watch *Spider-Man* before school?'

'Only if you go to sleep.'

'I'm thirsty.'

Having root canal work would be more pleasurable than this. I get up and pass him a drink.

'Now sleep.'

'I don't know how.'

'Just close your eyes. Think about something nice.'

'But that keeps me awake.'

'So don't think of anything at all.'

'My eyes won't close.'

I reach over and gently push his eyelids closed. 'There. Now if you say another word, I'm going.'

'But, Daddy . . .'

I get up to leave the room.

'OK, I'll try my best to go to sleep.'

It doesn't matter how much we've tried to exhaust him during the day, getting Alfie to sleep is always a complete nightmare. We've tried everything. When he was a baby, we went through what I now call the 'white noise' period of our lives, existing to a soundtrack of an untuned radio.

After that, we tried child mediation CDs, but Alfie got so swept up in the 'relaxing' adventures it woke him up even more. Audiobooks failed for the same reason. Whale song just prompted a load of questions – *what are the whales singing and where did they learn the songs from anyway, because CD players don't work under the water?* We even bought a book that had hundreds of five-star Amazon reviews saying it was a miracle cure for insomniac children, but I read it night after night (and it was long and tedious) and, every time, I'd keep glancing over at Alfie excitedly to see if it had worked and, every time, we'd reach the last page with him bright-eyed and bushy-tailed.

I sit back down and open up Facebook on my laptop. It tells me that my best friend from university has just posted thirty-three photographs of his latest trip to Venezuela. I click on the down arrow at the top of his post and choose 'unfollow Martin', feeling a deep sense of satisfaction as the arty shots of him drinking Polar with the locals disappear into the digital abyss.

After several more attempts to initiate conversation (*what if a monster climbs up the wall and through the window? How is it fair that teachers get cake at playtime and I only get fruit? Is it true that if you hold your breath and touch a stinging nettle it doesn't hurt?*), Alfie finally falls asleep and I go downstairs to the lounge. Jemma is sitting with her laptop on her knees, occasionally glancing up to survey the television. Her shoulder-length blonde hair is pushed off her face with a hairband and she has no make-up on. When you draw a face in art class and are given the correct proportions to follow, that's Jemma's face. Completely symmetrical. Everything in the right place. Although these days it's usually shrouded in whatever negative emotion she is feeling towards me, her face is still unequivocally beautiful.

I lie down on the other sofa. Jemma doesn't look up. I don't expect her to. Most of our evenings are spent in silence like this, with only the murmurings of the television in the background. There was a time when our house was filled with noise. Not the kind of discordant noise the days are filled with now. But the noise of laughter, glasses being chinked, animated conversation. At first, I found the whole dinner-party thing a bit pretentious. I was more of a 'beer in a cosy pub after a surf' kind of guy. But over time I got used to it. I even started to enjoy it. I still had to tune out sometimes, when some of the blokes Jemma worked with started spouting self-important drivel about their latest super deal or which fancy car they were going to add to their collection. But in many ways I enjoyed being part of the 'in' crowd. I never had been at school. I didn't play football or rugby. I preferred to sit in the corner and read rather than working out in the school gym. I was a latecomer when it came to girls – always 'the friend' rather than the hot bloke whose name they doodled on their exercise books despite the fact he treated them like crap. So when Jemma came up to *me* in the university bar, I thought maybe it was a wind-up. But it turned out, for some reason, that I was exactly what she was looking for.

But then Alfie came and the dinner parties were whittled down, and all our conversations became about how to 'mend' Alfie. And then, when we realized those conversations were fruitless and that anything we did have to say to each other was neither entirely pleasant nor productive, we just stopped saying very much at all.

But I can't let this one lie. 'Why didn't you tell me Alfie had sworn at school?'

Jemma stares intently at something on her screen. 'Oh, it was nothing.'

'I'd rather decide myself which of my son's actions are important and which aren't, thank you very much.'

She looks up at me, contempt filling her eyes. 'Give it a rest, Jake. You don't tell *me* every single time the teacher wants to talk to you about something.'

Because you don't care.

'I tell you the important stuff, and him getting into trouble for swearing is pretty bloody important.'

Jemma raises her eyebrows. 'I wonder where he gets it from.'

'Oh, fuck you.'

She smirks and I want to put my fist through the wall.

'You want to know why I didn't tell you? Because I didn't want a repeat of what happened last time, especially not with a teacher.'

I don't want to bite. I really don't want to. But it's like she actively seeks to provoke me, so that she can sit on her high horse and say, 'See, told you you're too angry.'

'How dare you? I stuck up for my son. *Our* son. You do remember he's our son, don't you?'

'Don't be an idiot, Jake. Just because you're the stay-at-home dad doesn't mean I love him any less than you or that he is any less mine.'

I take a deep breath. She doesn't get it. It's not about her decision to work. I support that. It's that she's not 'present' even when she's with us.

'Look, can you just tell me next time something happens at school? It's important that I know.'

'Fine.' Jemma resumes her typing and I know that's the signal that the conversation is over.

There is so much more to say, but I haven't got the energy. On my way to our bedroom, I peer into Alfie's room. He has tossed the cover off and is lying like a starfish in the middle of the bed. His pyjama top has risen up and his little outie belly button is poking out. He looks so young. So innocent. It's amazing how insanely in love with your child you feel when they're asleep. I stroke his hair – golden and straight, just like his mummy's – then gently kiss his forehead, careful not to wake him up.

Emily

Every day at work I find myself staring at the clock on the end wall of the café. It has this aggravatingly loud tick that repeatedly shouts 'THE SECONDS OF YOUR LIFE ARE TICKING BY, THE SECONDS OF YOUR LIFE ARE TICKING BY.' Obviously it doesn't actually shout that. I'm not sure there's a place in the market for a verbally abusive cuckoo clock, but that's what I hear as it tick-tocks through my day.

The café is quiet today, which is the last thing I need when my period's gone AWOL and I am definitely not in a position to be celebrating that news with the purchase of a cute little pair of booties from Baby Gap. To distract myself, I take the latest batch of brownies out and retrieve my trusty ruler from my bag. I get a bemused look from one of the smattering of customers but there's nothing worse than the person you're with getting a bigger brownie than you.

Sitting in the corner of the room, there's a teenage lad, his face covered in acne. He has long hair, dyed black, greasy, and he wears it swept across his face like a shield. He alternates between taking a bite of his panini and tapping away on his phone. A few tables across from him, there's a group of jocks. Every now and again, they look up at him and laugh and he tries his best to pretend he doesn't notice them, but it's obvious he does.

Two of the jocks begin whispering to each other and then one of them, his idiot status highlighted by his backward-facing cap, screws up the wrapper from his sandwich and launches it at the poor long-haired boy, hitting him right in the face. It leaks remnants of salad all over his black Slipknot top. The other lads start creasing themselves and slapping the big shot on the back in congratulation.

I put down my ruler and go to collect the empties on the tables next to them. There's a half-drunk mug of hot chocolate so I pick it up and – I can't resist – as I walk past the lad in the cap, I tilt it towards him and the shit-coloured liquid falls on to the crotch of his jeans with a satisfying splash.

'Ah, fuck's sake.' He slides his chair back and starts scrubbing his jeans with a napkin. 'Watch where you're going, will you?'

I give him an overly apologetic look and speak in my sweetest beauty pageant voice. 'Sorry. It was an accident.'

I'm not a confrontational person. I just can't bear injustice. There are too many people in this world who feel they can waltz around treating others like dirt and no one ever calls them out on it. The long-haired boy looks over at me, a quiet gratitude spreading across his chapped lips, and I give him a conspiratorial nod of the head, then return to the counter.

I bob down to check how much milk we have left in the fridge and when I pop back up there's someone waiting to be served. My chest suddenly feels tight, like an elephant's just trampled on top of me. It's Alex. Trust it to be today that I finally bump into him.

He's looking up at the menu on the wall and hasn't noticed me yet. I wish he looked like crap, but he's effortlessly cool in black jeans and a lumberjack shirt, his hair glistening and bouncy like he's just walked out of a bloody Head & Shoulders advert. Why oh why did I shave my head?

As his eyes meet mine, his head jolts back in surprise. 'Shit, I'm sorry. I thought you still worked in the pub.'

'No, it didn't work out.'

'Oh, right. Sorry.'

I wipe the counter even though it's already clean. 'Nice to know you're avoiding me, though.'

Alex shakes his head. 'I didn't mean it like that. I just didn't think you'd want to see me.'

I don't. And I do. And it's a horrible confliction.

'So, how are you?' he continues, glossing over my lack of response. 'Things going OK?'

Yep, couldn't be better. Other than the fact I'm possibly carrying your illegitimate and unwanted baby, everything is fine and dandy.

'I'm good. So, do you want a coffee?'

Alex looks at me like coffee is a newfangled product he's never heard of. 'What do you mean?'

'You're stood at the counter of a café, Alex. I figure you came here for coffee?'

'Oh, right. Yeah. A cappuccino, thanks, to take away.'

While I'm making his drink, he says something, but the machine's so loud I can't make it out.

'What did you say?'

'I said I'm sorry how everything turned out.'

How it turned out? Like it happened *to* us, two automated beings with no say in our actions. I should've known better

33

from the start. I *did* know better, but I'm ashamed to say it didn't stop me. I was taking a night course at the local college. Creative photography. He was the tutor. Charming, talented, married. I'd love to say he'd lied about the last bit, but he didn't. I knew that after shagging me in the darkroom he went home to his wife and nine-year-old daughter. It's a poor attempt at absolution, but I was drinking a lot – a somewhat inaccurate use of the past tense considering my Chardonnay-and-Mars-Bar breakfast. It just happened. And then, like rolling down a hill, you suddenly gather momentum and can't stop. He fed me the usual rubbish – he wasn't in love with his wife any more, he'd fallen head over heels for me, he just needed time. Stupidly, I believed him. He made me feel special, beautiful, like I was the only girl in the world worth losing everything for.

It went on for a few months. Until one night, unbelievably *after* we'd had sex, we were putting our clothes back on and I could see it, even in the dark, written all over his face.

'Look, Em, I really . . .'

I grabbed my bag and headed straight out the door. Because I knew what he was going to say and I didn't want to hear it. It's always the same. No one ever sticks around for long. That was the last time we had spoken.

I hand over his coffee, wishing it was hot enough to scald him. 'It was for the best.'

The relief is palpable in the way his features relax. Behind him, a group of teenage girls move towards the counter, giggling and chatting about some boy they've just bumped into. I want to slap them and tell them to get a grip.

'Well, I suppose I better let you get back to work.'

I nod and he gives me this look. I can't quite place the

emotion on his face, but I'm pretty sure it's sympathy. He goes to walk away but then turns back.

'I like the hair, by the way. Very Sinead O'Connor.' He smiles, the exact same cheeky smile that made me fall for the cheating bastard in the first place.

Clearly needing a slap around the face myself, I force myself not to smile back. 'You're showing your age there.'

He laughs and I can tell he thinks he's got off scot-free, but then I guess he has.

* * *

Back at my flat, I put my work clothes away in the wardrobe, grab my joggers and hoody and then locate the packet in the bottom of my bag. I read the instructions carefully. It says I can either piss in a pot or wee directly on to the stick, being careful not to go above the blue line. I'm not sure how you wee with that much precision without a penis so I go for the first option, still managing to get some on my fingers as I aim for the glass.

When it's been dunked for at least fifteen seconds, I put the test on my bedside table, set a timer and sit on my bed. At times like these, I always feel the best thing to do is to write a list. The 'why being pregnant would be a disaster' side is pretty easy to fill. *Useless married baby daddy. No money. Barely room in my flat to swing a cat. Having to give up alcohol. Ability, or lack thereof, to look after a baby.* The list goes on. Then, just as I finish writing the one and only pro I can think of, the timer starts beeping. With my heart in my throat, I scoot across the bed and force my eyes to look at the test.

A single blue line stares back at me. I hold it up to the

light, searching frantically for a second line as if I want it to be there. But it's not. And I don't. I only have to look at my list, like a one-legged man, to know this is, without doubt, the best outcome. And that this feeling in my chest, like a sinking stone, is just a strange form of relief.

* * *

As I walk down the dingy corridor of the block of retirement flats my nan lives in, the yellow strip lights, dated carpets and smell of overcooked vegetables make me instantly depressed (brimming with joy as I was when I arrived). I knock on her door but she doesn't answer, so I let myself in.

Nan's leaning forward in her chair and shouting at the television. She's incensed. Apparently the detective in the murder mystery she's glued to is missing a vital and obvious clue. It's called suspense, Nan. They do that on purpose.

I touch her lightly on the shoulder so as not to scare her. 'Hi, Nan, I've brought Chinese.' I hold up the plastic bag containing the food.

She looks surprised, as she always does when she sees me standing here, despite the fact I've been visiting her every week for the past six years, since we met at Dad's funeral. Then she crinkles her nose as if detecting a particularly repugnant smell. 'What have you done to your hair? You look like one of them queers.'

I run my hand over my bristly head. 'Nice to see you too, Nan. And they're called gay or homosexual. You can't say queer any more.'

'I'm eighty-six. I'll say what I bloody well want.'

I decide to let it go and smile. 'I guess I just fancied a change.'

'You want a change, you get a perm or something. Dye it a different colour. Don't make yourself look like a bloody cancer patient.'

I smile again. 'I'll just go and sort your food for you.'

'Oh, you know I only like sweet and sour, don't you, love?' Her face is etched with concern.

'I know, Nan.' I place my hand on top of hers. 'Don't worry, that's what I've got.'

'And you haven't got that strange eggy rice stuff, have you?'

'No, Nan. Chips. Just how you like it. I'll put it out on a plate for you.'

I go through to the tiny kitchen and manage to find two clean plates in the cupboard. There's a huge pile of washing-up that's clearly been there for days and I make a mental note to talk to the staff again. They mentioned that they 'weren't really there for that sort of thing', but what exactly are they there for? Twiddling their thumbs until it's time to do their daily rounds or some poor old biddy's had a fall? It's not acceptable leaving Nan with rotting food in her kitchen.

I take the Chinese through, slide out Nan's lap table and place her plate on it before sitting on the adjacent sofa with mine on my lap.

'Thanks for this, Em, love.' Nan scoops up some chicken, spilling sweet and sour sauce down her chin as she eats. It makes me want to reach out and hold her. 'So have you still not found a nice boy to be spending your evenings with?'

'Rather than have dinner with you? No way.'

'Seriously, Em, an attractive girl like you. You must have boys flocking around you.'

'Oh yeah, I'm beating them off with a stick.' Inwardly, I smile at the accuracy of my comment.

'Mind you, with that hair, I'm not surprised you're sitting here with me. You look like that Gail Whatshername. She was such a pretty thing till she got rid of all her hair. You know, the one that used to present *Top of the Pops*?'

'She didn't get rid of it, Nan. She has alopecia.'

'Well, what's your excuse?'

I wanted to become invisible. I remember coming home from the pub, still shaking from what happened, struggling to hold the scissors as I hacked at my jaw-length bob, followed by the razor, all the time watching myself in the mirror, the tears falling alongside the clumps of hair.

'I don't know. Poor judgement?'

'You want to get married, don't you, love? Have babies and all that?'

I shrug. 'I guess so. Just not found my Prince Charming yet, I suppose.'

Nan looks at me like I've said I'm waiting for a million-pound lottery win. 'Don't be a plonker, Em. There's no such thing as Prince Charming. Just find a half-decent one and hold on to him for dear life.' She puts a chip in her mouth and chews it while she talks. 'I know you never met your Grandpa Joe, but he was a mardy old bugger half the time. Used to argue like cat and dog, we did. But he went to work every day. He paid the bills. He never hit me or had any floozies. That's all you can ask for.'

'You're probably right.'

'I'm always right. You want kids, you need to get on with it.'

I inadvertently touch my tummy. 'I'm not sure I'd be a very good mum.'

'What are you on about? You'd be fine. You do the best you can and the rest is just luck. I probably should've given your dad a few more clips around the ear but I tried my best. He was fed and watered, he had a roof over his head and clothes on his back. If it hadn't been for the drugs, I think he would've been all right. He was a good boy really. But you can't wrap them up in cotton wool forever, can you? Anyway, you couldn't do a worse job than that mother of yours, could you? No offence, love.'

It's a fair point. She'd be hard to beat in the 'World's Worst Mum' awards. 'None taken.'

Nan pushes her food around the plate with her fork. 'I think I've had enough now. Be a love and put it in a bowl for tomorrow, will you?'

She's barely eaten any, but I take it into the kitchen, add the remains of mine to it, wrap it up and put it in the fridge for her. I do the washing-up and quickly and quietly put the things away in the cupboards so she won't notice what I've done.

'Got any plans this week?' I call through from the kitchen.

'Well, Amy's coming to tidy up my hair on Tuesday. And it's Betty's funeral on Thursday, Bert's on Friday. I might as well just take up a permanent position in that church until it's my turn.'

I walk back through to the lounge and start to collect my things, trying to ignore the lurking thought that one day Nan will be out of my life and then I'll have no real family at all. 'Don't be silly, Nan, plenty of years left in you. Look, I better get going now. I need to sort the flat before work in the morning. Anything else you need?'

'Some great-grandchildren?'

I kiss Nan on the cheek, her skin soft and papery. 'You take it easy.'

'Not much choice about that these days, love. See you soon?'

'Of course.'

'And grow that bloody hair back, will you?'

* * *

With the vastness of the night looming ahead of me like an exam I haven't studied for, I text my best friend, Alice.

> Can you squeeze in one drink
> at the wine bar? xx

A few minutes and another glass of wine later, my phone buzzes.

> Would love to but I'm in bed
> already. Billy's teething and
> my boobs seem the only way
> to placate him. Argh! Oh, how
> I miss sleep, boobs that don't
> leak at the mere sound of the
> cat crying, my sanity, oh, did I
> mention sleep . . .? Can't wait
> to see you on your birthday.
> Love you xx

I text a reply.

> To be fair, the little man has a
> point. They're great boobs.
> Love you too xx

I scroll through the rest of the names in my phone – a bunch of people I never talk to – resist the urge to call Alex and then, because I'm clearly a glutton for self-torture, open Facebook. It really should come with a health warning: do not open if drunk, angry, mildly depressed – basically in any state other than thinking your life is as perfect as humanly possible, and even then it might convince you you're wrong. If I'm not careful, I'm going to end up putting a sarcastic comment on one of the many wonderfully cute baby photos that pop up endlessly on my timeline, or posting one of those cryptic *feeling confused* statuses or, even worse, the classic *I know most of you won't read to the end of this post but if you did, you'd see it was full of self-pitying, attention-seeking crap so I'd trust your initial judgement and not bother.* I think the safest thing to do is to turn off my phone, go to bed and binge on Netflix.

*   *   *

When I wake up in the middle of the night and can't get back to sleep, I switch on my lamp and locate my pregnancy pros and cons list in my bedside table drawer. The one and only pro sits on the page, ridiculous in its purely emotion-based rationale, and yet it is the reason that jumps out at me, lying in my bed with acres of space around me. *You will love it and it will love you back.*

Jake

'Hi, everyone, I'm Emily.'

One of her legs is propped up on the other and she jigs it up and down, frantic, like a crack addict in rehab. It's infuriating. It's like sitting next to Alfie – whether we're eating, playing a game or reading a story, he's always moving, wriggling, falling off the chair, walking his legs up the wall. *Just sit still.* Her eyes are the same, wandering around the room, like she's searching for something but can't find it.

'Look, I might as well be honest. I don't need to be here.'

An audible sigh travels around the room.

'No, I'm not in denial or anything. I really don't have an anger problem.'

The hostility in the room grows like the tension at a football match, steadily rising before it explodes and a brawl breaks out between the opposing fans. Despite the fact she didn't pull any punches when attacking me last week, I almost feel sorry for her. It's not nice to see a person being vilified en masse, however unlikeable that person may be. And to be fair, I feel the same. Yes, I get angry, but so would anyone walking in my shoes.

Watching Emily, I can't deny she's striking. She has one of those faces you can't help studying. Maybe because you don't see many people that look like her. Her eyes are huge, almost creepily so, exaggerated by the lack of hair and the heavy black eyeliner. It wouldn't surprise me if she'd been a Goth at school. I can picture her in black, sitting in the corner of the common room, listening to heavy metal from a ghetto blaster and slashing her arms at the weekend. Today, she's wearing an oversized stripy knitted jumper and jeans that look like they've been sprayed on to her stick-thin legs. Against her skin-tight jeans, her bulky leather biker boots appear almost clown-like.

Sam steps in. 'Can you tell us why you are here, Emily? No one is here to judge you.'

Surveying the glaring faces, I'm not sure this is strictly true, but Sam's read the mood in the room and is doing his best to improve it.

'Perhaps I could go first?' I say, raising my hand.

Emily looks as if I've just saved her from the death penalty.

'Would that be OK, Emily?' Sam asks.

She nods and I take centre stage.

'Hi, everyone, I'm Jake.' They all mouth hellos back. 'A bit like Emily, I didn't really think I had an anger problem before I came here. I'm still not sure if I do.'

It's a risky strategy, relating to the black sheep, but I'm pretty sure I can make it work in my favour. It's one of the few bonuses of having been a teacher: I'm used to performing to a large group of people. The fact that they're angry adults instead of apathetic teenagers hopefully won't make too much difference. Successful public speaking is like mixing a cocktail. You need the right balance of confidence and self-deprecation, a drop of humour and a large swig of humility.

'My wife asked me to come, well, she *told* me to come, and any married men here will know that you do what you're told.'

43

Smiles from both the men and the women. A positive start.

'And maybe she's right. Maybe I do have a problem. I do feel angry a lot.'

Because my wife is self-obsessed and my son belongs in a mental hospital.

'And, yeah, it makes me say things and act in a way that I'm not proud of. I could be a better husband, I'm sure, and I could definitely be a better father to my son. He's just turned six – lovely but totally maddening. So whether or not I've got an "official" anger problem, I know that I could be better. I'm sure all of you will be able to help me find some ways to do that.'

At this point I give my most sincere-looking smile. To my relief, the room reciprocates the gesture. Except for Emily. I'm well aware it's going to take a lot more than a semi-heartfelt speech to get a smile out of her. I'm not sure she's even capable of it; maybe her face has a design flaw that means it just won't move in that way.

The focus of this week's session is how to respond in a non-aggressive way to the triggers we identified last week. Everyone has chosen to sit in the same spaces as before so, for my sins, I'm paired with Emily.

'Now I know you don't have an anger problem, so I guess we'll have to work on my triggers?'

Emily glowers at me. OK, there may have been a hint of sarcasm in my tone, but you'd think she'd at least be a little bit grateful that I just saved her arse. 'Can't wait.'

'Right, well, I suppose my main triggers are my wife and my son.'

'The fact they exist?'

God, this girl. She even makes my wife seem tolerable.

'No. There are specific things that they do. Not just them in their entirety.'

'Like what?'

'My son is very particular. He has to have everything done a certain way, he is unable to wait for anything, impossible to reason with . . .'

'Sounds pretty standard.'

'You got kids, then?'

Emily shakes her head and something in her face changes, like she's thinking about something she doesn't want to, or maybe she's just planning her next insult. 'Maybe you just need to understand him better.'

If you didn't have to be the other person in conversation with her, Emily would be fascinating. There's no filter, as if she's entirely unaware she's being a bitch.

'I do understand him. I've spent every single day of the past six years with him.'

Except, I don't. Even after all these years, I still can't work him out.

Emily holds both hands up. 'All right. Chill out. Bloody hell, you really do have an anger problem, don't you?'

I'm surprised to find myself laughing. 'You just keep attacking me. I feel the constant need to defend myself.'

'I was only trying to help. If you could see where the behaviour was coming from, perhaps it wouldn't piss you off so much. Just an idea.'

'Maybe. What makes you such an expert, anyway? You doing some kind of child psychology degree?'

'I'm not claiming to be an expert. That's just the sort of crap they spout in counselling. Never made any difference to me, but it might help you out.'

She starts rummaging in her bag, taking stuff out and dumping it on the floor in an attempt to reach whatever it is she is looking for. I want to ask her why she's been in counselling but I can tell she'll only give me a glib answer. She's happy to delve into my private life and tear shreds off me, but I reckon all hell would break loose if I did the same to her. Pulling out her camera, she extracts a piece of chewing gum from the bottom of her bag.

'Nice bit of kit.' It's a Canon 5D Mark IV – the camera I've always wanted but never had the talent to justify. I feel guilty for thinking it, but I did not expect *her* to have a camera like that.

'Yeah, it's not bad.' She puts everything away and pushes the bag under her chair.

'Not bad? Are you a professional photographer, then?'

Emily shakes her head. 'I did a bit of family photography for a bit, but nothing much. It was a gift.'

'Wow, that's a pretty extravagant gift.'

'It was more like a hand-me-down. A friend had bought a new one so he gave this one to me.'

'Well, I'm a definite case of "all the gear, no idea". I've got a 6D and a load of lenses but I'm no good at it, really. I got carried away buying stuff when Alfie was born, but I've still not managed to get a decent photo of him.'

'I see. Makes a bit more sense now.' Emily unwraps the piece of gum and pops it in her mouth. 'I did think it was a bit creepy how you were ogling my personal belongings.'

I smile. 'Don't worry. Your luck's not so bad that you've ended up sitting next to a wife beater *and* a thief.'

Emily's cheeks colour, a tiny glimmer of humanity inside her prickly shell. 'So how come you're really here, then? There must be a reason your wife made you come?'

I consider lying but there doesn't seem much point. 'I got into a fight with a parent at the school gates.'

I shouldn't have pushed Matt. I'm not proud of it. Well, my inner youth is slightly proud. I was never 'radical' enough to be involved in a fight when I was younger. But I'm aware it wasn't my finest choice. It's just that he stands in the playground all superior with his perfect little boy, George. The child who will always win first place at sport's day and receive the best player trophy at football club week after week. And every day, I have to quell an intense desire to punch Matt. So when he started mouthing off to me because Alfie had apparently pushed George, I just lost it.

'What about?'

'It was nothing.' I shake my head. 'It was stupid.'

'But you were about to smash his face in? Over nothing?'

'I wouldn't exactly say "smash his face in".'

'Let me guess, his son's on a higher reading level than yours?'

'Exactly. Little shit!'

Emily smiles. A fanfare plays in my head.

'He called my son autistic.'

'And he's not?'

'No, he's not.'

Matt wasn't the first person to suggest Alfie might have something wrong with him. Jemma and I have battled back and forth about it on and off since he was born. She wanted a reason for why we found him so difficult, a label. I even questioned it myself for a while. The extremity of his tantrums. The total inflexibility. But I've watched *The A Word*; I've read up about the various conditions. It's not Alfie. He's not non-verbal – he never bloody shuts up. He 'gets' emotion. He looks you in the eye, he smiles, he responds, he interacts. Besides, I don't want my child pigeon-holed, a teaching assistant permanently attached to his side like a stamp on his forehead that reads 'odd-ball'. I've been in education long enough to see people seeking it out as an excuse. *Oh, he's not naughty. He's got ADHD. Bang him on Ritalin and he'll be a model student.* And I've also seen the judgement. Teachers whispering 'That's the autistic one', with pretend-sympathetic faces like the poor kid's got the plague.

But I eventually gave in to Jemma's badgering and, when Alfie was three, I agreed to take him to the doctor's. I can still picture the doctor's face when Jemma explained his 'difficulties'. *He needs to be in control at all times. He wants everything a certain way. He has huge meltdowns if we say no or try and get him to do something he doesn't want to do.* He practically laughed in our faces and handed us the details of a parenting course.

So after that, Jemma went from blaming the world to blaming me. As the main caregiver, it had to be my fault. Some days, I'd not set clear enough boundaries. Other days, I'd been too strict. I should've socialized him more, stimulated him less. Although the exact details of my mis-demeanours varied, the ultimate truth remained the same: I'd ruined our son. Who knows? Maybe she's right.

The sharp sound of the triangle cuts through my thoughts.

Sam looks around the circle. 'So who would like to share today?'

A woman on the opposite side of the circle raises her hand. I think her name's Sharon. She's wearing black PVC trousers that make her legs look like two overfilled sausage skins and heels so high they must be a health and safety hazard.

'Sharon. Thank you.'

Another useless skill gained from teaching – the ability to remember names.

'I'm still having problems with my daughter. This week took the biscuit. So now, apparently, not only is it my fault she can't hold down a job, I'm also the reason her boy-friend's walked out on her when she's seven months' pregnant.' She looks to the sky as if this is the most absurd thing she's ever heard. 'I'm not saying I've been the per-fect mum, but she can't spend her life blaming me for every mistake she makes.'

From the look on Sam's face, I get the feeling he's spent a number of these sessions listening to the saga of Sharon and her daughter. 'So did you manage to come up with a non-aggressive way to respond?'

'I've stopped seeing her. Cut the negativity out. I feel better already.'

Emily sniggers and the whole room turns, an eager audience sensing a catfight.

Sharon leans forward, propping her hands on her knees. 'Oh, you think differently, do you?'

Emily locks eyes with Sharon but doesn't say anything.

'Do you have a different strategy to help Sharon, Emily?' Sam asks, his eyes pleading with her.

Emily uses one nail to clean the dirt from underneath the others. 'I just don't think you should cut someone out your life because they make you face up to how you messed up. Maybe you *are* the reason her life's so fucked up. Shouldn't you be trying to make it better, not just pretending it's not your fault?'

Sharon looks like all her muscles have been pulled taut by some invisible puppeteer. 'Coming from you? You won't even admit you've got a problem.'

'Because I haven't.'

Sharon's eyes search the room for support. 'See what I mean?'

'OK. Well, thank you for sharing, Sharon. And for your input, Emily.' Sam offers a well-practised smile. 'I would just ask you both to consider our ground rules. They're pinned up over by the refreshments table, if you want to give yourselves a little reminder in the break. Mutual respect of each other's views is key in these sessions.'

Emily and Sharon both nod, but they look like two boxers being told to tap gloves at the start of a fight.

'I hope that together we can find a way for you to have a positive relationship with your daughter, Sharon, but you're right, one strategy is to remove certain triggers from our lives. And, yes, sometimes that includes people, although when it's our loved ones, obviously we'd hope to find an alternative solution if possible. Has anyone come up with any other methods to respond positively to triggers?'

Tim raises his hand. 'Well, chatting to Nathan here, I think we might have come up with a possible solution to deal with my dog.'

'Fantastic.' Sam beams, clearly thankful for the glimmer of positivity. 'What is it?'

'Snuggle time.'

Tim's face is as straight as a ruler. Out of the corner of my eye, I can see that Emily is trying as hard as I am to conceal her amusement. And for the first time since we met, I wonder for a moment if we could end up being on the same team.

'I'm going to give Bouncer five minutes dedicated snuggle time when I first get through the door,' Tim continues, clearly pleased with himself. 'Then he'll have to learn I need my space.'

'Brilliant. Thanks so much, Tim, and Nathan, of course, for helping you to reach a positive outcome. Great stuff, guys.'

I have the feeling this is going to be a long twelve weeks.

* * *

The second I get through the door, I'm greeted by the all-too-familiar sound of Alfie yelling. Every time I walk into my house, it's like the air is getting thinner and I imagine how amazing it would feel to march back out, the cold autumn air filling my lungs.

I follow the noise and trudge up to Alfie's bedroom.

'What's up?'

Alfie is lying on his bed, a pillow over his head, kicking the wall so hard that all the Lego on his shelves vibrates. Sitting on the floor, her head in her hands, Jemma is surrounded by scattered Monopoly pieces, paper money and chance cards.

'I told him we were going for a walk at the arboretum when you got home. He's been like this ever since.'

Jemma rolls her eyes and I smile. Very occasionally, we have these conspiratorial moments and I cherish them. I just wish we had them more often.

'Come on, Alfie. You like the arboretum. We'll take your scooter and I'll even throw in a hot chocolate. That's a great deal.'

It's an Alfie phrase. Before he agrees to anything, he always starts his negotiations with 'here's the deal', like some kind of corny game-show host. Then he reels off the conditions that must be met before he'll commit to doing whatever it is we've asked of him.

Alfie lifts the pillow off his head but continues to kick the wall. Clearly, the conditions I'm offering on this occasion are not good enough for him to sign on the dotted line.

'I'm not going.'

I sit down beside him and hold his legs. He's surprisingly strong and releases them easily, kicking me in the chest in the process and causing my patience to dwindle.

'Look, we're going and that's the way it is. You've got five minutes to get your joggers and your shoes on or the iPad goes in the loft.'

Alfie puts the pillow back over his head. 'I don't care. I'm not going.'

It's the same every time we suggest going anywhere, whether he likes the proposed destination or not. I just don't get it. It makes me want to either become a recluse or leave the house forever without him.

'Come on. Let's just leave him.' I hold out my hand to

Jemma and pull her up. Alfie throws the pillow at us, but it misses.

Then he starts really crying. It's not for show any more. The angry dents in his forehead disappear, his bottom lip rises, tears pocket in his lower eyelids and then they slide down his face in a straight line.

'You said we would just do Lego and games. You never said about going out.'

He looks like he's in real physical pain and, if it wasn't so absurd, I could believe that asking him to go out was actually hurting him.

Jemma rubs her fingers along the line of her eyebrows. I imagine she's hashed this out a hundred times already. 'The sun's shining so Daddy rang and suggested the arboretum. You'll like it when you get there.'

'But you promised we would stay in all day. You lied.'

My whole body feels like it's attached to a torture rack – only minutes away from tearing. Why is *everything* such a trial?

'She didn't lie, Alfie. We changed our minds. Now we're going to go and get a box full of conkers. Stay here on your own, if you want to.' I turn towards the door.

I'm hoping the combination of getting more conkers – one of Alfie's latest obsessions – and the prospect of being left alone – one of Alfie's greatest fears – will be enough to swing it for me. Unfortunately, it's not. The protests intensify, the wall becomes his punching bag. I guide Jemma out of the room, shutting Alfie's door in a feeble attempt to contain him and the destruction he's about to cause.

It sounds like a catastrophic earthquake just hit the house but we try to ignore him and begin the military operation that is leaving the house with a child. Jemma packs a bag with all the things we might possibly need: hats, gloves, an activity book, pencils, snacks, drinks, plasters. The list seems endless and most of it will stay sitting at the bottom of the bag, the thing we really need sat at home, mocking us. I go downstairs and find Alfie's scooter, helmet and coat. We both know our roles. In situations like this, we're a good team.

Then suddenly Alfie goes quiet. I hear footsteps padding along the landing and then the sound of a small voice.

'Do you promise there will be conkers?'

It's like beautiful birdsong. I look up the stairs to see Alfie standing on the top step.

'Yes.'

Dear God, please let there be conkers.

'Can I take my special box to put them in?'

The settlement process begins.

'Yes, if you get dressed right now. I'll go and find your wellies.'

'And can we go to the conker tree first?'

This is a tricky one. I'm not even sure there's going to be a horse chestnut, let alone where it is in a place that is, by definition, an expanse full of trees, but I'm so close to sealing the deal that I've got to go with it.

'Absolutely. Now go and put your joggers and socks on. Time to go.'

Alfie plods up the stairs to his room and then reappears at the top still dressed in just his rainbow fleece and Batman pants but now carrying his special box in one hand and a pot full of Lego figures in the other.

'Alfie. Socks. Joggers.'

He scuttles back to his room. I hear the cupboard door slam and I'm hopeful. But then he returns and I look down at his feet to see bare toes sticking out from under his orange joggers.

'Seriously, Alfie. S, O, C, kicking K, S. Now.'

'Oh yeah, I forgot.' Alfie chuckles and slaps his forehead comically. Sometimes I wonder how he manages to be so infuriating and so adorable at the same time.

I lug out all the crap and put it in the boot of my car. When I return, Alfie is racing around the hallway with his socks on his hands while Jemma taps away on her phone.

'Why isn't he ready?'

Jemma looks at Alfie, as if she has no idea what this strange creature running circles around her actually is. Then she turns back to her phone. 'I've told him a thousand times, Jake. What else do you want me to do?'

I don't know. I don't know what to do. That's why I want you to know.

Alfie giggles and plays with the letterbox, opening it and slamming it shut over and over again, a manic look in his eyes. Eventually, I just pick him up, throw him over my shoulder still laughing and bundle him into the car, Jemma following behind carrying the wellies, his special box and his pot full of figures.

* * *

'But, Daddy, where are the conkers?'

'We need to find a conker tree. We will.'

I hope. Because if not, we're going to be driving around Gloucestershire trying to find one.

'Are you sure?'

'Yes, little man. Now let's just enjoy the rest of the walk. You scoot ahead and I'll race you.'

'No. I'm not scooting until we've found them. You promised.'

Jemma walks along beside us but doesn't say anything, just stares at the trees, their leaves falling off and creating a carpet on the ground. Sometimes I marvel at her ability to tune out. Other times, I want to do it too, just to show her how fucking annoying it is.

'I can't magic up a conker tree, Alfie. We'll find it when we find it.'

Alfie falls to the ground wailing, lies right in the middle of the path and refuses to move. People walk around him or step over him, but it's always with a backward glance. The looks he is given vary. Sometimes it's irritation, sometimes confusion, occasionally empathy. But there's always something. Some kind of judgement. Of Alfie, and, of course, of us.

It's clear nothing is going to placate him so Jemma and I walk on ahead until Alfie is just a tiny blemish on the beautiful landscape of brightly coloured trees. When we reach a point where walking any further would mean we might receive a call from social services, we reluctantly stop.

'Shall I go and get him?'

Jemma shakes her head. She looks as if even that slight motion has used up the last of her energy reserves. 'He'll come in a minute.'

'Have you met our son?'

Jemma smiles, but the humour doesn't reach her eyes.

Then, in the near distance, I see it. I couldn't be happier if there were bars of gold hanging from the branches.

'Alfie,' I shout. 'A conker tree!'

But he's too far away to hear me so I keep jabbing the air in front of us with my finger and move my hands in a way that is supposed to represent a tree but looks more like I'm outlining an apple-shaped female form. Surprisingly, Alfie must have worked it out because he stands up, abandons his scooter in the middle of the path, flies past us and starts scouring the ground under the tree. I take over his special box and join him in the search, while Jemma sits down on a bench on the opposite side of the path.

It's amazing how long it takes to fill a box equivalent to a two-litre ice-cream tub. The problem is this seems to be the only horse chestnut in the entire arboretum so it's already been raided by lots of other children, but I know we won't be able to leave until the box is full. I picture myself, reduced to just skin and bone, stuck here still searching until I keel over. But then I spot a large spiky conker case – the perfect size to fill up the remaining space in the box.

'How about this, Alfie? You can't have conkers without a shell to keep them safe in. Look, the spikes will stop anyone who tries to steal one.'

Alfie examines the shell. He tries out a few of his conkers to see if they fit inside. They do, thank the Lord.

'OK. Put it in the box.'

I want to jump up and down, as if I've just sprinted past Usain Bolt and won the 100-metre sprint. I quickly shut the lid of the box and go to put it in my rucksack, but Alfie insists on carrying it. Scooting with a box full of conkers under your arm, particularly one whose lid you have to hold closed, is a feat that would challenge even the most skilled of acrobats, but Alfie's determined to do it and I'm too exhausted to argue. He scoots over to get Jemma from the bench of indifference and we continue on, Alfie dropping the box and having to stop to gather up his conkers every few minutes until we reach the café.

'Right, you go and find a table with Mummy and I'll get the drinks.'

'No, I want to come with you.'

Please don't. 'OK, but no touching anything.'

The queue isn't long by normal standards, but there are three people in front of us so, with Alfie, it feels like being stuck in line on Black Friday.

'Will it have whipped cream and marshmallows?' Alfie runs his hand along the table beside us, nearly knocking off the ornate glass stands displaying the severely over-priced cakes.

I take his wrist and return his hand to his side. 'I don't know. I think so.'

'Last time they ran out of marshmallows.'

'Well, hopefully they won't today.'

'But what if they do?'

'Let's just wait and see.'

Alfie's body seems to have been invaded by a tribe of particularly lively jumping beans, his limbs twitching and banging into the table. 'I need to know now. Go and ask them, Daddy.'

'No. I can't push to the front. You just have to wait.'

The jumping beans seem to have gathered kinetic energy, ready to burst out at any point. There's a well-to-do older woman behind us and Alfie keeps accidentally knocking into her. Her response to my apologies started with a polite smile but now it's become a glare.

'Alfie, stand here. Stand still.' I position him in front of me and grip his shoulders, as if holding on to a criminal being transferred between one secure unit and another.

His questions don't cease and I'm just at the point where containing him is no longer possible when we reach the front of the line.

'Two cappuccinos and a hot chocolate, please.'

Alfie is jabbing me in the side, pulling on my jumper, while I try to find my credit card in my wallet. 'Do they have cream and marshmallows? Daddy, Daddy, do they? Ask them.' Then when I don't respond, he shouts, 'Ask them, stupid Daddy.'

I take a deep breath and smile at the woman behind the counter, who is unable to disguise the disgust on her face.

Alfie continues to tug on my jumper. 'Why aren't you asking them?'

Because the world does not revolve around you and your every whim.

She makes the cappuccinos first, on purpose perhaps, then makes the hot chocolate. As she reaches beneath the counter for something, I internally plead with a god I'm not sure I even believe in to please just save me. It's not until she lifts up the squirty cream canister, circles it on top of Alfie's drink and adds a handful of marshmallows that I realize I've been holding my breath.

Alfie grabs the drink off the counter, nearly spilling it all over the floor.

'Um, excuse me, young man, have you forgotten something?' The woman taps her well-manicured nail on the counter.

Alfie's eyes search the empty surface in confusion.

'Your "thank you", perhaps?'

At first, Alfie just stares at her. Then I nudge him in the back and he mutters a barely audible 'thanks' before rushing with his drink to the table.

For maybe five seconds, while Alfie spoons the cream and marshmallows off the top of his drink, he is silent.

'So do you think Adam's going to go for your idea?' I ask Jemma.

'I think so. He seemed to like it, but then you never know with Adam. He has a tendency to . . .'

'Can we go to the playground now?' Alfie pushes his half-drunk hot chocolate into the middle of the table.

'No, finish your drink. We'll go in a minute.' I push the mug back to him and turn to Jemma. 'Sorry, what were you saying?'

'Can we go *now*?' Alfie holds out his now almost empty cup.

'Alfie, Mummy and I are talking. We'll go to the park when we've all finished our drinks.'

Alfie rocks on his chair, nearly toppling back and crashing into the elderly couple sitting behind us. 'But when will we go? What time?'

Jemma reaches out and puts her hand on top of his. 'Five minutes, Alfie. Let us just finish these. And keep your voice down a bit, OK, darling? It's not fair on the other people trying to enjoy a quiet drink.'

'One, two, three, four, five, six, seven . . .'

'Alfie, we can't have a conversation when you're counting the seconds. Just wait.'

'Eight, nine, ten . . .'

I want to put my hand over his mouth. 'Alfie, stop.'

'But I want to go now.'

'Well, we're not. And we won't go to the playground at all if you don't stop hassling us.' I shake my head. 'I'm sure Adam will love it. You can't seem to go wrong in . . .'

'It's been five minutes. Look.' Alfie points to the clock on the wall.

I run my hand through my hair, pressing firmly on my skull. I just want to have a conversation with my wife. To enjoy a quiet drink with my family without there being a scene. Is that really too much to ask? 'We are going to finish our drinks, Alfie. However long that takes.'

'But I need to know. Just tell me when on the clock.' His voice is getting even louder and the number of looks coming our way is increasing one by one, like a Mexican wave. 'What time on the clock?'

Suddenly, Jemma slams her coffee cup down on the table. 'Alfie, please just stop. I can't breathe.' Her eyes are full of tears and she genuinely looks like she's fighting to catch her breath.

'I'll take him out. Finish your coffee.' I bundle Alfie out of the café, feeling the eyes of the other customers on my back, and Alfie darts straight off to the playground. I should probably chase after him, show him he hasn't won, but I can't manage it.

Later, when Jemma has emerged and we are sitting across from each other at a picnic table, surrounded by all the other middle-class parents in their Jack Wills jackets and Joules welly boots, watching Alfie running happily along the rickety wooden bridge and managing to finish our conversation, I realize this is how it should have been. This was what we always pictured.

I remember the exact moment Jemma suggested it – we were on holiday in Dubai. We'd spent the day jet-skiing across the harbour. Jemma had been reluctant at first, but I'd managed to persuade her to give it a go. So there we were, still high on the adrenalin, drinking cocktails in a bar overlooking the glittering skyline.

'I think it's time we had a baby.'

All I'd thought about at the time was getting her back to the hotel so we could practise making babies until I was so worn out I couldn't continue. And after we'd done just that and were lying naked on top of the sheets, watching the golden ceiling fan circle around and around, I agreed it seemed like the right time. We'd been married for nearly seven years. We'd travelled the world, seen amazing things, indulged in more extravagant cuisines than I'd even known existed before I met Jemma. A baby was the next step. The next adventure.

When we discovered she was pregnant with Alfie, we were like two kids on Christmas Eve. I got home from work to find a card addressed to me on the table. Inside, it read: *Hello, Daddy, I can't wait to meet you xxx*. At first, I hadn't got it. But then Jemma had appeared at the bottom of the stairs, tears in her eyes and an expectant smile on her face, holding out the positive pregnancy test. Wrapping my arms around her, I'd cried too and we'd spent the whole evening discussing baby names and whether it would be a boy or a girl and if it would look more like her or me. That night, we made love gently because I was terrified of hurting the baby, even though she assured me it wasn't possible. We were so happy. It was like surfing a wave of pure optimism. Every week we'd study *What to Expect When You're Expecting* and marvel over which fruit our baby was now the same size as, then I'd stop at the supermarket on the way home from work and buy whichever one it was. Once home, I'd hold it up against her tummy and we'd both laugh at the magic of it all.

And then he was born and he never stopped crying. I know babies cry. I'd expected a fair amount of noise and disturbed sleep. But Alfie cried from the moment he woke up until he finally went to sleep, fighting until the last second before he closed his eyes. Well-wishers would stop us in the street or at supermarket checkouts to give us insightful advice like 'perhaps he needs changing', as if we didn't spend every five minutes with our noses stuck up his backside hoping to decipher what the problem was. And colic, what the hell is that? It should be called your-child-never-stops-crying-itus, because that's all it actually means.

I can still picture Jemma pacing around the room, holding Alfie to her engorged breasts, her nipples cracked and bleeding like someone had taken a cheese grater to them, rocking this supposed bundle of joy and begging him to please feed. But he always just threw his head back and wailed. I'd come home from work to find him in a bouncy chair, screaming, Jemma frantically waving rattles in his face and him hitting them out of her hand. We didn't have sex. We never went out. Jemma went to bed as soon as Alfie fell asleep and I sat up and watched box set after box set until I fell asleep on the sofa.

One evening, as we hurried some food into our mouths while Alfie lay on his activity blanket, fussing but not quite crying, Jemma stared at me blankly.

'I'm sorry. I'm going back to work next week. I think it's for the best.'

My heart sank to the floor. 'Do you think you could just hold out until he's one?'

She dropped her eyes and shook her head. 'I wish I could. I've tried, Jake. I've really tried. But I just can't do it any more.'

I knew better than to try to convince her. I'd watched her slowly fade over those past six months with Alfie and I knew that in her mind it wasn't a choice.

On the day she went back, she asked me to take Alfie to nursery before I went to school. She made out she had an early meeting, but I'm pretty sure she just couldn't face taking him. She'd done all the research. Found one with a large outdoor space for when he was bigger. A variety of toys and activities. A high staff-to-child ratio.

I parked on the road outside and got Alfie out of his car seat. As if trying to bargain with me even at that young age, he gave me a rare smile and I kissed his soft crinkly forehead. As we passed the floor-to-ceiling window that looked on to the road, all the children stared out at me, their noses touching the glass, and I felt sick.

We went in and I handed Alfie's nappy bag over to his key worker. She was in her early fifties and had a friendly but somewhat weary demeanour, as if she'd been in the job too long and forgotten what it was she had loved about it in the first place.

'He gets a bit grumpy when he's tired or he's hungry.

Well, he's grumpy quite a lot, but he likes playing peekaboo. That seems to snap him out of it for a few minutes. Oh, and he loves having his nappy changed. It's strange, but he loves it. We tend to risk leaving his nappy off for as long as possible just for a bit of peace and quiet, but it does have the downside that you occasionally end up with wee in your eye.'

I laughed and she gave me a we've-seen-it-all-before smile. 'Your wife has told us everything, Mr Edwards. Don't worry. Alfie will be fine. We often find that watching all the other children distracts them from their woes.'

I wanted to scream that he wouldn't be fine. That she didn't know my boy one bit. But I handed him into her arms. And as I did, he gave me this look. There was no mistaking it. Pure fear. And all I could think about was my mum. How she'd swapped her swift rise up the career ladder to spend her days stuck in our crumbling Cotswold stone cottage with only me for company. When I look back on my childhood, she's part of every memory. Whether it's her delicate hands kneading bread or teaching me how to make pretend food for my action figures out of modelling clay, the feel of her hairy jumper on my face as she read me stories, the warmth of her body as she held me close when I woke up from a bad dream, the smell of her perfume – she always wore the same one – as I sat on the end of her bed and watched her getting ready every morning . . . she's always there.

I couldn't expect Jemma to do the same, to feel how I felt, but there was no way I could leave him there. So I grabbed my son out of the stunned key worker's arms, took him home, handed in my notice and never returned to nursery.

But now, as Alfie repeatedly runs over to check whether

anyone has touched his special box while all the other children chase around the playground without a care in the world, I wonder whether it would've been better for everyone if I'd ignored the guilt pulsing through me, the ridiculous sense of duty, and left him there, got in my car and driven to work.

* * *

Jemma rolls over in our king-size bed so that she is lying behind me, her bare breasts lightly touching my back. She starts to stroke my leg, softly running her fingers up and down my thigh. This is how Jemma always initiates sex. It's been a long time since we've even had sex, let alone since Jemma last initiated it, but I'm in no doubt that that is her intention and her touch makes me instantly hard.

'Are you suggesting what I think you're suggesting?'

She shrugs coyly. 'If you fancy it?'

'What do you think?'

It starts well. My foreplay seems effective. She's making the right noises. Showing all the right signs. It's the same old pattern, of course, but we've been married for nearly fourteen years so that's to be expected. Unlike normal, she doesn't take a lot of warming up and jumps on me pretty quick. We do it in the usual position, on our sides facing each other. I'm close to coming within a few minutes (to be fair, it's been a long time) but then I open my eyes and she looks so vacant, staring over my shoulder at the wall, that I stop thrusting.

'Are you OK?'

Jemma looks at me, as if she'd forgotten I was even there. 'Yeah, I'm fine. You nearly there?'

I know she's not into it and that I should just stop, but it's been so long I don't have the willpower.

'Yeah. Do I need to pull out?'

'No, it's fine. My period's due in a day or two. We're safe.'

We get back into our tried-and-tested rhythm and I manage to finish. It feels amazing for about six seconds, but then I just feel empty. Not a good, satiated kind of empty. A regretful, sad empty. I pull out of her and roll on to my back.

'You want me to finish you off?'

Jemma curls up like a hedgehog that's been poked. 'No, it's OK. It was lovely, but I'm tired.'

I imagine this is how it would feel to have sex with a prostitute. I don't know why Jemma initiated it, but her desire for me certainly faded fast. I know I'm out of practice but I didn't think my performance was that dismal.

She reaches into her drawer and takes out her eye mask. 'Night.'

'Night.'

I pick up my book and try to read but my eyes just scan the pages, so I give up and switch off the lamp. The light from the moon sneaks through the slats in our shutters and illuminates the side of her face.

'Do you ever wonder what it would've been like if we'd had a second child?' she asks, turning towards me and pushing her eye mask up on to her forehead.

'I don't know. I guess. Maybe.'

Despite initially having plans for at least two children, once we'd had Alfie, Jemma never brought up the topic of another child, so neither did I. Just dealing with him was more than I could cope with most days. Then the years passed and Alfie was suddenly six and it had become an unvoiced agreement that he was going to be an only child.

'I do. I think about it a lot.'

Really? The last thing I can imagine Jemma thinking about is another child. She barely seems to think about the one we've got.

'You've never said anything.'

'Because I was scared about what you'd say.'

'That I wouldn't want one?'

'Maybe. Or maybe that you would. I don't know.'

'Do you want one?'

The pillow rustles as Jemma shakes her head. 'No. Not now.'

'But there was a time when you did?'

'Sometimes. On the good days. And occasionally on the bad. But no, not really.'

It's completely unfair, considering I don't want one either, but it makes me sad that my wife no longer wants to procreate with me.

'Why on the bad days?'

'Because maybe another child would be different.'

I've thought the exact same thing on more than one occasion, but hearing it said out loud makes me realize what a terrible, ungrateful thought it is.

I reach over to hold Jemma's hand but I accidentally brush her thigh and she flinches, misreading my intentions. We lie in silence for a while, completely stationary, as if we're afraid to move. Then she props herself up on her pillow.

'Do you think we should take him back to the doctor again?'

I can't help but expel a deep sigh.

'I just think maybe it would help,' she continues, unde-terred. 'They could give us some strategies to deal with him better.'

I shake my head. 'They're just going to say it's our parent-ing, Jem. He's fine at school, a bit quiet maybe, a bit socially awkward, but he's not causing them any problems.'

Jemma sits more upright, leaning against the headboard. 'But I recently read this article about children with autism masking at school. It's really common, apparently.'

'He's not autistic, Jem. I think we just need to accept we were blessed with a difficult one. Or maybe we're just get-ting everything wrong. Who knows?'

Jemma nods, settles back under the covers and pulls her eye mask down over her eyes. 'I should get some sleep. I've got a lot of work to do tomorrow.'

'OK. Good night. See you in the morning.'

I turn away from her, staring at the stripes of light on the wall and wondering what else she thinks about that she doesn't tell me. I'm sure we used to know all of each other's thoughts, except for the really dark ones that no one ever shares with anyone. We'd been so close, but now we lie in the bed with a gap between us as wide as the Pacific Ocean. And it suddenly dawns on me how much I miss her.

Alfie

I open the lid of my special box and check the conkers are still there. I put them in the box last night and then hid it under the bed. I don't think anyone could get under there while I'm asleep but I want to check just in case a monster or someone sneaked in through the front door. Daddy says it's very safe here but Mummy makes me bring my bike in because someone might steal it and I don't know why a bad man would steal my bike but not come in the house and steal my conkers.

They're still there. I take them out of the box and count them. There's sixty-three and one in the shell so that's sixty-four. My conkers feel really smooth. I rub them on my face. I love them. They are my favourite thing as well as my Lego. Daddy says I'm obsessed with them. Obsessed means when I get something in my head and I can't stop thinking about it and talking about it. Daddy is mean to me when I get obsessed. He shouts and tells me to go and do something else like a normal child. I think he means like the other children along the street or at school. Maybe they don't have special things like I do. I like it when my favourite things get stuck in my head. Then there's no room for the worries. Except when I get obsessed with things I can't have. I don't like that because it goes round and round in my head until Daddy gets it for me and then I feel better. But sometimes he says no and that makes me cross and then I cry and my head hurts. I hate Daddy when he says no. Sometimes my brain tells me I want him to be dead so he can't say no and I can make all the decisions like a grown-up. I don't think I want Daddy to be dead because I love him, but sometimes my brain says things like that. I don't like it when my brain does that. I think maybe I'm Horrid Henry because he's naughty too. I don't want to be him but sometimes my brain tells me I am.

I count my conkers again just in case I've lost one. Once I've counted one, I put it out on the bed like Daddy showed me so I don't get muddled and count the same one twice. Sixty-three and one in the shell. Sixty-four. My favourite one is in the shell – it's the biggest and it's magic. I put it in there because then if anyone went to take it, they'd prick their fingers.

I check my Joker clock. I have to press Joker's head to make the light come on so that means it's too early. Mummy says if I have to press his head to see the numbers it means I have to go back to sleep. It says five then two then three. I'm allowed to get up when it says seven then zero then zero. That means seven o'clock. I press Joker's head again. Five then two then four. I can't get back to sleep. I need Daddy to check my conkers in case I've counted them wrong. If I wake him up, he'll be cross, but what if one's been stolen and I don't realize? Daddy will say I have to wait, but I can't. I need to know now. I press Joker's head again and then climb out of bed to go and wake him up.

Emily

I sort through the pile of post scattered across the rug in the communal hallway. It must be a couple of days' worth, but no one except for me ever bothers to pick it up. I organize it into five piles, one for each flat, and leave them on the side next to the withering pot plant, gasping at me for water like a fugitive in the desert.

My post consists of two handwritten envelopes. I open one to find a marketing pamphlet from a local MP, full of false promises, and I know what the other one is without even opening it. More false promises. Some years it's there. Some it's not. Sometimes, if I'm really lucky, she even puts a tenner in.

I go back into my flat and sit on the window ledge, leaning out to smoke my cigarette. Ripping open the envelope, I find a clear illustration of the fact my mum knows nothing about me; it's one of those awful tacky cards you get in Clintons with 'To my wonderful daughter' in a swirly embossed gold font on the front and a cheesy sentimental verse inside. Her handwriting is so poor I can barely read it.

To my baby girl, it's your birthday!!! I'm taking you out. Boston Tea Party 7pm, my treat. Love always, Mum × PLEASE COME!!!

I last saw her just over a year ago. In some lame attempt to impress me, she suggested meeting in this stuck-up café where a coffee and a slice of cake cost the same as my weekly shop. As I walked in, everyone looked at me as if I was about to raid the till. To top it off, like holding up a banner saying 'we got lost on the way to McDonald's', she staggered in twenty minutes late completely off her tits. I didn't even stop to talk to her, just stormed out and went straight into Vodafone to get my mobile number changed. I haven't spoken to her since. A few months ago, she sent me her six months' clean coin and asked me to meet her at the park, but I didn't. I got halfway there and then turned around and went home.

Reaching up into the top of the wardrobe, I retrieve my shoebox-full-of-inane-sentimental-junk and put the card on top of my collection – other birthday cards from Mum and Nan, letters from childhood boyfriends, old photos of Alice and me with an array of hairstyle disasters, a swimming certificate from when I was seven and my foster mum took me to lessons, and a faded Polaroid of me as a newborn in Mum's arms, Dad wearing the regulatory hospital hat and gown, grinning gawkily over her shoulder – the same large eyes and prominent jawline I see reflected in the mirror every day. I try to wedge the shoebox back into its former position but something else has slipped into its place, like Tetris, so I plonk it at the bottom with my extensive collection of trainers and my only childhood teddy bear.

* * *

Eating my Wilko's pick-and-mix, a luxurious birthday treat, I settle into my seat. I'm not your typical 'mini morning' customer and get a few funny looks from the parents sitting near me, but I love kids' films. I'm sure if I'd revealed this to my counsellor, she'd have had a field day psychoanalysing the reasons why – the desire to reinvent my childhood, a need for predictability and happy endings – but as far as I'm aware, without delving too deeply into my subconscious, I just like the bright colours and catchy songs. Counselling was a total waste of time. School made me go, because I kept bunking off and they thought it was because I had unresolved issues from my time in foster care. I kept trying to tell them that that was the good bit – it was being returned to Mum that was the problem, and I couldn't be bothered to talk about that – but they didn't listen. I quit after a few sessions. They tried to convince me to go back, but I didn't.

On the other side of the aisle, I notice a little boy counting out each piece of his popcorn on to the arm of his chair. It's exactly what I used to do when I was little. On the rare occasion I was given a treat, like Smarties or chocolate buttons, I'd first check how many I had and then count them down every time I ate one, as if it helped them to last longer. The boy's dad says something to him and then scoops all the popcorn back into the bag, probably reprimanding him for making a mess or exposing himself to germs. Like a trapped bird, the boy starts flapping around in his chair, shouting his objection. His dad tries to quieten him, even putting his hand over the boy's mouth, but it doesn't work so he picks him up, holding him out at arm's length like he's infected with a highly contagious disease, and carries him out of the cinema. Poor kid.

The film starts. It's *Trolls*. Exactly what the doctor ordered. A Technicolor land and the dulcet tones of Justin Timberlake to lose myself in. About ten minutes into the

74

film, the boy and his dad return, along with a couple of other irritating halfwits who can't manage to arrive before the film starts, despite the fact, with the numerous adverts and trailers, it's over half an hour later than the listed time. One of them, infuriatingly, has a seat at the other end of the row I'm in so I have to re-close my pick-and-mix, take my jacket off my knee and squish my body as far back into my seat as possible. All so that the man with no time-management skills and his no doubt soon-to-follow-in-his-footsteps son can get past.

Once they're no longer inconsiderately blocking my view, I see the popcorn child walking up the central aisle facing me and I realize it's the little boy from anger management, accompanied by Jake. I duck down as low as possible in my chair, but luckily Jake seems too distracted with stifling his son to notice me.

After the film – great music but a slightly questionable message: that the 'ugly' troll needs a makeover in order to win the boy – I treat myself to a hot chocolate from the cinema bar. All the tables are empty, probably because the drinks are overpriced and the girl making them is slow and sour-faced, but it's my birthday so I can't just go home and sit around waiting until it's time to visit Alice (as if having hot chocolate makes my solo trip to the cinema somehow less tragic).

I take my pick of the tables and sit bang in the middle. On my phone, I read the birthday messages on my 'wall' from people I barely ever see. I can just imagine them getting the reminder – 'It's Emily Davies' birthday today. Send her good thoughts!' – and succumbing to the virtual guilt trip to post a celebratory greeting.

Suddenly, Jake appears with a tray of goodies and plonks it on to a table nearby. I stare at my phone in that preposterous way people do, as if not looking at someone makes you somehow invisible. But then, out the corner of my eye, I see he's walking over so I look up, feigning surprise.

'I thought it was you,' he says. 'What are you doing here?'

'Surprisingly, I've just been watching a film.'

'Yeah, sorry, dumb question.'

In his defence, it's not a dumb question, more a turn of phrase, a stereotypical greeting. But something about Jake brings out my facetious side.

Alfie looks up at me with a mystified expression. 'You're the one that gave me the biscuit.'

'Well remembered. I am.'

'And Daddy took it off me,' he says, accompanied with a frown.

I smile.

Jake gestures to his table and says with as much conviction as he can muster, 'Join us, if you want.'

I'm well aware neither of us wants to spend the next ten minutes thinking up things to talk about and then fabricating an excuse to leave.

'It's fine. I'll let you enjoy your drinks in peace. It was nice to see you again, Alfie.'

'I could show you my Lego figures!' Alfie says it like he's offering me an all-expenses-paid holiday to the Caribbean.

I'm not usually that fussed about kids. I mean, I love Billy, Alice's little boy, but that's because he's part of her. Usually when I encounter children, they're either whining or bashing their trolley into my ankles. But there's a certain charm to Alfie. I can't quite put my finger on what it is, but it's hard to resist.

'Well, in that case . . .' I pick up my cup and my remaining sweets and sit down on the chair next to Alfie.

He pulls his figures out one by one. They are in what was once a vitamin pot and, looking at the worn-out label, I'm guessing it travels everywhere with him.

'This one's Hulk, this one's Martian Manhunter, this one's Braniac.'

I hold out my hands and he places the figures into them.

'This one's –'

'Spider-Man. I know that one.'

He looks at me for a moment, and I'm not sure if he's impressed that I know who the figure is or annoyed at me for interrupting him.

'How did you know that?'

'I'm secretly a bit of a superhero fan.'

'This one's my favourite,' he says, putting it on the table while he takes the others off me and puts them back into the pot. 'Loki.'

'Thor's brother.'

He shoots me a puzzled look. 'Yeah, that's right.'

'I thought Antman was your favourite,' Jake says. So drab is his personality, I'd forgotten he was even there.

'No, Daddy. You're so silly. That was last week. I told you yesterday it was Loki,' he says in an exasperated tone. Then he turns to me and shakes his head. 'He never listens.'

I imagine it's something he's heard his mummy say, and he's perfected the expression that accompanies it.

Jake pinches Alfie's shoulder muscles and he giggles.

'I do listen, monkey. It's just hard for an old man like me to keep up.'

Suddenly distracted, Alfie points to my paper bag on the table. 'Did you have pickle mix?'

'Oh, pick-and-mix. Yes, I did.'

Alfie crosses his arms. 'I wanted pickle mix, Daddy. It's not fair.'

'You had popcorn and you've now got a huge slice of cake. I think you've done pretty well.'

Alfie's expression doesn't change.

'I'll let you in on a little secret, Alfie,' I whisper. 'I only had pick-and-mix today because it's my birthday. I wouldn't normally have it.'

Jake looks up from his phone. 'Oh, happy birthday.'

He says it in the way someone says, 'That's nice,' when you've been telling them about something and they haven't listened to a word you've said.

'Thanks.'

'I'm six now,' Alfie says, putting his hands on his waist. 'It was my birthday yesterday.'

'Wow!'

'Not yesterday, little man, but it was a few weeks ago,' Jake says.

'So now you're six. Well, that is a super-special age. Happy birthday for a few weeks ago.'

'I had a Batman cake. And I got Jokerland.'

'Sounds amazing. Did you have a party?'

Jake visibly winces and I get the feeling it's a touchy subject. 'We had a family one, didn't we?'

'Well, that wasn't really a *party*.' Alfie says it as if his dad has no idea what the word 'party' actually means.

I try to change the subject. 'So tell me all about Jokerland.'

'Well . . .'

It turns out Alfie can tell me every single detail of his new Lego set, down to the individual colours of certain pieces. I love how he talks, his facial expressions and hand movements somehow out of sync with his words. He's a stunning-looking boy. Huge rich-chocolate eyes and thick long eyelashes. His hair is straighter than Jake's and golden blond with natural highlights.

Once Alfie's talked non-stop about his Lego set for over five minutes, Jake puts his empty mug on to the tray and lifts Alfie's cup and wipes underneath it with a napkin.

'I think that's enough about Jokerland now, little man.' He puts his hand on Alfie's shoulder, but Alfie shrugs him off.

'No, I haven't told him about the cannon yet.'

'It's not "him", Alfie. Remember I always tell you, girls are "her", and her name is Emily.'

Alfie doesn't respond, just presents his dad with a laughably cross face.

'It's fine, honestly. I've been called a lot worse.'

Jake forces a smile and unhooks their coats from the backs of their chairs. 'Not everyone wants to know every detail of every Lego set you own, kiddo. Come on, we should be getting back.'

'I am not going until I've finished telling him about my Lego.'

I can see it on Jake's face, the switch, as if he's a werewolf that's just spotted the light of the moon and realizes he can no longer hide his true self.

'We're going *now*. Nice to see you, Emily.'

'Your Lego sounds amazing, Alfie,' I say, trying to counter the fact his dad's being a grumpy git. 'In fact, I might have to go and buy some myself.'

'You won't be able to afford it. It's so 'spensive.'

I smile at this clearly regurgitated information. 'Maybe I could just come and see yours one day, then?'

It's just a throwaway comment, I'm trying to be kind, but I can tell by the look on Jake's face I've said the wrong thing again. It seems there's no pleasing some people.

'Can he come now please, Daddy?'

Jake shakes his head. 'It's "she". And, no, Emily does not want to come and see your Lego right now.'

Alfie writhes in his seat like he's got worms. 'He does want to. Don't you?' The volume of his voice is steadily increasing and Jake shoots a look at the door, as if plotting his escape.

'I can't come today, Alfie.' I look directly into his eyes. 'I have to go and see a friend and I'm late and she'll be sad if I don't go now.'

Alfie's eyes dart around my face. 'But you could come after you've seen your friend, you could . . .'

I cut him short. 'Not today, Alfie.' I enunciate each word slowly like I'm giving directions to a foreigner. 'But I will talk to your daddy to sort out a time I can come and see the Lego. And, in the meantime, can you do something for me? Can you take some photos of Jokerland on Daddy's phone and send them to me?'

He doesn't answer immediately but then he looks up at Jake. 'Can we do that, Daddy?'

At this point, I'm pretty sure Jake would say yes to

donating his kidneys just to keep Alfie quiet. 'Yep, sounds good.'

'Fantastic. I'll write down my number and you and Daddy can send me the pictures later.'

With a face like a slapped arse, Jake reaches into his rucksack and pulls out a pen. I scribble my phone number down on a napkin, holding it out for Jake to take, but Alfie quickly intercepts.

'I'll look after it. I'll put it in my special pocket.' He looks around for his coat and yanks it out of Jake's hand. 'Look, it's got a zip so nothing can fall out.' He squeezes the napkin into his pocket before zipping it up.

'Perfect. Right, I have to go. Thank you for showing me your Lego, Alfie.'

Alfie doesn't reply and Jake pokes him. 'Say bye, Alfie.'

'Bye.' Alfie barely looks up. Instead, he's preoccupied with opening and closing the pocket on his coat, pulling out the napkin a little each time he does and then pushing it back in.

* * *

'Happy birthday to you, happy birthday to you, happy birthday, dear Emily, happy birthday to you!'

Alice's husband, Ben, carries the caterpillar cake while she walks along beside him carrying Billy, who has a wide toothless grin planted on his face. He's clearly excited by the simultaneous combination of chocolate cake, candles and singing. He bobs up and down in Alice's arms and attempts to clap his hands together, but they don't fully meet.

Ben holds the cake in front of me so that I can blow out

my candles, then puts it on the worktop, hugs me and kisses me on the cheek, the wiry hair of the beard he is growing (not his best look) tickling my face.

'Happy birthday, Em. Even more gorgeous with every year that passes.'

'Thanks, Ben. You're an excellent liar. And thank you both for the cake. You really don't have to do this every year.'

'Nonsense. It's another excuse for cake. You know I'd never turn that down.' Alice wraps her free arm around me, and Billy squeals as we squash him between us.

'Sorry, gorgeous,' I say and kiss Billy on the head. He has a smattering of silky ginger hair and smells like talcum powder. For a second, a baby's face flashes through my brain – a mop of dark hair like Alex's and my blue eyes – but I push it into some distant corner so that it's a tiny spark, just able to sit and flicker but not enough to really burn.

'Let me take the little monkey off your hands so you ladies can chat.' Ben takes Billy out of Alice's arms. 'Come on, let's go and do something manly, like racing cars or bashing the hammer bench.'

'See you in a bit, my gorgeous boy,' Alice says, lifting Billy's top and blowing raspberries on his tummy. She's such a natural mother. Despite having the pick of practically any career and finally settling on law, she only ever really wanted to be a mother. I always envied her surety. The way she knew exactly what would make her happy, complete. I've still got no idea.

'What about me?' Ben puts his arm around Alice's waist, pulls her into him and kisses her.

I look away, not wanting to intrude on their moment.

'I'm sorry, baby. You know you don't get a look in now this handsome chap has arrived,' Alice teases.

Ben holds his fist to his heart and pretends to sob theatrically. 'He's taken my place.'

Alice slaps him on the bottom and sends him on his way. Usually, couples as openly in love as they are make me want to smash their self-satisfied heads together. It always feels like pretence, showmanship. But with them, it's real. They found the elusive fairytale. And they deserve it. Alice is the best person I know and, although I put the poor man through a rigorous testing process in order to prove it, it turns out Ben is probably the only man on this planet worthy of her.

I met Alice at grammar school. She was the only person who didn't look at me like I was playing at being there – like I really belonged at the comp with all the other rough kids from my estate. She's genius-category smart, gorgeous and utterly hilarious. Typically, that kind of perfection in a person would make me run a mile, but hidden behind her wild red curls, I recognized a deep insecurity that matched my own. I noticed she never put her hand up even though, when a teacher called on her, she always knew the right answer and then some. Then one day, in the school toilets, I was washing my hands and she was standing at the basin reapplying her eye make-up.

'Do you think it's too much? The blue? Does it look silly?'

I looked around to check that she was actually talking to me and, realizing we were the only two people in the toilets, responded, 'It looks great.' Because it did. She always looked amazing. I examined myself in the mirror. 'Mine looks like I applied it with a shovel. But then I need to.'

Alice took a step back and looked directly at me. 'Are you kidding me? You're stunning. You're Emily, aren't you? We do art together.'

'Yeah, we do.'

'Well, next lesson, will you please come and sit by me? I can't stand the pretentious idiots I'm on a table with.'

And that was the start of our friendship. As well as our self-doubt, we connected over shitty home lives and an unwavering love of *Dirty Dancing*. I always thought people with money had perfect lives, but her dad was an alcoholic. Her parents split up when she was nine and continually used her to score points off each other. Every Friday night we'd sit in her bedroom while her mum was out on yet another date and we'd drink her mum's wine and smoke her cigarettes and swoon over Patrick Swayze, hoping one day we'd meet someone who'd tell our parents not to put us in the corner.

'Right. Wine.' Alice opens the fridge and starts to fill two glasses with rosé.

I sit at their oak dining table and Alice places my wine in front of me.

'I'll just grab my laptop,' she says. 'I can't wait to see these photos.'

As she leaves the room, I look around me. I love their house. It's muddly, the walls could do with a fresh lick of paint and the leather on the sofa is worn at the corners, but it screams home. Every knick-knack is a keepsake from some great place they've visited; all the photographs are full of joy.

Alice sits next to me and hands me her laptop.

'I wouldn't get your hopes up. They're really nothing special. I'm sure you've got better ones you've taken yourself.'

'Come on, Em. You can't get away with that humble shit with me. I've known you far too long.'

Every woman needs an Alice in her life. However many times I mess up, she doesn't seem to see it. The guy was a shit, the job wasn't good enough, the scumbag deserved it. She has an unfaltering belief in me that I'll never understand.

I pop my memory stick in and thumbnails of the images of Billy pop up. I start the slideshow, handing the laptop back to her. It's silly – she's my best friend – but I'm nervous. The images flash up one after another and Alice stares at the screen but doesn't say anything. My favourite one pops up. Alice is tickling Billy and he's gazing up at her adoringly – exactly how she deserves to be looked at. I glance at her to gauge her reaction. Her eyes don't leave the screen but she reaches her hand over and puts it on top of mine.

When the slideshow finishes, she looks over at me and her eyes sparkle with tears.

'Oh, Em, I absolutely love them. They're perfect. He looks so gorgeous.'

'That's because he *is* gorgeous.'

She clicks back to a photo of Billy and Ben building a Duplo tower. 'He looks just like Ben, though, doesn't he? I'm hoping he grows out of it, of course.'

I smile. 'Of course.'

'Thank you so much. I'm going to pay you, though. I won't take no for an answer.'

'There's no way you're paying me. I owe you just for putting up with me.'

Alice taps my hand. 'I like putting up with you.'

I take a large gulp of my wine while Alice scrolls back through the photos.

'What was it Mr Peterson used to call you? "The bud of genius." Wasn't that it?'

I smile at the memory. 'He probably just wanted to get his leg over.'

'Well, you *were* the prettiest girl in the school by a mile.'

'Hardly. The easiest, maybe.'

'Don't you dare! That is not true and you know it.' Alice wraps one of her long curls around her index finger. 'Can you remember when I took all those photographs of litter? We had to do that triptych. I called it "The Deterioration of our Souls". Oh, don't you just love teenage angst?'

'Mine was called "Winter".'

'Yours was actually good. It was those portraits of that elderly couple at the beach, wasn't it? It was beautiful.'

'It was clichéd.'

Alice sips her wine. 'Stop putting yourself down. Mr Peterson was right. You *are* a genius. You should use your talent. Start a photography business.'

'And give up the joys of working in the café? No chance.'

'I'm serious.'

I shake my head. 'I hate all that selling-yourself stuff. It's not for me.'

'Well, I think you'd be brilliant.' She gets up and heads over to the kitchen. 'I think I might need nibbles to soak up this wine.'

Rifling through a cupboard, she pulls out half-eaten bags of popcorn and a range of puffed snacks for babies before locating a bag of Doritos and pouring the bright-orange crisps into a bowl.

'So how are you, anyway? Heard from Alex at all?'

I pick at the Play-Doh engrained into the ridges in the table. 'Actually, he came into the café the other day.'

Alice rushes over with the crisps and retakes her seat next to me. 'Why didn't you text me? What the hell did he say?'

I shrug. 'He pretended to be sorry that he just upped and left one day. And I pretended that I'm not still in love with him. So all in all, we put on a good show.'

'Oh, Em.' Alice places her hand in between my shoulders.

'I'm OK.'

'It's his loss. You do know that, don't you?'

'Yeah, sure. I'm a right catch.'

'You *are* a catch.' Alice takes a handful of Doritos and puts one into her mouth.

'My period's late.'

Alice practically chokes on her crisp. 'What? How late?'

'A week. I did a test. It was negative so I don't think I'm pregnant, but I wish the bloody thing would turn up so I could stop freaking out about it.'

'Did you tell Alex?'

'God, no. There's no way he'd want anything to do with it. He has his family. I was just a dirty mistake.'

Alice looks at me sympathetically but doesn't argue. What can she say? It's the truth. I don't know why I always do it to myself – choose guys that are entirely unsuitable. Anyone would think I want to repeatedly get my heart broken.

'So what are you going to do if you are pregnant?'

I shake my head. 'I'm not. The test would show it up by

now. It's probably just stress and exhaustion. I've been working a lot of shifts.'

Despite knowing that the arrival of my period is the desired outcome, I can't ignore my stupid nagging maternal instinct. It seems we're genetically programmed to want to procreate even when we know it's a terrible idea.

'Well, keep me posted, OK? You know I'm always here for you.'

'I know. Of course I will. So anyway, enough about me. How's Ben?'

'Oh, you know, he's a man. "Why is the house always a mess?" "Why is there never anything for tea?" "Why are we only having sex once a month?"'

I reach across her and take a crisp. 'He's not bad as men go though, is he?'

'As men go.' Alice brushes the crumbs off her jumper. 'If only we liked pussy, hey?'

I spit my wine on to the table and we both collapse into fits of giggles. Ben walks in carrying Billy, who, when he sees us, starts giggling too, which only makes us laugh more.

* * *

Later that evening, when I walk into the restaurant, I spot Mum sitting in a corner booth, tapping her hideous fake fingernails on the table. She's changed her hair since the last time I saw her. It's wildly permed and dyed a shade not unlike the purple of her nails, but at least it looks washed today. She keeps looking down at her phone and then looking around the room but she hasn't seen me yet.

There's still time to change my mind, to turn around and head for the vodka bar, spend the rest of my birthday obliterating myself with shots. It's tempting, but for some strange reason I don't understand, I walk further into the restaurant. Most of the time our shared genes mean nothing to me. But, occasionally, I feel the strands of DNA wrapping themselves around me and pulling me towards her. Like for a short time my memory's been wiped.

As soon as Mum sees me, her mouth forms a simpering smile of gratitude and I wish I'd turned around and walked back out. She stands up to greet me and hugs me tight. I let her hold me for a few moments, then pull away and sit down in the booth.

'It's amazing to see you. I'm so glad you came. Oh, it's so good to see you. You look thinner. Are you eating? I hope you're OK. You look amazing, though. You've always been so beautiful. I can't believe you really came.' When Mum talks, it's like a stream of consciousness. She barely takes a breath. 'Things are going to be different this time, I promise. It's going to be perfect. Oh, look at you. You're so beautiful. It's so good to see you.'

She reaches over and puts her hands on my cheeks. It irritates me, like she feels being my mum gives her some kind of God-given right to touch me. All the times I needed her to hold me, she didn't. I move my head away and bury my face in the menu. I don't fancy any of it. I'm not hungry. Mum pretends to study hers but I know she'll wait for me to order and then have the same. I suppose I should find it endearing but it just pisses me off.

'What do you want, sweetheart? It's my treat. Have anything that you want.'

She reaches over and places her hand on my arm. It feels like a tarantula, her fingers digging into my skin. *Get off me.*

'Don't be silly, Mum. You have no money. I can buy my own.'

'It's your birthday. I'm treating you. No argument. Anyway, I've got a job interview next week. I'll be able to take you shopping. We could even do a spa day.'

I still find it astounding just how much she hasn't got a clue. 'I don't want your money, Mum.'

'I didn't say you did, love. I just want to be able to treat you. You know, to make up for the fact I never could when you were little.'

I take a deep breath. 'I never cared about the money.'

I wanted you to protect me.

The waitress comes over and I order a ham and cheese toastie because it's the cheapest thing on the menu and a large glass of white wine because it's the only way I'm going to get through this. As predicted, Mum orders the same but with a Diet Coke. Screw her and her turning-her-life-around bullshit. She couldn't do it when I needed her to. But now that the damage is done, she's as clean as a whistle.

'Actually, I'll have the tuna melt.' I say it just as the waitress is walking away so that Mum doesn't have time to change her order. It's petty and stupid – I don't even really like tuna – but I can't help it. Whereas being around some people makes you a better person, Mum brings out the very worst in me.

'So what are you doing with yourself at the moment, Em? You working?'

'I work in a café. It pays the bills.'

'You should be a teacher or a doctor. Something like that, clever girl like you.' The waitress brings over our drinks and Mum takes a sip of her Coke while I take a large gulp of wine. 'Not sure where you get it from, though. It's not from me, I was useless at school, and it certainly wasn't from that waster father of yours.'

'You need a degree for those jobs, Mum, and university was never really on the cards for me, was it?'

'Why not?' I can see I've touched a nerve. 'We would've supported you. We never stopped you from doing anything you wanted to.'

I don't respond, just drink more of my wine. I wish I could tell her all the ways she made it nigh on impossible for me to make anything of my life. In my head, I've explained it to her in brutal detail, but when I see her, the words freeze in my throat and I end up swallowing them back down.

Our order arrives and we both pick at our food. Mum's never been a big eater, always been rake-thin. When I lived with her, whenever she saw me tucking into food, like if Shane brought a KFC home or something, she'd always say, 'Careful you don't get fat,' and pinch my tummy, like she was on a mission to give me an eating disorder.

'Remember that time we went to the zoo?'

I know exactly which story she's going to tell. She tells it every time I see her without fail. It's because it's the only good day we had together. You think she'd realize how shit it is that we have only one good memory to reminisce about, but it's like she thinks reliving it will bring us closer, that perhaps I'll focus on that day and forget all the rest.

'You dropped your banana in with the gorilla, remember? He plodded over, gobbled it up and he definitely smiled. I don't care what anyone says. He smiled.'

Mum chuckles to herself. To be fair, it was really funny.

'I'm so happy to have you back in my life, Em. I'm going to hold on tight to you this time.'

'Don't get ahead of yourself, Mum.'

'What do you mean?'

Her hand shakes as she picks up her glass. She's so frail, so weak, and I know that I can break her with just my words. I want to scream at her to get a grip. I want to shake her.

'You still with Shane?' I ask casually, but his name feels repulsive in my mouth, like a slug slithering along my tongue.

She nods and I feel sick. 'He's really changed, Em. He's working at Smith's. They're even looking to give him more shifts because he's been so reliable. He takes good care of me.'

I push my semi-eaten plate of food away and search in my bag for a twenty-pound note.

'What are you doing? You're not leaving, are you?'

'I'm sorry. I thought maybe I'd come here and feel different, but I don't.'

Mum reaches over and grips my wrist. 'Please, Em. Please just stay a little longer.'

I reclaim my arm. 'I can't.'

Mum's jaw tightens and I can see she's getting angry. I'm glad. It's easier for me to walk away when she's like that.

'Nobody's perfect, Em.' She picks at the skin near her thumbnail and I realize that's who I get that delightful habit from. 'I know I've made my mistakes but I always loved you and I'm here now, aren't I? I'm trying to put it right.'

I swallow down the bile rising in my throat. Why do people think that loving someone is some kind of achievement? An absolution. It's her fucking duty to love me. She's my mum.

'I wish you'd left me with Tina. I was happy, Mum. Things could've been so different for me if you'd just let me be.'

It's a metaphorical sword to the heart. Her shoulders hunch and her head drops like it's too heavy for her to hold up any more.

I stand up and put on my jacket. 'Bye, Mum.'

The restaurant is packed now and it's hard to weave my way through the overcrowded tables. I turn around just long enough to see Mum slumped in the booth, head in her hands, crying, and the waitress walking towards her with a birthday cake topped with glowing candles.

* * *

On the way home, I stop off at my local. It's as busy as it ever gets. The landlord, Andy, is flirting with a group of women at the bar. The majority of Andy's hair was last seen in the nineties but he refuses to let the last few strands go, sweeping them across from one side of his head to the other. His stomach squashes against the bar as he leans over and whispers something in one woman's ear and she laughs as if it's the funniest thing she's ever heard (it won't be; I've spent many a night listening to Andy's jokes).

When he sees me, he excuses himself and heads over to my end of the bar. 'What are you doing here? I thought it was your birthday today.'

I'm oddly touched that he remembers.

'It is. Happy birthday, me.'

He takes the house rosé out of the fridge and pours me a large glass. 'You look like you need this. Happy birthday.'

'Thanks.' I wince at the sharpness of the wine. 'A quarter of a century.' I raise my glass.

'And spending it with me? That's what dreams are made of.'

I down the rest of the wine in one mouthful. If Mum taught me one thing in life, it's how to get smashed. Without asking, Andy refills it and then goes to serve some young lads. I'm pretty sure they're not old enough to be out drinking. One has attempted to grow stubble and it looks like the fluffy down on a chick, but Andy doesn't bother checking for ID. I expect he's glad of the business.

I feel someone's eyes on me and turn to see Sam sitting in a booth with a friend. Automatically, I hide my face. I know it's anger management, not Alcoholics Anonymous, but it feels wrong getting drunk in front of him, like eating a sugary cake in the doctor's waiting room.

Out the corner of my eye, I see him saying goodbye to his friend. I focus on tracing the droplets of condensation on my glass and wait for him to leave. A minute later and there's a hand on my back.

'Emily, I thought it was you. Are you waiting for someone?'

'Um no, just having a quick drink before heading on. It's my birthday. Some friends are throwing me a party.' I lie, because the truth – that I'm spending the night of my twenty-fifth birthday sitting alone in a crappy pub – is just too humiliating to admit.

'Oh, happy birthday. Can I join you for one?' Sam asks.

My head is beginning to spin and I'm not sure I'm in a fit state to have a sensible conversation with my group leader, but I don't feel like I can say no. 'Yeah, of course.'

'Do you want another drink?'

Absolutely. I put my hand over the top of my glass. 'No, I'm good with this one. Thanks.'

Sam orders a beer and Andy looks him up and down while pouring it for him.

'So have you had a good birthday so far?'

'Yeah, it's been brilliant. I went to . . .' I'm not sure what happens mid-sentence. Maybe it's the wine, or Sam's caring eyes and the fact he's trained to help people open up to him, but suddenly I'm sick of the bullshit. 'I just met up with my mum. It didn't go well.'

He nods slowly, a quiet realization filling his face, and it suddenly dawns on me that Sam probably knows a lot more about me than I'd like him to.

'Do you want to talk about it?'

Yes, and no.

'I walked out. She cried. She'd organized a birthday cake. They brought it out as I was leaving so now I feel guilty, and that makes me hate her more. It's been a great birthday.'

'I'm sorry. But well done for going to meet her. It can't have been easy.'

'Thanks.' I finish my wine. 'I bet I don't come out very well on paper, do I?'

Sam shakes his head. 'You come out just fine.'

I raise my eyebrows. 'Really?'

'I've learnt not to judge anyone by what I read about them.'

'So I *do* come across badly?'

Sam adjusts his position on his bar stool. 'I didn't mean it like that. I just meant . . .'

I place my hand on his arm. 'It's OK. I'm winding you up.'

Sam tilts his head towards my empty glass. 'Well, can I buy you a drink now, birthday girl?'

'I probably shouldn't.'

'Come on, think of it as a present.'

I'm surprised how laid-back he is, how completely non-judgemental. It's refreshing.

'OK, go on then. Thanks.'

'You're welcome.'

Sam raises his hand and Andy skulks over, pouring the drinks Sam orders with a sour look on his face. I'm not sure what's got into him, but if I didn't know better, I'd think he's pissed off I'm drinking with another man.

When Andy's out of earshot, I say, 'Sorry about him. He's not normally this grumpy.'

'We all have our off days. Not a problem.'

'Really? I don't believe that for a second. I can't imagine you ever being grumpy.'

I fear the wine may be loosening my tongue.

'It happens. Occasionally. If I forget to get something out the freezer in the morning for tea, that sort of thing.'

Although I initially found Sam's impenetrable happiness off-putting, it's uplifting to be around him. Maybe it's the beer goggles, but he has a lovely face – not exactly striking, but warmly handsome.

'Have you always been this happy?'

Sam looks over my shoulder and, when his eyes return to meet mine, there's a sorrow in them that looks entirely out of place. 'Not exactly. My mum and dad died in a car accident when I was twenty-one. I started lashing out, got into a few nasty scuffles and one night I picked on the wrong guy.' Sam lifts up his top to reveal a long straight scar across his stomach. 'I realized that I could ruin the days I had left or try to make the most of each and every one. So I did that instead.'

'I'm sorry about your mum and dad. That must have been horrendous.'

'It was. But the way I look at it is at least I had twenty-one idyllically happy years with them. Not everyone has such a great start.'

I wonder whether the notes he has about me are just a brief summary of dates or whether they go into detail about the events of my crappy life.

'I guess not.' I spin the stem of my glass. 'So is this against the rules, socializing with me outside of class?'

Sam shrugs. 'I don't think so. I'm not sure. It's never come up before. Well, I won't tell anyone if you won't?'

I pull an imaginary zip across my lips and Sam smiles.

'It's nice to talk to you, anyway. You don't say much in group.'

'The things I have said haven't exactly gone down well. I thought Sharon was going to throttle me last week.'

Sam smiles, but he looks uncomfortable, like he doesn't want to say anything unprofessional. 'Give them time. You'll be OK. It might help to tell them why you're there, you know, when you feel ready to, that is.'

'Maybe. Or it might make them hate me more.'

'They don't hate you. They just don't know you. Let them in. You might find them worth getting to know.' Sam climbs down off his bar stool. 'Anyway, I'd better let you get to that party of yours.'

I wish I hadn't lied about having somewhere else to go. Sam's presence is like being wrapped in a fleece blanket and I don't want to be thrown out into the cold, to face another night with only my TV remote for company.

'Yeah, I expect they're wondering where I am.'

Sam drinks the last of his pint, then, taking me by surprise, he kisses me on the cheek and I feel it going red. 'Tell them you ended up having a drink with a handsome stranger.' He smiles, puts on his coat and stands up, placing his hand on my shoulder. 'Oh, and just between us, I think the guy probably deserved everything he got.'

I'm not sure what to say. 'Thanks. And thanks for the drink.'

'You're welcome. Have a great night.'

As soon as Sam's gone, I order a taxi, finish my drink and then stagger outside to wait.

* * *

On the way home, before I can think clearly about what I'm doing, I ask the driver to drop me off at the vodka bar. I head straight for the bar and order myself a shot. Sure enough, after I've been sitting there for about ten minutes, some loser approaches me and starts buying me drinks. I let him; I even flirt a little bit to ensure they keep coming. I know that I will end up going back to his flat, that we will have crap sex and he won't make me come. That I'll lie there for a few minutes and he'll tell me how incredible I am and ask for my number, even though he has no intention of calling me, not that I'd answer if he did. But at least I won't be lying in my bed alone, thinking about Alex or Mum or all the other stuff I struggle to block out. So for now I drink as much as I can, so that the memory of tonight will be like a photo I've taken with too high an aperture and too low a shutter speed, where you can only make out the shapes and none of the details.

*   *   *

The next morning, I stumble in through my front door. The telltale cramps come first and then later, like a belated birthday gift, my period arrives in full force. I text Alice.

The witch arrived x

I follow it with a smiley face, despite the fact my face as I'm sending it is anything but. Then I scroll through the photographs of Alex on my phone, deleting them one by one, not bothering to even try to stop the tears flooding down my cheeks.

Jake

'Daddy, can we go and buy the batteries now?'

'Go back to sleep, Alfie.' I turn away from him and pull the cover up over my shoulders.

'You said we could get them today.'

He's slapping my back. My eyelashes feel like they're ripping as I try to open my eyes. I can just about make out it's still dark outside.

'It's the middle of the night, dude. You're going to be ill if you keep doing this. Go back to sleep.'

'No. I need the batteries now. You promised.'

I've got no idea what he's talking about. I don't recall making any promises, especially not about batteries, but I was probably just trying to redirect another storm. I pad the quilt next to me, but Jemma's not there.

'Mummy must be downstairs. Go and ask her.'

It's a temporary solution, but it should buy me about five minutes extra sleep, until Jemma tells him no, we can't get batteries at the crack of dawn and he comes charging back up to scream at me.

I'm right, only it's three minutes, not five.

'Mummy says we might have some somewhere in the house and you'll know where they are.'

Unbelievable. Not only has she sent him back to me, she's done it in a way that means I have to get out of bed and pretend to search the house for something she knows we don't have.

'We don't have any, Alfie. Go to sleep.'

'I want to play with my walkie-talkies. We could go to the shop.'

'The shops are closed.'

'There's that one we go to when we have to get up to go on holiday in the middle of the night. That will be open.'

It's at times like this I wish Alfie wasn't so bright and didn't have a superhuman memory.

'But I am not going to the shop in the middle of the night and you have no one to talk to on your walkie-talkie anyway.'

It's a bit harsh, I know. In my defence, it is five o'clock in the morning.

'I don't care. I want to get them ready.' He's shouting now, his fists clenched and his elbows sticking out. 'Go and look. Mummy said we've got some.'

This is one of the many reasons why Alfie and I are such a terrible match as father and son. I hate being told what to do. It's like when Jemma tells me not to stack the cups on top of each other on the draining board because 'the water gets stagnant inside them' or some such rubbish. I like to think I forget not to do it, but secretly I think I might do it on purpose, as a sort of subconscious reaction to her bossing me around.

'Well, tell Mummy to find them then.'

I pull the cover over my head and he stomps back downstairs. Within seconds, the door opens. Only this time it's Jemma.

'Jake, will you just find some batteries in another one of his toys or something?'

'Why can't you do it?'

'Because I'm working. I didn't get up this early for nothing, did I? What exactly are you doing?'

'It's called sleeping, Jemma. It's this thing that normal people who aren't obsessed with their jobs do. You don't understand it when he's fixating on stuff, but you're just as bad.'

'My work is important, Jake. Batteries are not. There's a difference.'

'But they *are* important. They're important to me.'

I hadn't heard Alfie come up and immediately feel bad that he's overheard our conversation.

'Please, Daddy,' Alfie continues, his face full of anguish. 'If you just find the batteries, I'll let you sleep.'

Somehow he manages to make it sound so reasonable and, consequently, makes me feel guilty. But I know that as soon as I've found the batteries, they'll be forgotten and he'll be on to his next obsession, his next demand. Every day is the same. His suffocating intensity starts before the sun's even risen and lasts well beyond the time it sets. There's no escape, and if I don't make a stand about the little things, he's never going to learn. It's never going to change.

So I turn my head away and enjoy this moment, this refuge under my quilt, before the room-shaking tantrum begins. It'll almost certainly be the high point of my day.

*　*　*

We are already five minutes late leaving for school. I've now asked Alfie sixteen times to get his school uniform on. I know it's sixteen because I've started keeping a tally. It's one of the fun little things I do to keep myself from running out in the road in front of the next passing car.

'If you don't get your clothes on in the next second, I am going to take you into school in your pyjamas and you can explain to Mr Frampton why you are incapable of putting your uniform on.'

I'm shouting from downstairs and it's gone very quiet so I pop up to check what Alfie's doing. When I enter his room, he's got his pants on his head, his T-shirt on back to front and is currently tying his socks around his bedpost.

I can't keep the exasperation from my voice. 'What are you doing? We are late for school. You need to get dressed.'

I grab Alfie's hand and he pulls it away, laughing and running off around the house.

'I can't create any more time, Alfie. We have to go. Now get dressed.'

Alfie appears in the doorway, a slightly insane smile on his face. And then, before I can grab him, he runs away again. Sometimes he seems to find such delight in pissing me off, it just makes me more furious. We get caught in this vicious circle that I can't see a way out of. Taking an extended breath in, I think back to one of the strategies Sam taught us at the last session. *When you feel like you're about to snap, close your eyes and think of your happy place.* I stand in Alfie's room, trying to block out the sound of him crashing around and, although I feel like an idiot, I close my eyes and try to picture the sea, the waves lapping in and out, in and out. Is this seriously supposed to help?

I open my eyes and search all the rooms for Alfie.

Finally finding him hiding underneath my bed, I pull him out, carry him into his bedroom and lay him on his bed. I straddle my legs over him so he is pinned down and begin to dress him. He hates it when I do this but it's often the only way I can get him out of the door in anything more than his underwear.

'Stop, you're hurting me. I can't breathe. I can't breathe.'

I'm not hurting him. He's fine. He just hates that I am finally the one in control.

'Well, you should've put your clothes on when I asked you to, then.'

I battle his clothes on, Alfie getting more and more hysterical with each item. When I've finished, I climb off him and he's like a wild animal that's just been released from its cage, his legs kicking out with all his might, but I move away just in time.

'I'm going to find your book bag. I expect you downstairs in one minute with your shoes on.'

Alfie leaps off the bed and runs towards his desk chair, picking it up and threatening to hurl it towards me.

'I wouldn't, if I were you. Now get your shoes on.'

He clenches his teeth and utters a low, strained, almost inhuman sound, then slams the chair down on the floor. I leave him circling his room, searching for something to trash, and scour the house for the bits and bobs he needs for school, which are scattered improbably far and wide.

With a dramatic change of mood (very typical of Alfie), he dawdles down the stairs a few minutes later.

'Right, shoes on.'

Alfie sits on the bottom step and turns his head away. 'I can't.'

'Of course you can. You're six. Stop being silly.'

Alfie holds out his hands in front of him. 'I'm not being silly. I can't touch my shoes.'

'Seriously, Alfie, I'm going to lose it in a minute. We're late. We have to go. Now get your shoes on and get in the car.'

'No.'

It's this blatant defiance, this total refusal to perform the simplest of requests, that riles me more than anything else. *Just do what you're told. I'm not asking you to wash the dishes or iron my shirts or climb up a sodding chimney and sweep it. I just want you to put your shoes on.*

I take his shoes off the rack and throw them towards him, and they land at his feet. 'I'm getting in the car. Go to school in your socks, if you want. I really don't care any more.'

Here come the waterworks. The screaming so loud I think it pierces an eardrum. Then, as I turn towards the door, Alfie throws one of his shoes and it hits me right in the centre of my back.

I turn around and march towards him. 'How dare you?' I pick him up under his armpits and carry him out to the car while he tries to kick me with his dangling legs.

'I hate you, Daddy. I hate you, I hate you, I hate you. I'm never talking to you ever again.' Then just to really hammer the point home, 'Ever.'

'Great. I can live the rest of my life in peace. Fantastic.'

As I bundle Alfie into the car like a tent that refuses to go back into its bag once it's been used, I notice our next-door neighbour standing on her doorstep having a cigarette, trying to pretend she's not looking at me, and I know she thinks I'm utterly incompetent. Just like the parents who watch Alfie charge out of the car when we get to school, turning around to shout at me and then nearly bumping into a parking car. But he always stops when we get to the playground, where he stays close to my leg and shuffles inaudibly across the tarmac, as if he's purposefully trying to convince the teachers that the only problem is my parenting or that we're making everything up.

When we get there, I position myself next to the small group of dads. There're usually a few, doing the drop-off before heading to work, and we tend to congregate together, exerting our manliness with regular one-upmanship. Ted, the trendiest and best-looking dad at the school, is currently telling one of his fascinating stories about his weekend adventures. He's some hotshot events organizer and is always getting free tickets to parties attended by the local celebrities who have second homes in the area. Ted's a bit of a twat really, but the other dads stand and guffaw at his self-indulgent storytelling, as if some of his 'coolness' might rub off on them and their boring lives. I tune out and listen to the mums' conversation beside us.

It's funny how the dads always talk about themselves and the mums always talk about their kids. This particular conversation is being led, as usual, by Penelope. She's probably my age, maybe a little older, she dresses as if she's attending Ladies' Day at the races and her voice is both too loud and too high-pitched. Every morning, I walk past the drop-off area in the staff car park and her sodding great Land Rover is parked there, despite numerous letters home asking parents not to do that. Typical privileged upbringing – the rules clearly don't apply to her. As usual, she's yacking on about her 'perfect' daughter – the precocious Annabelle – who I often see punching her mum when she doesn't get her snack quickly enough after school.

'I just can't believe they're expecting her to learn her letters alongside all the other children. I mean, she's been reading for over a year. It's preposterous. And they sent us that homework, what was it? Ordering numbers to twenty. I wrote some three-digit additions at the bottom for her to solve and sent those back.'

'I know. It's very basic, isn't it?' Daisy this time. Mum to pristine blonde Amelie, unnaturally polite and exceptionally pink. 'Can you believe it, they put a photograph of Amelie on Tapestry writing the word "cat" on a whiteboard, as if that was some kind of great new achievement. I marched straight into Mr Frampton's office and complained.'

The other mum in the group smiles, but the look on her face makes me suspect her child isn't reaching quite such heady academic heights and I wish I could reach out to her and say, 'Hey, don't worry about it. Mine neither.' But she'd never admit to it in public. No one ever does. It's all 'best face forward' in the playground.

During this time, the children chase around, alternating between running races and tag, but Alfie always skirts around them, close enough to look like he's joining in, but really he's on the periphery, wearing a strange glazed expression like he's not entirely sure what's going on. I wonder if he knows he's not really part of the game. He doesn't seem to. I guess it's better that way, not being aware you're the outsider, but, at the same time, it makes me sad that he's not striving to get in.

It's a relief when his teacher appears. She's probably only

in her early twenties, but she's one of those people who seem old before their time, wearing a high-necked cashmere sweater, a beige knee-length skirt with thick black tights and pumps my nan might have worn if she were still alive. She seems nice though, smiling warmly at the children and ruffling their hair as they walk past her. I give Alfie his book bag and kiss him on the forehead, but he barely acknowledges me, lost in some faraway land that I have no map for. Like a machine in a production line, he hooks his book bag over his head and trails into the classroom. And as soon as he's gone, I experience the same feelings I always do: regret, sadness, and the desire for one morning with no arguments, no screaming. Just one morning when I can walk away from school feeling anything but this.

* * *

Despite Jemma leaving the house before us as usual, her car is there when I pull into the drive. I go straight up to the bedroom, where I can hear her bashing around, and open the door.

When she sees me, she looks flustered and stops what she's doing. There's a half-packed suitcase on the bed and she's been filling it with clothes from the wardrobe.

'How come you're back? I thought you'd left for work. Are you going away again?'

Jemma sits on the bed and pats the quilt beside her.

I join her, but I feel unnerved. 'What's going on?'

'This isn't working, is it?' She looks me straight in the eyes and I feel a sudden sense of panic about where this conversation is about to go.

'This meaning us?'

'Jake, you know what I mean.'

'No, I don't. Please elaborate. What exactly about me doing everything to support you, your career and look after our son isn't working for you?'

Jemma gives me an I-don't-know-why-I'm-bothering expression, stands up and pulls more of her clothes off the hangers in the wardrobe, stuffing them into the case with less precision than before. 'I should've guessed we couldn't do this reasonably.'

'Reasonably?'

'I need some time away from all this.' Jemma gestures around the room, as if our bedroom contains everything that is wrong with the world.

'And Alfie?'

'He can come and visit. I'll Skype him all the time.'

'Skype him? You're going to parent him via Skype? Are you serious?'

'He'll be fine. Better off, probably.' Jemma looks like she's on the run, frantically squashing more and more clothes into the case – there's no way it's going to close. 'Look, I don't have all the answers, Jake. I just need to get away. I can't explain it any better than that.'

'And where exactly are you going?'

'I'm going to stay with Laura. Work have agreed to give me a six-month sabbatical.'

'Laura? Please don't tell me you mean your sister Laura?'

Not looking at me, she nods.

'You're going to Paris?' I find myself laughing. 'How the hell is Alfie supposed to visit you in Paris? When did you agree this with work? How long have you been planning all this?'

I've got so many questions; I don't know which one to start with. I know our relationship's not great right now. The last conversation we had that lasted over two minutes and wasn't an argument was about what we needed to put on the online Waitrose order, and even then we couldn't agree on whether to get frozen fruit or fresh, chopped tomatoes or plum. But this? I would never leave Jemma, even if at times I've wondered whether I'd be happier if I did.

'But we had sex last week,' I continue, my voice coming out as a squeak. 'You initiated it. You never do that.'

'I was trying to . . .' Jemma stops.

Suddenly the penny drops and, with it, my heart. 'To make yourself love me again?'

Jemma pauses, long enough for me to know that yes, that was exactly what she'd been trying to do. 'No. Let's not make this any harder than it already is. I just can't live here any more.'

Jemma fiddles with the clasp on the suitcase. When it won't close, she starts rummaging through her clothes, pulling items out and throwing them on the bed.

'And you think I don't feel like that? You think I don't want to run away?'

It's the truth, I do. Even though I hate myself for it.

'I'm sorry.'

'You're sorry? That's it? So are we getting a divorce or do you expect me to wait for you? You go off and refresh yourself in Paris, then come back and we act as if you never left?'

Jemma shakes her head, as if trying to explain something incredibly simple to someone incredibly stupid.

'No. I don't expect anything from you. We don't need to think about divorce yet. I just need out. I'm so miserable, Jake.'

I swallow down the hurt and try not to focus on her use of the word 'yet'. 'And what exactly are we going to do about money? We have a mortgage to pay, bills, our child needs to eat. Have you thought about any of that?'

There's a sudden shift in Jemma's mood. The untrained eye might have missed it, but it's very clear to me.

'Have *you*? Have you thought about any of that? I've all but supported you for the past six years. Perhaps it's time *you* put the food on the table and kept the roof over your own head.'

'Are you serious? I've been looking after your son. God knows, you certainly had no intention of doing it.'

From the look on Jemma's face, I think that if she wasn't leaving me there's a high chance I'd be found in a few months' time buried under the decking. 'Why does it always come back to this, Jake? You think you're a better parent, no, a better person, because you stayed home with Alfie. You're right. I wouldn't give up my career. I would've been one of those parents you despise and put him into nursery. And who knows? Perhaps then he wouldn't be such a fucking mess.'

I can tell that Jemma knows she has overstepped the mark because she leaves the room. I know that she will come back in a bit and apologize. But I also know that deep down in her heart, she does think that. Because I think it too.

I sit on the bed, trying to take in what's happening. After a few minutes, Jemma comes back in, rushes over to me and gives me a hug. I breathe in the familiar smell of her shampoo and it almost makes me cry. After a while, we both pull away.

'I'm just going to finish off packing and then I'm going to go. I don't want to drag this out for any longer than we have to.'

'What about Alfie? Won't you stay until he's home and say goodbye?'

'I can't. My flight's at two.'

I can't believe she has a flight booked. Up until this moment, it's felt like just another fight where threats are made and not followed through. But now it's hitting me that my wife is actually leaving me.

'But what about the anger management? I'm doing that for you. Aren't you even going to give me a chance to change?'

I hate how desperate I sound. Like it's all my fault. But I just don't want her to go.

Jemma shakes her head. 'It's so much more than that, Jake. I thought that might make a difference, but it's not just you. It's me. It's Alfie. It's everything. I feel like I'm slowly dying here.'

I chew my bottom lip, trying to stop the tears in my throat from reaching my eyes. 'So how exactly do I explain this to Alfie, Jem?'

'I don't know, but I know you'll find a way. Whatever I've said in the past, we both know you're much better with him than I am.'

During other fights, this kind of platitude would've calmed me. It wouldn't have meant that the argument was over, but it would've been a turning point towards resolution. Jemma is well aware of this. She thinks she's being clever, but it's not going to work today.

'Don't try and get out of it like that, Jem. It's your job to tell your son you're abandoning him. Not mine.'

I expect her to tell me to fuck off, that she's not abandoning him, that I'm being a prick. But she doesn't. She collapses on the bed, puts her head in her hands and sobs. Embarrassingly loud sobs that make her body convulse.

'I've thought about it over and over, Jake,' she says through the tears. 'I'd never do anything to hurt him. But I've got to leave. I'm no good to Alfie like this. That's why I think it's better that he just comes home and I'm not here. I don't want a painful goodbye. I'm not sure I'd be able to leave if he was here. And I need to, Jake. I'm so sorry, but I need to.'

I put my arm around her and she rests her head on my chest as her sobs gradually turn into sniffs. There was a time, when Jemma first started working late every night and in the study all weekend, that I wondered if she even loved Alfie. But then I'd catch her at night, sitting at the end of his bed just staring at him. Sometimes she'd be crying, other times smiling. And I knew that she adored him. Just like now I know she really believes it's best for her to sneak away.

'OK, I'll tell him.'

Jemma looks up at me in surprise. 'Thank you so much.' She tries to hug me tightly, but I sit there, my body frozen.

Then I suddenly stand up, because if I don't, I might fall to my knees and beg her to stay. 'I'll leave you to finish packing.'

'Thanks.'

Our actual goodbye is less than dramatic. She brings her case down into the hallway. I potter in from the kitchen. She gives me a kiss on the cheek and I offer her a half-hearted smile. I don't say all the things I want to say. She picks up her case and walks out.

Later, when she's been gone about half an hour, it hits me. I collect up the clothes she's left on the bed and throw them across the room. I run my arm across shelves – books, candles and her stupid bowls of pot pourri spilling on to the floor. I take our wedding photo off the wall and smash it against the top of the cabinet, the glass only splintering feebly, remaining mostly intact. I search the house for something, anything, that she cares about. The vase sits on the dining-room table. It was a gift from her parents and I always hated it – the intricate flowers and butterflies adorning the ceramic. Jemma knew I hated it, that I thought it was too showy, but she still insisted we used it as a centre-piece so I had to look at it every time I sat down for a meal. As I launch it at the wall, it shatters into pieces, shards scattering far and wide across the floor. For a very long time, I sit amongst the chaos with my head in my hands, feeling as broken as the ceramic that surrounds me.

Then I spend the rest of the day tidying so that Alfie won't wonder what's happened, and trying to mend things that can't be fixed.

* * *

'Can we send Emily a message? Can she come now?'

'Alfie, I don't think you are really listening to what I'm saying.'

'Please, Daddy.' Alfie waves his arms around manically,

the napkin with Emily's number on it gripped firmly in his hand.

I bend down so that I'm at his eye-level and hold his arms still by his side. 'Alfie, I said that Mummy has gone to live with Aunty Laura in France for a while. Do you understand what I'm telling you?'

'Yes.' A short pause. 'Now can we call Emily?'

This isn't the reaction I was expecting. I've been avoiding telling Alfie that Jemma's not coming home for several days. I even bought him a Lego set to calm the inevitable meltdown. But he seems less bothered than if I'd told him I'd forgotten to record the latest episode of *Gigglebiz*.

'Alfie, I don't think you're getting it. Mummy isn't going to be living with us for a while.'

'I know. Like when she's away for work and we see her on the computer and she brings me home the shampoo bottles from the hotel.'

'Not quite like that, little man. It'll be longer than normal. But, yeah, we will still talk to her on the computer.'

'And will she bring me the little bottles?'

'Well, no, she's not staying in a hotel.'

'But I want the little bottles.'

'I'm sure we can get you some of those from the shop.'

Alfie ponders this for a minute. 'OK. Can we send Emily a message now? It's been ages and you promised she could see the Lego.'

'Look, we're not texting Emily, Alfie. She doesn't want to see your Lego. She was just being nice.'

At this, huge waves of tears ensue – just as one set dies down, another rolls in. 'You're being so mean, Daddy. Why are you being so mean?'

Alfie starts pulling the cushions off the sofa and throwing them around the room, then he looks around to see what else he can propel and decides on the magazines neatly positioned in a wicker basket. In mid-tantrum, Alfie still looks like a toddler. Sometimes, when he's answering me back and arguing with every word I say, it's easy to forget he's still so young.

'I'm sorry.' I pick him up and hold him on my lap, my arms encapsulating his so he can't lash out. 'I'm so sorry for all this, Alfie.'

'Please can we invite Emily over to see my Lego?'

I've just told my son his mum's left him so I know that I've got to say yes. I take the napkin from Alfie. He somehow still manages to have Emily's number firmly clasped in his hand, even after throwing around most of the contents of the lounge.

'OK. I'll send her a message. But she might not be able to come, OK? And it won't be today.'

'Oh, I want to see her today. Please.' He elongates the 'ee' sound and opens his eyes as wide as they'll go.

'It'll be bedtime in a couple of hours. She's probably busy. Look, I'll try. I'll text her now.' I hold out my phone as evidence.

'Make sure you put pretty, pretty please.'

I laugh. 'Of course.'

Alfie appears satisfied that this'll do the job and that Emily will be turning up shortly. Unbelievably, within ten minutes she texts me to say that she will be.

I have a quick straighten up, gathering up all the crap – the empty beer bottles on every surface, the dirty bowl from last night's impromptu midnight pie, five or six of

Alfie's socks (all odd), his school trousers and pants on the bathroom floor where he's taken them off and left them – then I run the Hoover round and lightly wipe the surfaces. I don't want it to look like I've tidied for her arrival, so I leave out a few bits, choosing the ones that paint me as a good father – the book I read to Alfie at bedtime, one of his completed puzzles on the lounge floor, the home-made hovercraft from the one time we did a science experiment out of the book we bought him for Christmas. I take the last painting he did at school out of the recycling bag and Blu-Tack it to the dining-room wall.

When Emily arrives, I welcome her into the hallway and quickly kick the dirty socks I missed under the shoe rack.

'Come on in. Do you want me to take your coat?'

I don't think I've ever offered to take anyone's coat before.

'Thanks.'

She takes off her leather jacket and I hang it on the coat rack. She's wearing a long-sleeved top that hangs off one shoulder and, seeing her exposed shoulder blade, it's noticeable how painfully thin she is. For a second, it makes me feel strangely protective.

We walk into the dining room and she pulls the cuff of her top over her hand. 'Is your wife here?'

'No, she's . . . just had to pop to Paris on business. She's a highly successful marketing executive so she spends a lot of time travelling. Look, there's a photo of her on our wedding day.' I point to the now slightly cracked picture of us on our photo wall – the frames organized in a purportedly random configuration that actually took hours and a lot of swear words to put up.

Emily glances up at the photo and nods.

'I know, I'm punching. Everyone always says it.'

Why am I saying all this?

If Jemma were here, she'd glare at me and slyly dig me in the ribs. When we first met, Jemma found my tendency to over-explain endearing. I'd take a shirt back to the shop for a refund and regale the shop assistant with a fabricated tale of why I once thought it suitable but how unfortunately it no longer was and Jemma would lean in, kiss me on the cheek and whisper, 'You're bumbling again,' like I was some kind of adorable Hugh Grant figure in *Four Weddings and a Funeral*. But over time, the novelty wore off and her affectionate reaction gradually turned into an embarrassed, 'Jake, just shut up, will you?'

'She's very pretty.'

I nod, my eyes drawn to the photograph, Jemma looking up at me, her eyes brimming with love, my hand on her face. I never quite worked out why she loved me so much. I remember the day I proposed, standing at the edge of the Grand Canyon on our extensive tour of America's west coast, terrified that she would say no. My heart was beating so fast I was sure I was about to end up as a newspaper headline: 'Man dies during histrionic proposal'. I got down on one knee, pulled out the Tesco carrier bag I'd used to disguise the ring box and held it out to her. She laughed, 'That's a dramatic way to hand me my sandwiches,' before I removed the little red box from the bag and asked her properly. When she said yes, it was relief I felt first and then euphoria, as she kissed me and everyone around us cheered and whooped in the unashamed way the Americans do best.

I suddenly realize that Emily and I have been standing in silence and, for once, am glad to hear Alfie bounding down the stairs ready to dominate all conversation.

He runs up to Emily and holds the cannon from his Jokerland Lego set right up to her face. 'Look, this is just a tiny part of it. Come upstairs and see the rest.' He looks down at Emily's biker boots. 'You have to take your shoes off, though.'

'It's fine. Don't worry,' I say, with a wave of the hand.

'But you always say we have to take our shoes off.'

'But Emily is a guest.'

It dawns on me that, other than family, we haven't had many visitors to the house since having Alfie.

'It's fine.' Emily removes her boots. She's wearing odd socks, one of them pink with luminous yellow stars and the other sporting a Christmas pudding with a smiley face. If someone had asked me what kind of socks she wore underneath her boots, I definitely would not have predicted those.

'Do you want a cup of tea? Coffee? A glass of wine?'

'Coffee, thanks.'

'OK, I'll just get you one. Alfie, be gentle with our guest.'

Alfie's clearly not listening. He tugs at Emily's sleeve and starts pulling her up the stairs.

'Alfie.'

'Don't worry, it's fine,' Emily says. 'Come on, Alfie. I'm super-excited about seeing the rest of Jokerland.'

I'm glad of the breather. After the swathe of negativity I've had so far from Emily, her being here feels like a test I'm desperate to ace. I'm determined to prove her wrong, to show her I am a good dad and decent husband – even though, as my son spends most of his time hating me and my wife is currently hundreds of miles away, both are debatable.

I take up two coffees and a hot chocolate for Alfie (piled high with marshmallows in the deluded hope that sugary treats will make up for Jemma's absence). He and Emily are on the floor playing with Lego. She looks different; her face is relaxed and childlike as they take turns to send a figure through the Joker's mouth, down the slide and into the pot of pretend gunge. As each figure lands, they both chuckle and send down another one until the pot is overflowing.

'Empty it. Let's do it again.' Alfie grabs the pot and shakes the figures out on to the floor.

I put the drinks on Alfie's desk. When Emily notices me, her face changes entirely, as if she has quickly pulled down a mask.

'I'll put the drinks here. Clumsy-pants, make sure you don't knock them over.'

'It's your turn, Emily.' Alfie prods her arm and hands her a figure.

Emily sends it down the slide, but not with the same gusto as she did before.

'I'll leave you guys to it.'

I take my coffee to my room and sit on the bed listening to Emily and Alfie giggling. It's nice to hear him laugh. It reminds me how happy it makes me when he's not enraged or obsessing about something or trying to manipulate me.

When I open my laptop, there's an email from Jemma.

Here safe x

I picture her and Laura in Paris, having a champagne toast to Jemma's freedom on the deck of the Eiffel Tower. I type a reply, delete it and then type it again.

Come home x

I can't stop thinking about something my mum said, while I sat on the edge of her bed after she'd got so sick that she could no longer get up without being supported. *I don't mind what you do with your life, Jake. Just promise me you'll be two things. Promise me you'll be kind. And promise me you'll be loyal.* I nodded, shredded to pieces at the thought of a time when she'd no longer be there, but determined never to disappoint her. I just hope Jemma will eventually feel the same way. *For better or worse,* isn't that what we promised each other?

'No.' Alfie's voice is raised. 'We have to put them down in the right order. It's Spider-Girl next, not Magneto.'

Great. This is all I need. It had been going so well. Too well. I should've known it was only a matter of time before Alfie resumed his typically humiliating behaviour.

I walk across the hallway and stand at Alfie's door. 'It doesn't really matter which order the figures go down in, does it?'

Emily holds up her hands. 'It was my mistake, sorry. I didn't realize.'

'It does matter, Daddy. They go in a line like this.' He points to his figures carefully organized in a row, ready for their turn on the slide. 'Emily was doing it wrong.'

Emily sips her coffee, hiding behind her mug.

'Excuse us a minute.' I pick Alfie up. He yelps and

resists, but I manage to carry him across the landing to my room and put him on the bed.

'You do not speak to visitors like that, Alfie. Do you understand? It's rude.'

Alfie turns his face away. 'She was doing it wrong.'

'No, she was being kind and playing with you and you're just making a fuss about the stupid order.'

'You can't say "stupid".'

It's one of Jemma's rules – you have to say silly instead. Stupid rule.

'Go back in and apologize to Emily and then it'll be time for bath and bed.'

Alfie climbs down off the mattress and goes back to his room and, for a minute, I think he's taken on board what I've said and is going to apologize. But then there's a crash and I know he's thrown some of his Lego across the room. Please, God, don't let it be the Batmobile. That thing is a nightmare to build.

I peer into his room. It's the fucking Batmobile.

'Right, it can stay like that. I'm not wasting any more of my time building Lego sets for you to smash them up when you don't get your own way.'

Alfie scrambles on to his bed, builds a wall across the corner with his pillows, climbs over and hides in his makeshift den.

I turn to Emily. 'I'm sorry. It's been a hard day.' *Unlike all the others. They're a walk in the park.* 'Feel free to go. I need to get him bathed in a minute, anyway.'

'Oh, OK. I'll just say bye to him.'

I take the hint and go downstairs. It's about ten minutes before Emily appears in the doorway to the lounge.

'Thank you for the coffee. I'll see you on Saturday.'

I struggle to push myself up off the sofa. Since Jemma left, it feels like I'm three stone heavier and twenty years older. 'Look, I'm sorry about that. I didn't mean to make you feel awkward or anything. It's just he needs to learn he can't get away with that sort of behaviour.'

Emily shrugs like a teenager who's been asked if they had a good day at school. 'I didn't feel awkward.'

There's a subtle but definite emphasis on the 'I'. Meaning what, that *I* should?

'Well, that's good then. I needn't have worried.'

I'm not sure whether Emily picks up on the hostility in my voice or not. She's always so po-faced when she's around me, it's hard to tell.

'Oh, just so you know, he's fixing the Lego. I told him I wouldn't tell you, so act surprised when you go up.'

Great. Now I feel like even more of an arsehole.

'OK, I will. Thanks for coming. It will have made his day.'

'No problem.' Emily looks down, her demeanour still petulant.

'See you Saturday.'

She leaves and I feel my whole body relax. When I get to Alfie's door, I stand there and watch. He's putting the finishing touches to the front of the Batmobile. He's got the instruction booklet out of the box and is studying it carefully so that he gets every piece just right. It makes my chest hurt. Most six-year-olds would've just thrown it back together any old which way, hoping it was roughly like the original model. In fact, that's exactly what I would've done. But Alfie's got it perfect – like mother, like son.

All of a sudden, I wish Jemma was still here. Because even though we'd be arguing over whose turn it was to do the bath and whose life is harder, at least I wouldn't be standing here alone with my son, not knowing what the hell I'm doing.

'Look, Daddy, I've mended it.'

It always amazes me how quickly children forget about arguments and move on. Jemma and I would've thrashed something like this out for at least three days.

'I can see, little man. Thank you.' I kneel down beside Alfie, close enough so that our bodies touch. 'I'm sorry that I shouted at you. Daddy was just cross because you shouldn't have thrown the Lego. That was naughty, do you realize that?'

'Yeah, but you hurt me and pushed me on your bed when I was playing with Emily.'

'No, I didn't. I just told you not to be rude to her.'

'I wasn't. Emily didn't mind. We were fine once I told her. I just didn't want her to do it wrong.'

There's such torture in his voice that I wonder whether the root cause of all this is really Jemma leaving, but maybe I'm just projecting my own feelings on to him. Either way, I'm failing. My son's just lost his mum and I'm screaming at him.

'Look, Alfie, let's just forget about it. I promise I'll try not to get so cross and you promise not to break your things. Deal?'

'We'll try our best?'

'Yeah.'

'They say at school you can only try your best and, as long as you are trying your best, then that's good enough.'

I smile, remembering all the mantras we had in teaching. Assembly upon assembly on bloody values. As if you can teach that stuff with a sparkly PowerPoint and a well-chosen story.

'This school malarkey is making you very clever.'

Alfie stops, a Lego brick held in mid-air. 'What does "malarkey" mean?'

'I don't actually know. Just being at school, that's what I mean.'

I watch as the answer filters through his ears, into his brain, pauses at his is-this-a-good-enough-response cortex and then, luckily, passes through.

'I like Emily.' Alfie puts the final brick on his model and carefully places it back up on his Lego display shelf.

I don't want to cause another argument now things are finally settled down, but I know I need to prepare Alfie for the likelihood that he won't be seeing Emily again. 'I'm not sure she's going to want to come over again, little man.'

'Why not?'

'I'm just not sure she really wants to be Daddy's friend. Not everyone wants to be friends with everyone, do they?'

'But she's my friend. Not yours.'

I marvel at his innocence. It's at times like this I don't understand why I find it so hard to get along with him. It's like there are two boys, one who I utterly adore and the other who drives me to the very cusp of my sanity.

'Please can she come over again?'

'We'll see. Now let's get you into your pyjamas.'

'Not we'll see, say yes.'

'Alfie. Pyjamas.'

'Not until you say yes.'

I'd rather sit through a One Direction concert than have Emily over again, but I don't want to argue with him tonight.

'OK, yes.'

'You're just saying yes because you want me to go to bed, aren't you?'

I laugh and kiss Alfie's head. 'No. I promise she can come over again.'

Trust my son to want to see the one person in the world who can't stand me.

Alfie

'Hurry up, Alfie.'

I walk to the car. One, two, three, four, five, six. There are six stepping stones and I have to count each one and not step on the cracks or I have to go back to the start. Covering my hand with my sleeve, I tug on the handle of the car door. It keeps slipping and I can't get it open.

Daddy leans over and opens the door from inside and he's got that cross face which means I'm not going to get a snack after tea today.

'Just get in the car.'

I step in, making sure I avoid standing on the ledge. Finally, I'm in. It no longer feels hard to breathe, like when I've got a cold and Mummy puts that smelly stuff on my pillow.

'Put your seat belt on, then.'

I want to say I can't. That it's really hard to put your seat belt on when your hand is covered up, but I know he'll tell me to stop being weird and I don't like it when he says that. It makes me feel funny deep in my tummy. A bit like when I eat too much cake at a birthday party and it hurts. So I use just two fingers and, after a few attempts, I manage to get my seat belt done up.

I hold my hand out in front of me with the fingers spread so that they don't touch. Some days I don't mind touching things. I don't even notice. But other days, my brain says if I touch things I have to say it out loud or I have to wash my hands. I can't say it out loud because Daddy will get cross and say, 'What are you on about, Alfie?' and when I say, 'I have to say it,' he'll say, 'Stop being silly,' but I'm not. When I'm silly, it's fun. I like being silly, but I don't like it when I have my funny hand days.

When I get into class, I'll tell Mrs Young that I need the toilet so I can wash my hands and she'll say, 'Why didn't you go before you came to school, Alfie?' and I'll say that I did but I just had a big drink at breakfast. Usually, she'll say, 'What are we going to do with you?' and smile and I know that means I'm allowed to go. But when lots of the other children are asking her questions or Archie is swinging his book bag around his head or throwing pencils across the room, she'll wave her hands and tell me to 'just sit down' and I'll have to hold my hand out until she lets me go and the other children will say, 'Alfie's trying to touch me,' and I'll cry because I'm not.

When we get there, Daddy says, 'We're late,' which means we'll go straight in. We're late most days and it makes Daddy cross. He says it's because I won't get ready. I don't like getting ready. I don't like it when Daddy tells me to do things because I want to choose what to do myself. Some days it doesn't make me feel so cross and I do try to put my clothes on, but I end up getting muddled and put things on in the wrong order, and I always lose my socks. Daddy says I have a cotton-wool brain but I'm not sure what a cotton-wool brain is. I think he means my brain forgets everything, but I'm not sure if I forget or if I just remember something different. It doesn't really make sense that he says I forget everything, because if I did, then I wouldn't remember all my Lego figures or the stories we listen to in the car. I can remember every single word of those in the right order and Daddy says I must be a genius, like Superman. I like it when he says that.

I climb out the car, swinging my legs a bit to get them over the ledge, and then kick the door closed.

'Do not kick my car,' Daddy shouts. He doesn't understand that I have to use my feet because it's a funny hand day.

Daddy holds my hood and pulls me along the pavement. I like the path to school because it's tarmac, it's got no cracks so it makes walking much quicker, but Daddy still thinks I'm too slow. If I run, though, he tells me not to go off ahead so I'm not sure what he wants me to do.

I arrive just in time to join the end of the line. When we get into the classroom, I'm happy because Archie is taken off with Miss Smith so Mrs Young is smiling and she lets me go to the toilet straight away.

I cover my hand with my sleeve and just about manage to turn the tap on. It's not easy because it's my wrong hand. It's not the one I hold my pencil in. It's the one that if I hold up my fingers like Mrs Young showed us it makes a capital L, which stands for 'left'. I wash my right hand and the feeling in my tummy like I might be sick goes away. I put on some more soap and wash it again. Bit more soap, then wash it again. First the front, then the back. I dry it with a paper towel and then put both hands in my pockets where they're safe.

I walk back into the classroom and Mrs Young looks at me.

'Take your hands out of your pockets, Alfie. There's a good boy.'

I don't do it straight away and her face begins to change to a cross face and I don't want to be sent to Mr Frampton so I do what she told me to. When I sit on the carpet, I keep my hands in my lap because I think they'll be OK there now I've washed them.

After register, Miss Smith asks me to read to her. I don't like reading out loud because the words jump about or the pictures get in the way and Miss Smith makes me go back to the start and try again. Today she asks if I'm OK and I say yes but she asks me again, so I'm not sure if yes is the right answer or not. She says if I ever want to talk to her about Mummy, then I can, but I'm not sure why I'd want to talk to Miss Smith about Mummy or what to say about her. I know Daddy told Mrs Young that Mummy is living in French at the moment because I heard him in the playground. She had a sad face but I'm not sure why, because when I asked Daddy, he said French is a lovely place to live.

Miss Smith has a sad face now too and puts her hand on my shoulder. I don't really like it because it feels hot and sticky but I don't want to get in trouble so I let her put it there. She asks if I have spoken to Mummy on the computer yet and I tell her no but I am going to tonight and she says, 'Good.' I don't really think it's good because Mummy's voice sounds funny on the computer, like a robot, and it keeps jumping like when CDs and DVDs get scratched because I don't put them back in their box. When Mummy's voice jumps, I can't understand what she's saying and she doesn't hear me and I have to keep saying the same things again, which is annoying. I want her to bring me back the little bottles so I can keep my magic spells in them, but Daddy says she isn't staying in a hotel so I won't get them this time. Luckily, when I told Emily, she said she had lots of them at home and would bring them over. I hope Emily can come over tonight. Daddy will probably say no but I'm going to send her a message myself because she's my friend, not Daddy's, and I want to see her so that's that.

Emily

On the way to anger management, I recite my confession in my head, making adjustments as I go, changing my tone of voice for certain parts. They all hate me anyway. Telling them why I'm here isn't going to make it much worse. It's like a serial killer saying they wouldn't give up their seat to an old lady on the bus; it loses its impact somewhat. I march in, ready for action, ready to prove I don't belong here. Then I look around at all the faces and it feels like I'm shrinking.

Sam clangs the triangle and welcomes everyone. Then the group members bow their heads and I do the same, trying to ignore how my heartbeat has got all overexcited and doubled in speed. After that, it's the dreaded declaration. Jake doesn't bother to hold out his hands now, as he knows I'll refuse to hold them.

'So, before we start, does anyone want to share anything?'

It's Sam's stock opening phrase, but today it feels like he's talking directly to me. He surveys the room and when his eyes reach me, he pauses, and I'm just about to say yes when his eyes pass me by and the moment's gone; and alongside the relief, I feel an unexpected sense of disappointment.

'Right, well, today you're going to be thrilled to hear we're going to do some role play.'

An audible groan travels around the room and Sam smiles.

'I know people don't like role play, but it really does help to try some of the strategies out, rather than just talk about them. You might not appreciate it now, but when a conflict situation arises, you'll be better off for having had a go.'

I'm not seven. I think I can make the giant mental leap from discussing a strategy to using it in everyday life.

'So I'm going to give out a range of hot topics, the types of things that tend to stir up a bit of debate. If you find you both share the same view, perhaps one of you could pretend to oppose it so you can practise some of the language choices that help deal with a difference of opinion in a positive way. Then I'll call you back so we can share ideas.'

Sam circles the group, handing each pair a folded piece of paper.

I open ours. *Me Too campaign.* When I hold it up for Jake, I notice my hand's shaking so I quickly drop it to my lap. 'I mean, there's nothing to discuss really, is there? Unless you agree with sexual abuse, it's pretty clear-cut it's a great thing women are finally standing up and saying enough is enough.'

Jake nods, but there's no commitment behind it.

'Do you seriously think differently?'

'I just think maybe it's gone a bit far, that's all. It seems you can't even compliment a woman or touch her on the arm these days without being accused of sexual harassment. My friend got a formal warning the other week for trying to kiss one of his colleagues in a bar, when she'd been the one flirting with him all night and encouraging him to buy her drinks.'

An image comes into my head. My short skirt. A row

of empty shot glasses lined up on the bar. 'So that makes her fair game, does it?'

Sam wanders over. 'Right, I can see you guys have a difference of opinion, which, for this exercise, is great.'

I pick at the rough skin round my thumbnail, then stop myself as I picture Mum doing the same.

'So let's see if we can discuss this in a way that is respectful to both viewpoints,' Sam continues. 'Because, ultimately, the best conflict resolution is that which seeks to empathize with the other person, to recognize and accept a different view to our own by showing the other person the respect they deserve.'

Jake offers Sam an ingratiating smile, then turns to me. 'Look, I'm sorry if my opinion upset you, Emily. Perhaps I didn't explain myself clearly.' *Suck-up.* 'I merely meant that if a woman has been giving a man the right signals all night, I don't think you can call it harassment when he tries to kiss her.'

I wrap my arms around my body. 'So because a woman's nice to you, it gives you permission to do what you want to her?'

Jake takes a sharp intake of breath. 'That's not what I'm saying.'

Sam puts his hand on my shoulder. 'Em, try not to hear something negative in Jake's words. Try to have empathy for his viewpoint.'

I bite down on my thumb until it starts to hurt.

'Of course I don't think a man should touch a woman if she doesn't want him to, even if she's been flirting all night,' Jake continues. 'Maybe my friend misread the signals, it happens, but he only leant in to kiss her and as soon as she said she wasn't interested, he stopped. Surely he shouldn't be persecuted for that?'

I can still feel clammy palms gripping my wrists. His breath – hot and wet – in my ear. 'As long as he stops when she tells him no.'

Jake nods, his eyes suddenly appearing to read something in mine. 'Of course. No question.'

Sam stands up. 'Well done, guys. I can see it wasn't easy, but you worked hard to resolve the conflict.'

Sam heads over to another pair and Jake rests his head on the back of his chair. 'Well, that was fun.'

He laughs awkwardly and I grab my cigarettes out of my bag. 'I'm just going for a smoke.'

Outside, I struggle to steady my hand enough to light a cigarette and then, once I've managed it, take a long, hard drag. The thing I hate most about what happened is how it pounces on me when I least expect it. I expect it to wake me up in the night, sweaty and panicked. But sometimes it's when I'm just driving along thinking about something else entirely, or when I'm in the supermarket and I see someone with the same colour jacket as he had on, or now, standing here innocently trying to have a smoke, like I was that night.

I rub my face and my head hard, trying to get rid of the images, some painfully clear, some muddled like a toddler's scribbled all over the memory. And that feeling, like an elastic band stretched too many times. Surely it was inevitable I was going to snap?

* * *

As I leave anger management, I spot Alfie outside, repeatedly climbing on to a wall and then jumping off. There's an older man with him, handsome in a classic Robert Redford way, and I can tell straight away he's Jake's dad. They have the same deep-brown eyes and chiselled jaw, although the skin around his dad's is a little looser with age.

When Alfie spots me, he runs over and grabs my legs.

'Hey, buddy, how are you doing?'

Alfie turns to Jake and starts jumping up and down. 'Daddy, Daddy, is Emily coming to play?'

'No, kiddo. Emily and I just go to the same class together.'

Jake's dad slyly gives me the once-over. It's fair enough. I accept it doesn't look good – a skinhead who's just stepped out of anger management and appears to have a relationship with your grandson.

'Can we go to the park, Daddy? Can Emily come?'

'Emily's probably busy, little man, but yeah, we can go to the park, if you want.'

'Are you busy, Emily?' Alfie looks up at me, perfecting the puppy-dog eyes that will one day bring a girl to her knees.

'Well, I've got to go and see my nan soon, but I could come for a little bit if it's OK with Daddy?'

'Of course, but only if you want to. Don't let Alfie pressure you.'

'It's OK. I'd like to come.'

Alfie grabs my hand and starts pulling me in the direction of the park.

'Hold on, Alfie, just say bye to Grandad first,' Jake says, laughing.

Alfie runs back and gives Jake's dad a cursory hug. 'Aren't you coming, Grandad?'

Jake's dad kisses the top of Alfie's head. 'I think you've exhausted me enough for today. I'll see you soon though, OK?'

I imagine he was the sort of dad who helped build sandcastles and read bedtime stories. It would've been nice to have a dad like that.

Alfie returns his attention to me. 'Come on, Emily, let's go. I'll show you where it is. I can switch on my supersonic map brain.'

'Wow, why don't I have a supersonic map brain? Come on then. Nice to meet you . . .'

Alfie pulls me away.

'George,' Jake's dad calls out. 'Nice to meet you too, Emily.'

* * *

Alfie charges around the park. He appears to have no awareness of his body, accidentally bumping into other people, crashing into posts. He begins to climb up the slide, despite the queue of children at the top.

'Alfie, you have to go down the slide, not climb up it,' Jake says, a nervousness on his face, like a clairvoyant who's just seen something terrible in their client's future.

With a look of pure mischief, Alfie ignores him, but just as Jake is about to grab him, he jumps off the slide and darts towards the cargo net, clambering up it and waving at us from the top.

'Disaster averted for a second,' Jake says.

We slowly trace Alfie's movements around the park and watch as he struggles down the other side of the netting and then starts jumping along a set of logs, going back to the start every time he falls off. The silence between us feels uncomfortable, so I rack my brain for something, anything, to break it.

'You look just like your dad, by the way.'

'Do you think? I always thought I looked more like my mum.'

'Well, I've not seen your mum, but you definitely look a lot like your dad. Same eyes. Same face shape.'

Jake looks solemn, like he's just remembered some bad news. 'My mum died when I was eighteen. Cancer.'

'Oh, I'm sorry.'

'Yeah, me too.'

I can't help but feel guilty for giving him a hard time over the past few weeks. It's irrational really – experiencing loss doesn't suddenly make you a decent person. It's like when the biggest bitch at school got leukaemia – suddenly everyone wanted to be her best friend. But ultimately, although of course I felt sorry for her, it didn't make her any nicer a person.

'Look, I'm sorry I pissed you off earlier. It certainly wasn't my intention.'

I shake my head. 'Don't worry about it. I was probably being oversensitive.' I quickly change the subject before he has a chance to delve any deeper. 'So are you finding it useful? The anger management?'

'Well, it hasn't saved my marriage. I lied when you came over. My wife's not away on business. She's gone to stay with her sister in Paris. A trial separation, I guess you'd call it.'

'I'm sorry.'

'It is what it is. I just hope Alfie's OK.'

'I'm sure he'll be fine. They say kids are pretty resilient.'

Jake massages the skin around his temples.

'And you? Are you OK?' I ask, because he doesn't look it and I feel I should.

Jake gives his best nonchalant shrug. 'Yeah, I'm fine.' He pauses. 'I mean, being a single dad isn't exactly a walk in the park. But in terms of the marriage, it's probably for the best. I think we both felt the same way, really. That it wasn't working.'

I call bullshit. A man who attends anger management to save his marriage doesn't sound like someone who was ready for it to end. But I let him keep his pride. Let's be honest, it's all he's really got.

'So I guess you could quit the anger management? The ultimatum doesn't really apply now, does it?'

'True. I hadn't really thought about that.'

Alfie waves and we both wave back.

'I don't know,' Jake continues. 'I might stick with it. Who knows, maybe it'll help with the road rage I've always struggled with. It can't be good for my blood pressure. Maybe she'll end up saving me from a coronary.'

'Every cloud and all that.'

Alfie runs over and grabs my hand. 'Come and help me with the *Ninja Warrior* course.'

I'm guessing by the *Ninja Warrior* course he means the two balance beams, the rope bridge and the monkey bars.

'I'd love to.'

Jake follows us over and I hold Alfie's hand as he tracks along the beams. I hold him up as he grips on to the monkey bars. He's surprisingly heavy for such a skinny little kid, like he's filled to the top with sand. He scuttles across the rope bridge on his own and then he's back.

'I did it.'

'High five!' I say and he slaps my hand as hard as he can. 'Ow.'

Alfie thinks this is hilarious and we repeat it several times, with no sign of him getting bored.

'Enough now, Alfie,' Jake says. 'See if you can do the course on your own.'

'Only if you stay here and watch,' he says to me.

'Of course.'

Alfie goes back to the start and balances along the beam, falling off a couple of times but persevering until he completes it in one go.

'It's really odd. Normally, he won't even look at strangers. Just goes all quiet and hides behind me. He's really taken to you.'

'Yeah, well, I'm pretty irresistible.'

Jake laughs. A little too hard for my liking. In all honesty, I have no idea why Alfie wants to spend time with me either. But I'm glad that he does, because, to my surprise, I like spending time with him too.

I check my watch. 'I better go. My nan will be getting hungry. I take her round Chinese.'

'That's nice of you.' Jake's unable to hide his surprise, like he thought I was the type of person who'd sneak money out of my nan's handbag rather than take her highly processed take-out food. 'Yeah, I suppose I'd better get back and do Alfie's lunch.'

'I'll just go and say bye to him. See you next week at group?'

He sweeps his hair off his face. It's so buoyant, it's like it's mocking my measly stubble. 'Yeah, see you there.'

Alfie is dangling off the first monkey bar, unable to get enough momentum to reach the next one. When he sees me walking over, he drops to the ground.

'I'm going now, Alfie. See you soon, yeah? You'll be on *Ninja Warrior* before you know it.'

'Can you come to my house again?'

'Yeah, sure, one day.'

'How about today?'

'I've got to see my nan today, Alfie, but another day would be good.'

He looks at me like I've just snatched his teddy off him and Jake shambles over, like a weary soldier trying to muster up the energy for his next combat.

'Daddy, can Emily come over tomorrow?'

I can see Jake's brain turning over, desperately searching for an excuse. 'Um, well, I'm not sure what we're doing tomorrow.'

I'm surprised to feel a flicker of hurt. I don't know why. It's not like I want to see him either. 'Honestly, it's fine, Jake. I think it's pretty clear there's no love lost between us.'

'Please, Daddy.' Alfie pulls at Jake's jeans, then turns his attention to me. 'I've got a new Lego set. It's Riddler's car. It's got Calendar Man in it. He's so cool.'

Jake places his hand on Alfie's head, like he's trying to steady a dog, then he looks at me. 'See, the problem I've got is that, for some unknown reason, you are very much flavour of the month. So despite the fact you're right, I don't have a burning desire for you to come over, he really does.'

I definitely don't fancy another uncomfortable visit to Jake's house but there's something about this little boy that makes it hard to disappoint him.

I crouch down in front of Alfie, thinking of the gentlest way to say no, and then somehow the words 'I'd love to see your new Lego, buddy' pop out.

'So can you come tomorrow?'

I look up at Jake. He looks like he's fallen twenty feet down a well, searched every possibility for a way out and resigned himself to the fact he's never going to see the light of day again. 'I ridiculously bought a whole chicken for the two of us, so you're welcome to join us for Sunday lunch, if you can bear to try my roast?'

It suddenly feels like a more formal visit than I'd anticipated, but looking at Alfie's expectant face, I know there's no turning back. 'OK, then.'

'Yippee,' Alfie says, twisting his feet in the mud. 'Except I hate roast.'

'You don't hate roast. You have it every Wednesday at school.'

'But I hate your roast.'

Jake crinkles his forehead at me. 'Hopefully you won't feel the same.'

'I'm sure it'll be great. See you tomorrow then, Alfie.'

'See you tomorrow.' Before he's finished speaking, Alfie's off, running back towards the balance beam with Jake trailing unenthusiastically behind him.

* * *

From the moment I arrive, I wish I hadn't come. Jake's flustered, tiny beads of sweat forming a row along his hairline and, from the brusque way he greets me at the door and then storms through to the kitchen, I'm guessing he's regretting inviting me over.

When I enter the steam-filled kitchen, there's stuff everywhere: vegetable peelings, pans bubbling over on the hob, knives, chopping boards, kitchen foil, and the distinct smell of burning.

'Do you want a coffee?' Jake almost throws the box of coffee capsules at me and then stirs a pan on the hob.

I'm desperate for something stronger, but I study the pods in the tray. They're all different colours and there's a menu, like with a box of chocolates, but I have no idea what any of the names mean. It was bad enough when I had to learn all the drinks at the café – macchiato, masala chai, blonde double shot, espresso con panna – why can't they just call it what it is? Not much milk. Lots of milk. Strange-tasting spiced tea. It'd be much easier for all involved. I don't recognize any of the names on the capsules so I choose my favourite colour, purple – 'Arpeggio' apparently – and hope for the best.

'Thanks,' I say, handing it to him.

He opens a flap on the coffee machine and turns the capsule over in his hand a few times before popping it in. There are two buttons on the top and he presses one, but nothing happens so he smacks the other one, more aggressively than the task warrants, in my opinion. A small trickle of what looks like very strong coffee comes out and half fills the cup.

He hands it to me and I wonder if I'm supposed to add milk, but I don't want to ask so I take a sip and try to disguise the way my body baulks at the bitterness. When

Jake's finished making himself one, he swirls the contents of the cup and drinks some, his eyes narrowing like he's just happened upon a cardamom pod in his chicken korma.

He pours his down the sink and opens the fridge – it's one of those posh ones hidden behind a cupboard door, like a strange game of hide-and-seek – then he slams a bottle of milk and a pot of sugar down in front of me. 'I'm not sure if you want these. It's Jemma's bloody machine. I've never used it before. I should've just made instant.'

'It's fine. I'll just add a splash of milk, thanks. It's nice.'

I pour in the milk and, despite wanting more, spoon in a fleck of sugar, worrying nonsensically that having lots would make me appear more common.

Jake pulls a tray of potatoes out the oven, then jumps back. 'Shit.'

'Are you OK?'

He flicks his hand in the air, then runs it under the tap. 'Yeah, it's nothing. Just the bloody oil spitting at me. Alfie's upstairs in the bath, if you want to go and see him. He was getting a bit overexcited waiting for you and the water tends to chill him out a bit. I won't be long.'

'OK.'

'Just check he's not flooding the bathroom floor, will you?' Suddenly, Jake seems to recognize the abruptness of his tone because he adds more softly, 'When I checked on him a minute ago, he was getting a bit too trigger-happy with a Calpol syringe.'

When I get upstairs, I can see Alfie through the bathroom door, playing with an array of bright plastic toys. He's jumping his Spider-Man figure over various obstacles – a boat, a tub of some sort, a swirly bath toy. He repeats it several times, in the same order, with the same phrase, 'Spidey to the rescue. One, two, three,' said in an Americanized voice.

'Who's he rescuing?' I ask and, seeing the expression on Alfie's face when he notices me, I instantly know why I've come.

'He's on a mission to save Superman from Doc Ock.'

'Ah, I see.'

'He has to do it like this.' Alfie replays his routine and then, all of a sudden, he stops playing and drops his figure into the water. 'I want to get out now.'

'Oh, OK.'

'What are you waiting for?'

'Sorry, do you want me to go?'

'No, you need to wash my hair, silly, then I can get out.'

'Oh, right.'

'You use that cup to pour the water on my head, then the shampoo is the green stuff just there.' Alfie points to the things I need.

I pick up the cup and pour the water over his head. He splutters as it goes in his mouth.

'Not like that,' Alfie laughs. 'You need to put your hand on my head like a shield.'

He shows me what to do and I try again. I massage some shampoo into his hair so gently I'm barely touching him. I've never washed a child's hair before. It's strangely terrifying.

'That's it, now make the shield and pour the water over my head until all the foamy stuff is out.'

I fill the cup again and pour the water over Alfie's head,

my other hand desperately trying to block any liquid reaching his face. I repeat the process several times until I'm pretty sure I've got all the shampoo out.

'What's going on?' Jake asks, appearing at the door.

I jump. 'Sorry, Alfie asked me to wash his hair.'

'Alfie, you shouldn't have asked Emily to do that. You should've called me to come up and do it.'

I wonder if this is really aimed at me, whether I've overstepped the mark.

'I showed Emily how to do it. She only got the water in my eyes one time.'

The bathroom suddenly feels incredibly small. 'I'll leave you to it.'

I go into Alfie's room and sit on his bed. The room is beautifully decorated. There are alphabet stickers around the top of his wall and ones spelling out his name by his bed. One wall is covered with a gorgeous zoo-themed mural and he has a large stylish clock with wax-crayon hands. One whole wall is shelved and, of course, all the shelves are covered with Lego models and Minifigures, lined up in neat rows. It's the perfect kid's bedroom, and a harsh reminder of how completely devoid of any care mine was.

It's a four-bedroom house, which seems excessive considering they only need two, but there you are. The distribution of wealth and all that. Other than Alfie's room, all of the decor, the furniture, the trinkets on the shelves, it's all very elegant, very elaborate, but somehow devoid of any real personality, like it's been plucked out of the pages of *House & Garden* magazine.

There's some banging and splashing from the bathroom

and then Alfie runs into his room shouting, 'Stop, stop, it hurts.'

Jake follows Alfie in, puts the towel on his head and starts rubbing. 'It doesn't hurt, silly. I'm just drying your hair.'

Alfie wriggles away again. His hair is standing on end like a mad scientist's and his face is crumpled like a discarded piece of paper. 'It *does* hurt.'

'Normally we get this about having it washed as well. You were very privileged,' Jake says to me before turning back to Alfie. 'Now, let's get you some clothes. Emily does not want to see your naked bottom running around.'

As soon as Jake says this, Alfie starts dancing around, wiggling his bum at me and giggling.

'Alfie, come on. Not with visitors.' Jake looks like he wants to teleport into another person's body like Sam Beckett in *Quantum Leap*.

'Don't mind me, honestly, it's fine.' I smile, but it doesn't do anything to alleviate the discomfort written all over Jake's face.

'Come on, Alfie. Clothes. Food's nearly ready.'

If Alfie hears his dad, he doesn't show it; he just keeps charging around the room and stopping every few seconds to wiggle his bare bottom in my face.

'Sorry. Look, I'll have to take him out.' Jake picks his son up and Alfie jerks his arms and legs like a crab being pulled out of a rock pool.

I search for anything to diffuse the tension and spot a Batman costume in the corner of the room. 'Hey, Alfie, why don't you put that costume on? I'd love to see it.'

Alfie looks at me and then gradually his limbs still and

147

Jake plonks him back on the ground. He picks up the costume and starts putting it on. 'It's awesome, look at the muscles.' Alfie tenses his arms like a bodybuilder and I laugh. 'Wait until you see the mask.'

'Can't wait.'

'Daddy, Daddy, where's my mask?'

Jake looks as if Alfie's just asked him the meaning of life. 'I have no idea.'

'But I need it.' Alfie pulls at his costume and stamps one foot.

'So find it, dude. I'm going to go and plate up.'

Alfie's bottom lip begins to tremble and, as Jake goes off to sort the food, I suddenly feel scared to be left alone with him. It feels like I'm walking through a field of landmines, one wrong move and it's devastation. I kneel down beside Alfie and put my arm around his shoulder.

'How about we go on a hunt together?'

Alfie pouts and shakes his head. Where to step next?

'OK, I'll go on a hunt. You count and see how long it takes me. See if I can do it in ten.'

Alfie points his forefinger to the sky. 'No, I've got a better idea. Let's have a race. You search the playroom and I'll search the lounge.'

Mission accomplished.

'Deal. You ready?'

Alfie nods.

'OK. Ready, set, go.'

* * *

Alfie climbs on to his chair and stares at his plate of food. 'Yuck. I hate this. I'm not eating it.'

148

Jake doesn't respond. Instead, he tucks into a roast potato, the sound of cutlery on plate echoing pointedly around the walls.

Alfie rocks on his chair so its feet repeatedly smash on the wooden floor. Then he stops, puts his feet up on the table and accidentally knocks Jake's arm as one foot slips off, followed by the other.

'Just sit still, will you?' Jake moves Alfie back on to his chair and pushes it closer to the table. 'And eat your food.' Then, as if he remembers that I'm there, he adds, 'Please.'

'But we don't have it very often. It's strange. I can't feed myself when it's strange. You have to feed me.' Alfie bangs his fork on the table.

Jake grabs Alfie's hand to hold it still. 'It's a roast. You have it every week at school. You're six. I'm not feeding you.' He keeps his tone measured, but I can see the deep breaths he's sucking in as he tries to stay calm.

Alfie crosses his arms and turns his head away from Jake. 'Then I'm not eating it.'

'I'm sorry about this,' Jake says to me.

I hold up my hands in an attempt to dismiss his concerns.

'I'm going to watch *Peter Rabbit*.'

'No, Alfie, you need to eat your lunch.'

He starts to climb off his chair but Jake holds him back. 'You'll do what you're told. Now eat it, or no snack.' Then in a more bargaining tone, he says, 'Remember we bought cupcakes?'

Alfie looks like he's about to yell, but then he looks at me and reluctantly puts a carrot into his mouth. 'Urgh.' He spits it on to the plate, chewed-up orange goo falling out of his mouth. 'It's got broccoli on it.'

Like when you open a can of Coke that's been shaken, Jake erupts, throwing his fork on to his plate, and Alfie and I both jump. 'You do not spit your food out, Alfie. There is no broccoli on your plate. Now stop being silly and just eat it.'

'There is, there is! It's there, look.' Alfie points to a fleck of broccoli the size of a grain of rice on the surface of one of his carrots.

Jake pushes his chair back, stands up and lifts Alfie out of his seat. 'Just go. I am not having this behaviour at the table.'

Alfie looks amazed that he's getting away with not eating his food and runs out of the dining room before Jake has a chance to change his mind, loudly banging the glass door shut as he goes.

I focus on what's left of my plate of food, Jake's outburst still bouncing around the room. He's overdone the chicken and it's quite dry, so I cover it in gravy and try not to chew too obviously.

'I'm sorry about all that. It's a daily occurrence, so it's very hard not to react.'

I continue to eat my food, unsure of what to say. While I'm trying hard to avoid eye contact, I notice the Rauschenberg print on the wall behind Jake's head. It's one of my favourites. A beautiful mix of typography and bold splodges of paint.

'So are you the Rauschenberg fan?'

Jake follows my gaze. 'Oh no, that's Jemma's.' Jake looks around the room. 'In fact, pretty much all the decor is Jemma's creation. I'd have driftwood and lighthouse pictures. I suppose I could now.'

I nod, wondering if he can hear the bitterness in his voice.

'How come you know about Rauschenberg, anyway? I didn't take you for a modern art connoisseur.'

'Jake, I'm poor, not thick.'

Jake bangs his beer bottle down on the table more forcefully than I think he intended to. 'I didn't say you were. God, why do you always think the worst of me?'

His eyes are puffy and his frown lines are so deeply engraved they look like they've been drawn on with black fineliner. He looks like a tree that's been battered by a particularly bad storm, like any minute now he might crash to the ground, so I decide to go easy on him.

'I went to art college for a while, but working evening and weekend shifts wasn't enough to pay the bills so I had to quit. That's where I really got into photography.'

'So what do you do now?'

'Oh, I work in a café. It's thrilling.'

'Try being a stay-at-home dad.' Jake smiles but I can tell he's not joking. We've both finished our food so he clears the table and takes our plates to the kitchen. 'Do you want any pudding? A glass of wine?'

As he says the word, I can almost feel the warmth of the alcohol trickling down my throat.

'I'm full, thank you. It was lovely. And I have to drive, but thanks.'

'Another of my delightful coffees?' It's only a tiny crack, but I can just make out a chink of light shining through Jake's dejected exterior.

'I think I'll pass, as great as it was.'

'Wise decision. Right, shall we go and find Alfie?'

Jake seems to gather himself for his next encounter with his son, grabs another bottle of beer out the fridge, opens it and brings it through to the lounge with him.

Alfie is sitting on the floor. He's set up a game of Monopoly and is sharing out the money.

'Oh no, not Monopoly,' Jake says with mock exasperation.

Alfie giggles. 'Yep, your favourite.'

'OK, but I'm only playing if you play fair.'

'I will.' Alfie holds up a handful of playing pieces to me. 'Who do you want to be? You can't be the zebra.'

'It's a dog,' Jake says.

'No, it's a zebra.' Alfie shakes his head. 'Silly Daddy.'

'I'll be the iron,' I say.

'That's a shield. See.' Alfie holds it up, wielding an imaginary sword and putting on a warrior face.

'Oh, yes, silly me.'

Jake chooses the car and we put our pieces on the board. The game goes well to start with. Alfie's like a property tycoon, expertly weighing up cost versus revenue when choosing which properties to buy. We circle the board several times, Alfie getting more and more agitated when he doesn't land on his treasured dark-blue street. On our fifth time round, he's two steps away from Park Lane and throws a three.

He quickly scoops up the dice and moves himself two spaces. 'Yay. Finally. A two!'

Jake moves him on a space. 'No, it was a three.'

To add insult to injury, Alfie's ended up on Super Tax and owes one hundred pounds.

He throws the dice across the room and it hits the window. 'It was a two.'

'You either play fair or we stop playing. Up to you.'

Alfie crosses his arms and I retrieve the dice and have my turn. 'Oh, great. I landed on you, Alfie. What do I owe you?'

'Twenty-six pounds,' he says grumpily and takes my thirty, efficiently doling out four pounds change.

Next, it's Jake's turn. He throws a six, counts his car round and, in a cruel twist of fate, ends up on Park Lane. 'Buying it.'

Fair play, he's got balls. There's no way I'd have bought it if I'd landed on it.

'No. The dark-blue ones are mine. It's not fair!' Alfie drops to the floor like he's been shot. It would almost be comical if it wasn't for the intensity of the torment on his face, like an athlete who's just crashed out of the Olympics.

'It's only a game, Alfie. There's no point playing if we don't play properly. You've got loads of other properties.'

Alfie lets out a cry of what sounds like pain and sweeps his hand across the board, sending cards, houses, hotels and pieces flying. He picks up the board and starts repeatedly hitting Jake with it like someone's swooped in and taken control of his body.

I look up at Jake and see any semblance of calm is gone. 'I'm not having that. Thinking step.'

Jake picks Alfie up and carries him past me. I can hear the struggle outside the door, Jake trying to get Alfie to do his allotted time and Alfie charging up the stairs to escape. It feels like listening to a couple having sex, like I should be covering my ears. It's time to leave.

I sneak into the hallway. Jake has his thighs over the top of Alfie's legs so that he can't move, and Alfie's squirming and hitting him, literally unwilling to take his punishment lying down.

'I'm going to go.' I have to raise my voice to be heard over Alfie's protests.

Jake's sweating and out of breath. He doesn't say anything, just nods. Alfie seems too lost in his rage to even notice me so I put on my boots, grab my jacket and skulk out the door.

It's like stepping out of a sauna when you've stayed in there too long – when you can feel the pulse in your forehead and your vision blurs. I locate my car keys in the bottom of my bag, then hear the front door open and Jake appears with bare feet, his hair blowing into his eyes.

'Just hold on a minute.'

I stand behind my open car door.

'I'm sorry you had to see all that. I know it looks like I'm a terrible dad but I'm not.'

'Seriously, Jake. You don't need to explain anything to me.'

'But I want to. If you lived with him every day, you'd get it. You'd understand. It's . . .' He pushes his hair off his face with both hands and shakes his head. 'But you come over and you see these tiny snippets that make me look like a prick and then I feel even angrier that I'm made to look like that. Does that make any sense at all?'

I don't know. I feel like I've run a marathon. I'm drained and unfit to think clearly about anything.

When I don't respond, Jake continues. 'Well, I'm sorry. And I do love Alfie, I really do.'

'I'm sure you do. Look, thank you for the meal. It was lovely. Please say goodbye to Alfie for me.'

'I will.' Jake trudges back to the house and I get in my car and drive home, feeling like I've just been engaged in a spar and taken one too many knocks to the head. Being in Jake's house is so intense, so stifling, I'm not sure I can go back. And yet there's something about Alfie that draws me in. I can't help feeling that behind the difficult behaviour, there's a little boy crying out to be heard. And I know exactly how that feels and how desperate it makes you when no one seems to be listening.

Jake

'Look, Dad, I need a favour.'

We are sitting at the dining-room table drinking tea. Alfie keeps popping in and out to look for things for his latest 'project'. He is trying to build some kind of contraption to allow him to reach and open the loft door. I've told him he's not allowed up there over and over again but he won't let it go. I know he'll never achieve it and it's keeping him quiet, so I let him try. So far, cushions and a small bin have been taken upstairs. I've had to wrestle a chair off him. Now he appears to be attaching straws together to create some kind of stick to loop into the hole and pull the hatch down. When I'm not caught up in the middle of a battle with Alfie, I have to marvel at his determination and creativity. I'm envious. Mine disappeared a long time ago. Six years ago, in fact. Funny, that.

'I've had to get a job. We need the money.'

I see the realization the moment it appears on Dad's face, like he's just seen an army of flesh-eating zombies march past the window. 'You want me to look after Alfie?'

'I wouldn't ask if I wasn't desperate.'

He sips his tea, probably buying himself time to think up an excuse. 'How long for? Would it be every day?'

'It hopefully won't be for long. I'm sure Jemma and I will sort things out soon and, if not, I can get something more permanent arranged. Please, Dad.'

I hate having to beg. Jemma always said I should just ask my dad for help when I need it. He has the time. He has the money. I'm an only child so he hasn't got anyone else to deal with. But I've always felt that if he doesn't offer, I'm not going to ask. This time, I have no alternative.

'Why can't you just send him to a childminder? I'll pay, if you're worried about the money.'

Coming from the stingiest man on earth, this would be funny – if it didn't hurt so much.

'Wow, you really don't want to spend time with my son, do you?'

'Come on, Jake, that's not fair. I love that boy. Of course I do. But I'm too old. I haven't got the energy he requires. When I looked after him the other day while you went to your class, it nearly killed me. Can't Jemma's parents help out? She's the one that landed you in this mess. Plus there are two of them. I'd be doing it on my own.'

Even before 'the incident', I hated taking Alfie to Jemma's parents' house. It always felt like he was a ticking time bomb and I was just waiting for the moment he was going to explode. They have hardly any toys there (they don't understand why he won't just sit and colour like Jemma and her sister always did) so he gets bored, and Bored Alfie is a disaster waiting to happen. Anyway, about five months ago, we went there for Sunday lunch. Alfie spent the entire meal climbing both under the table and on top of it while Richard and Wendy stared at him fearfully like he was an escaped chimpanzee. And, to be fair, that's exactly how he looked, surrounded by their pristine china. Trying to do the decent thing, I decided to remove him from the room, but when I went to grab him off the table, he dodged and bashed his head on their glass chandelier, which probably cost more than my car. With the most horrendous smash, it fell right into the dish of roast potatoes, shattering into a thousand pieces. Needless to say, they've not invited us over since. Instead, they conveniently choose to meet us when we're going to some sort of wide-open space.

'I can't do that to Alfie. And I can't leave him with a childminder. He wouldn't cope.'

Dad sniffs.

'What?'

'Nothing.' He circles his watch around his wrist. 'Just that all the other children these days have to do it and they don't seem mentally scarred. It's the norm now. It wasn't when you were little.'

'So you think Mum would've put me in childcare, do you? If it had been the norm then?'

'I'm not saying that, Jake. I'm saying that just because your mum had strong views about it, she wouldn't be disappointed in you. Cut yourself some slack. You do what you have to do. And actually, all my friends' grandchildren who are in nurseries seem very happy, very well adjusted and very well behaved.'

'Unlike Alfie?'

'That's not what I said.'

As if to make the point, there's a loud crash from upstairs and, a few seconds later, an anguished scream. I run upstairs to find Alfie's created a gigantic tower of sofa cushions, quilts, pillows, a beanbag chair, an upturned plastic bin and his little stool, and has gone flying off the top of it all and bashed into the wall.

I pick him up and rub his head, which he is holding in both hands. 'I told you not to try to get in the loft. This is why. You need to listen, Alfie. You need to start understanding no.'

I say it loudly, mostly for Dad's benefit, to show him I'm not just letting my child run amok. So what that he nearly committed accidental suicide – at least I'm reprimanding him for it.

Alfie wriggles away from me. 'If you'd just let me go up, I wouldn't have hurt myself.'

He storms into his room and slams the door. I go back down to Dad, who is putting on his coat.

'I'm sorry, son. I hope you sort something out. If you need me for a few days while you get sorted, I'll do it, but I can't commit to longer. It wouldn't be fair on Alfie. He needs someone who can run around with him and stuff, not an old man like me. I am sorry.'

I nod. There's no use trying to persuade him. When Dad's made up his mind about something, there's no budging him. A family trait. And besides, he's probably right. Alfie would be too much for him.

'Your mum would be really proud of you, you know?'

It seems to come out of the blue and I look away, suddenly scared I might cry. We're men. We don't do emotion. Dad didn't even cry when Mum died, well, at least not in front of me. But then I never cried in front of him either.

'It's not easy in this day and age to go against the grain. The decision you made to give up your career and look after your boy, it was a noble one. I just don't want to see you killing yourself in the process.'

He pats me on the back, the closest we've ever got to a

hug. In contrast, Mum was so physically demonstrative I'd often have to pull away. Her motto was 'you can't leave a room without a cuddle', even if I was just going from the lounge into the kitchen. As a teenager, I'd slink away from her affection, embarrassed, as if accepting it made me less of a man. I wish I hadn't. I wish I'd cherished it. I wish, instead of moving away, I'd held her tighter and longer. But I was too young to even consider that her cuddles and kisses might not be infinite. That one day, far too soon, they would run out.

'Thanks, Dad.'

He swats my words away with his hand, as if to stop them piercing his carefully constructed exterior. 'Cheerio then, son. Let me know if you need me to have Alfie for a few days until you find someone else.'

'Thanks. Bye.' I watch him walk up the path to his car, his body showing the gradual signs of age, that bit slower, that bit more hunched, but still far stronger than I'll ever be.

* * *

Alfie repeatedly bashes his head against the wall.

'Alfie, please don't do that.' I put my hand in between his head and the plaster.

'I don't want to go to the childminder,' he says, each word staccato and accompanied by a backwards thrust of the head.

'I've got no choice. We have to have money to pay for this house and for food and toys.'

'I don't mind not having the house or food or toys. We could sleep in the tent.'

I pull him towards me and put my arm around him.

'Look, little man, hopefully it won't be for long. Just while Mummy is away.'

Alfie shuffles away from me, takes a cup off the windowsill and throws it across the room. Luckily, it's empty. 'No. I am not going and that's that.'

I understand this is hard for him, but all the other kids have to do it and my patience is rapidly deteriorating.

'It's not my fault, Alfie. If you want someone to blame, blame your mum. She's the one who walked out.'

I regret it as soon as the words leave my mouth. Since Jemma left, I've vowed to myself that I will never become one of those people who bad-mouths the other parent. But I didn't realize how hard it would be to be the parent left behind, getting all the grief for what the other one has done.

'Look, I'm sorry. I didn't mean that. Mummy loves you.'

Alfie looks distracted and then, suddenly, his face brightens. 'I've got an idea.'

Relief washes over me like a hot shower. 'What's that, kiddo?'

'Emily can look after me.'

The hot shower of relief is sucked away again, like water down a plughole. 'Emily?'

Alfie looks like one of those nodding dogs you used to get in the backs of cars. 'Emily would love to look after me. That would be OK. I wouldn't mind you going to work then.'

He looks very pleased with himself for finding a solution to my problem and I feel the familiar rise of dread in my stomach, as I know I have to tell him that she can't.

'I'm sorry, Alfie, but we barely know Emily. I can't ask her to do that.'

'We *do* know her. She's my friend. We don't know the childminder, do we? I've never even seen her.'

Alfie has an uncanny ability to always find a fair and reasonable counterargument.

'But it's the childminder's job to look after children. She knows what she's doing.'

'But I can teach Emily. Like I did with washing my hair.'

I look at his face, full of innocence, his eyes pleading with me. I want to put his life back together and I can't.

'OK, I'll ask her. But she will say no, Alfie, so please don't get your hopes up.'

Asking her is win-win. She'll refuse, I'll look like the good guy and the blame will be pushed her way.

'She won't say no.'

'She will.'

'She won't.'

Just as I think we are going to be trapped in this panto-esque exchange for the rest of the evening, he skips out of his room and into the playroom, singing the *Peter Rabbit* theme tune (with his own unique version of the lyrics) as he goes.

* * *

After school the following day, we meet Emily at Star-bucks. When we arrive, she's sitting at a table in the corner and already has a drink, so I order myself a coffee and a gigantic piece of chocolate fudge cake for Alfie in the hope that it might keep him quiet for five minutes.

We join Emily and start with the usual social niceties before falling into an awkward silence. Alfie's so engrossed in his cake that even he doesn't offer the usual distraction.

'Look, I might as well cut to the chase.' I search my brain for some way to say it that doesn't sound ridiculous and decide on the direct approach. 'I need someone to look after Alfie and I wondered if you might be interested?'

Emily scrunches up her face like a bulldog. 'Tonight?'

'No, I mean because Jemma's decided to take a sabbatical and swan around Paris, I've got to get a job. It's just a maternity cover so it's not permanent.'

'And you want me to look after Alfie?'

She gives me an am-I-hearing-this-correctly look and, alongside feeling stupid, I'm surprised to realize that I was hoping she'd say yes. I'm fast running out of options and anything that makes Alfie happy ultimately makes my life a lot easier.

'I'd pay you, of course. It would just be looking after him for an hour or so in the morning before taking him to school and then a few hours after picking him up. I'll be home about six. There might be a few days in the holidays when I need to go into school. I can't pay you tons but I'd beat what you get in the café.'

'But I've got no experience of working with children. Why don't you just pay a childminder?'

It's the question on everybody's lips. 'Because he asked for you.'

An unreadable emotion flickers in Emily's eyes, but she doesn't respond. Alfie scrapes the last fleck of cake off the bottom of his plate and then looks up at Emily, chocolate smudges covering his face. Somehow, he's even managed to get crumbs on his eyebrows.

'So are you going to look after me, Emily?'

Emily studies him for a minute. 'I don't know. I mean . . .'

'Please, Emily,' Alfie says, his eyes imploring.

'Come on, Alfie. I told you Emily would probably say no. It's not fair to put pressure on her.'

Alfie sticks out his bottom lip and drops his chin to his chest. He looks so utterly dejected even I'd find it hard to say no to him.

'OK. I'll look after you, buddy.' Emily ruffles Alfie's hair.

I feel like a ventriloquist's dummy, my mouth falling open.

'Yay!' Alfie throws his arms around Emily with such force that she falls back in the chair.

Looking at them together – Emily's pale skin looking even more ghostly against her black leather jacket, her harsh shaved head – I just don't get it. When you picture an adult who will appeal to children, it's the candyfloss-and-rainbows type of person you see on CBeebies, all over-exaggerated facial expressions and Technicolor clothes. And yet I've never seen Alfie hug anyone other than Jemma or me like that.

'Seriously?' I ask.

Emily sits back up and Alfie climbs down on to the floor and starts tying his napkin around the table leg.

'I'm not sure I'll be any good, but I'll give it a shot. Has to beat working in the café.'

'You have met my son, haven't you?'

Emily smiles. 'So when do you need me to start?'

'I start in a fortnight.'

'OK. I'll hand my notice in tomorrow.'

'Wow. Thank you so much. You're a lifesaver.'

It all feels too simple, too easy, and I have a sudden

panic that I've just asked a relative stranger with no experience of working with children, no CRB check and no qualifications to take care of my only child. And don't even get me started on the unknown reason she's been forced into anger management.

As if reading my mind, she says, 'Don't worry, I'll take good care of him.'

'Yeah, I know you will. You'll do a great job. Better than me, that's for sure.'

'Do I still have to go to school? I want to stay home with Emily.' Alfie emerges from under the table.

'I'm sorry, little man. You still have to go to school.'

I prepare myself for battle but luckily Emily steps in first. 'We'll have loads of time to play after school though, Alfie.'

'And in the morning?'

'Oh yeah, I forgot about the mornings. Loads of time to play then.'

Alfie seems satisfied with this and returns to his position under the table. He has managed to find several more napkins and adds them to the table leg, like a row of garters on a bride's thigh.

'So is there anything in particular I need to know?'

I think about the past six years of looking after Alfie and how to condense it all into a conversation over coffee. How you need to tell Alfie something a minimum of seven times before he'll take it in. To talk through every aspect of the itinerary for the day until it's engrained in his head and give him a serious heads-up if you plan on changing anything, although even that probably wouldn't prevent the meltdown, just perhaps reduce the ferocity of it. To be prepared to negotiate everything, to answer a thousand questions a day, to justify your every move. There's so much about my little boy you need to know just to survive the day with him, but I've got a funny feeling that Emily will figure it out on her own. She might not be the type of person I want to spend an hour in the pub with, but she seems to instinctively know what to say when it comes to Alfie.

'Well, I'll put you together a schedule with times, places and stuff. We have certain rules. Only healthy snacks after school, thinking step for five minutes if you have to give him more than one warning, no screens in the morning, that sort of thing, but I'll write all those down too.'

As I'm saying it, I feel like a fraud – remembering all the times I hand him his tablet the second he wakes up just to keep him quiet and get five minutes more sleep. When we first had Alfie, we had all these principles. No dummies, no screens of any description before the age of three, no E-numbers, no tablet until he started secondary school. And then, after ten days of solid screaming, survival mode took hold: we shoved a dummy in his mouth, plonked him in front of CBeebies and, from that point on, all our embarrassingly naive ideals went out the window.

'OK. No problem. I'm sure we'll be fine.'

If I'm not mistaken, a glimmer of doubt streaks across her face, but I try to ignore it and the slight panicky feeling in the pit of my stomach. How bad can it be?

* * *

At about ten o' clock, Jemma rings. It's odd because our conversations so far have been limited to a few words before I pass the phone over to Alfie, but she knows he'll be in bed at this time so she must be calling to speak to me. I can't help hoping it's to say she's coming home.

'What's up?'

'Nothing's up. We've been married nearly fourteen years. Does something have to be up for me to want to talk to you?'

She sounds like she's outside and walking, her breath uneven.

'I guess not. It's just the last time I checked, this whole marriage thing we've got going on wasn't going too swimmingly.'

There's the sound of a siren in the background.

'I just wanted to ask you how Alfie is. Is he doing OK with all this?'

'Yeah. He's good. He misses you, of course, but we're getting by.'

I'm not sure if he misses Jemma or not. I'm guessing he must do, but he hardly mentions her. I can't tell her that, though.

'Good.'

As soon as I think about the fact she's abandoned our son, I can't help but feel my animosity towards her building. Though I spend the majority of my days longing for escape, I know that, if I left, after the initial intense feeling of calm, the ache would start. Just like it did when I dropped him off on his first day at school, and, inexplicably, intensely missed him.

'So, I got a job. I start next week.'

'That's good.' It seems to take her a moment to remember the reason I haven't been working for the past six years. 'But who's going to be looking after Alfie?'

I know this isn't going to be the easiest thing to explain.

'It's a little complicated. There's this girl, woman, at anger management.' As I hear the words coming out of my mouth, I know I'm going to have to lie. 'She happens to be a nanny so I asked her to do it.'

'You've asked a woman from anger management to look after our son? Are you crazy?'

I have to move the phone away from my ear she's shouting so loud.

'But *I'm* in anger management. Does that make me a bad person? Am I not capable of caring for our son?'

Jemma's exaggerated exhalation makes a rustling sound down the phone. 'Look at it from my side, Jake. Surely you can understand where I'm coming from?'

I can, but I'm still pissed off. I'm the one who's here, having to make the difficult decisions.

'I didn't have a lot of options.'

'Because of course you couldn't just put him in regular childcare?'

'Let's not start this. Alfie asked for her. He likes her.'

'How does he even know her?' Jemma's voice has the distinct tone of someone who is trying to sound calm but failing.

'We just bumped into her a few times. She doesn't look at him like he's a spoilt brat. Do you know how rare that is? She's actually really good with him. I mean, she's far better with him than –'

'I am,' Jemma interrupts.

'I was going to say than I am. Come on, Jemma, you can't exactly be angry with me. You chose this, remember?'

I can picture Jemma running her hand through her

blonde hair. Her perfect face only slightly marred by the anguish spread across it.

'That doesn't make it any easier, Jake. I know I'm not entitled to say that, but it's the truth.'

'You know, Jem, you could just come back home. I wouldn't make you pay for this, well, not too badly, anyway.'

I can almost hear Jemma smile and it makes me want to jump on the next flight to Paris and bring her home in some fancy Hollywood gesture.

'I can't, Jake. It's easy to stand here listening to your voice and imagine it's just like it used to be, when we'd talk on the phone into the early hours when I was away for work. I used to physically ache with missing you.'

Her use of the past tense is like an elbow in the ribs.

'But you know if I came back, it'd only take five minutes before we'd be arguing again, scoring points against each other, resenting each other, just making each other miserable.'

I know she's right. I know it's easy to romanticize things now she's not here, but even if Alfie isn't showing any signs of missing her, I am. I don't miss what we'd become, but I do miss her.

'Do you think if we hadn't had Alfie, we'd still be happy?'

I know it's a terrible thing to say, to think even. But it's something I wonder about a lot.

'You can't think like that, Jake. It's like wishing him away.'

'I'd never wish him away. Of course I wouldn't. But we were good together, weren't we? You and me, before, I mean?'

'We were the best.'

I think we were. I remember being really happy, but it seems so long ago that sometimes I wonder if I've reinvented the memories.

A door bangs in the background and I can tell she's gone inside.

'I'm going to go and make some supper now. I'll call Alfie again in a couple of days. Give him a kiss from me.'

'I will. And, Jem? I still love you, you know?'

'I know. Bye, Jake.'

She puts the phone down and the bed, the room, the whole house suddenly feels so much emptier than it did before.

I know she's right. If she came back, I'd forget this feeling in a few days, maybe sooner. The minute she waited for me to respond first before dealing with Alfie, I'd resent her. Or picked me up on how I'd chosen the wrong clothes for the woods because they were smart clothes and he needed scruffy ones for somewhere muddy. How the hell can you tell what's smart or scruffy? They all look the same to me and, whichever I choose, you can guarantee I'll get it wrong.

But right now all I can see is Jemma on our first date. We'd chatted a few times at the university bar, but it was the first time we'd gone out, just the two of us. She organized it all, which was something I wasn't used to, but was secretly chuffed with, as it meant there was no danger of me disappointing her. She chose this ultra-stylish bar and when I arrived, she was already there, sitting talking to the barman, who was clearly flirting with her.

'Ah, here you are. I was just telling Rich all about you.'

'What about me, exactly?'

'Oh, just that you're some hot surfer dude. Shit, I got the wrong person, didn't I?'

'You're funny.'

'You're cute.'

'Cute?'

'Yes. Trust me, I know a lot of knobs. Cute is definitely a good thing.'

She told me all about her marketing degree. How she was going to work for an agency called Abbott Mead Vickers because apparently they were the best of the best. I still remember her response when I asked her how she knew they'd give her a job.

'Because I'll work my butt off until they see it's in their best interest to employ me. And if that fails, I'll use my feminine charms on them.' At that point, she flicked her then long hair and pouted her lips, and we both laughed.

'Well, how could they possibly resist?'

'Exactly.'

It was that simple for her. She believed the world was a wonderful place and that she deserved to experience everything it had to offer. I've always had a fair bit of cynicism, but back then Jemma had none. It was one of the main reasons I fell in love with her.

That night, we went back to my halls and, as we walked in, my room-mate winked at me and excused himself. Jemma giggled and, when the door shut, she pushed me up against the wall and kissed me. And, all of a sudden, I began to believe that dreams could come true too.

But now, well, now I can't help wondering what we've done to each other.

Emily

The first couple of weeks with Alfie haven't gone quite as I'd hoped. I had some misguided vision of making magnificent Lego creations, producing inspiring works of art to put up on the dining-room wall, teaching him new skills, sharing unique experiences. Of course, I knew he could be challenging. I'd seen him kick off with Jake. But I thought maybe he'd be different with me. If I'm totally honest, I hoped I could show Jake how to get it right.

But it turns out Alfie is actually really hard work. Smash-your-head-up-against-a-wall kind of hard. So far, key highlights have included him refusing to get dressed for school and lying outside the front of the house in his pants while all the neighbours watched me try to bundle him into the car with his uniform tucked under my arm, an extraordinarily loud and physically encompassing tantrum in the doorway of the local Sainsbury's because I needed to pop in to buy some carrots I'd forgotten to pick up while he was at school (I've not forgotten anything since) and an hour-long screaming fit that I think might have permanently damaged my hearing because I told him his time was up on his tablet.

This morning he is refusing to put his seat belt on.

'Come on, Alfie. We're late for school. Just pop it on, will you?'

Alfie doesn't do anything so I put the gearstick back in neutral and pull the handbrake on.

'What's up?'

'I can't do it.'

'Don't be . . .'

I'm about to say 'silly' but looking at Alfie's expression, that's not the Alfie I'm sitting next to right now. I've discovered that Alfie has a number of faces, a number of guises, like costumes he slips on and off. Silly, manic, nothing-you-say-will-get-through-to-me Alfie has a fixed grin like the Joker, and darting eyes. This Alfie – eyes staring ahead as if he needs switching on – is not Silly Alfie.

'Do you want me to do it?'

Alfie nods and I reach over and fasten his seat belt. He relaxes back into his seat.

'Right, let's go to school.'

* * *

The school playground is a terrible place. Seriously, I didn't realize before how lucky I was to be missing out on this shit. It's like being back at school myself, but worse. Because the people staring at you like you're a piece of crap are no longer girls struggling to hide their acne with thick orange foundation but beautiful, confident, successful women.

The cliques are similar, but there's not the same sense of hierarchy as there was at school. The ones who would've been geeks now have multiple degrees, successful businesses and children on the 'gifted and talented' register. The arty ones are no longer relegated to the corner of the common room – they're right in the middle of the playground, happy and self-righteous in their charity-shop clothing with their free-range toddlers running around bashing their scooters into people's legs and munching on organic carrot sticks. The sporty ones still gather together, confidently dressed in Lycra or running shorts, but no one seems intimidated by them any more. As long as you're in a group, it doesn't appear to matter which one you're in. The killer situation is standing on your own, like I am right now, with everyone glaring at me like I'm an escaped convict about to abduct their child. I've been here every morning and afternoon for the past two weeks, and not one person has spoken to me.

Alfie leans his head on my thigh, then tugs at my jumper. I crouch down so that I can hear him over the noise of all the other children playing.

'Did you put my book in my book bag?'

'Yes.'

One day, I forgot to put his reading record (a Big-Brother-type document in which you have to write every single night that you've heard the child read or there'll be a punishment worse than death) into his bag. Now, every day without fail, he checks that I've remembered.

'And did Daddy write in there that I read?'

I pull the yellow book out of his bag, open it and show him where Jake has written the page numbers. 'Yep. See, there.'

I put the book away and Alfie wraps his arms around me, squeezing me tight. For a few seconds, it's a normal cuddle, but then, as often happens with Alfie, it turns into something more akin to a chokehold. I try to remove his arms from around my neck, but he just grabs me tighter so that I tumble back on to my bottom. Out the corner of my eye, I catch the group of sporty mums staring at me.

'Stop now, Alfie.'

He giggles in my ear.

'Alfie. Stop.' I manage to move him off me.

Now, right there, that's the face of Silly Alfie.

When his teacher emerges from the classroom door, I give Alfie a kiss and hang his book bag over his shoulder. 'See you after school, buddy.'

Alfie joins the line, tripping over a box of wooden building blocks as he glances back at me on his way into the classroom.

* * *

As soon as I pick Alfie up from school, he's on one. Swinging his book bag round in the middle of a busy playground, running into the road, purposefully putting his shoes up on the dashboard to make muddy footprints. We get through the door and he's on a mission for a biscuit, enraged at the injustice of not being allowed to have one (and when you get Feeling Wronged Alfie, God help you). He climbs up on to the worktop to reach the biscuit box in the cupboard and I lift him down. We do this three times, like a disc jammed in the same spot, until he, very sneakily, pretends to have given up and then darts back and vaults on to the worktop while I'm putting something away.

I walk over and hold the cupboard door closed. 'No chocolate, Alfie. A piece of fruit, a fruit bar or a cracker.'

'A cracker with Nutella.'

'That's chocolate, Alfie. What about some peanut butter? That'd be yummy.'

'No, I want chocolate.'

'No chocolate, Alfie. You know the rules.'

'The rules are stupid.'

I tend to agree with him on that one. I'm desperate for a biscuit and Jake's pointless law means I have to sneak them when Alfie's on the toilet, like I've got some dirty crack habit.

'Either way, those are the rules. Come on down.'

He tries to pull my arm away from the cupboard door so I carry him off the worktop again. He fights his way out of my arms and runs into the lounge. I leave him for a minute but I can hear banging and crashing so I know I'm going to have to go in. I take a deep breath and put my game face on. If I show any sign of weakness, he'll jump on it.

He takes a run up and storms into the glass doors.

'Alfie, you're going to break the glass. You can't do that.'

It's like he doesn't hear me; he just keeps doing it over and over, getting slightly more forceful each time. I can just imagine Jake's face if he comes home to find an Alfie-shaped hole in the patio door.

'Come on, Alfie, let's go and build something with your Lego.'

'No, I want to run.'

'Then let's go and run outside.'

'No, I want to run here.'

'Well, you can't. You're going to break the glass.'

'No, I'm not.' Alfie takes a big run up and then bashes into the door, shoulder first.

'Alfie, I'm going to count to three and then if you don't stop, I'm going to have to put you on the thinking step.'

Alfie covers his ears.

'One.'

Bash.

'Two.'

He looks at me and I think he's going to stop. I will for him to stop. Because trying to get Alfie to sit on the thinking step is like trying to get a piece of wool through the eye of a very tiny needle. But then he takes another run up and I know he's going to charge into the door again.

'Three. Right, Alfie, thinking step. Five minutes.'

I know he won't go of his own accord so I pick him up and his flailing legs kick me in the stomach, but I try not to show it hurts. I place him on the step and put my hands on his shoulders to keep him there. He wriggles free and runs up the stairs, laughing. I chase him, pick him up and carry him back to the step. This time, I sit next to him and hold on to him so he can't move.

'Stop, you're hurting me.'

'I'm not hurting you, Alfie. I'm just stopping you from running away. If you just sat here and did the five minutes, then we could go and play. You know I have to start the timer again every time you run away.'

'I won't run away.'

'Promise?'

'Promise.'

I let him go and the second I do he belts upstairs again. It takes everything I've got to follow him up. When I reach his room, he's sitting on his bed.

'Come on, Alfie. I'll sit with you. Let's just do the five minutes, yeah?'

Alfie lowers his chin to his chest and crosses his arms.

'Why won't you do it, buddy? Just get it over with so we can carry on having fun?'

Alfie doesn't speak, just stares at his quilt.

'Please, I don't want to have to fight you back on to the step.'

'I'm not doing it.'

'Then I've got no choice.'

I pick him up again, and he screams and hits my back with his fists. I just about manage to carry him to the stairs, then sit on the top step with him on my knee, my arms clasped tightly around him as he tries to fight free. Tears are streaming down his face and his cheeks are bright red.

'Stop, Alfie. Please stop fighting.'

I'm begging but he's not listening. Just screaming and kicking, my shins taking blow after blow. When I can't bear it any more, I release him and he runs away. I hear his bedroom door slam and I lie back on the stairs and know there's nothing I can do to stop the ambush of tears. I just let them fall, welcoming the release. Once they've passed, I wipe my face with the sleeve of my hoody and check in the mirror that my eye make-up hasn't run. I lick my finger, wipe away a rogue bit of mascara and take a deep breath.

When I enter Alfie's room, he is sitting on his bed with a box of conkers. He takes them out one by one and puts them in a circle on top of his quilt.

'Wow, that's a lot of conkers.'

Alfie looks up at me. His face is puffy from crying and he looks suspicious of me, like he's not sure whether I come in peace or whether my friendly comment is to disguise my next attempt to capture him.

'There's sixty-four. Sixty-three and one in the shell. That's sixty-four.'

178

'Cool. I wish I had sixty-four conkers, especially one in a shell.'

Alfie smiles, clearly proud of his collection. He carefully opens the shell and takes out the conker from inside. 'This one's magic. If you hold it, it makes you super-strong. Look, I can even lift my bed up when I'm holding it.'

Struggling with the conker still in one hand, he manages to lift his bed a centimetre or so off the floor. 'See.'

'Wow, Alfie. That's amazing.'

'Do you want a go?' He holds the conker out to me.

I take it and then lift the bed. 'Oh, yeah! It really is magic. I can't believe how strong it makes me.'

Alfie smiles, takes the conker off me and returns it to its shell. 'Do you want to help me put them in a circle? Then I'm going to do a square and then a triangle.'

'I'd love to, buddy.'

I sit on his bed beside him and run my hand up and down his back. I want to tell him I'm sorry, that the thinking step is a load of bollocks, but I know that I can't. So, instead, I help him make the different shapes out of conkers and just enjoy spending some time with this Alfie before I next have to face the other one.

* * *

The following day, the conflict begins as soon as we get home from school. 'I want to go to the park.'

Hands are on hips. Heels are dug in. I can see we're in for the long haul.

'It's pouring with rain and freezing. We can do anything else, just not the park.'

'The Xbox, then.'

I sigh, but secretly I'm impressed by his resourceful-ness. 'That's the only other thing we can't do. Come on, it's not good for you to be staring at screens all the time.'

'Which is why I said let's go to the park.'

I can't help it. I have to laugh.

'Normally I love the park, but seriously, in the pouring rain?'

'I'll wear my coat and my waterproof trousers.'

'And what about me?'

'You can wear Daddy's snowboarding trousers. They're waterproof.'

'You have answers for everything, don't you? Come on then, let's get you dressed.'

It's freezing at the park and the ground is like a mud bath. Alfie's covered within seconds, but he doesn't notice. He's got the place to himself and he makes the most of it, charging from one piece of apparatus to the next. Running up the slide as many times as he wants because there is no one to move out the way for.

The rain is dripping off my hood and on to my nose but I realize that there are no arguments, no negotiations or tantrums. Shivering and soaking is a small price to pay for a break from all that. For once, Alfie's face is not twisted with angst or rage. His eyebrows are relaxed, his eyes gleaming and there is a smile that fills his face. I wish I could show Jake.

Then I have a brainwave. It's a rare occurrence, so I jump on it.

'Alfie, I'm going to grab something from the car. I'm just there.' I point at my car parked right next to the fence. 'You'll be able to see me the whole time.'

'OK.'

I run to the car and grab my camera out of the boot. I sort the settings while I'm slightly sheltered and then create a makeshift rain cover by ripping a hole in a plastic bag and posting the end of the lens through.

Alfie is running up the slide, then letting himself fall back down, chortling away to himself. There's so much mud on his face it looks like camouflage paint. I snap away, capturing him just as he lets go and begins his descent, as this is the moment when he always giggles. I take more pictures of him on the swings, in the tunnel and lying on his back on the roundabout. It feels great to be behind the camera again. For the first time in a long time, it feels like it has nothing to do with Alex. In fact, without even really noticing, I'm thinking about him less and less. The wound is definitely still there, but I think it's healing.

Just as the rain eases, Alfie decides he wants to go. We get in the car and I remove my camera from the plastic bag.

'Can I see the pictures?'

'Of course.'

I scroll through the images for Alfie. He laughs as he sees himself covered in mud.

'Can I take some pictures?'

I put the camera back in its bag. 'Well, it's pretty tricky.'

'You could teach me. Please.'

I'm reluctant. Alfie's all fingers and thumbs and my camera is the only possession I have that I'm precious about. To be fair, it's the only thing I own of any value. But looking at the excitement on his face, I can't say no.

'OK. I'll teach you later.'

I'm hoping he'll forget all about it, but as this is Alfie we're talking about, I know that's highly unlikely.

The second we get home, he grabs my camera bag and carries it into the house. My heart feels like it's imitating a techno beat. I take the bag off him and remove the camera.

'OK. Look, I'll show you. But you must look after it. It's very expensive and precious to me. You must always wear it round your neck and hold it at the same time and press the buttons gently.'

'I promise I will. Can I have it, then?'

'Wait, I've got to teach you how to use it first.'

I switch it to auto and show him the basic controls. He listens carefully but he can't sit still. It reminds me of my first driving lesson. My instructor always smelt of cheese-and-onion crisps. I swear he must've gobbled a pack before every one of our lessons. On our first lesson, I sat in the driver's seat, a mixture of nerves and excitement, with my hand on the key, ready to turn it. I couldn't believe it. I only got to drive for the last fifteen minutes of that forty-five minute lesson. The rest was spent listening to him drone on about the mechanics of driving. How when you pressed this pedal it affected this pulley or some rubbish like that. All I wanted to know was how to make it go, what gear to have it in and how to make it stop. I didn't care about the technicalities of how it all worked. So I keep it simple for Alfie and concentrate on the basics of zooming and focusing. Then, like it's a newborn baby, I reluctantly hand the camera over.

At first, Alfie snaps randomly and I'm sure we're going to end up with a lot of close-ups of cupboard handles and the carpet. But then he goes into his room and starts to position his figures. He has the camera around his neck and it bashes against the carpet every time he leans over.

'Let me hold that for a bit while you're sorting out where you want your figures to go.'

Alfie turns his body away. 'No, I want it.'

'I look after it or no more pictures. Simple as that.'

Alfie pushes out his bottom lip, but he doesn't fight as I lift the camera from around his neck.

'I'll hold it just here until you're ready.'

He gets more figures down off his Lego shelf and grabs the Batmobile. He puts Batman in and then sets up a row of baddies that I'm assuming are about to get run over.

'Can I take a picture now?'

I hand Alfie the camera, reminding him which button he needs. He struggles to look through the viewfinder so I hold my hand over one of his eyes. He twists the lens to zoom out and then presses the shutter.

We look at the photo on the back of the camera. It's blurred but he's managed to get the whole scene in view.

'Good one. Next time, just remember to press the button super-gently until it beeps and then keep pushing it the whole way down. Don't take your finger off.'

Alfie creates another scene as the Batmobile crashes into the row of baddies and the Joker and Bane topple over.

'I need to take another picture.'

I hand Alfie back the camera and this time he manages to focus properly and gets a pretty decent shot, if a little wonky.

'I'm making a story.'

Unexpectedly, I have my second brainwave of the day.

It's like my brain's been in hiding and suddenly decided to reveal itself.

'We could make a stop-motion film, Alfie! We could use the pictures and turn them into a proper film, like your Lego superhero ones.'

Alfie opens his mouth in wonder and I'm suddenly aware that, in my excitement, I may have slightly over-played exactly what we can achieve. Now Alfie's expecting a Hollywood movie rather than the amateur creation we'll be able to muster.

'I mean, it won't be exactly like the ones on TV – they use a special program on the computer that we don't have.' Alfie's face falls. 'But it will be a film. And we can add sound effects and stuff.'

We did a project on stop-motion films at art college and I have a vague recollection of spending hours making tiny adjustments to clay figures. In fact, now I come to think of it, it was a tediously long-winded process.

'Actually, Alfie, I think your idea of just taking photos to tell the story is much better. We could make it into a comic. That'd be cool.'

'No. I want to make the film.'

There's no point arguing. I put the idea in his head – I have to live with the consequences. 'OK.'

'So what do we need to do? Let's make a list.'

It's one of the many great things about Alfie. Despite being only six, he has a clear understanding of the impor-tance of a list.

'Right, we need to decide on a story, then list the key scenes, then we take pictures of each scene, put it on to my computer and then we can add the sound effects. You can even speak into the computer and put your voice on the film.'

'Really?'

I can't help but be infected by Alfie's enthusiasm. 'Come on, let's decide what story you want to tell.'

Well, Alfie being Alfie, of course the story he wants to tell is long and complicated. It involves pretty much every Lego figure and every Lego creation he has (and he has a lot) but I don't have the heart to scale down his big idea. While Alfie dictates the story, I write down his ideas in bullet-pointed scenes, until he gets to the part where Spider-Man is declaring his love for Gwen Stacy.

'Hold on a minute, I thought Spider-Man loved Mary Jane.'

Alfie gives me a look that says *bless, you haven't got a clue, have you?*.

'Daddy says that's what everyone thinks but in the real story it's Gwen Stacy he loves, but the Green Goblin throws her from a bridge and Spider-Man tries to catch her but he doesn't and she dies so he marries Mary Jane. But in one episode, when he gets to live his perfect life for the day, he chooses to spend it with Gwen Stacy, and Daddy says that's because Gwen Stacy is his true love.'

'Good remembering, little man,' Jake says, popping his head round the door.

Amid all the excitement, I hadn't heard him come home. 'He was just correcting my inaccurate knowledge of Spider-Man.'

'It's an easy mistake to make. Only real geeks like me overanalyse Marvel comics.'

'I'm right though, Daddy, aren't I? Gwen Stacy is super-special because she's the one Spider-Man really loves?'

'Well, he loves Mary Jane too, but, yeah, she's his one true love. She's the one he would've chosen.'

'Except he didn't catch her?' I lift my eyebrows. 'Even though he's got, like, super-strength and speed and stuff?'

Jake smiles. 'Even heroes make mistakes.'

Alfie jumps up, taking the story plan off me and waving it in Jake's face. 'We're doing a story, Daddy. We're going to make a real film and I can even talk on it. We'll be able to watch it on the television.' Alfie looks up at me, concern suddenly filling his face. 'We will be able to watch it on the television, won't we?'

'Yes, buddy. We will.'

Hearing Alfie so animated about something I've suggested feels good. Making the perfect cappuccino never brought quite the same job satisfaction.

'Sounds great,' Jake says warily. I can tell he thinks I've bitten off more than I can chew. He's probably right, but I'll enjoy the moment while it lasts.

'Can I start doing some photos?' Alfie picks the Lego figures he needs for the first scene off the shelf.

'Well, I'm going soon and I need to take my camera with me, but I promise I'll bring it back on Monday, OK?'

'But . . .' Alfie starts to protest but Jake shuts him down.

'I know how much that camera cost, Alfie. There is no way we are being responsible for that over the weekend. If you make a fuss, Emily won't bring it back next week.'

Alfie doesn't look happy but he doesn't object. 'OK, can I play on the tablet then, Daddy? I've not played on it all week.'

'I said he had to check with you,' I say to Jake. 'I wasn't sure when he was allowed it back.'

Alfie told me, with surprising honesty for a boy his age, that Jake had banned it because of some Lego-smashing misdemeanour.

'Oh, go on then,' Jake says, squeezing Alfie's shoulders. Going back to work seems to suit him. It's like he's removed the weights from his shoes.

'Thanks, Daddy.'

Alfie runs off to locate his tablet and Jake releases his tie and pulls it out from the neck of his shirt. 'I'm just going to get changed.'

'Right, well, I suppose I better get going. Shall I put the oven on? You've got lasagne tonight; I hope that's OK? My repertoire of meals is somewhat limited.'

'Don't be silly. It's amazing. Thank you. I told you that wasn't part of your contract.'

'And I told you I can't have you pay me the equivalent of a day's work and not clean the house or make the meals.'

Since I've started looking after Alfie, things with Jake have been a lot better. He greets me with a smile when I arrive in the morning and always seems really appreciative of everything I've done when he gets home. But I can't help feeling like a fraud. I'm sure if Jake saw the screaming fits, the chaos when he's not here, the constant state of panic I'm in because I don't know what to do with his son, he'd be slamming the door in my face and telling me never to return. I always tell him everything's great, but I'm convinced one of these days Alfie's going to dob me in.

'Well, at least have a glass of wine before you go? I'm just about to open a beer.'

I usually leave almost immediately after Jake's come through the door. 'Um . . . I don't know. I should probably be going.'

'Come on, one drink. You've been looking after my son all day; there's no way you're not in need of a glass of wine.'

He's right. I am. 'Oh, go on then. Just one.'

'Great. Go down and help yourself. I'll be there in a sec. We've lost Alfie to the land of *Where's My Water?* for at least an hour.'

I head to the kitchen, take a bottle of white wine out the fridge and get the bottle opener from the cutlery drawer. It feels weird knowing where everything is. I can imagine Jemma, when she moved in, deciding where she wanted everything to go, and now some stranger is rifling through her carefully organized drawers.

The wine glistens in the glass like a precious jewel and it takes every ounce of my willpower not to down the whole lot in one go. I find a beer for Jake and remove the top.

When he comes down, he's wearing black joggers and a long-sleeved Volcom top, the stone logo emblazoned on the front. There's no denying it: he is very attractive – his deep-brown eyes, like Alfie's, his tanned skin and tousled dark hair. I know it's stupid but it puts me on edge slightly. I'm not sure what it is about good-looking men, and I'm not proud of it, but being around them always makes me feel self-conscious. I hand him the bottle.

'Oh, thanks.' He straddles the stool opposite me at the breakfast bar and glugs his beer. 'So, how's your week been?'

I shrug. I haven't got the energy to lie. 'It's been OK.'

Jake raises an eyebrow. 'That good, hey? Please tell me you're not about to throw in the towel?'

'No, of course not. I'm just tired, I guess. You know what it's like.'

'I certainly do. Before Alfie, I thought teaching was exhausting, but I guarantee my week dealing with the predicaments of melodramatic teenagers has been a walk in the park compared to yours.'

'It's had its moments.'

'Well, Alfie seems happy, so you're obviously doing something right.'

'We went to the park today. It was nice. And he seems excited about the film, although I'm not sure it's going to live up to his expectations.'

Jake gets down off the bar stool and walks to the sink. He starts putting away the crockery I've left on the drying rack and I suddenly worry that I should've done it. 'You went to the park? In this weather?'

'Yeah, he wanted to. We wore waterproofs.'

'Fair enough. But just because Alfie wants to do something, don't feel you have to do it. You can say no.'

I know he's trying to be supportive, but it feels like a criticism. 'I know. I do say no. Sometimes it feels like the poor kid's whole life is one big no.'

'Right.'

I can see I've pissed him off and it's the last thing I need right now. I'm dog-tired and, besides, I need this job. I don't want to go back to the café. But there's this constant niggling feeling in my stomach that I can't ignore ... guilt, sadness, I'm not sure. I just keep seeing Alfie's face as I held him down on the stairs – at first surprise, like he'd thought

I was going to be different, and then disappointment, as he realized I wasn't. It feels like I'm betraying him, and every time I do, it's like I'm making yet another tiny crack in the delicate relationship we've formed.

'I just feel like every time I start to make some forward progress with him, I ruin it by forcing him to sit on that bloody naughty step because he's dared to ask for a biscuit or something equally minor.'

'So what do you suggest? We just give in to him about everything?'

'No. I just think maybe if you said yes a bit more, he wouldn't fight so much.'

Jake snorts. 'You're right. Let him have his own way all the time and he'll be a doddle.'

'Forget it. I'm wasting my time.' I down the last of my wine, start to gather my things and put them in my bag.

'No, come on. You tell me what to do with him. How are you going to solve Alfie's behaviour?'

I take a deep breath. 'I don't know, Jake. Maybe it doesn't need solving. Maybe he just needs to be cut some slack. I mean, do you ever want a treat when you get home from work? Would you like to be forced to sit on the thinking step every time you disagreed with the way something was done?'

Jake throws the cutlery into the drawer. 'He needs to understand consequences. He needs to learn.'

'I get that. It just doesn't feel like anyone's learning very much when I'm physically holding him down and he's fighting me to get off.' The oven light goes off and I put the lasagne in on the middle shelf. 'Look, I've got to go. The food will be about half an hour. I'll put the timer on for you.'

Jake nods. 'Thanks.'

Before I leave, I go up to find Alfie, but he's so engrossed in his game on the tablet that he doesn't even acknowledge me, so I kiss the top of his head and leave him be.

*   *   *

'Right, we're halfway through the course, so I want you to consider if there was one thing in your life you could change right now to make you feel less angry, what would it be? Instead of getting you to work in pairs this time, I'm going to give you ten minutes to think about it on your own, make some notes if you wish, and then we'll discuss as a group. After today, you have a break for half-term, so you might want to try putting your chosen change into action and see what effect it has.'

Sam hands us all a piece of paper and a pen, and I stare at mine, the blankness almost commanding to be filled. What *wouldn't* I change?

'Remember, it needs to be something you *can* change,' Sam adds, as if reading my mind. 'Not something you can't.'

I look around at all the others, scribbling away frantically, and start to doodle a picture of a flower, going over and over the petals until the pen makes a hole in the paper. I think it's probably too late for me – that any damage to my psyche is most likely well and truly done – but sometimes I wonder how it would feel to confront Mum and Shane about what happened. Would it be like bursting a blood blister – an immediate release? Or would it make no difference at all, and therefore make me feel even worse?

Sam claps his hands (he seems to have left his triangle at home) and I cover my paper with my hand.

'Right, who'd like to go first?'

As expected, Sharon raises her hand. 'I've been thinking about moving away. Maybe I should just take the plunge. It can't be good for my anger, living around the corner from my main trigger.'

Believe me, I guarantee she feels the same way.

'Maybe I should do the same,' Bill says. 'Find myself a nice deserted cottage in the country where I don't have to be surrounded by idiots day in and day out. I suspect I'd soon feel better.'

Sam smiles. 'Well, I guess controlling our emotions would be easier for all of us if we didn't have to interact with anyone else, but it might get a bit lonely, hey, Bill?'

Bill shrugs. 'I don't know. I quite like my own company.'

Sam gives him this look – I'm not quite sure what it means but there's a definite sadness behind it. Then he turns back to the rest of us. 'Anyone else?'

Jake shakes his head, as if disagreeing with his own thoughts. 'When you said it, the first thought that came to mind was that I'd change my son. That makes me a right arsehole, doesn't it?'

Yes, actually, it does.

'It doesn't make you an arsehole,' Sam says. 'But often with parenting, we need to change ourselves in order to see changes in our kids.'

'I know. I'm trying. I really am. But it feels like everything I try, the behaviour never gets any better.'

I sigh loudly. I can't help it. He says he's trying to change it, but he's not. He's too pig-headed to even consider a different approach.

'Emily?'

'I don't know, I thought I might take up yoga. That's supposed to chill you out, isn't it?'

Jake rolls his eyes and I notice Sharon looking over at him approvingly, sensing an ally in her crusade against me.

I hold out my hands. 'What? What's wrong with yoga?'

Jake looks like he can't be bothered to explain it to me. 'Nothing.'

Sharon, however, is more than happy to grab hold of the baton. 'What he's trying to say is that we're all here baring our souls and it feels like you're just taking the piss.'

'I'm being serious. Yoga is supposed to be very cleansing. At least my suggestion is focused on changing myself. You're all just blaming other people.'

Sharon laughs bitterly. 'According to you, it's someone else's fault you're even here.'

As she says it, the whole group looks at me, waiting for an explanation, but I drop my eyes to the floor. I sense Sam surveying me, weighing up whether or not I want to take this conversation any further, but I'm not going to give Sharon the satisfaction of being the one to force it out of me. Sam seems to take the hint, standing up and clapping his hands.

'OK, everyone, coffee time. After the break, I'll show you some clips about people who did decide to change something big in their lives and the impact it had. Ten minutes.'

I thank Sam with a flick of the head and then hurry outside for a cigarette.

* * *

'So, tell me all about this strange new job of yours?'

Alice pours two large glasses of wine and joins me on

the sofa. The late-afternoon sun shines through the patio doors, giving the room that soft orange glow you only get at this time of year.

'I'm a nanny for this little boy called Alfie. He's six.'

'So did you say on the phone you met the mum at anger management or something?'

'Well, the dad, but yeah.'

'Ah, now it's making more sense.' A broad smile fills Alice's face.

'Oh, give it a rest. It's definitely not like that at all.'

'Like what? I didn't say anything. I can't imagine what you might think I was insinuating.'

I smile. 'I just happened to bump into him a couple of times with Alfie. He's an unusual kid. He's not easy. For some reason, he seemed to take a shine to me. I have no idea why. Probably saw a kindred spirit.'

'So how's it going? You enjoying it?'

I hold up my empty glass.

'That good, eh?'

Alice tops up my wine and I notice she's not even halfway through hers. Note to self: must stop drinking it like water. I know she'd be supportive if she found out my penchant for an alcoholic beverage or two had become a bit more intense recently, but, truth be told, I don't want her to try to stop me. I like drinking. It makes me feel better. I'm not ready to be saved.

'He's challenging, you know? He finds rules tricky.'

Alice looks at me as if I'm stating the obvious.

'I know no kid is going to be thrilled at being told what to do but he seems to really struggle. If things aren't fair, he just doesn't get it. And Jake, that's the dad, he makes me stick to all these bloody rules, like he's not allowed a biscuit when he gets home from school and he can't take the dining-room chairs into the lounge to make a den because they make a mess. And every time he does something he's not supposed to, I have to make him sit on the sodding thinking step for five minutes.'

Alice laughs. 'I like it. The considerate parent's naughty step.'

'It's ridiculous. Calling it a thinking step doesn't suddenly make it a place for great enlightenment. It's age-old dictatorship. Do as I say or I punish you.'

'I didn't realize you were such a politician, Em.'

Alice opens a bag of sweet-chilli crisps and empties them into a bowl. I tuck in and realize I'm starving.

'It just makes me mad, you know? I'm the one who has to deal with him every day and yet I have to abide by these stupid laws. Thinking about it, perhaps I'm not the best influence on this kid.'

'Seriously though, Em, how would you deal with him? If he was your son?'

I think it over for a second. 'I'd let him have the bloody biscuit when he gets home from school, because I'd sure as hell want one after a day stuck in a classroom. I'd let him build his den – we can tidy it up. I wouldn't force him to sit on the sodding thinking step, that's for sure.'

'Then do it your way.'

'But my kids would probably be completely wayward and end up in prison aged sixteen. What do I know about parenting? I've never even had any real parents to learn from. I've got no nieces or nephews. No experience. Plus he's paying me and it's his child. I can't just change everything.'

'But like you said, you're the one who has to cope with him every day. Try it your way. If it doesn't work, go back to the old way. If it does work, you're the genius nanny who learnt how to deal with his son. You might even get a pay rise. Plus I can steal all your ideas when Billy turns into a little brat.'

I smile. 'We both know that'll never happen.'

'So anyway, come on, is he hot?'

'Who?'

'Oh, come on, Em – the dad, silly.'

I shake my head. 'A hot mess, more like.'

Alice strokes her chin like a wise professor with a slightly sinister glint in her eye. 'I knew it. He's a hotty.'

'He has a pleasing face, I suppose.'

'A pleasing face? Ha! You're classic, Em, you really are.'

'It's really not like that, though. We can't spend more than five minutes with each other without falling out.'

Alice smiles, a crisp paused at her lips. 'It'd never work, anyway. Different parenting styles.'

Alfie

When I grow up, I am going to be the man that made the *Lego Batman* film. Emily says if I do that I'll be able to have a massive house with a swimming pool. I don't want to live in a different house. I want to live in my house forever with Daddy and Mummy and Emily, but I do want to make the films. Daddy says Emily can't live with us because there's not room and she has her own house but I don't think that's true because we have an extra bed and she can just have two houses. I *would* like a swimming pool but we will just have to put it in my garden next to the climbing frame. I think it would just about fit.

Emily says I'm super-clever because I've made a film already and I'm only six. I took some of the pictures but I didn't like the camera because I couldn't see through the hole. Emily kept putting her hand over one of my eyes but then I just saw a pinky-grey smudge and not my figures. So Emily took the rest of the pictures and I moved all the figures around. I love making my films. I get to choose exactly what happens and what to do and no one tells me off for being bossy. Emily said I was the most patient boy in the whole world because it took a long time making all the changes and I didn't mind waiting for all the pictures to be taken. But Daddy says I'm rubbish at waiting so I'm not sure Emily is right that I am the most patient boy in the *whole* world. Maybe just in our land but not other lands like when we go on holiday.

Mummy is in a different land at the moment but I think she will be coming home soon because it's been a very long time and she always says 'see you soon'. I hope if Mummy comes home, Daddy will still go to work and Emily will still be my nanny. I like having Emily looking after me. When I have my funny hand day and I can't do stuff like my shoes or my seat belt, she just does them for me. And she lets me choose whether I have my twenty minutes on the iPad before my reading or after. When she lets me choose how we do things, I don't feel so cross.

Emily bought me a timer for when I get dressed. It's really cool. It's got orange sand, my favourite colour, and when the sand all goes from the top to the bottom, it means three minutes are up. We play a game and I have to get dressed before the sand is at the bottom. I always beat it. It's really fun.

I have to go and do my teeth now. I have a special chart with all the things I need to do in the morning and it's got Velcro on like my shoes so I can stick the things on when I've done them. I've already stuck the getting-dressed one on, next is my teeth, then my book bag, and then there is a special chart down in the hall for the picture of my shoes because I was worried about getting mud on the carpet running back upstairs.

Jake

After a day dealing with a teen pregnancy announcement, a fight in the canteen that resulted in a broken nose and a drugs raid because one of the kids had been spotted with MDMA in the common room, the last thing I need is another awkward encounter with Emily. Before the end of last week, a friendship between us had seemed a possibility. But with Emily, it's always one step forward and two steps back.

When I get to Alfie's bedroom, he and Emily are sitting on his bed with her laptop in front of them, falling about laughing, tears spilling down their cheeks. I can't help it, there's a flash of jealousy that there's stuff I'm missing out on now. That I don't share absolutely everything with Alfie like I used to. But, in general, returning to work has been easier than I thought it would be. Having that breathing space definitely makes Alfie's intensity easier to deal with. And it helps that he's clearly happy.

When Emily notices me, her face immediately becomes more serious. 'Oh, hi. Sorry, we just got the giggles about our voice-over.'

'Daddy, have a listen, have a listen. It's so cool. It's actually us on the film.'

I sit down on the bed and Emily starts their stop-motion film. It's jerky, there's very little continuity between scenes and Alfie's hands are apparent in most shots, but I can just make out some sort of story. Spider-Man's fighting with an array of baddies, there's a car chase and a lot of smashing figures together, then Gwen Stacy appears, stuck in the Hulk Lab Smash jail until Spider-Man rescues her in his helicopter. The voice-over is hilarious: Alfie attempts a gruff voice for the baddies and an American accent for Spider-Man, and Emily is a posh Gwen Stacy. Then it becomes clear why they're wetting themselves. Right in the middle of the kissing scene, there's a squeaky parp and then Alfie suddenly blurts out, 'Oops, I farted,' completely unaware that it'll appear on the film. I can't help but laugh along with them.

'Did you hear me, Daddy? I said, "Oops, I farted." Did you hear me?'

'Yeah, I heard you, little man. Silly billy.'

'Do you like our film?'

'I think it's the best film I've ever seen.'

Alfie examines my expression. 'Really? Are you teasing, Daddy?'

I sweep Alfie's fringe out of his eyes. 'No, I'm not teasing. I love it. I can't wait to see the next one.'

'Can we make another one, Emily?'

Emily's face suggests this creation has been a little bit more taxing than she expected. 'Yeah, we'll do another one soon.'

'Now?'

'No, not now, buddy. Soon though, I promise.'

'When? Tomorrow?'

'OK. We'll start doing the photos tomorrow. Why don't you plan another story?'

'Will you help?'

Emily looks like a drooping flower. I'd say *no, do it yourself.*

Let me breathe. But Emily seems to have an endless well of patience with Alfie that I just don't have. Maybe if she lived with him, she'd understand that if you let him he'd suck every last drop of blood out of you like a leech. That's why I have to shut him down sometimes. It's a survival technique.

'OK, the deal is you choose the figures you want to include and I'll help you with the story in the morning. Daddy's back late tonight because he had a meeting. Time to get ready for bed.'

'But I want to do it now.'

'It's a great deal, Alfie. I'd take it,' I say.

Alfie contemplates his response and looks at Emily. 'Only if you stay and read me my bedtime story?'

'I think Emily's tired, dude.'

Emily rubs her eyes. 'It's fine. I'd like to do that, I mean, if you don't mind me staying a bit longer?'

'No, it's fine.'

Alfie climbs on to the desk and begins selecting figures off his shelf and Emily tidies away some miscellaneous Lego into the boxes. Clearly already indoctrinated, she makes sure to sort each piece by its colour.

'We've already eaten,' she says. 'Yours just needs zapping in the microwave.'

'Yeah, sorry, my meeting went on and on. Thanks for tea.'

'No problem. I'll get him ready. You go and eat.'

I wonder if it's her way of calling a truce or whether she just wants rid of me. I suspect the latter.

* * *

Once I've finished eating, I go upstairs, stand in the hallway and peer through Alfie's door. Emily and Alfie are lying in his bed, under his Avengers quilt. He has his head on her chest and is staring intently at the story she is reading, while she strokes his hair. It's the Disney Storybook version of *Peter Pan*, one of Alfie's favourites. He is so still, so calm, so focused – it's hard to imagine this is the same child who can't stay on his chair for more than fifty seconds at mealtimes or who often chases around so manically that he damages either furniture or body parts.

'Why don't they stay in Neverland forever with Peter Pan?'

It's the same question he always asks me when we get to the end of the story.

'Well, because they miss home. They miss their mummy.' Emily's answer is the same answer I always give.

Alfie looks deep in thought.

'Do you miss your mummy, buddy?' Emily asks, lifting her head to meet his eyes.

I quietly crouch down and sit outside the door with my back to the wall. I probably shouldn't be listening in but I'm fascinated to hear what Alfie says.

'I'm not sure. Daddy says he misses her but I'm not really sure what "missing" feels like.'

It's at times like this I want to freeze Alfie so he doesn't get any older, any more worldly-wise.

'That's a very good point. It's hard to describe. I guess it's a feeling in your tummy, like you really want to see someone and show them your new toys or tell them something you've done, and I suppose you feel sad that you can't.'

There's a pause and I picture Alfie giving this serious consideration. 'I think I miss you sometimes, then. Because I want to show you my Lego and stuff and I feel sad when

Daddy says no. Like at the weekend, because Daddy says you're not working then so we can't invite you over.'

Another pause.

'I do miss Mummy's porridge,' Alfie continues. 'She used to make it for me on a Saturday and a Sunday and it was super-yummy. Daddy's not very good at porridge.'

'Exactly. I think you've got it there, Alfie. I think sometimes we miss the things they did. How about my porridge? Is it OK when I cook it for you?'

'It's not as good as Mummy's but better than Daddy's.'

I smile at his honesty.

'I'll take that. I'm sure it's a bit strange having me looking after you so much now and not Mummy and Daddy. That's OK. I don't mind.'

'I like having you looking after me. Mummy always says "in a minute" and then I'm sure I count one minute but she still doesn't come so I ask again, but then she gets cross because she said in a minute but I'm sure I've waited like a hundred minutes and she still doesn't come and help me.'

My heartstrings feel like they're about to rip.

'I guess it's tricky being a mummy when you're super-busy.'

'And Daddy is a bit of a grumpy-pants. Especially at bedtime and in the morning. I don't like Daddy at bedtime and in the morning.'

It's a fair criticism, but it's still hard to hear.

'Shall I tell you a little secret?' Emily says in a hushed voice. 'I'm really grumpy in the morning too.'

'Not when you get to my house. You always smile and that's not grumpy.'

'Ah, but that's because I'm seeing you.' I hear Emily kiss Alfie, and it feels odd that this stranger has been getting so close to my child without me even realizing it.

'My mummy used to get cross with me when I kept asking her for stuff too,' Emily continues. 'You know it doesn't mean they don't love you more than anything in the whole world, don't you?'

'And what about your daddy?' Alfie asks. 'Was he grumpy in the morning?'

'I didn't really have a daddy.'

'Doesn't everyone have a daddy?'

I hope this isn't going to turn into a conversation about the birds and the bees, although Emily would probably do a much better job of explaining it than me.

'Well, yes, everyone has a daddy, but my daddy went to live somewhere else when I was little and I didn't see him again until I was a big girl.'

I realize this is probably the most I've learnt about Emily in all the time I've known her.

'Big like me?'

'No, much bigger than you. Thirteen.'

'I'm six.' I can almost see Alfie pushing out his chest with pride.

'I know you are. So I was a lot bigger than you.'

'One, two, three, four, five, six, seven, eight, nine, ten, eleven, twelve, thirteen. Wow, that's really big.'

'I know.'

Alfie goes quiet for a while and then asks, 'Why didn't you see him until you were thirteen?'

'Some daddies, and some mummies, I suppose, just don't see you. I don't know why, Alfie, but what's important is that *your* daddy sees you all the time. So even if he is a bit grumpy sometimes, he still always wants to see you. That's what matters.'

'So like my mummy doesn't want to see me any more?'

I feel a lump in my throat.

'No, gorgeous. Not like that at all. Your mummy has to work away at the moment, but she still wants to see you. That's why she rings you on the telephone and you talk to her on the laptop. That's because your mummy wants to see you lots and lots. And it won't be long before she comes to see you properly again.'

'Like in real life?'

'Yes, in real life. Now go to sleep, buddy. I'll see you in the morning.'

I hope Emily's right. I don't want Alfie to be the product of yet another fractured marriage. I want my family back. Because although it wasn't perfect, it was better than this.

'Emily?' It's his question voice and I wonder, anxiously, what he's going to ask her. 'Do you have a little boy?'

'No.'

'Would you like one?'

'Only if he was just like you.'

I expect Alfie to question this, about whether it's possible for anyone to be just like him, but he doesn't so he must be tired. After a few minutes of silence, I guess Alfie's drifting off so I sneak back downstairs before Emily catches me.

* * *

When Emily finally surfaces, I'm sitting in the lounge with a beer and a tub of Ben & Jerry's, watching an old episode of *Game of Thrones*.

'I'll see you in the morning, then,' Emily says, peering around the door, her jacket draped over her arm.

'Hang on, come in for a minute.'

Emily keeps hold of her jacket, a signal to me, perhaps, that I'm on borrowed time, and sits on the other sofa.

'Do you want a drink?' I ask, putting off my apology.

'No, I'm OK, thanks.'

'Ice cream, then? Come on, I'll even get you your own spoon.'

Emily starts to put her arm through the sleeve of her jacket and I know I can't put it off any longer. I have to be the bigger man. After listening to Emily and Alfie's conversation, I know he needs her in his life right now. So whether or not I agree with some of the stuff she says, I've got to try to make this work.

'Look, I'm sorry about last week. I seem to have an uncanny knack of pissing you off.'

'You can't help it.'

I'm not sure if she's joking or not at first, but then the corners of her mouth turn up.

'I don't have all the answers with Alfie,' I continue. 'Far from it. I'm just trying to follow the recommended strategies. Supernanny made a lot of money coming up with these miracle cures. I can't have the only child in the world who can't be trained.'

I'm being flippant but Emily flinches and I know it's my use of the word 'trained'. But surely that's part of my job as a parent? To mould Alfie into someone who can function in society?

'Look, if you think you've got some better strategies, I'm willing to listen to alternatives. All I ask is that we're on the same page. Alfie needs consistency, so whatever methods we choose, we both need to be using them.'

Emily's finger circles her temple. 'I get that. I do understand he needs consistency, Jake, but you need to understand I'm trying to survive.'

I can't help feeling I misread her the other night. That it wasn't an 'I know better' attack, it was a cry for help.

'I've not got any magical solutions either,' she continues. 'I just wonder if we tried not sweating the little stuff, like the biscuit, maybe he'd be more receptive to the important rules, like not smashing into the glass doors. But I'm not an expert. I'm not even a parent, so feel free to ignore me. I just find it hard to enforce the naughty step. It drains me. And it just feels a little pointless, but I might be wrong.'

When I really listen to Emily and I'm not caught up with being a defensive idiot, what she says makes quite a lot of sense.

'OK. No more *thinking* step. And one biscuit. Just one.'

'OK. As Alfie would say, it's a deal.'

'Ice cream?' I hold out the tub.

Emily looks at it as if she thinks it might be poisoned, then goes out of the room and comes back with a spoon. She sits at the other end of the sofa. 'Hand it over then.'

She digs around, then eventually spoons out a huge chunk of cookie dough.

'You can't just eat the cookie dough, you know? You have to eat the ice cream too.'

At first, Emily looks like she's about to throw the spoon at my head, but then she laughs. 'I'm sorry. I'm not used to sharing. I usually just dig the cookie dough out and throw the rest away.'

I hold out my hand. 'My turn.'

Emily hands me the tub and I spoon some out. 'See,' I say, modelling the process, 'you just dig in randomly and see what you get.'

Surveying the room, her eyes stop on the CD rack. 'Interesting collection.'

I study Jemma's selection of cheesy dance compilations and her comprehensive history of boy bands, starting at East 17 and going all the way up to 5 Seconds of Summer.

'They're Jemma's. Mine are relegated to the study.'

Emily looks like she's trying to find the thumbprint embedded into my skin. 'So what sort of stuff are you into then?'

'Nirvana, the Foos, anything heavy.'

'Seriously? Mr Clean-cut is into grunge?'

I dishevel my hair with the palm of my hand. 'I'm not clean-cut.'

'OK. Sensibly middle-class.'

'I'm a radical surfer and snowboarder, thank you very much.'

Emily looks softer tonight. Her hair is a little longer and she's bleached it white blonde.

'You growing your hair out?'

Emily rubs her head. 'Oh, I don't know. I guess I just haven't had a chance to shave it again.'

'It looks nice.' Emily visibly baulks at the compliment so I change the subject. 'So, while we're not arguing for a nanosecond, tell me something about yourself. It's dawned on me that you're looking after my little boy every day and the only thing I know about you is that he thinks you're the best thing since sliced bread.'

At the mention of Alfie's affection for her, Emily's eyes sparkle. Her face is always brighter when she's around him. It makes me feel bad that he doesn't have that effect on me. Like I'm so caught up with the trials of looking after him that I'm missing the magic.

'What do you want to know?'

'I don't know. Do you live with anyone? What films do you like? Anything. You've seen my house, met my son, you know my wife walked out on me, you know I couldn't cook a decent roast if my life depended on it. I know nothing about you.'

'It wasn't that bad. The roast, I mean.'

'You're avoiding the question.'

Because Emily doesn't smile very often, when she does, it's more rewarding, like getting an A from the teacher who consistently gives out Cs.

'OK, I live on my own in a flat at the bottom of town. And it's embarrassing to admit, but I like romcoms.'

I nearly choke on my beer. 'No way do you like romcoms.'

'I know, I know, it's hard to believe that the girl with the shaved head who wears hoodies and biker boots is a romcom fanatic, but it's true.'

'It's not because of how you look. You just seem too . . .' I search for the word.

'Much of a bitch?'

'I was going to say cynical. Sorry, that's really rude of me, isn't it?'

Emily shakes her head. 'It's a fair description.'

She's so much more easy-going than she was earlier. She reminds me of Alfie. You never quite know which version you're going to get.

'Well, I know all about your brilliant job. What else is there? Are you with anyone?'

Emily sucks the ice cream off her spoon. 'No. We split up a few months back.' Then, by way of explanation: 'He was a prick.'

'Seems there's a lot of us around.'

That smile again. Bonus points.

'Any hobbies?'

'What is this? A job interview?'

'I'm just being polite.'

'I don't know. I've never had much free time because of working so much, I guess. I used to do a lot of photography. It was the only thing I've ever really felt passionate about. God, I sound really boring, don't I?'

I shake my head. 'There's quite a few words I'd use to describe you, but "boring" isn't one of them. So how come you *used* to do a lot of photography?'

Emily bites her nail. 'It's a long story.'

'Fair enough. I get the feeling there are a lot of "long stories" in your life.'

Emily stares out of the patio door and I worry I've said the wrong thing again.

'Sorry, I didn't mean that in a negative way. I just mean there seems a lot to you.'

'It's fine. You're right about the long stories. But I'm not so sure that makes me interesting. Just hard work.'

It's the most she's ever opened up to me and it makes me want to know more. She hands me back the tub of Ben & Jerry's and there's a fleck left at the bottom.

'Well, I've also discovered that you're a terrible person

to share with. Jemma only ever had a few spoonfuls and then left the rest of the tub for me.'

'Sorry.'

I scrape out the remains and put the tub on the coffee table. 'Truth be told, it used to drive me mad. It's hard to properly tuck into your food when you've got someone picking at theirs like a sparrow opposite you.'

'Much better when someone gobbles it down like a pig?'

'Exactly. Except when we're sharing, then I'd choose the sparrow every time.'

Emily puts her jacket on. 'Right, now I've eaten all your ice cream, I better get home. I've another exhausting day looking after your son tomorrow.'

'True. So, are we calling a truce? For Alfie's sake?'

Emily stands up with a smile. 'OK. For Alfie.'

With most people that I meet, I can figure them out within a few minutes. I know almost immediately whether they're someone I'm going to get on with or someone I'd rather avoid. But Emily's so all over the place, so Jekyll and Hyde, that I can't get the measure of her. But, for the first time ever, I'm not in any desperate hurry for her to leave and, when she does, the clunk of the door closing echoes around the empty house.

*　*　*

I grab another bottle of beer from the fridge and, because I no longer have anyone to answer to, take it up to bed with me. I remove most of my clothes and sit on top of the covers in my boxers. I power up my laptop to peruse the latest articles on *Den of Geek!* and it opens on my Skype page. I notice that Jemma's online. Without thinking, I click on her name and select 'call'. It rings for a minute or two and then her face appears on the screen. She's standing in her sister's spare bedroom wearing a skimpy red dress. The laptop must be on the bed because she leans down to look into the camera.

'Is everything OK, Jake?'

She says it with a why-the-hell-would-I-want-to-speak-to-you expression and I suddenly feel stupid.

'Yeah, I just saw you were online so I pressed call. I'm not sure why.'

Jemma sits down on the bed and pulls the laptop on to her knees. 'How's Alfie?'

'He's good. Exhausting. You know, he's Alfie.'

She offers a sad smile. 'I almost booked a flight home the other day. I got right to the bit where it says pay now and then I shut my laptop down.'

My shoulders tense, the anger flooding back.

'So why did you stop yourself?'

How can you call yourself a parent?

'He's better off without me right now.'

It's an easy excuse. A way to make the really shitty thing you're doing sound less shit. But it doesn't wash with me. What she's done is still the shittiest of the shit to me.

'Of course he's not better off without you. You're his mum. Every child needs his mum. But he's doing OK. We're making the best of a bad situation. Emily's been making these stop-motion films with him and it seems to have really captured his imagination.'

'That sounds good,' she says, but her face says something very different.

'Yeah, it is. Turns out he's pretty creative.'

I don't think I'm saying this stuff to hurt her, but I might be. I'm on a roll, so I continue.

'Emily thinks we've got too many rules. That if we had fewer nos it'd be easier to stick to the ones we do have. We're going to drop the thinking step for a while – see if she's got a point. I'm not sure, but I reckon it's worth a go.'

Jemma nods. Her mouth's clamped shut and I know I've pissed her off but I don't care. She's not here, so why should she get a say in how I'm dealing with Alfie?

'Emily this, Emily that. This Emily seems to be having a big impact on both your lives.'

'Seriously? You want to go down that road?'

Jemma shakes her head. 'No. Sorry. It's just hard to be so far away sometimes.'

So come home.

'Where have you been tonight, anyway? You look very swish.'

'Oh, we're just about to go out.'

'Now? It's ten o'clock. Where are you going?'

'It's just a few drinks with some of Laura's workmates.'

'Male workmates?' Naively, up until this point I'd not even considered that Jemma might be spending time with other men.

'Jake, it's really not like that.'

'So they are men?'

'It's a group of people. Male and female. There's nothing going on.'

But it suddenly dawns on me that even if she's telling the truth on this occasion, in the not-too-distant future, there could be another man. Jemma's stunning. I'm sure there are hundreds of suave French twats dying to get their hands on her.

Jemma pushes a strand of hair off her face and checks herself out in the camera. 'I've got to go. Tell Alfie I love him.'

'Do you?'

'I haven't got time for this now, Jake.'

'Of course not. When do you ever have time?'

Jemma sighs. 'Look, I didn't want to have this conversation right now. I was going to call you when we had more time to talk properly, but since you're pushing me, I might as well say it. I hate missing out on stuff with Alfie. I hate the thought of you two starting a new life without me. But I don't miss this shit between you and me, Jake. I don't miss the arguing, or the scoring points, or feeling like a terrible person. Being here, I finally feel like myself again.'

'So what are you saying?' I ask, even though I'm pretty sure I know the answer.

'I think maybe we're better apart.'

I shut my laptop. I can't listen to any more. I imagine her in some sophisticated Parisian bar, dressed up to the nines, free and happy in her new life, and I feel sick. I naively thought that time away from us would make Jemma realize what she had, but instead it's made her realize what she wants. And that's clearly not me any more.

Emily

'Come on, Alfie, it's this way.'

I drag Alfie down the corridor until we get to Nan's door. I don't want her to have to get up, so I let myself in. Alfie shuffles along beside me, hiding behind my leg. Nan's watching the *Some Mothers Do 'Ave 'Em* box set I bought her last Christmas and laughing like a drain.

When she hears the door click, she looks up. 'Oh, Em, you really didn't need to come. I'm fine. They make such a fuss here sometimes. It was only a little fall.'

'Don't be silly. It's fine. Alfie here wanted to come and meet you anyway, didn't you, buddy?' I put my arm around his back and manoeuvre him out from behind me. 'Come on, don't be shy.'

On seeing Alfie, Nan's face breaks into a wide smile. 'Ah, so you're Alfie! I've heard all about you. Would you like some chocolate?'

Alfie nods. It's a sure-fire way to win him over.

Nan pats her chair. 'Well, come and sit down and Emily will get you some chocolate buttons. They're in the cupboard by the fridge, Em.'

Alfie walks towards Nan and, rather than choosing the sofa opposite, sits on her chair next to her.

Nan shuffles along to give him space and pulls him further back from the edge. 'There you go, perfect. Shall we find you something to watch? What do you like to watch, young man?'

It's like Alfie's perfect afternoon. Chocolate and unlimited TV. Alfie takes the remote from Nan and starts typing in 'Peter Rabbit'.

'Wow. You're better with this than me. *Peter Rabbit*? Do you like that? I used to read that to my little boy. I had a little boy like you once, you know.'

I hate the thought of my dad as a child, just starting out, so full of potential. It makes me so mad that he just threw it all away.

'I'm six.'

'Six? Well, you're a big boy then, aren't you?'

Alfie smiles proudly, then the *Peter Rabbit* theme tune starts to play and he jigs in his seat and sings along. Nan giggles and then turns to me. 'Don't just stand there gawping at us, Em. Get those chocolate buttons, will you?'

'Oh, yeah. Sorry.'

Alfie shakes his head. 'Silly Emily.' And Nan laughs.

I grab the chocolate buttons from the cupboard, bring them through and hand them to Alfie. 'What do you say, Alfie?'

He looks up at Nan. 'Thank you.'

'You're very welcome.' Nan taps Alfie's hand.

Alfie starts counting the buttons out into three piles on the arm of the chair. Once he's finished, he holds a handful out to Nan and one out to me. 'Here you go.'

Nan looks at him like he's just offered her a palmful of gold. 'Oh, thank you, Alfie. No, they're for you.'

'Emily?' I can tell by his face he hopes I'll give the same response.

'You keep them, buddy.'

'What a lovely boy you are,' Nan says.

'No, he's not. He's a pain in the bum really, aren't you, Alfie?' I squeeze his shoulder.

'No, I'm not. I'm awesome.' He says 'awesome' in an American accent and tries to wink while making a clicking sound with his tongue.

We both start giggling and Nan looks at us like we're mad. Once we've calmed down, Alfie turns his attention to the television and, soon after, there's a knock at the door.

'That'll be his dad come to collect him.' I stand up to open the door.

'Oh, good, it's the right place,' Jake says, slightly out of breath. Then he looks me up and down like he's trying to work something out. 'You look nice.'

I look down, hoping he can't see the heat flowing into my cheeks. 'I always look like this.' I stand back to let him into the flat, then close the door. 'Anyway, thanks for coming. I didn't want to leave her on her own, just in case,' I say quietly.

'I might be old but I'm not deaf, Em. And I don't need you to look after me. I'm fine.'

Jake walks past me into the lounge. 'Lovely to meet you . . .'

'Edith.'

Jake grasps Nan's hand between his own. 'Lovely to meet you, Edith. I see you've met my son. You OK, little man?'

Jake sits on the sofa beside me. Alfie's so immersed in *Peter Rabbit* he doesn't even seem to notice him.

'Well, I can see where Alfie gets his good looks from,' Nan says, a cheeky glint in her eye.

'I could say the same about Emily.'

Nan giggles like an infatuated schoolgirl. 'Charmer.'

'Just being honest.'

I've not seen Charismatic Jake before. It feels strange.

'So what is it you do then, Jake?' Nan asks. 'Obviously something important with that smart suit.'

'Oh, I'm just a teacher.'

'Ooh, very fancy. You must be very intelligent.' Nan's of the generation that still sees teachers as higher beings.

'No, not at all. It's more that I'm on their wavelength. I hated school so I wanted to try to give the children a better experience than I had.'

Hearing Jake talk, I suddenly feel guilty that I've only ever seen him in relation to Alfie. I've never considered him as a person in his own right, with a past, interests, a job that he's possibly very good at.

We all sit and watch *Peter Rabbit* until the episode finishes. Nan raises her leg on to the coffee table and pulls up her highly attractive support socks.

Alfie gives her a concerned look. 'How did those worms get in your legs?'

'Alfie!' Jake looks mortified.

Nan laughs. 'It's fine. I like someone who says what they're thinking. Everyone's so politically correct these days. He's curious, like all good children should be.' Then she turns to Alfie. 'They're veins, love. Give me your hand.' Alfie holds out his hand and Nan takes it and turns his arm over. 'Look, you've got them too.' She runs her finger along the veins in his wrist. 'It's just that when you get older they sometimes stick out, like mine.'

'Yuck. I hope mine don't do that.'

'Alfie.' Jake covers his face with his hands.

Nan smiles. 'Well, make sure you get lots of exercise and don't get fat like me, OK?'

Alfie nods.

'I'm sorry about that,' Jake says, standing up. 'I'll take the little monkey off your hands.'

Nan waves Jake's apology away. 'Not at all. It's been a real pleasure.'

'Can't I just watch one more?' Alfie says, leaning back in Nan's chair.

'No, it's teatime, but how about we go for a McDonald's on the way home?'

Alfie leaps out of the chair. 'Yay!'

Jake leans down to kiss Nan on the cheek. 'Well, I hope to see you again soon, Edith.' Jake puts his hands on Alfie's shoulders and leads him to the door. 'Say bye, Alfie.'

Alfie looks at me, then turns to Jake. 'Isn't Emily coming?'

'No,' I say, 'I'm just going to stay here for a bit. I'll see you soon though, OK?'

'Tomorrow?'

'Well, no, it's the weekend tomorrow. And then it's half-term so you have a week with Daddy.'

'We're going to go to the beach, Alfie. It's going to be awesome,' Jake says, as if he's trying to convince himself as much as Alfie.

'Will you come too, Emily? Please.'

'Well, I think you're going to go with just Daddy.'

Alfie runs over to me, climbs on to my lap and puts his arms around my neck. 'Please, Emily. Please come.'

I look over to Jake, who I can see is getting anxious about the potential colossal meltdown brewing.

'I'll call Emily later and we'll talk about it then, OK, Alfie? Come on. Those chicken nuggets are waiting.'

'Yeah, quick. You don't want them to sell out.'

'OK. But you have to come to the beach.'

I smile. 'I'll talk to Daddy about it later. Go on.'

'Kiss first,' Alfie says.

It takes me aback – he's never asked for one before – but I kiss him on the cheek and he pulls me in tight to him. Over his shoulder, I meet Nan's eyes, but I can't quite tell what she's thinking.

*   *   *

'How about we go for a drive and park up somewhere with a view? I can stop off and get sandwiches and we can eat them in the car.'

'Um, I'm not sure really, love. It takes me such a long time to get anywhere these days.'

'Come on. We'll steal one of the wheelchairs in the corridor, take it for a joyride.'

Nan pushes a loose grey curl off her forehead. 'Oh, go on then. You only live once, right?'

We drive out to Crickley Hill and I park up so we have a view of the valley below us. The sky is clinging on to the last of its pinky-orange glow before the sun retires for the day and the lights in the house windows punctuate the landscape like decorations on a Christmas tree. It's nearly November and there's a definite sense that autumn is being left behind and winter will soon be upon us.

I pull the sandwiches out of the plastic Sainsbury's bag and hold Nan's out to her. 'Egg and cress?'

'Oh, thanks, love. My favourite. What have you got?'

I hold up the packet to show her. 'Coronation chicken.'

Nan wrinkles her nose like a rabbit. 'Smells funny. Are those raisins in it?'

I nod, taking a bite.

'Well, each to their own, I suppose.'

We sit in silence for a while and eat our sandwiches. The cold from outside starts to seep into the car so I switch the engine back on and turn on the heater.

'That Jake's a bit of a catch,' Nan says, removing a piece of cress from her teeth. 'Clearly got a soft spot for you, as well.'

'He's married, Nan. And he definitely has no interest in me.'

'I thought his wife had left him? Isn't that why you're looking after his boy?'

'It's a trial separation. I'm not sure when she's coming back. I don't talk to Jake much. I leave once he gets home from work.'

Nan nods, but she doesn't look convinced. 'Well, Alfie seems like a sweet boy.'

'He is. He has some . . . difficulties, I suppose. But he makes me laugh. He's so funny, some of the stuff he comes out with. He's such a character. You can't help but feel brighter when you're with him, you know?'

Nan offers a faint smile and then, suddenly, there's a bang and a burst of light as colourful sparks fall from the sky.

Nan's eyes open wide. 'Fireworks!'

It's amazing how fireworks never lose their magical beauty. No matter how many times you've seen them, they still make you feel like a tiny kid again, wrapped up in gloves, hat and scarf, standing outside on an ice-cold night, watching them for the very first time.

We sit and gawk at them for a while, oohing and aahing at the pops, crackles and sparkles.

'I remember when I first took your dad to the fireworks. He was about five. Cried like a baby, he did. The big wuss.'

Nan stares through the windscreen, her eyes suggesting her mind is a long way away.

'I should probably take Alfie. I don't know if he likes them or not.'

I might be wrong but if feels as though Nan is stopping herself from saying something. The fireworks finish and I throw my empty sandwich wrapper in the plastic bag. Nan still hasn't finished hers and, as I watch her eating, I notice her hands are shaking and her face looks drawn. Her hands probably always shake, maybe it's just more noticeable because she's sitting so close to me, but I want to bring the sandwich to her mouth for her, as if she were a small child.

'Are you eating enough, Nan? Are you getting enough sleep? You look tired.'

The crinkles around her eyes bunch together as she smiles. 'I'm just old, love.'

Sitting in the car, only darkness surrounding us, my emotions feel amplified and I wish I hadn't brought her out.

'Right, shall we head back?' I pull my seat belt over my shoulder.

Nan looks into my eyes. 'Thanks for bringing me here,

love. I haven't seen fireworks for years. I always hear them overhead but by the time I've got out of my chair to look out the window, they've gone.'

'It's a pleasure. Any time.'

Nan tries to put her seat belt on but she can't quite reach. I undo mine so that I can lean over and pass hers to her. She holds on to it, then I help to pull it down and click it in. As I do, she grasps my hand. Her skin feels so thin, like she's down to the last few layers.

'Just remember you're not his mum, Em. Eventually you're going to have to give him back.'

I shrug. 'Of course. I mean, he's not mine to give back. It's just a job.'

'It's not like loving another adult.' Nan continues as if she hasn't heard me. 'When you love a child, it's . . .' She shakes her head, as if no words can explain the feeling. 'And then if you lose them, well, I'm not sure you're ever quite the same.'

I pull my arm away to put my seat belt back on.

'I never knew what it was tormenting your dad. Then when I found that photo of you in his wallet and he finally told me the truth, suddenly it all made sense.'

It still hurts that he didn't tell Nan about me for all those years. Like I was just a dirty secret. An embarrassment.

'Well, he kind of brought that on himself, to be fair.'

Nan squeezes my arm. 'Partly. I know it's hard for you to believe after everything you were told all those years, but he really did love you, Em. You only have my word and I only had his, but I know he tried to see you.'

'Let's get back. It's getting cold.'

It was the first thing she told me when we met. It was

at Dad's wake and I was sitting in the corner of the church hall, drinking a glass of wine and trying to avoid talking to anyone. I really didn't want to hear people's condolences for losing my dad when the truth was I'd never really had him. Nan walked straight over and, after a brief introduction, she launched into a spiel about how my dad had tried his best to see me over the years, but Mum had taken a restraining order out on him. Mum said he hit her; Nan says that's bollocks, that she got the bruises elsewhere. Either way – that, paired with the drinking and petty drug use – he was refused access. Nan says he sent letters, birthday cards, but I never got them. Mum still sticks to her story and I guess I'll never know the truth.

In the end, it doesn't really matter. The fact is, from the age of four I didn't have a father. He turned up to my thirteenth birthday party. I call it a party – Mum subsidized what I'd saved of my pocket money to take Alice and another friend from school bowling. I have no idea how he found out we were there, but he turned up with this silver 'best daughter' necklace he probably found on the pavement. He looked a mess, like he hadn't washed for weeks, and he smelt stale, of fags and alcohol and burgers. When he tried to hug me, Mum must've spotted him because she sent Shane over, who swore at Dad, pushing him away and embarrassing me in front of my friends. Dad fought back for a bit but, when he saw that I was in tears, he agreed to leave.

The only other time I saw him was about six months before he accidentally overdosed on pain meds. Somehow he must've persuaded Mum to give him my mobile number. I didn't answer at first, not recognizing the number, but after four calls in a row I picked up out of curiosity.

'Hi, Emily, it's your dad.'

I put the phone down. He called back a few minutes later and I rejected the call. Then he called again so I reluctantly picked up.

'Please just hear me out, Em.'

I hated how he called me Em – as if he knew me, like we had some kind of relationship.

'Please just come and meet me. If after you've spoken to me, you never want to see me again, I'll leave you alone forever.'

I don't know why I agreed to go. Because I was intrigued, maybe? Because I wanted to tell him how much I hated him? I'm not sure, but we met about a week later in the park. As I walked over the bridge and saw him sitting on a bench staring at the lake, his face a near reflection of my own, my stomach did somersaults. He had a bunch of flowers in his hand. Gerberas. My favourite. Not that he could possibly have known that. He just got lucky, I guess.

When I got to the bench, he stood up and embraced me, tears in his eyes, and I stood like a statue in his arms. He asked me questions about myself, my life, my hobbies – like he thought showing an interest in who I'd become would make up for never seeing any of the things that had led me there. I gave him one-word answers and didn't ask him a thing. He said he was finally practising clean-living, that he was going to put things right, but he never called me again and six months later he died from an overdose so I guess that was just more bullshit.

I still remember the last thing I said to him, as I stood up to leave and he begged me not to hate him.

'I don't hate you. I feel no more for you than if you

were a complete stranger that I just sat down next to on a bench. Because, let's be honest, that is all you are.'

He'd looked at me like I'd just stuck a knife in him and twisted it round multiple times. And I walked away wishing what I'd said was true. When Mum called me to tell me he'd died, all I could think about was his face right then, as he sat on that bench.

* * *

We reach Nan's flat and I grab the wheelchair that I left in the car park, open the passenger door and help to man-oeuvre her into the chair. It's so cold I can see our breath so I race Nan into the flat, turn her heating up and settle her in her chair.

'Thanks again for taking me out, love. I do appreciate you, you know?'

'I know, but it's a pleasure. You never have to thank me, Nan.'

I put the television remotes on the arm of her chair and kiss her crêpey cheek.

She puts the palm of her hand against the side of my face. It's still cold from outside. 'Bye, love. Don't forget I love you.'

I squeeze her wrist. 'Love you too, Nan.'

'And just think about what I said about Alfie, will you?'

I nod, offer her a half-smile and head home.

* * *

Despite Jake and I fabricating ingenious reasons for why I couldn't come to the beach, Alfie picked them apart with the skill of a world-class detective and made it impossible for us to say no. And sitting with the sand between my toes, it actually feels good to be here. The last time I went to the coast was when I was eight and my foster mum took me to Weston-super-Mare and, let's be honest, the swathes of mud and dingy water there don't really constitute the seaside.

'Let's go and jump the waves,' I say, attracted by the glistening aquamarine water and deceived by the warmth of the autumn sun on the back of my dark hoody.

Jake looks at me like I just suggested getting naked and having sex right here on the sand, but Alfie's straight off, running towards the water.

'Wait, Alfie!' I run after him. 'You need to take your trousers off.'

He removes his trousers mid-run and leaves them lying on the sand halfway down the beach. Within seconds, he's in the water, jumping over the line of white froth. I pull up the legs of my jeans so that they're above my knees and follow Alfie in. The water's icy and when it splashes against my shins, it makes my legs cramp.

'It's freezing.'

Alfie looks at me, his face full of joy. 'No, it's not. Come on, let's play chase the waves. We have to wait for one to come and then run away as fast as we can.'

'OK.'

While we wait for the next wave, I jig my legs around in the water to stop them from seizing up completely and landing me face-first on the seabed. Then a wave splashes down against the shore and we race each other back up the beach.

Jake's there waiting, his jeans rolled up. 'I must be mad.'

Then we all run in and wait for the next wave. When it comes, we charge back up on to the sand.

'Can we do it again, Daddy?'

Jake shivers loudly. 'Go on, then.'

'I'll be back in a sec. I just want to get something,' I say.

'Oh yeah, good one. You suggest this, then abandon us.'

I smile. 'Promise I'll be back in a minute.'

I run back to the picnic mat, pull my camera out of my rucksack and zoom in on Jake and Alfie, staying back so that hopefully they can't see what I'm doing. I take a few shots of them facing out to sea, the vast landscape surrounding them. And then I catch their faces as they turn, their laughter as they run away from the rolling waves. They look like something out of a lifestyle magazine. Handsome dad and son frolicking in the ocean, except the backdrop is a lot less tropical than it would be on a double-page spread. I scroll through the images and, happy that I've got some good ones, put my camera in my bag and go back to join them.

By the time I get to the water's edge, I can see Alfie is dripping wet and crying.

'Oh no, what happened?'

'He fell in. It's OK. I've got a change of clothes in the bag.'

'Wow, look at you, Super-organized Dad.'

Jake licks his finger and then hisses as he puts it to his chest in an unbelievably camp gesture. 'Check me out.'

When we get back to the mat, Jake pulls out a towel and I wrap it around Alfie, then help to pull off his wet clothes from underneath. Once they're off, he lowers himself into my lap. He's shaking with the cold so I wrap my arms tightly around him. And I think it's now, with the weight of his body against me and the sun shining on our faces, that I realize Nan was right – I do love this little boy, possibly more than I've ever loved anyone. And that causes a strange concoction of emotions to swirl around in my stomach, the predominant one being fear.

'Ice cream?' Jake rolls down his jeans, dries his feet and puts on his socks and trainers.

Alfie jumps out of my lap. 'Do we have to have lunch first?'

'Nope. We're on holiday, little man. Normal rules don't apply.'

Alfie does a little dance on the sand.

'Come on,' Jake says. 'Get your clothes on. Let's go.'

'A sugary snack? Before lunch? Surely it isn't so?'

Jake shoots me a look, then dresses Alfie, while I put on my shoes and fold up the picnic blanket.

We eat our ice creams on the wall, Alfie ending up with most of his on his face. When he's right at the bottom of the cone, he holds it out to show me.

'Look, I got the ice cream to the bottom, just like you taught me.'

It's funny the bits children take in. After school one day, I'd taken Alfie for an ice cream in the park. He'd moaned that he didn't like the cone once the ice cream had all gone so I showed him how to push down with your tongue to get the ice cream all the way to the end. The fact that he's remembered inexplicably makes me want to cry.

'Well done, buddy.' I turn to Jake. 'Look, I'm going to let you two have some boy time. I'll meet you in the hotel lobby about five and we can go and grab some food?'

'No. I want you to come and help me build a sandcastle,' Alfie says, listening in.

'I've got a few things to do. Daddy will help you build your sandcastle.'

'Yeah, I'll do that,' Jake says. 'Let Emily have some time on her own, Alfie. She doesn't want to be stuck with us all day.'

Alfie looks like he's just discovered Santa's not real and I feel terrible, but I have a sudden and desperate urge to get away.

I bend down and meet Alfie's eyes. 'It's not that. I love hanging out with you. It's my favourite thing to do. I just need to do a few jobs. We'll have fun at the pub later though, OK, buddy?' I kiss him on the forehead. 'I might have a special surprise with me for you.'

Alfie's face immediately transforms. 'What is it?'

'Well, then it wouldn't be a surprise, would it?'

Alfie wiggles on the spot. 'Please tell me.'

Jake puts his hand on Alfie's shoulder. 'You'll have to wait and see. Come on, let's go and build that sandcastle.'

I watch Alfie dragging his feet all the way back down to the beach, and then head into town where, thankfully, I find a Co-op. I buy a bottle of wine, making sure it's got a screw top, and walk along to the headland, where I stop and sit on a bench overlooking the sea. I pull my phone out of my pocket and google train times, opening the bottle of wine and taking a large swig. I find a train that leaves the local station in the next hour, but then I spot Jake and Alfie, two dots surrounded by an expanse of sand, and I picture Alfie's face if he were to turn up at the hotel and find me missing. I put my phone away, get up and leave the bottle of barely drunk wine by the foot of the bench.

* * *

'So, are you going to tell me what's going on?'

We're at the pub. Alfie's busy building the helicopter from the Scarecrow Fearful Face-Off Lego set I bought him while Jake and I scan the menu.

I focus on the words in front of me. 'Nothing. I'm fine.'

Jake raises his eyebrows. 'I might not know you that well, but I'm not stupid.'

'You can't say stupid,' Alfie chips in. I hadn't even realized he was listening.

'Sorry, I meant silly. I'm not silly. One minute you're like an excited kid, dragging us into the sea, the next you can't get away from us quick enough. I've racked my brain but I can't think of anything I might have said or done to upset you. I know it's usually my fault.'

I find the bits that Alfie needs for the next part of his build and put them next to the instruction booklet for him. 'You didn't do anything to upset me. I'm sorry. If you did know me better, you'd know that these kinds of little freak-outs are actually pretty common.'

'Can you find me the next bits?' Alfie says, having deftly put the other pieces on already.

'You're so speedy. I can't keep up.'

Alfie smiles and puffs out his chest, and I feel that pang of fear again, starting deep down in my tummy and rising into my throat. I try to wash it away with more wine.

231

'So am I allowed to ask what the freak-out was about?'

'You can ask.'

Jake nods. 'Fair enough.'

The waitress comes over. Jake and I order a steak each and we get chicken nuggets for Alfie. When the waitress leaves the table, there's a moment of awkward silence, Jake's question lingering in the air like a burnt-out firework.

'It just suddenly dawned on me that when your maternity cover finishes or Jemma comes home I'll be out of a job.'

Jake looks confused. 'Don't worry. I'd keep paying you until you found something else. You gave up your job for me. I'm not going to leave you in the lurch. Besides, the way things are looking, I'll have to find another job when this one's up.'

I can't help it. I'm relieved. I don't want Jemma to come home, even though that makes me feel terrible because I should want Alfie to have his mum back. I finish my glass of wine and Jake calls to the waitress to bring me another.

'It's not the money.'

'Then what?' I can see in Jake's face that he suddenly understands. 'You'd miss Alfie?'

I glance at Alfie, who is fully absorbed with his Lego, and feel my eyes blurring. 'Like crazy.'

I can't look at Jake as I say it. He reaches over and touches my hand, then rapidly moves it away again, like it gave him an electric shock. 'Look, Em, you've got a friend for life there. There's no way you're getting rid of him, even if you stopped officially being his nanny. Why do you think I'm bothering to make friends with you? It's only because I know we're stuck with you now.'

I smile and pull Alfie along the bench towards me. 'How are you getting on with that helicopter, buddy?'

Alfie holds it out for me to see. He's nearly finished already.

'Wow, that's awesome.'

Alfie points at the instruction booklet. 'Look, we get to make pumpkin bombs next.'

I squeeze him tight, then he wriggles out of my arms to continue building.

I turn to Jake. 'Thank you.'

'What for?'

'For introducing me to your son. I think he might just be my new favourite thing in the world.'

'Well, the feeling's mutual, that's for sure.'

Alfie stops building for a minute and looks up at me. 'Will you spend all day with me tomorrow?'

I nod. 'Every second.'

'As soon as I wake up?'

Jake laughs. 'Even Emily won't want to see you as soon as you wake up, kiddo. How about we knock on Emily's door on the way down to breakfast?'

'What time will that be on Joker clock?'

'I don't know, Alfie. We're not going to set a time. Let's just see when we wake up and Emily can call us when she's ready and then we'll go down.'

Alfie bangs his fist on the table. 'But I need to know the time.'

'Alfie, calm down,' Jake says in a low voice. His eyes

scan the pub. A few people glance over, an automatic reaction to the noise, but nobody seems bothered.

Alfie swivels around on the bench so that he has his back to us.

'Let's say seven thirty, Alfie. That's seven, three, then zero on Joker clock. If that's OK with Daddy?'

Jake nods, but I can see Alfie's outburst has pissed him off.

Alfie pauses for a moment, then turns his body back to face us. 'Only if I can have croissant with Nutella for breakfast?'

'I'm sure we can manage that, don't you think, Daddy? As it's a holiday?'

'OK. As it's a holiday.'

The squall passes. Alfie alternates between eating and building and we manage to enjoy our steaks. By the time we get to the question of whether or not to have dessert, Alfie's bubbling. It's easy to spot now I know the signs. He's jostling, going under the table and pulling our legs, climbing up on the table and tapping us on the head with his knife. It's time to leave.

I look at Jake. 'Ice cream from the shop on the walk home?'

Jake grabs his wallet. 'Perfect. I'll go and pay the bill.'

Alfie peers out from underneath the table. 'But I want ice cream here.'

'Trust me, Alfie. I saw the ice creams at the shop earlier. They're much better,' I whisper to him, hoping he'll feel like he's in on a top secret.

Alfie gives a comical evil smile. 'OK. Shh.'

I hold my finger up to my lips. When Jake returns, Alfie

and I creep out of the pub like two burglars in a picture book minus the stripes, and Jake looks at us like we've lost the plot, making us both giggle.

* * *

Back at the hotel, Jake goes down to the bar to get us some drinks and I lie next to Alfie, downloading the images from today. He's had three stories and a hot chocolate with four marshmallows (managing to wangle one more than my suggested three with the insistence that there needed to be an even number).

As I watch the images flash up, I feel giddy, like I used to when I first discovered the joy of taking pictures. Before all the stuff with Alex made photography yet another thing tainted by my bad choices. There are a couple of images that I love. It's nothing to do with my photography skills: Alfie's an easy child to capture. As long as you get the light and the focus point right (not rocket science), his huge dark-brown eyes will always make for a striking photo. He and Jake look so happy, their faces a mirror of each other; I can't help but smile looking at them.

Once I've added the images to Lightroom, I find my favourite and begin editing it. There's not much to be done. A little more contrast, slightly less exposure and just upping the clarity on Alfie's eyes and it's pretty much complete. I add a radial filter and lessen the sharpness of the background just to isolate Alfie and Jake a little more, and I'm done.

Alfie pushes the cover off and then turns on to his back. Distracted by editing, I hadn't noticed he was still awake. He stares at the ceiling as if it has a drawing on it he can't quite make out.

'You OK, Alfie?' I brush his fringe off his face. 'Is it a bit strange sleeping in a different bed?'

'No. I can never get to sleep.'

'Well, I'd just close your eyes and think of all the nice things we did today and all the adventures we are going to have tomorrow. You'll fall asleep eventually.'

'That's what Daddy says. Doesn't work, though.'

I close my laptop, put my head on the pillow and snuggle up next to him. 'Sometimes when I lie in bed, I can't sleep either. My head gets too busy. Is that what happens to you?'

Alfie nods. 'Daddy says I have to switch my brain off, but I can't. It's just too full of worries.'

'What kind of worries, buddy?'

'Yesterday, Molly fell over and hurt herself and I'm worried I thought it was funny.'

'Well, did you laugh?'

Alfie shakes his head. 'But my brain tells me I think it was funny. I don't think I did. I don't want Molly to cry. My brain just tells me I think that.'

I feel a bit out of my depth. I'd expected being scared of the dark, monsters. But I'm not quite sure what to do with this. 'I'm sure you didn't think it. But don't worry, we all think unkind things sometimes. Try to get some sleep.'

Alfie's eyes remain wide open.

'Look, I'm not sure if this'll work for you, but sometimes what I do is I imagine a special box in my head and I picture all the worries running around and I pick them up and put them in the box.'

'Like the worries are little people, like Smurfs?'

'Well, I hadn't thought of it like that, but yeah, that's a really good idea.'

Alfie screws his eyes shut. 'OK, I'll try.' Seconds later, he lets out a loud sigh. 'It's not working.'

'OK, let me show you how.' I close my eyes tight like he did. 'Right, there's a worry, got you. Another one, got you.' I mime picking up the worries with my fingers. 'No, worry, get in that box. It's trying to escape, naughty thing. Get back in that box, you little monkey.'

Alfie starts laughing.

'Now it's your turn. Close your eyes.'

Alfie closes his eyes, trying to suppress his smile. 'Go on, worry, get in that box,' he says through splutters of laughter. 'Stop running away.'

I kiss him on the forehead and he opens his eyes. 'See, your worries have gone away. Now, time for sleep or you won't have enough energy to build our amazing sand Batcave tomorrow.'

'Yeah,' Alfie says excitedly, 'and then Joker can smash it down.'

'Can't wait. Batcave smashing sounds awesome. Night, buddy.'

Alfie turns on to his side and I return to my editing.

'Emily?'

'Yeah?'

'What if the sea washes away our Batcave when we're still building it?'

'It won't. We'll do it far enough away from the water's edge.'

'But what if a really big wave comes?'

'We'll do it so far away that even the biggest wave in the world couldn't get it.'

'But what if it does?'

'Don't worry, it won't.'

'But . . .'

I place my hand on Alfie's shoulder and then stroke my fingers up and down his arm. 'Alfie, get some sleep. I promise I won't let the sea ruin your Batcave.'

Alfie yawns and rubs his eyes. After a while, he starts to give in to the exhaustion, his eyes getting heavy before his breathing changes and he finally drifts off. The door clicks and Jake appears with a pint of beer in one hand and a glass of wine in the other.

'Shh, he's just gone,' I whisper.

Creeping over, Jake hands me my drink and sits on the bed on the other side of Alfie.

'Well done. I thought he'd take ages to go down,' Jake says in a low voice.

'Must be the sea air.'

Jake smiles and looks wistfully out the window. 'You can't beat the sea air.'

I can see in his face how much he misses it. He's talked before about how, since having Alfie, he never gets to surf or snowboard any more, and I always felt like he was being ungrateful, but now I see that was unfair. That it's hard to give up the things you love, however valid the reason.

'Why don't you go for a surf tomorrow? Alfie and I are going to be busy sand-Batcave building, anyway.'

'Oh, it's OK. I didn't bring my board. But thanks for the offer.'

'Hire one. I saw a place right by the beach.'

Jake seems to contemplate this for a few moments. 'Well, if you're sure? But I didn't invite you here to be his nanny for the weekend.'

'We'll be glad to get rid of you. I insist.'

Jake looks me directly in the eye and smiles. 'OK. Thank you.' Then he looks at my laptop screen and I realize I forgot to close it.

'Wow, that photo's amazing!' He says it like he's just realized I'm superhuman. 'I didn't know you were so talented.'

I push the screen down and place my laptop on the bedside table. 'It was a lucky shot.'

Jake gives me an I-wasn't-born-yesterday look. 'That was not a lucky shot. I've managed to get some lucky shots in my time and they do not look anything like that.'

I pick up my wine. 'Look, I'm sorry I freaked out and didn't spend the day with you guys today. I feel like an idiot.'

Jake shrugs. 'Starting to really care about someone is a scary thing. It must be even worse if it's a child. With a partner, if they leave, you can kid yourself you're better off without them and they're not worth it. But it's not like that with a child, is it?'

'Thanks for getting it. For not thinking I'm crazy.'

'Woah, hang on, I didn't say that. I still think you're crazy.'

I jab him in the ribs and he laughs. Perhaps it's because we've both had a few drinks but things feel so much easier between us, and I realize that I'm actually really enjoying his company.

'So is that what you are trying to do? Kid yourself Jemma's not worth it?'

'Maybe. Or maybe she's actually not. I haven't worked that bit out just yet.'

'Well, imagine you got back tomorrow and she was there waiting for you. Would you take her back?'

'After my last conversation with her, I'm pretty sure that's not going to happen. But, hypothetically, if it did . . . I just don't know. I still love her. Of course I do. But is that because she's Alfie's mum and because of all the great times we had together? Am I still in love with her or am I just clinging on to what we once had? I mean, we haven't been happy for a very long time. I know that. How do you know if you're still in love with someone, anyway? If you're fucking miserable every day, does that mean you're not in love with them?' Jake shakes his head. 'Sorry, I'm sure you have no interest in any of these internal meanderings.'

'I asked.'

'True. You did bring it on yourself.'

Alfie sniffs and rubs at his face and I put my index finger to my lips.

'So how about you?' Jake whispers. 'You over your ex?'

Alex's face pops into my head. The thought of him no longer makes my stomach hurt.

'Yeah, I'm pretty sure I am.'

I think, with distance, I can see what we had wasn't real. I allowed myself to get swept up in it for a while, but deep down I always knew it wasn't going anywhere. Maybe that's why I chose it.

'Any other victims in line?' Jake's face when he's teasing me is exactly the same as Alfie's when he lies about how many biscuits he's had or the fact that Daddy lets him eat his tea in front of the television.

'Why are you always so mean to me?'

'Take it as a compliment. I'm only mean to the people I like.'

I raise my eyebrows.

'Honestly, taking the piss out of someone is how I show we're friends. Thinking about it, maybe that's why I don't have many friends.'

'Possibly worth considering.' I fluff up the pillow and prop it behind my back. 'No, currently no victims in line. I'm too busy looking after your son to have time to start a relationship.'

'Oh, I do apologize for getting in the way of your sex life.'

'I said no time for a relationship. I'm still getting plenty of sex.'

Jake coughs, a small amount of beer shooting out of his nose. 'At least one of us is.'

'You should get back out there. You're not completely hideous. I'm sure *someone* would want to sleep with you.'

Jake smiles, but it doesn't reach his eyes. 'As utterly ridiculous as it sounds when my wife is probably getting boned daily by French blokes, I'd feel like I was being unfaithful.'

'Yep, sounds totally ridiculous to me.'

As we both laugh, Alfie turns over and we simultaneously cover our mouths.

'It's funny, when I see him in profile like that, I just see my mum.'

'Did you get on with her? Your mum?'

Jake runs his finger along his bottom lip. 'She was the best. Like all young lads, I probably didn't show her very much, but I worshipped the ground she walked on.'

'I'm sure she knew.'

'I hope so. How about you? You get on well with your parents?'

When I've been drinking, I always feel like blurting out everything, like passing on a hot potato – it's a relief to be rid of it. But Jake already thinks I'm common as muck; I don't want the details of my shitty background to enhance that perception.

'Oh yeah. They're great. Happily married for twenty-seven years. It's incredible, really.'

Jake's eyebrows twitch, like he's confused about something, but then he appears to shift whatever it was he was thinking.

'You thought I was one of those people who has seven siblings all with different surnames, didn't you?'

Jake shakes his head forcefully, his mouth full of beer. 'No, I don't know where you get this impression of me. Anyway, what kind of person is that? At this rate, that could be Alfie in a few years. Well, maybe not seven siblings. I'm not sure I'm quite that prolific.'

I smile.

'Seriously, though,' he continues, 'my dad worked in a factory. He eventually worked his way up to manager level, but we never had much money. We didn't go abroad until I was fourteen. My mum stayed home with me. The big house, the fancy things, it's all Jemma's.'

The more he opens up with me, the more I wish I'd been honest with him. It's like I can feel the lie wedged between us, making everything less comfortable than it was before.

I look at my watch. 'I suppose I better get back to my own room. Busy day of Batcave building tomorrow.'

'OK. Well, thanks for coming. I know it means the world to Alfie.'

'Thanks for letting me. I'm sure you can think of better ways to spend your half-term.'

Jake sticks out his bottom lip. 'Not right now, no. It's a sad state of affairs, isn't it, when going to the freezing-cold English seaside with your infuriating son and his emotionally stunted nanny is as good as it gets?'

I punch his arm and he grabs on to his bicep dramatically, then I push myself up off the bed. 'Right, I'm off to my room.'

'See you bright and early. Seven, three, zero. We'll pick you up from your room on the way down.'

'I might be there. If you're lucky.' I grab my jacket off the back of the armchair and root in the pocket for my room key. 'And I am not emotionally stunted.'

Jake laughs. 'I knew you wouldn't be able to let that pass. Night, Em.'

*   *   *

Jake sits out at sea on his board, patiently waiting for another set of waves to roll in. When he sees one in the distance, he manoeuvres on to his stomach and starts paddling towards it, then turns his board, waits, and then frantically sweeps his arms through the water, jumping up on to his board and riding the wave all the way to the shore. When he surfaces, I can hear him yelping. It makes me laugh.

I take a few photographs of Alfie studiously working on his Batcave, which he has been creating for the past hour and a half. 'You done yet, buddy?'

'No. It's not right yet.'

'It looks pretty good to me,' I say, watching him through the viewfinder.

'It has to be perfect. It's OK. I'll get there eventually.'

Sometimes Alfie is so patient, so meticulous, it's easy to forget he's only six years old.

'I've got no doubt about that. Good for you.'

I feel a splash of water on my back and Jake appears behind me, placing his board on the sand. 'Ah, that was amazing. Thank you so much. I'd forgotten how good it feels.' I can't believe how different he looks. Like Alfie when he's hurtling down a slide.

'No problem. Just glad you enjoyed it.'

Alfie stands up and puts down his spade. 'Can I come, Daddy? Will you show me how to surf now?'

Jake goes over to him, picks him up and swirls him around. 'Of course! I'd love to.'

Jake puts Alfie down and he rushes straight to the bag we've brought with us, pulls out his wetsuit and starts putting it on. 'Awesome. Will you come too, Emily?'

I look at Jake. 'No, it's OK. I haven't got a wetsuit. I'll just watch.'

'I've got a spare one in the car. Come on, it'll be fun. Alfie and I can laugh at you when you fall off.'

Alfie giggles at his dad's joke.

'Charming.' I gaze out at the sea. 'I don't know. I wouldn't want to show you up.'

Jake smiles, pushing his wet hair off his face. 'I'll take that chance. I'll go and get that wetsuit.'

'But I want to go in now, Daddy,' Alfie says, folding his arms in front of him.

'I'll go and get it,' I say. 'You guys go in. I'll join you in a minute.'

'OK,' Jake says, widening his eyes. 'As long as you promise not to chicken out.'

'I promise.'

I watch them run towards the water, both with an extra bounce in their step, then I go back to the car to get changed and dash into the waves after them.

Jake

School holidays are supposed to be the major perk of being a teacher. Oh, and obviously making a huge difference to the lives of young people, I shouldn't forget that bit. BA (Before Alfie), Jemma and I would've spent October half-term exploring a European city or lying by a pool in Morocco. We'd always have great sex on holiday, as if somehow being away from it all made us infinitely better lovers. But now, half-terms are not a perk. Now, half-terms are a survival challenge that could rival Bear Grylls dumping you on a deserted island with a few measly preparatory lessons, like how to make a fire or catch a crocodile. Luckily, it's Friday. Nearly there.

Today's gem is a trip to Legoland. It's a rite of passage for every parent. With its overpriced food and overcrowded pathways, it's something that has to be endured at least once in a lifetime. I've managed to avoid it thus far, using the excuse that Alfie wasn't big enough to go on a lot of the rides. But after Alfie making me measure him twice a week for the past two years, the dreaded day has come when he has grown beyond the required one metre and Emily has insisted that we take him.

As we drive past the large welcome sign made out of thousands of tiny bricks, Emily and Alfie can barely contain their excitement. It's a side to Emily that still surprises me, considering her default setting when we met was bite-your-head-off. She's jigging around in the seat next to me, gasping at every new model that we see. I can't help but chuckle to myself. That is, until we reach the car park.

'Five pounds? Seriously? We have to pay five pounds for parking on top of the extortionate ticket prices?'

'I'll pay for it. Take a chill pill.'

I shake my head. 'I'll pay. It's the principle, that's all. We'll probably be ripped off in the shop too when I could get all the stuff cheaper on Amazon.'

'Aah, but where's the magic in that? Come on, grumpy, let's get going. We want to go into Legoland, don't we, Alfie?'

'Yeah, come on, Daddy.'

As we walk towards the entrance, Alfie's eyes look up at the huge Legoland sign as if it's the Angel Gabriel leading him to Jesus, and he starts running.

'Alfie, wait.'

Emily puts her hand in the middle of my back and pushes me forward. 'No, come on, let's run after him.'

I know there's nothing in it from her side and she's definitely not aware of the effect it's having on me, but it's something she's started doing – this touching me thing. It's only a punch in the arm here, a jab in the ribs there, usually in response to me teasing her, but whenever she does it, it causes this feeling in the pit of my stomach. If it didn't sound so downright ridiculous, I'd say it feels like butterflies.

Reluctantly, I jog to keep up with them. The queuing process is as painful as I expected – four questions on a continuous loop: how much longer is it going to take? (we are going as quick as we can), is the dragon ride open?

(yes), am I tall enough to go on all the rides? (yes), can we go in the splash park? (no: too cold). After what feels like a lifetime, we enter the park. As I feared, Alfie looks utterly overwhelmed and begins pacing back and forth.

'I want to go on the dragon but I want to go to the shop too. The dragon might get really busy if we don't go straight away but the shop might sell out of all the make-your-own Minifigures. Oh, I can't decide.'

The torment on his face is palpable. I shoot a look at Emily. I told her he wasn't going to cope with this trip, but she assured me we'd have a great time.

She crouches down and holds Alfie still. 'They have thousands of Minifigure parts. Whenever the boxes run out, they just keep refilling them. So I promise they will be there. Let's go to the dragon ride because, you're right, that could get busy soon.'

Alfie's eyes dart back and forth between the shop and the rest of the park. 'Are you sure? Are you sure they just keep refilling it?'

Emily nods.

Alfie turns and looks at me. 'Is that true, Daddy?'

It's rare for him to seek my opinion. I'm strangely touched. 'Absolutely.'

'But what if the box they're using to refill the other boxes runs out?'

I shake my head. 'It never does. It's magic.'

Large dents form at the top of Alfie's nose and he turns to Emily. 'Is it really magic?'

Emily glances at me, then nods. 'We're in Legoland, Alfie. Of course it's magic. Now come on, let's get to that ride. You need to hold my hand, though. I'm scared.'

Emily grabs hold of Alfie's hand and pulls him along.

'I'm not scared. I'll look after you,' he says, running to keep up.

When we arrive at the dragon ride, I'm glad to see that the queue isn't too long. Still long enough to cause a huge meltdown, but better than I'd expected after reading the reviews on TripAdvisor. As we wait, Emily plays game after game of I spy and manages to keep Alfie in high spirits. I enjoy the break and just watch, marvelling at Emily's endless patience and her ability to know just what to say and do to keep Alfie calm. It used to piss me off, the fact that she was so much better with him than I am, but now I feel grateful that he's found someone who seems to make life easier for him and, besides, I treasure the respite.

We get to the front of the queue and Alfie's ecstatic because he gets to be in the front cart with Emily. I sit in the cart behind them and lean forward to whisper in Emily's ear.

'How come you're so good with him?'

Emily shrugs and remains facing forward, but I can tell from her coy expression that she's happy to receive the praise, if not a little uncomfortable. It's actually quite endearing. She came across as so cocksure when I met her, but now I can't help feeling I might have got her all wrong.

After the ride, we go to the booth to see the photograph of ourselves caught in mid-fall. I hate this kind of thing. Another way to rip families off. Some hideous over-saturated photo of everyone looking demented to stick on the fridge.

'It's not there, it's not there.'

Alfie's climbing the desk at the photo kiosk, his eyes searching for the image of us.

'Don't worry, it will be.' Emily puts her arm around Alfie, but he wriggles away and continues climbing and falling, climbing and falling, much to the annoyance of the miserable lad behind the desk.

'Look, there it is.' I point to the picture as it appears on the screen.

We are all clearly in shot, smiling manically with our hair shooting up into the sky. I want to hate it, but Alfie looks so happy, so free from the usual stresses that cause his face to crease and contort into strange expressions. He just looks like a normal boy having fun.

'Shall we buy it?' I ask.

'Yeah, yeah.' Alfie jumps up and down.

'Are you sure you want a photo of my ugly mug stuck on your fridge?' Emily asks.

'I'll just get one of those stickers from an apple and put it over your face.'

'He's teasing, isn't he?' Alfie asks.

'Yes, I'm teasing.' I pat Alfie on the head and go to buy the overpriced print.

Alfie won't let go of the photograph all day. Even when he goes on the rides, he puts it behind his back and leans against it to make sure it doesn't slip out. At lunch (fifteen pounds for a cold burger and a few burnt chips), he puts it on the bench and sits on it so that it doesn't get covered in ketchup.

Alfie spends the day ordering us around the park like a mini army sergeant and Emily casts me a look whenever she notices my irritation building. Like she told me on the phone last night, it's his day and I need to take a back seat and let him rule it.

And by allowing Alfie to be in charge, we actually have a great day. The expected major breakdowns never come. They threaten occasionally (when we have to deviate from Alfie's plan to stop for lunch, go to the toilet, or when I suggest we visit the *Star Wars* exhibition) but Emily skilfully negotiates with Alfie and brings the outbursts down from a ten on the Richter scale to a less dangerous four. After I've sulked for a good twenty minutes about the *Star Wars* exhibition (like father, like son), Emily takes Alfie to his next destination without me so that I can indulge my inner geek and witness the Millennium Falcon made entirely from Lego.

Finally, after Alfie asking so many times it feels like the words 'can we make the Minifigures?' are forever stamped into my brain, we reach the shop. Alfie rushes straight over to the boxes of decapitated bodies, heads, hair, helmets, legs and accessories. He rummages through, oohing and aahing whenever he finds a piece he's not seen before.

'Right, Alfie, you get to make three figures, OK?' Emily says. 'There's the special box they go in when you've chosen. See, it's got three spaces, so that's three figures, OK?'

I know that narrowing down his creations to only three is going to take Alfie quite some time, so I grab a seat next to him and begin building my own strange crossbreeds: a pirate with a witch's hat, a tennis player with a peg leg, a ninja with a wand.

Emily looks over at me like I've just done a shit on the Queen's lawn. 'What are you doing?'

'What?' I hold up my hands.

'You can't mix them up any which way. You have to find the parts that go together.'

I laugh. 'OK, Mrs OCD. I can see why you and Alfie get on so well now.'

Emily gives me daggers, but I can tell she's not really angry.

'Look, I've made me, Daddy,' Alfie says, holding up his creation. The body is sporting a doctor's uniform and it's holding a spiky club but it does have Alfie's yellow hair.

'Looks just like you, son.'

Emily stifles a smile.

'I'm going to make you next, Daddy, and then you.' Alfie points at Emily, who looks concerned.

'Why don't you make your mummy instead? Then you'd have your family. You, Daddy and Mummy.'

Alfie clearly doesn't get it. 'No. I want to do you.'

I put my hand on top of Alfie's. 'Em's right. We could Skype Mummy later and show her. I bet she'd love it.'

Alfie pulls his hand away from me and crosses his arms. 'No, I'm doing Emily and that's that.'

'OK. That's fine.'

I'm not going to push it. It's not like Alfie's representations are accurate enough for Jemma to make out who the figures are anyway. And, besides, she's not here and Emily is.

When we reach the till, Alfie holds up his figures to the cashier.

'Oooh, what have you made?' she asks, feigning interest for probably the thousandth time that day.

Alfie points to each figure in turn. 'This one's me, this one's Daddy and this one's Emily.'

'What a perfect family.' The young cashier smiles.

There was a time when it would have seemed strange, this selection of people, a mum called by her Christian name. But this girl has probably seen a million so-called 'modern' families passing through her shop. Maybe she's even part of one.

'Oh, I'm not . . .' Emily begins but trails off. 'Thank you.'

Maybe I'm mistaken, but I think Emily purposefully avoids my eye contact. A week ago, misunderstandings like this would've been a source of amusement, but since she came to the beach with us, everything feels different. Like we're operating at a different frequency.

* * *

When we get home, Alfie's exhausted but, in true Alfie fashion, it still takes him about an hour of Emily and me sitting with him before he goes to sleep. It drives me insane. I'm sure he's taking years off my life expectancy.

Anyway, he's asleep now. I have beer. For a short period of time, all is right with the world.

'Thank you for persuading me to go today. I had a great day.'

We're sitting on the sofa, our backs against opposite arms like bookends. My legs are out in front of me, bent at the knee, and Emily has hers crossed.

'Get your geek fix with the *Star Wars* exhibition?'

'Yeah. Thanks for that too.'

'It's OK, I've never really got the whole *Star Wars* thing. I was happier doing multiple rides of the Fairy Tale Brook boat trip. Lego seven dwarfs, now that's what you call impressive.'

I rub the moisture off the label on my beer bottle. 'How many times did he make you do it?'

'Seven, and one more for luck.'

I smile.

'I think the guy operating it thought we were slightly insane, but I enjoyed it.'

Every time Emily's knee brushes against my feet, my heartbeat becomes tangible in my chest. It's snuck up on me all of a sudden, like a well-disguised trick-or-treater, but somehow I find myself wanting to be around her. I'm not sure if it's a knee-jerk reaction to Jemma's rejection of me, the fact she makes Alfie more bearable to live with or maybe just pure desperation affecting my eyesight, but I suddenly find her really attractive. And I don't just mean she has a pretty face. I've always known she was striking. But now, when I look at her, it's like, *Man, you are seriously hot.* With her bright-white choppy hair and toned physique, she looks like the surfer chicks I used to fantasize about as a teenager. I know the feeling's not mutual and it's not like I'd act on it even if it was (despite the fact my wife has made it crystal clear she doesn't want to be with me), but it's still a confusing development that I'm not sure what to do with.

Emily studies me for a second and I pray to God she can't read my mind. 'I enjoyed masquerading as Alfie's mum today. The only downside was people thinking I was your wife.'

I take a swig of my beer. 'Now you know how Jemma felt.'

'True. And I only had to bear it for one day. How long were you guys married?'

'Over thirteen years.'

It makes my head hurt to think of all the time we spent together.

'Oh, yeah, I'd have run a mile long before that.' Emily's huge blue eyes peer at me over the top of her wine glass as she drinks. Surely she's wearing contacts? I'm convinced her eyes weren't that blue before. 'Do you miss her?'

'Not right now, no.'

'I have to admit I find it strange she doesn't miss Alfie. Well, I'm sure she misses him but I mean so much that she has to come home. I even miss him at the weekends.'

With Emily in such close proximity to me, I'm too distracted to really focus on what she's saying.

'Sorry, it's really not my place to say anything about Jemma,' she continues. 'I didn't mean to offend you.'

I realize I must've gone quiet. 'No, you didn't. I was just thinking . . .' *about you naked* '. . . how glad I am that you like being with Alfie so much.'

I feel like a teenage boy again. What has got into me? I'm embarrassed for myself. I finish my beer and use it as an excuse to get up off the sofa and head to the kitchen for a breather. 'More wine?'

'I'm driving.'

'I can book you a taxi or you can stay here, if you like?' My mouth seems to be speaking without the permission of my brain. 'We have a spare bed.'

'I don't know. I think I'll just drive back.'

'Come on, it's been a long day. You deserve a drink or two.' I try to sound as nonchalant as possible. 'Besides, I have cheesecake. You can have your very own slice.'

Emily narrows her eyes. 'OK, then.' She hands me her empty glass. 'I don't suppose you've got any Baileys, though? I don't fancy wine and cheesecake.'

'I think I can manage that.'

In the kitchen, I cut two slices of the leftover cheese-cake in the fridge and put them in bowls. I locate the Baileys from the back of the cupboard and pour her a glass, dropping in a few ice cubes. Once I've grabbed another beer, I put it all on a tray and take it through to the lounge, all the time trying to convince myself that my intentions are entirely pure.

Emily's pulled the throw over her legs. I hand her one of the bowls and her drink and settle back in where I was at the other end of the sofa.

'So, have you ever thought about having your own kids?'

Emily looks down and begins to move the silver squares along her bracelet. 'I've not really thought about it.'

'Well, I think you'd be a great mum.'

'Thanks.' Emily smiles but she looks momentarily sad. 'Need to find a decent man first. Although isn't that an oxymoron?'

'Oh, come on, you must have guys throwing themselves at you. I mean, obviously when they realize you're a psychotic ice queen, they might take a step back, but you're probably just about hot enough to counteract it.'

Emily pretends to look affronted. 'Thanks. Is that how it works for men?'

'Pretty much. An attractive face and a hot body can make up for most personality defects.'

I suddenly realize I'm feeling quite drunk. Only having a sandwich for tea in the car on the way home wasn't such a good idea. I put down my beer and tuck into the cheese-cake in the hope it might soak up some of the alcohol before I say something I regret.

'I'm not sure what's worse, the fact you think I've got a personality defect or the fact you've actually managed to win me over with the pretty face and hot body comment.' Emily tucks into her cheesecake. 'Do you really think I'm a psychotic ice queen?' She says it like a child asking if you're still cross with them.

'Not any more.'

'To be fair, I thought you were an arrogant chauvinist who beat up his wife, so I suppose neither of us are great with the first impressions.'

'Why did you think I was arrogant?'

Emily's cheeks flush. 'Because you're quite good-looking, I suppose, and most of the good-looking men I know are arrogant idiots.'

It feels like the moment in a film where the leading man and the leading lady look into each other's eyes and then finally share the passionate kiss everyone has been waiting for. Except it doesn't quite go like that.

'Daddy, Daddy, I've had a bad dream.'

We both jump as Alfie comes shuffling into the room. His eyes are puffy with sleep and he looks tiny standing there in his pyjamas, clutching the teddy bear he's had since he was born. Not even seeming to notice Emily there, he clambers on to my lap and drifts back to sleep.

Emily slowly moves away and puts her full glass on the mantelpiece. 'I think I'll go.'

'No, it's OK, you don't have to go. I can take him back up in a minute. He'll probably settle back in his own bed.'

She begins gathering her things together. 'No, you stay with Alfie. I'll see you both on Monday.'

'OK, well, at least let me call you a taxi.'

'I only had a sip of this. I'm fine to drive.'

She strokes Alfie's hair and leaves. And, once she's gone and the air feels clearer, I realize that Alfie may have just saved me from a humiliating moment of madness that I never would have lived down.

* * *

The microwave tings and I retrieve Alfie's porridge, which is just about to turn stodgy. I put in a spoonful of Nutella and hand it to him. He's sitting at the breakfast bar, tracing his finger along the path of one of the mazes in his activity book.

'Is Mummy going to come home soon?'

'I don't know, little man. I don't think so. Not at the moment.'

Alfie takes a spoonful of his porridge from the edge of the bowl where it's not too hot, just like I've shown him.

'You do know Mummy loves you, though, don't you? Even though she's not here, she still loves you more than anything.'

Alfie nods. 'She tells me when I talk to her on the computer.'

I realize it's still that simple for him. If someone says they love you, they love you. No questions asked.

'And Emily loves me,' he says, blowing at his spoon so hard that squidgy lumps of oats fly off in multiple directions.

I stop tidying away the cereal. 'Has she told you she loves you? I know she does, of course she does, how could she not? But has she said she loves you like Mummy does?'

Alfie shakes his head. 'Not like Mummy does. Emily

says, "I love you more than curry," but Mummy just says, "I love you." I don't like curry. They have it at school on Tuesdays and it smells yucky. But Emily says it's her favourite food in the world so that means she loves me the most in the world so I said I love her more than ice cream because that's my favourite food in the whole world.'

I swallow hard. 'And you love Emily that much, hey?'

Alfie nods, but then he looks alarmed. 'But I can still have ice cream *and* Emily, can't I? I don't have to choose?'

'Of course, little man. You can have ice cream and Emily.'

And as I say it, a not entirely innocent image runs through my head and I fear that my feelings last night weren't just the result of too many beers, that things might be about to get complicated.

Alfie

Mrs Young is talking about the story we are learning. I want to cover my ears but we have to do SHELL, which means something like Sit, Hands, Eyes, Lap or something. I can never remember what each of the letters means, but when they say 'shell', we have to sit with our hands in our laps and look straight at the teacher so she knows we are listening.

But I don't want to listen because the aliens from the story were in my dream last night but instead of stealing underpants they were trying to blow up the world. I don't want the world to blow up. It's not what happens in the book but now, when we do the retell, my brain keeps saying the bad ending from my dream and it makes my tummy feel funny.

'So which bit are we going to write today, Alfie?'

I'm not sure what Mrs Young is talking about because my head is too full of worries, so I just don't say anything.

'Away with the fairies again? You need to try to listen or you won't know what we're doing, will you?'

Her voice is a bit cross but she's smiling, so I don't think she is telling me off. I'm not really sure.

We sit down to do our writing. I don't like writing because Miss Smith keeps coming over and saying my letters are the wrong way and I have to rub them out and start again so I'm always the last to finish, which means I get stuck with the yucky carrots at the bottom of the fruit bowl at break time. I like carrots at home but not the ones at school because they taste funny. Today, I'm last again but luckily there is one apple left, so I eat that.

At playtime, I want to play the shark game where we chase each other and then we have to fight, but Molly and James don't like it and say they won't play with me. So I ask them to play the Secret Seven game, except we are just the Secret Three because there's only three of us. But they say it's not fair because I'm always the leader, but I have to be the leader because otherwise they won't do it right. If I'm not in charge, then they just change bits of the story and make things up and they don't follow the rules. And then we end up arguing because they're ruining the game and they tell a dinner lady and I get into trouble and it's not fair. It's not fair because it's their fault they aren't playing the game properly, not mine.

After I've been told off, I play on my own. It's better for a while because I know what the right password is and what the adventure is. I pretend the tree is Janet and I'm Peter and we have our meeting. The password is 'stinky socks' and we discover there is some missing treasure at the beach. I don't really go to the beach; it's just the bottom playground, but I pretend. But after a while, if I'm not playing with anyone, my brain has the silly thoughts again and I can't make them go away. When I'm with my friends or doing learning, they usually disappear, but they come back if I'm on my own. I worry that I am just dreaming and that I'm not real. I'm just pretend and everything in the school is pretend and the whole world is just a pretend world, like when I'm asleep. It makes me feel dizzy when I think it and I don't like it. I hit my head because I want it to go away.

Emily

'So why exactly did you want me to meet you here?'

We are standing in the car park of the mall. Jake has done as instructed and changed out of his work clothes, but he looks exhausted and I suddenly worry that my idea of a fun after-school surprise will not match his.

I open the door to my car and Alfie jumps out. When he sees the shopping centre, there's a look of genuine fear on his face. 'Why are we here? We're not going shopping, are we?'

They both look to me for an answer and I feel the weight of expectation on my shoulders and realize why I don't normally arrange surprises for people. I'm not sure why I made an exception this time. I think it might have been because of something Tim said at group this week. When he first started talking about spreading positivity, I wrote it off as something more befitting a hippy commune, especially after the whole ridiculous snuggle-time thing. But, actually, the more he talked, the more sense it made. Maybe making other people happy does make you happy.

But as we round the corner and I catch a glimpse of the ice castle, glowing purple, it doesn't look as impressive as it did in the photos, and it's packed, and I wonder if I should have just picked Alfie up from school and driven home.

'No, we're not going shopping. It's this way.'

As we get closer, I look down at Alfie to see him staring open-mouthed at the giant sheet of ice we are going to be expected to stand up on, and I feel a renewed confidence.

'Come on, let's go and get our boots. We're going ice-skating. Have you ever been before, Alfie?'

Alfie doesn't talk, just keeps staring.

I touch him on the shoulder. 'We need to get special boots to skate on the ice. I've hired you a penguin – see, that little girl has one. It'll help you to get your balance, if you need it.'

Alfie pulls me towards the queue of people getting the obligatory footwear. A teenage girl with too much make-up trades our shoes for boots and mutters her way through a safety talk before setting us free on the ice. As soon as we step on to the rink, Alfie falls on to his bum and I prepare myself for a scene, but he just holds out his hand with a smile and I pull him up. Once he's gripping on to the penguin, he's off, leaving Jake and me clinging on to the edge, trying to make forward progress.

'Come on,' Alfie calls, looking back at us over his shoulder.

Jake and I waddle forward, then Jake tries to pick up speed and crashes to the floor, his legs ending up like two crossed fingers to the side of him.

Alfie giggles and I slowly totter over to Jake and hold out my hand. 'Need some help?'

Jake untangles his legs. 'Looks that way, doesn't it?'

He reaches up and grips on to my hand. As I try to help him up, I lose my balance and hit the ground with a thump right next to him. We look at each other, marooned on the cold wet ice, and both start laughing.

'Whose great idea was this?'

'I'm sorry. I thought it would be fun,' I say, floundering like Bambi.

Jake manages to get into a crouching position and then pushes himself up. He bends down, puts his arms under my armpits and hoicks me up. And I might be imagining it, but it feels like he holds on to me longer than he needs to before releasing me.

'It *is* fun. Thank you,' he says into my ear.

We both attempt to skate again. Annoyingly, Jake suddenly seems to get the hang of it and catches up with Alfie. Then they both look back at me, urging me on.

I try to take bigger slides, but it feels like my feet are weighed down with bricks. Jake skates back to me and takes my hand.

'Come on, slowcoach. I'll pull you along.'

Once I'm up and going, my natural reaction is to let go of Jake's hand – Miss Independent – but Alfie keeps looking back at us with a huge smile on his face, and it actually feels nice to have Jake to steady me when I start to wobble. So we continue to skate along hand in hand, Alfie ahead of us clutching on to his penguin.

* * *

When I finally get home, after not one, not two, but three bedtime stories, I'm exhausted. I immediately head to the kitchen, open the fridge and pour myself a glass of wine. Watching the condensation form on the outside of the glass, I suddenly wonder – when did drinking stop being a decision? Purely autopilot? Like breathing, or putting one foot in front of the other to walk down the street? I push the glass to the back of the worktop and put the kettle on. I'm not sure I even enjoy the taste of it any more. And I definitely don't enjoy turning up at Alfie's door each morning with a hangover, the undercurrent of nausea, the general numbness, like when you fall asleep leaning on your arm and wake up with pins and needles.

Taking my cup of tea and the biscuit jar through to the lounge, I lie on the sofa, surf the channels and settle on one of those parenting programmes where some woman who doesn't have any kids of her own solves the parenting woes of the nation. In this one, a room of experts are sitting around a television watching clips of the problem child and his family. At first, it's the usual complaints – problems with bedtimes, mealtimes – but then the camera zooms in on the child's face as he's having a meltdown about putting his shoes on for school, and it's just like watching Alfie. It's not unruly disobedience I see on his face, acting out for attention and taking pleasure in it: it's something more, something different – fear, concern. Everything the mum says rings true: the daily battles over the simplest requests, the need to control everything and everyone around him, the meltdowns when plans change.

After watching the clips, the experts look at each other and nod simultaneously to show the viewer they are in agreement. Then they call the parents in to the conference room and they sit down at the table; the little boy is on the floor in the corner, dismantling a train track.

'It's a distinct form of autism called Pathological Demand Avoidance.'

The mum breaks down in tears and the dad puts his arm around her. The experts start reeling off the typical signs and symptoms and I grab my laptop and google the condition. Hours pass as I take in all the information. I find a forum on the PDA Society website and read post after post from exasperated parents wondering what the hell to do with their children, who just don't fit the rulebook. I pick up my phone to call Jake but then I see it's gone midnight.

Suddenly it all makes sense – the meltdowns, the inflexibility, the bossiness – it's all because of how anxious it makes Alfie not to be in control. It feels like I've solved the last clue of the crossword. Like, finally, I might be able to make life better for Alfie and Jake.

*　*　*

'Ready, steady, go.' I turn the timer over. 'Remember, when the sand gets to the bottom, you need to be dressed. I'm just going to get your book bag sorted.'

I leave Alfie in his room and collect all the things he needs for school. The timer has been a revelation. No more fights about getting his clothes on, no more Alfie running around with pants on his head and his legs through the arms of his T-shirt – he just gets dressed and appears in the hallway with a smile on his face and the timer in his hand to prove the sand is still running down.

But not today.

'Come on then, buddy. Timer must be up,' I call up the stairs.

Alfie doesn't appear so I go up to his room and find him sitting on the floor, his school clothes in a pile in his lap and tears in his eyes.

I sit on the carpet next to him and put my arm around him. 'What's up?'

'I don't want to go to school today. I want to work on my film.'

'Well, we can do that after school.'

Alfie shakes his head, but his face isn't full of its usual defiance – he just looks drained.

'Has something happened at school? Is that why you don't want to go?'

Alfie shakes his head again. 'I just want to do my film. I'm at the best bit. Superman and Batman have just found out that Supergirl is trapped in Joker's dungeon so they're going to go and rescue her.'

As he talks about his film, his face lights up. Then it falls again, each one of his features taking a downward turn.

'School's boring. All we do is writing and I always get told off because my letters are the wrong way and I forget my finger spaces. Mrs Young keeps saying I need to start trying my best but I am trying my best.'

I can just imagine Alfie's little face, wanting so badly to get it right and not understanding where he's going wrong.

'I know you're trying your best, buddy. I'll let you in on a little secret – even teachers get things wrong.'

'And I always end up playing on my own and I don't like being on my own.'

I feel my heart breaking with each word he says.

'Please don't make me go, Emily. Please.'

Looking at Alfie's distressed face, I imagine how school must appear to him with all its implied and explicit demands and expectations. I look at the clock. Even if we leave now, we'll be at least ten minutes late and we'll have to go through the office and sign in, which will only stress Alfie out further.

'OK, just today.'

Alfie throws his arms around my neck so hard that he nearly headbutts me. 'Thank you, Emily.'

'Everyone needs a break sometimes. Come on, let's go and get a hot chocolate and decide what we're going to do.'

Without the pressure of the school run, it's like I've broken free of the shackles. 'We could do anything, Alfie. Where do you want to go? A safari park? Climbing? We could learn a new skill. What about skiing? I've always fancied learning to ski. We could get a lesson.'

Alfie scoops the gooey remains of the marshmallows off the top of his hot chocolate and it drips down his chin.

'What do you think, Alfie?'

He slurps his drink noisily. 'I just want to finish my film.'

'Well, of course we can do that, but we have the whole day free. Where do you want to go?'

'I don't want to go anywhere. I just want to stay here.'

So that's exactly what we do. Alfie spends the day in his pyjamas. He sets up the last few scenes for his film and I take the pictures. While I import them into iMovie, Alfie creates his own Lego Joker limousine, cleverly sticking to the trademark purple and green palette. We add sound effects and a voice-over to his film and then we cuddle up in front of *Peter Rabbit* and eat popcorn. We make a shepherd's pie for tea – Alfie thrilled that I allow him to help cut up the vegetables with a grown-up knife. Alfie organizes a party for me and insists I wait in a different room.

When he reveals the party room – his bedroom with the blinds down and his pebble light cycling through its sequence of bright colours – he's thought of every detail. There's a little table he's brought through from the play-room with paper plates and plastic cups on top. He's found a birthday banner from somewhere and Blu-Tacked it to the wall. His portable CD player is blasting out bubble-gum pop. He's even made party bags – one for himself, one for me and one for Jake when he gets home – full of a range of his toys, a packet of Haribo and a fun-sized Milky Way.

'I love it. It's perfect,' I say and grab his hands.

And it is. I swing him round and we dance to the music. We play musical bumps, even though there's only two of us and he has to stop the music and fall to the floor at the same time. We have a dance competition, complete with *Strictly*-esque scorecards that he's made. It's the perfect end to a perfect day. Not a disagreement or meltdown in sight. And it makes me realize that I have to do every-thing I can to make life less challenging for him.

* * *

'Wine?'

Alfie has finally fallen asleep and I am sitting at the dining-room table while Jake puts away the last of the Waitrose order. When he called to say he was working late, I rushed Alfie through bath and stories and practically closed his eyes for him so he wouldn't have the chance to drop me in it about not going to school today. But now I wish Alfie had told him, because I wouldn't be sitting here feeling like a kid about to confess that I've smashed the neighbour's window with a football. I'm hoping I can soften the blow with my pathological demand avoidance discovery, but I'm not quite sure how he's going to take that either.

'No thanks.'

'Seriously? You don't want wine?' Jake helps himself to a beer out of the fridge. 'You feeling OK?'

'It's the new me.' I flip my hands out in front of me like a magician revealing his assistant has not really been sawn in half.

'What was wrong with the old you?' Jake takes a sip of his beer.

I was putting vodka in my orange juice for breakfast.

'I'm just doing one of those detox things. Your body is a temple and all that.'

Jake shrugs. 'Each to their own.' He starts throwing the tins into the cupboard any which way and I have to force myself not to take over and order them by category. 'So, have you had a good day?'

I know I have to tell him but I feel sick. It's farcical. It's not like I spent the day introducing Alfie to the delights of wacky baccy or soft porn.

'Alfie didn't go to school today.'

'Oh no, was he ill? He seemed fine when I left.'

I chew a rough bit off my thumbnail. 'Not exactly. He was tired. He wanted to work on his film. He needed a break.'

Jake bundles the pasta into a cupboard that contains baking ingredients. 'So you just let him have a day off? Did you call the school to let them know?'

Yes, yes, I did. See, I am a responsible adult after all.

'Of course I did. I left a message to say he was exhausted and feeling under the weather.'

Jake raises an eyebrow.

'See, the thing is,' I continue, making the most of the fact he's not yet shouting at me, 'I think sometimes it gets a bit much for him. Keeping everything in at school.'

'What do you mean?'

'Well, the other night I was watching this programme called *Born Naughty*. It was about these challenging children and they got experts in to decide whether they were just naughty or whether they had an underlying condition.'

I can see Jake's jaw clenching.

'There was a boy quite a lot like Alfie on it,' I continue, although I wish I'd never started. 'They discovered he had this newly identified condition called Pathological Demand Avoidance. It's on the autistic spectrum, but it's quite distinct from typical autism.'

'And let me guess, their recommended advice was to let the child take a day off school when he can't be bothered to go?'

'No. It wasn't like that. If you'd seen him, you'd know . . .'

You know what? Fuck you.

'He needed a break, Jake. Don't you ever feel like you need a day off?'

'Of course I do, but I can't just take one. Kids need to learn about responsibility.'

'And they need to learn about compassion, about empathy too. I saw that he was struggling and I supported him.'

'He wasn't struggling. He just couldn't be bothered to go.'

I'm tempted to leave it, but I can't. It's not fair on Alfie.

271

'Look, I googled this PDA thing. There's a forum full of parents experiencing exactly what we are, well, what you are. It was like reading about a thousand Alfies. I mean, of course there were differences, no child's the same, but so much of it rang true. It's all about anxiety, Jake. All of it. He needs to feel in control and at school he has to bottle all that up. It must be impossible for him. If you'd just look at it, you'd see that –'

Jake holds up his hands, like Simon Cowell when he's seen enough of an act on *The X Factor*.

'I told you before, Em, we went down this road. I've been back and forth about this so many times with Jemma. We took him to the doctor's. They told us quite clearly there's nothing wrong with him.'

'But they're wrong. Loads of the parents on the forum said the doctors dismissed them too. You need to go back.'

Jake rams something on to the overfilled freezer shelf and it knocks the peas out; they spatter all over the floor like green polka dots.

'For fuck's sake!' He pushes the now half-empty bag of peas into another drawer and then slams the freezer door. 'I'm tired. I need to sort all this out, then I'm going to go and watch some TV. I'll see you in the morning.'

If I leave, I know Jake is never going to allow me to raise this topic of conversation again, so I give it one more try.

'Please just look at the website. Read some of the posts in the forum. If you still think I'm talking nonsense, then I'll never mention it again, I promise. But I really think some of the strategies could help Alfie. He deserves for us all to try to understand him better.'

Jake doesn't speak for a minute, just sweeps at the peas

with a brush. But when he looks up, I can see in his eyes that he's raging.

'You're not his mum, Em. You're his nanny. You've known him, what, ten weeks, something like that? I've spent pretty much every day of the past six years with him. So how dare you tell me what my son deserves, because you've watched some bloody TV programme and read a few posts from a bunch of whining parents with nothing better to do?'

His words are like a slap around the face.

'You're right. I'm not his mum. But just so you know, I'm not trying to be. I'm just trying to help him out because, as far as I can see, his mum doesn't seem too bothered about doing that. And neither does his dad, come to that.'

I storm out of the kitchen, grab my things from the hallway and leave, slamming the front door as I go. Once I'm in my car, I put my head on the steering wheel and let it engulf my sobs.

Jake

As soon as I get through the door, Emily grabs her stuff to leave. It's been two days since we fell out and both days she's avoided eye contact and bolted the second I got home from work. I wish I hadn't been so harsh to her, but the truth is what she said hurt. For the first time ever, I thought I'd found someone who 'got' Alfie, who didn't think there was something wrong with him, but now it feels like she's just like everyone else.

'He wants to bake a cake. I said you might not want to.'

Might not want to is an understatement. Cooking with Alfie is akin to enduring a severely turbulent flight with a toddler repeatedly jabbing you in the back, but I can tell Emily thinks there's no way I'll do it so I'm desperate to prove her wrong.

'I'd love to. Can't wait.'

'Great,' Emily says, heading to the door and slamming it on the way out.

But after a traumatic trip to the supermarket with After-School Alfie (i.e. a child who acts like he's off his head on speed), I realize that my initial standpoint was correct – never cook with Alfie.

I put all the ingredients and a big mixing bowl out on the worktop and search the cupboard for the scales. When I turn around, Alfie has his hand in the bag of flour, which is dispersing through the air like a cloud of fog.

'Alfie, hands out of the bag. Don't touch anything until I say.'

I continue to search for the scales and find them underneath the huge casserole dishes. Who would think that was a good place to put the scales? And why do we need casserole dishes that are so cumbersome they could feed all the children in a large orphanage?

I just about manage to lift the dishes enough to pull the scales out. This time when I turn around, Alfie is munching away on the chocolate buttons we've bought for decorating the cake.

'Right, that's it. We can't make a cake if you can't listen to instructions.' I practically throw the scales down on the worktop and then quickly press the on button to check I haven't broken them.

Alfie jigs up and down on the bar stool. 'I will, I will, I promise.'

'OK. Last chance.'

I'm determined that we will successfully make this cake together if it's the last thing I do, which it might well be if he continues to raise my blood pressure any further. I put the mixing bowl on the scales and hold the sieve so that Alfie can pour in the flour.

'Gently. We only need it to get to one hundred and seventy-five.'

Alfie slips with the bag so the kitchen looks like a crack den.

'Seriously, Alfie. I said be careful.' I snatch the bag out of his hand and start spooning flour back in until the scale gets down to two hundred. 'Right, that'll do.'

'I thought you said it needed to be one hundred and seventy-five.'

'It's close enough.'

Alfie grabs the spoon off me and starts removing flour from the bowl until the scales say exactly one hundred and seventy-five. 'There you go.'

The sugar goes in without too much being spilt and then I cut a few slices of butter and Alfie begins to stir, half the mixture flying over the edge of the bowl.

'Can I lick the bowl now?'

'No, Alfie. At the end.'

Alfie puts his finger into the mixture, scoops up a blob and puts it into his mouth.

'Fine, you can't lick it at the end now.'

'Please, I just wanted to try a bit.'

'But you need to listen, Alfie.'

In some ways, I'd like to bottle Alfie's exuberance so I could use it myself on a grey day. But trying to do anything with him feels like being thrown around on a white-knuckle ride – eventually you just need it to stop.

'Please can I lick the bowl at the end?'

'Maybe.'

'You have to say yes.'

'Maybe.'

I can tell by the way Alfie's body is twitching that he's getting really agitated. I know how he feels.

'Please say yes. Please say I can lick the bowl.'

'If you listen from now on.'

'Then I'll definitely be able to have it?'

'Yes. Now we need to do the eggs.'

I take an egg out of the box.

'I want to do it. I want to do it.'

'No, I'll do this bit.'

'Emily lets me.' Alfie grabs the egg out of my hand with such force that it cracks and snot-like goo falls on to the worktop, down on to the stool and eventually lands with a plop on the floor, mixing with the flour to make a delightful congealed paste.

'For God's sake, Alfie, just get out.' I lift him down off the chair and place him on the kitchen floor away from the mess.

Before I can stop him, he runs towards me and steps right in the glue-like mixture.

'What are you doing? Use your brain. There's crap all over the floor.'

Alfie runs out of the kitchen and up the stairs to his bedroom, his socks leaving sticky footprints every step of the way.

I follow him up. 'Now it's on the carpet. Take your socks off.'

He crosses his arms.

'I'm going to count to three and if you haven't taken off your socks, you can go straight to bed and you won't come out until morning.'

Alfie puts his chin to his chest.

'One.'

'I'm not listening to stupid Daddy.'

'Two.'

Alfie's eyes don't leave the floor.

'Three.'

Alfie pulls off his socks and charges towards me. Just as I think I've won the battle, instead of handing them to me, he holds them in his fist and punches me straight in the nuts. Without thinking, I lift my arm and the noise of the slap seems to ricochet off the walls, as my palm makes contact with his cheek.

For a moment, Alfie stops still and stares at me, a look of utter confusion spreading across his features. Then come the tears and the screams as he pushes against my thighs, managing to shove me out the door, which he then slams in my face.

I try to get in but it won't budge. I slide my back down the door and let my head fall against it, imagining Alfie, a mirror image of me, on the other side. And then, for what is probably only the third time in my adult life, I start sobbing. I'm like a pipe that's suddenly been unblocked, like my body is purging all the pent-up crap that's been stuck inside me for so long.

I've heard friends talk about smacking their kids. None of them seem proud of it, but they're not overly bothered either. But it's something I've always sworn I would never do. I was hit as a child, not in a 'call social services' way, just in the way lots of kids were when I was little. You knew if you messed up, you'd suffer for it. But I still remember each and every time Dad hit me. I can picture where we were, whether I'd really deserved it or not and, most importantly, I remember exactly how I felt. Betrayed. And that's exactly what I just saw in the eyes of my little boy, and I know I need to do whatever it takes to never have to see that again.

'Alfie,' I splutter through the tears. 'Alfie, open the door.'

I hear the swoosh of boxes of Lego being poured out on to the floor. 'No. I hate you. Go away. You're never coming in.'

'Alfie, I'm sorry. Please let me in. I just want to give you a cuddle. I'm sorry, Alfie. I didn't mean it.'

More Lego crashes on to the floor and then Alfie starts throwing things at the door. 'Go away. You are not my friend any more, Daddy. Never, ever again.'

'Well, you'll always be mine, little man. I'll come back in a bit and keep checking on you until you let me in.'

I go into my room, slump on my bed and reach underneath it to find my laptop. I open the PDA Society page and try to take in all the information: *anxiety-driven need to be in control and avoid other people's demands . . . underpinned by an intolerance of uncertainty . . . uses social strategies such as negotiation as part of the avoidance . . . meltdowns should be viewed as panic attacks . . . excessive mood swings . . . obsessions.* I click on the strategies to try at home. *Adjust your mindset. 'Being told' cannot solve the problem and nor can sanctions. Pick your battles and try to balance tolerance and demands.* It's like a punch to the chest. Before she even knew about PDA, Emily managed to work out what Alfie needed – and I just made him worse. My eyes fall on a quote from a child with the condition: *Although I'm acting angry, what I'm feeling is terror.*

I shut my laptop and go straight to Alfie's room. When I push the door, it opens and my heart throbs as I watch Alfie sitting amongst a huge pile of Lego, sensibly sorting it back into its coloured boxes. He's done the box of yellow and is now working on the red. With a sick feeling in my stomach, I notice an inflamed patch on Alfie's cheek where my hand met his face.

'Can I help?'

Alfie looks up at me and I'm sure he's going to scream at me to get out, but he doesn't. 'Yes, but make sure you get them in the right boxes. You do the blue and purple. Not the pink, though. That goes in my box with the red.'

'OK, I'll try my best, but you know Daddy is a bit colour blind, don't you? Silly Daddy.' I tap my head.

I'm thankful when Alfie smiles.

'How about I check any of the pieces I'm not sure about with you before I put them in?'

'OK, Daddy. That's a deal.'

I pull Alfie on to my knee. 'Come here, little man.'

I hold him tight and he strains against me, as he tries to continue to sort his Lego.

'You know Daddy's so very sorry, don't you?'

Alfie grabs a handful of red Lego and drops it in the box.

'I promise I will never, ever hurt you like that again.' I can't bring myself to say the word 'hit', but it's the word that's in my head, blazing like a beacon. 'Daddy loves you more than anything in this world, you know that, don't you?'

Alfie shuffles off my knee to reach some more of the red Lego pieces scattered around his room.

'Are you going to do the blue and purple ones, Daddy?'

'Yes, little man. Of course.' I kiss the top of Alfie's head and then start sorting the Lego. 'How about we put your favourite song on while we tidy?'

'Yeah. Yeah.' Alfie runs straight over to his portable CD player and scrolls through to track ten.

The overfamiliar notes of 'We Are Never Ever Getting Back Together' come booming through the speakers. Alfie tries to sing along but he only manages to get the odd word in and I laugh. When it gets to the chorus, we both sing at the tops of our voices and Alfie starts dancing in his jerky trademark-Alfie way.

And, somehow, Taylor Swift manages to lighten even this darkest of days.

* * *

Emily makes a point of not sitting by me. She walks in, observes the space next to me and then sits on the only other empty chair, next to Bill.

Sharon's away so Sam steps in to do the declaration with me. As much as Emily often made it tricky for me, I still wish it was her hands I was holding – or not holding. And although I'm extremely secure in my sexuality, grasping a bloke's hands and making promises to him isn't the most comfortable of experiences.

'So, as we're nearing the end of the course, I'd like to start today with a quick reflection on the progress you've made so far because, although some of you might not realize it, there will have been positive developments for each and every one of you. And also think about anything you still feel you need to work on, because personal development is never really finished, is it? So, anyone want to start us off?'

Almost without realizing I'm doing it, I raise my hand. 'I'll do it.'

Emily glances up at me in surprise, then carries on tying her shoelace.

'Jake. Thank you.'

I sit forward in my chair, my heart beating so hard in my chest I worry people can see it through my clothes. 'If I'm totally honest, I've never really thought my anger was any worse than the next guy's. I came here to try to save my marriage, which, incidentally, didn't work.'

A few of the group give me sympathetic smiles and I force myself to continue.

'It's not been a good few days. Firstly, I said some things to someone who I've begun to . . . to care about. Someone I was starting to think of as a real friend.'

I glance at Emily, but she doesn't meet my eyes.

'She was just trying to help me, I can see that now, but I was too proud to listen. So I'm sorry about that.'

At this point, she looks up at me briefly, offering me a cursory smile. I take my hands out of my pockets and try to find the right words for what I need to say next.

'But that wasn't even the worst thing I did. I slapped my son. Right around the face.'

As I say it, the words feel like they're burning the inside of my throat. Most of the people in the room look back at me supportively, as if they've heard this sort of thing a thousand times. But Emily looks just how I knew she would – horrified.

'There's no way I can excuse what I did. I won't try to. But to explain a little, I think my son might have a condition called pathological demand avoidance. It's an autism spectrum disorder.'

When I look up, I spot a single tear sliding down Emily's nose.

'I always knew he was different. My wife was convinced he had an underlying condition but I thought we were just rubbish parents. I kept saying we needed more rules, more boundaries, when all along, the more demands I put on him, the worse his anxiety got. I made him worse. I failed my son.'

I shake my head, as if it will help to expel my next thought.

'I've never admitted this to anyone before, but sometimes I just thought he was a horrible person. That we'd ended up with a dud. How terrible is that? My little boy. How could I think that about him? How could I not like my own son? I've resented him for ruining my life, my marriage. I was so fucking angry. I didn't even realize how angry I was. And all along, he was just struggling.'

Emily wipes at her face with the palm of her hand.

'Thank you, Jake, for your honesty,' Sam says. 'Feel safe in the knowledge that none of us are here to judge in any way. It sounds as if, although it's been a challenging few days for you, you've also made some great progress and I'm sure things are going to improve from here on out.' Sam offers me a comforting smile, then turns back to the rest of the group. 'Would anyone else like to share?'

I can't concentrate on anything the others have to say. I just want to talk to Emily. When it's time for a coffee break, everyone leaves the circle but I stay seated. To my relief, Emily comes over and sits beside me.

'I'm really sorry about the stuff I said to you,' I say. 'I know you were just trying to help. I was an arse.'

Emily just looks at me and, for a moment, I'm scared she might hit me, but then her face softens. 'You *are* an arse. Present tense.'

'Come on. Surely even you can be gentle with a guy when he's at his lowest ebb?'

'OK. Apology accepted.'

'And I'm so sorry for what I did to Alfie, Em. Please

283

understand I am not that guy and I will never do it again. I don't know what came over me.'

Emily nods, but I still get the feeling she's disgusted with me. 'At least you realize you were wrong. A lot of people hit their kids every day and don't see a problem with it.'

'Well, I am not one of those people. I hate myself for what I did.'

Emily rifles around in her bag and pulls out a pack of Tic Tacs. She offers me one but I decline.

'I liked what you said, by the way.'

I shrug. 'I guess it shouldn't have taken me this long.'

'Better late than never.'

She smiles and I wish I could hold her.

'Alfie is desperate to see you. Will you come back with me after this?'

'I can't. I have to see my nan.'

'Oh, OK. Don't worry.'

'I could come after, though. Do bath and bedtime with you?'

It's a sudden release of pressure, like letting the air out of a balloon. 'Sounds great. Thank you for not hating me.'

'Who says I don't hate you?' When I see she's joking, I'm surprised just how relieved I am that I haven't ruined everything.

*　*　*

As soon as Emily walks through the door, Alfie comes charging down the stairs holding up his new Lego set.

'Daddy got me the Killer Croc set. It's so awesome. Look, it actually chomps.'

As Alfie demonstrates how to make the giant crocodile mouth open and close, Emily removes her boots.

'Guilt purchase?' she says, taking off her jacket and hanging it on the coat rack.

It hurts, because it's true.

'Lighten up, Jake; I'm only teasing.'

'I know. I'm just still struggling with it all, to be honest.'

Emily comes over and props herself up on tiptoes to whisper in my ear. 'Good. That means you're not an arsehole.'

'Look, Emily, here's the Killer Croc Minifigure that goes with it,' Alfie says, shoving it in Emily's face. 'It's got this super-cool bat tank with it too. You are going to love it. Come and see.'

And then they're off, leaving me alone with my guilt.

* * *

After Alfie's had his bath, he decides to make a bed on the lounge floor for movie night. He goes up and down the stairs, bringing down pillows and trailing quilts behind him. Once he's finished, he lifts up the top quilt.

'Come on, then.'

'What?' I ask, feeling suddenly nervous at what I think he's suggesting.

'Come and snuggle.'

I look over at Emily and wonder if she's feeling the same flutter in the belly that I am at the thought of sharing a bed with her, however makeshift that bed might be, but she doesn't give anything away.

Alfie lies down in the middle of the quilt he is using as a mattress and Emily arranges herself next to him. I lie on the other side of Alfie and he lifts the top cover over the three of us and then presses play on the film. Predictably, it's the *Lego Batman* film and Alfie whispers the dialogue at the same time as the characters.

Beneath the quilt, Emily rests her hand on Alfie's tummy. At the funny bits, they both laugh, but the film sweeps over me. I've seen it so many times and my mind is elsewhere.

I mirror Emily, turning my body towards Alfie and put my hand right next to hers on his tummy so that our little fingers lightly touch. It feels like a short circuit, sparks flying off at all angles, but then Emily moves her hand away.

By the time the film finishes, Alfie's eyes are heavy so I put on the end of *Strictly Come Dancing* in the hope it might lull him off to sleep. I'm lucky. It works.

'I'll carry him up,' I whisper. 'I'm going to get another beer. Do you want anything?'

'A hot chocolate would be great.'

'Wow, you know how to live.'

When I pick Alfie up, his arms and legs automatically wrap around me. With a flash of sadness, I notice how much heavier he is, how much more of him there is now.

Once I've deposited him in his bed and got our drinks, I return to the lounge and am glad to see Emily hasn't moved from the floor. I climb in next to her. We're not quite close enough to touch, but the absence of Alfie's body between us feels more prominent than its presence did.

'So how come you've given up the booze?'

I wish she hadn't. A few glasses of wine and she might give me some hint about how she feels about me. Most women are relatively easy to read but it's like Emily's written in a foreign language.

'It was getting a bit out of hand. It's probably hereditary.'

'Are your folks big drinkers, then?'

'You could say that.'

We don't talk for a while, pretending instead to watch *The X Factor*, until Emily breaks the silence, her eyes still on the screen.

'I lied about my mum and dad. They're not happily married. In fact they never were married, or happy, for that matter.'

I nod. I don't want to say anything that might stop her in her tracks and prevent her from finally being honest with me.

'When I was four, my dad left and Mum fell apart. I didn't know it at the time, but she and Dad had always been drinkers, and they used drugs, but I don't think it was anything too heavy back then. Then when Dad left, the drink and drugs took over and she couldn't look after me any more so I was put into foster care.'

It's like that point in a puzzle when you've put in enough of the pieces for the picture to emerge.

'I'm sorry, Em. I can't even imagine how scary that was. To think of Alfie . . . well, I can't.'

Emily shrugs, but the pain is written all over her face. 'It was OK, actually. I had a few shitty placements to start with, but then they placed me with Tina. I remember missing my mum at first, God knows why. I'd actually sleep with a photo of her under my pillow at night.' Emily laughs, but it doesn't disguise the bitterness in her eyes.

'But then things got better. When I was hungry, Tina actually fed me. She used to read me a story every night. I loved it. Putting my head on her shoulder and getting swept up in whatever adventure she was reading me. I'd never had that before. Can you imagine never reading your child a story? There should be some kind of check before you're allowed to have a baby.'

'I'm not sure I'd have passed it, if there were.'

Emily frowns. 'You're a great dad, Jake. Don't be so hard on yourself. I'm not saying parents should be perfect, but they should give a shit. They should at least *try* to get it right.'

All this time, I've felt so judged by her, like she thinks I'm getting everything wrong, that I'm a failure as a father. It's noticeable how much it means to me that she doesn't.

'So have you ever thought about finding her? Your birth mum? For closure maybe, I don't know.'

'Oh, we're not estranged. She came back for me just before I turned nine. Apparently she'd stopped the drinking and the drugs and was ready to be a mum again.'

'I'm guessing that wasn't the case?'

Emily turns on to her side and I copy her so that our faces are close enough for me to feel the warmth of her breath on my skin, but then she rolls away and stares at the ceiling. 'She was better for a while. Being a mum didn't exactly come naturally to her but she tried, I guess. But then she met Shane.' She shakes her head. 'I moved out as soon as I could.'

'And your dad? Do you ever see him?'

'He died. Overdose.'

'I'm so sorry, Em.'

She shrugs. 'It's fine. I didn't know him.'

I prop my head up so I can look into her eyes. 'You don't always have to be so strong, you know?'

Emily looks away. 'I know.'

'So why did you lie to me about your family?'

'I get bored of talking about it. Everyone's always fascinated when they find out, like I'm a walking episode of *Jeremy Kyle* or something. But when you live it, it's just dull.'

I wish she felt she could be more honest with me. I want to hold her, to comfort her, but I know that the moment to get close to her has passed and her barbed-wire fence is firmly reinstalled.

As predicted, within about five minutes she's making her excuses and I get up to see her out. As she opens the front door, there's a moment when she hesitates and I wonder if she might change her mind and stay, if maybe she is feeling what I'm feeling, but then she leaves and I question whether it was all in my head.

* * *

The next morning, I'm woken by a text from Jemma.

Available to Skype?

I look at my watch, disorientated, and force my eyes to focus so I can read the time. It's nine o'clock. Alfie hasn't slept in beyond seven in his entire life and he's usually hassling me well before six. I panic and run into his room naked. He's sitting at his little table, bits of paper scattered around him, busy drawing.

'You OK, Alfie?'

Alfie looks around. 'Yeah, I've got this amazing idea,

Daddy. We could make a Christmas Lego superhero film. Look, I've drawn the story.'

Alfie says all this without taking a breath. He holds up several pieces of paper. There's no way I can tell what's supposed to be happening. Drawing isn't exactly Alfie's strong point, but I feel a rush of happiness to see him so engaged and not needing my constant guidance.

'Looks amazing. But it's still quite a while until Christmas, little man. Perhaps you and Emily could work on it a bit closer to the time?'

'No, Daddy, please will you do it with me? I want to do it today.'

'Well, I'm not sure I've really got the skills.'

Or the patience . . .

'Please, Daddy.'

'OK, I'll give it a go. First, your mum wants to Skype you. Let's change you out of those pyjamas or she'll think I don't look after you properly.'

Alfie stares at my nether regions. 'Daddy, why is your willy like a mushroom?'

I suddenly feel very self-conscious and grab a pillow to cover my private area. 'We'll talk about that when you're a bit bigger. Let me just get some clothes on, then I'll get you dressed.'

Jemma doesn't speak to Alfie for long. I stay in his room, out of view of the iPad, and listen to their conversation. Alfie's telling her all about his new Christmas Lego film, his arms gesticulating wildly as he explains the story in detail.

'Oh, and we went to Legoland, Mummy. It was awesome.'

I know this isn't going to go down well.

'So Daddy took you to Legoland, did he? Wow, that was pretty special. Daddy always said he didn't want to go there when I suggested it.'

I hate it when she does this. Subtly throws in a dig at me when talking to Alfie in the hope he might pass it on. I'm so tempted to bite, but I don't want her to know I'm in the room.

'Yeah, with Emily. It was so much fun, Mummy. Do you want to go when you get home?'

'Emily went too?'

'Yeah, Emily is my nanny. Remember, I told you a million times, Mummy.'

'I know, Alfie. I just wonder why you need a nanny at Legoland when Daddy is with you?'

She must know I'm in the room.

'It was Emily's idea to go.'

'Oh, right. I see.'

The poorly disguised fury in her voice makes me want to scream at her. How dare she play the victim in all this?

'I want to speak to Daddy now, darling. I miss you so much. I really hope to come and see you soon, OK?'

'OK, Mummy. Can we go to Legoland when you get back?'

'Of course. Pass me to Daddy now. Love you.'

Alfie passes the iPad to me and returns to his sketches.

'Can we do this now, Daddy?'

'In a minute, little man. Let me just speak to Mummy. I won't be long. You get all the characters off the shelf and everything ready, OK?'

'OK,' he says, drawing out the 'ay' sound.

I take the iPad into my bedroom and close the door so

that Alfie can't hear us. Jemma's hair is scraped back in a ponytail and her skin looks blotchy.

'What's up?' I don't bother trying to hide how pissed off I am.

'I just want to talk to you.'

'Go ahead.'

'Why is this Emily going to Legoland with you anyway?'

'If you're looking for a fight, I'm not interested.'

'I'm just asking you a question. You don't have to bite my head off, Jake.'

I take a deep breath. 'Let's not play games. I've got stuff to do with Alfie. Is there anything else?'

'I'm sorry. I'm just jealous of this woman spending her time with my two boys.'

I sigh. 'She's just his nanny. Anyway, I didn't think I *was* your boy any more.'

I feel immediately guilty for dismissing Emily like this. Because she's so much more than his nanny. She's a part of our life now. And unlike Jemma, she's here, putting in the time.

'I know I'm being unfair, Jake. I'm sorry. It's just I . . .'

'You what, Jemma? You're coming home? You want to be a part of our family again?' I pause to allow her to answer but she doesn't. 'No, I didn't think so. So you need to let me do this as I see fit. I'm the one dealing with Alfie. I'm the one trying to survive this.'

'I know, I know. I just miss you, OK? I know what I said a few weeks ago, but as time goes on, it's getting harder to be away from you and I'm starting to think that it wasn't us that was the problem.'

I tap the back of my head against the wall. If she'd said

this a month ago, I would've been elated. I would've begged her to come home and end this silly mess. But now? Well, now, when she says it, all I can think about are Emily's big blue eyes.

'You don't miss me, do you?' Jemma has tears in her eyes now and one escapes and trickles down the side of her cheek.

'I didn't say that.'

'You didn't have to. We're on Skype, remember? I can see it written all over your face.'

'Daddy, come on. You said you'd be super-quick,' Alfie shouts from the other side of the door.

For once, it's a relief to have him hassling me.

'I've got to go, Jem. We'll speak soon, OK?'

Jemma nods and then turns off her Skype. I watch as her face disappears and the screen goes blank.

* * *

I now see why Alfie loves making stop-motion films so much. He's learnt to use the camera and sits behind it on his bed, giving me precise orders about what changes to make to the figures. I'm basically his slave. It's perfect for him. I try my best to deep-breathe away my irritation, and sit and make minute adjustments to bits of plastic while he barks at me for not getting it exactly right.

'Now put Santa's hat on Spider-Man, Daddy, and hang him on to that bit on the Batcave.'

I start to attach Spider-Santa to the Batcave. It's all wrong, this mixture of Marvel and DC, but Alfie doesn't seem to get it when I say Batman and Spider-Man would never work together because they are from different worlds.

'Not that bit, Daddy. The bit with the computer.'

I smile, in the way a politician might when his rival is named the winner of the election. 'Well, you didn't say that, did you? You need to make your instructions clear if you want to be a director.'

I hear the passive aggressiveness in my tone and vow to try harder.

'Right, move out the way. Your hand is in the picture.'

'Sorry, boss.'

'I'm not called Boss, I'm called Alfie.'

'But you're my boss. You like bossing me around, don't you? Does it make you feel better, safer, to be in charge, do you think?'

I feel like I should have a clipboard in front of me and be making notes.

Alfie shrugs. 'I just like it when people do things right.'

'You mean when people do things how you want them to? Other people might want to do things a different way. It doesn't mean they're not right.'

Alfie screws up his face. Does not compute.

I continue with my feeble attempt at psychoanalysis. 'It's OK if people sometimes want to do things in different ways or want to do things that you don't want to.'

'But if you put the figures in the wrong place, then the story won't be right. It's my story, so I know where they go.'

'Yeah, with your film you do need to be in charge. You're right. But, sometimes, if Daddy wants to go somewhere you don't want to, that's OK too. And if someone at school doesn't want to play the game you choose – sometimes you can try playing their game.'

Alfie looks down and appears to be staring at something

on his quilt intently. Then after a while, he starts to speak. 'But I don't like it if I don't choose.' His voice wavers. 'Because they don't explain the rules and then they say I'm playing it wrong, but I'm not because they didn't say not to do that and I don't like it. I just want to play my game.'

I move on to the bed beside Alfie and wrap my arms around him. For a second, I can see the world just as it must appear to him, this huge terrifying place full of rules you don't understand and people who don't do what you expect them to.

'I'm sorry I've not tried very hard to understand, Alfie. I promise I'm going to try harder.'

I know Alfie's not listening, he's busy looking at the photos he's taken on the back of the camera, but really I'm saying it to myself, like a mantra, in the hope if I say it often enough, I'll be able to do it.

Emily

I've never really liked Christmas before. Mariah Carey and Noddy Holder on repeat. When I lived with Mum, it was just an excuse for her and Shane to get drunk. Then either they'd get all mushy with each other and overly physical, which made me want to regurgitate my turkey dinner, or they'd get lairy and start smashing plates like they were at a Greek wedding.

Since moving out, I've spent Christmas morning on my own in the flat with a Baileys for breakfast and *The Snowman* on the television. Occasionally, I get a mini pre-decorated tree from the garden centre, one you just have to plug in and the lights flash. But most years I don't bother. It always looks a little sad with the single present from Alice underneath it. Mum usually sends me a card containing a voucher for a shop I never go into. And since meeting Nan, I've spent the afternoon with her. I cook her Christmas dinner and we sit watching crappy Christmas TV while eating it. She always buys me a gift box of lavender toiletries, some socks and a box of chocolates. The same every year, as if she's forgotten over the twelve months that that's what she bought me the year before. I love Nan to bits and it's better than spending all day on my own, but it's not exactly the most exciting day on the calendar.

But this year, as the over-long build-up to the big day

begins, it's like suddenly I appreciate how pretty the lights making the trees sparkle down the Promenade are. I'm sure I must've noticed them before but I never realized how beautiful the town looked at this time of year. Maybe it's the Alfie effect. The way he oohs and aahs at all the little Christmas details and displays. Or maybe I've joined the sappy brigade now I have people to share it with.

We arrive at the garden centre (it's December the first so, according to Alfie, the tree must go up) and Alfie circles the various specimens, surveying each one to make sure he gets the biggest and the thickest. We have to go round four times before he chooses one, and even then he's having doubts.

'Are you sure this is the biggest one?'

'I reckon so,' Jake says.

'But does that mean you're sure or that you think it is but you don't know?'

'I'm sure, Alfie.'

'Can we decorate it when we get home?'

'Yes, I told you that earlier.' I can see Jake's patience dwindling with each new query. Since his big admission at anger management, Jake has been amazing with Alfie. He never talks about PDA, but I can tell he's looked up the strategies. He's trying so hard to allow Alfie to control the stuff that doesn't really matter, to recognize his need for certainty, his inability to wait, but I can see it still gets his back up.

'You promise the second we get in the door you will go into the loft and get the decorations down?'

'Well, I might just get myself a drink and take my shoes off . . .'

Alfie's face crumples. 'You promised you'd get them straight away.'

'Look, Alfie,' I say, putting my hand on his shoulder, 'I'll make the drinks and Daddy can get the decorations, OK?'

Perhaps a little selfishly, I don't want an Alfie tantrum to ruin this moment. It's my first time choosing a real Christmas tree. My first Christmas where I feel like I'm part of something.

Alfie contemplates my offer and then nods in agreement.

Jake leans his head towards me and his nose brushes my cheek. 'Thank you.'

I'm not really sure what's going on with Jake and me but these moments of physical contact seem to be increasing. And, sometimes, I catch his eyes lingering on me when he doesn't realize I've noticed. I don't know what it all means, but unlike everything else in my life, I'm trying not to overanalyse it too much. Because if I do, I'll probably end up picking at it so much that I pull the stitches out and it falls apart, and I don't want to do that with this. Because, in the simplest terms, when I'm with Jake and Alfie, I feel happy. And I've not felt that in a very long time.

'Come on then, Alfie. Let's go and buy this tree,' Jake says, struggling to pick it up.

'Shall we just check the others again so we're sure it's the biggest?'

I run my hand through Alfie's hair. 'It's definitely the biggest, buddy. Come on, the sooner we buy it, the sooner we can get home and decorate it. And I'll let you in on a secret: I brought mince pies with me.'

Alfie beams.

'Well, you can't do decorating without mince pies, can you?'

Jake goes to pay, and Alfie and I walk to the car, hand in hand. When I look back, Jake is following us hidden behind the ridiculously large Christmas tree, so that it looks as if it's walking on its own.

* * *

When I finally get back to my flat, after an evening of tinsel, baubles and Christmas lights, I walk through the door and remove the range of winter accessories adorning my body.

From the bedroom, I hear the sound of my phone buzzing against the surface of the bedside table where I've left it on charge. I run into my room and answer it.

'Hello, is this Miss Davies?'

'Yeah, who's this?'

'Oh, hello, Miss Davies. I'm calling from Broadlands Assisted Living Centre. It's about your grandmother.'

I worry she's had another fall. 'Is she OK?'

The man on the other end of the phone clears his throat. 'Well, no, I'm really sorry to have to tell you, but your grandmother died last night. We found her this afternoon when we did our daily rounds. She must have passed away in her sleep. I'm really very sorry.'

I don't speak. I can't. I want to be sick.

'Miss Davies? Are you OK? Shall I call back with all the technical stuff? I'll give you some time to process the news.'

I put the phone down and lie on my bed. I get up again and begin pacing the room. I don't know what to do with my limbs. I feel like I should call someone but I don't know who to call. I feel like I should be crying but no tears come. My chest feels so tight that I'm struggling to breathe. I go through to the kitchen and open the fridge. There's nothing. My stupid fucking no-alcohol pledge. I grab a hoody and head to the Tesco Metro on the corner. I buy three bottles of wine and hurry home.

As soon as I get through the door, I unscrew the top of the wine and drink it straight from the bottle. It's bitter and makes me shudder, but soon the desired dampening effect kicks in so I keep drinking until the bottle's gone and then move straight on to the next one.

I take it into the shower with me. Crouching down on the shower floor, I pour the wine down my throat and let the water wash over me, drowning the noise in my skull. I pick up the razor in the corner and start stroking it over my head, rhythmically, watching the clumps of white hair swirling around in the water by my feet. I finish the wine and stand up, smacking my head on the shower knobs, but I don't feel it.

Wrapping a towel around me, I stagger on to the sofa and allow my eyes to close.

* * *

The sound of a fist banging on my front door startles me into a semi-conscious state. I'm naked apart from a towel strewn over my legs so I stumble into my room, grab my underwear, some joggers and a T-shirt and struggle to the door. My head feels like someone's whacked me with a large heavy object.

'Where the hell were you? I've been calling you non-stop. I had to take the day off. Alfie's freaking out.'

Jake pushes past me into the lounge. I close the door and follow him, as yet unable to take in what he's saying. Then it dawns on me. Alfie. School. Shit.

'I'm sorry. I overslept. Is Alfie OK?'

'I told him I'd forgotten you'd told me you were busy today. So I got a fist to the bollocks and a torrent of verbal abuse, but yeah, he's at school and he's OK.' He lifts up the empty bottle of wine on the table. 'No wonder you overslept.'

'Fuck you, Jake. Take the Mr Perfect act elsewhere, I'm not in the mood for it today.'

Jake drags both hands through his hair and starts pacing the room. '*You're* not in the mood for it? I had to call the head at ten past eight and say I'd just been sick in the car on my way to work. I can't do stuff like that. Some of us have responsibilities.'

'Well done, you. You procreated and got yourself a mortgage. Big clap.'

Jake looks like he's about to blow, I fully expect him to, but then he stops and sits down on the sofa beside me.

'What's going on, Em?'

I shrug. I can feel the tears rising in my throat.

Jake places his hand on my leg. 'Come on. There's no way you'd let Alfie down unless it was something big.'

I shake my head and move away. I don't want to say the words because that'll make it true. 'It's nothing.'

'I know it's not nothing, because if it's nothing then you're an idiot, and I know you're not an idiot.'

I bite my lip and run my hand over my head. At first, I'm shocked to feel the bare skin but then I have a vague recollection of taking a razor to it in the shower.

'You don't know anything about me.'

Jake grabs my hand. 'So tell me. Tell me a thing about you. Because I really want to know.'

I pull my hand away. 'My nan died. They called last night.'

'I'm so sorry.' Jake shuffles along the sofa and pulls me into him.

At first I resist, but then I bury my face in his chest, as the tears come fast and heavy. 'She was the only family I had. I know everyone has to die some time, but I didn't want her to. I wasn't ready.'

Jake doesn't speak, just holds me tighter. His aftershave smells sweet and his arms feel comfortingly muscular through the wool of his jumper. Once my tears have run out, I sit up straight, suddenly feeling very self-conscious.

'You should go.'

Jake starts to take off his shoes.

'I said I think you should go.'

He stands up and puts his shoes on the mat by the door.

'Jake.'

He sits down at the end of the sofa. 'I'm not leaving, Em. So tell me what you need me to do and I'll do it. You want me to get you some breakfast? A coffee? You want to talk about it? Or we can sit here and not talk at all. Whatever you need. But I'm not leaving.'

There's an annoying, niggling part of my brain telling me to physically drag him to the door and push him out, but I just manage to hold it at bay.

'Will you just sit there, please?'

'Of course. But is it OK if I give you a hug first?'

I feel the tears blocking my throat again so I just nod and Jake puts his arm around me.

'Come here.' He lies back, moving me with him so that I am lying with my head on his chest. While we lie there in silence, he strokes my head and gradually I feel my eyes closing. For a little while, I fight it, but then I allow myself to fall asleep.

When I wake up, Jake's sitting at my feet, reading a book off my shelf. It's called *The Little Book of Hygge* – ideas from Scandinavia to create a happier you, bought in desperation a few years ago after yet another failed relationship, as if lighting a few candles and creating a book nook was suddenly going to make me all zen.

There are a few blissful moments before it hits me, when everything doesn't hurt and I don't feel sick. But then it comes at me like a train, the knowledge that my nan's dead and I'm never going to see her again.

Jake looks over. 'Hey, I made you a sandwich. I know you probably don't feel like it, but you should try and eat.'

He goes into the kitchen and comes back with the plate of food. It's just a cheese sandwich with a few crisps on the side, but it feels like the kindest thing anyone has ever done for me. He hands it to me and I sit up and nibble on a crisp.

'I'm not sure I can manage it.'

'Just take it slowly. No rush. I remember when my mum died, the whole world suddenly felt the need to feed us. Every five minutes there'd be a knock at the door from a well-meaning neighbour or family friend with yet another casserole or shepherd's pie. Why is it that when you least feel like eating everyone brings you hearty meals?'

'I'm sorry you had to lose your mum so young.'

Jake shrugs, but I can see in his face that he's still angry about it. 'I was lucky to have such an amazing mum in the first place, I guess.'

'True, you could've been blessed with my joy of a mother.'

'So you never really explained what happened when she came back for you? When she met that bloke, Shane, was it?'

I lick my lips.

'I'm sorry. You probably don't feel like talking about it right now.'

Except the strange thing is, I do.

'He didn't rape me or anything.'

Jake nods slowly. 'I didn't say he did. But, you know, hypothetically, if he had, it wouldn't make me think any less of you.'

Despite myself, I feel my eyes filling with tears again but I blink them away.

'He used to deliberately come into the bathroom when I was in the shower and just stand there looking at me with this gormless smile on his face.' I can't look at Jake. 'I'd run into my room but he'd follow me and hold me down on the bed. He'd cover my mouth with one of his hands and use the other one to touch me. I'd hit him and kick him but he'd just use the weight of his body to keep me down.'

The words feel weird in my mouth, like having a brace for the first time. I clamp my teeth together and swallow hard.

'Oh, Em.'

Jake turns his body towards me and puts his hands on my cheeks, rubbing my tears away with his thumbs. Then, very slowly, he leans forward and kisses me, just lightly at first, our lips barely touching, but then, when I kiss him back, it becomes more intense. It feels like putting my head under water, everything else around me blocked out.

When we come up for air, he sits there looking at me, the weight of expectation hanging in the air between us. And I'm not sure what comes over me, but I suddenly want Jake as close to me as he can possibly be. I lift my T-shirt over my head and drop it on the floor. At first he looks startled, a little afraid even, but then he runs the tips of his fingers up and down my arms, making my hairs stand on end. I pull off his jumper, throw it on to the chair and copy his movement, stroking my hands over his arms and then down his chest.

'Are you sure this is OK? We can stop if you don't feel comfortable.'

'It's OK.'

I remove my bra but, unlike all the other men I've ever known, Jake doesn't grab my boobs. Instead, he runs his fingers along my shoulder blades, up my neck and then holds my face in his hands and kisses me again.

'You're so beautiful.'

'Even with this?' I point to my freshly shaved head.

'Absolutely.'

I shake my head but Jake holds my face still.

'You are.'

I slip off my joggers and knickers and then pull down his jeans and boxers. Lying naked opposite each other in the bright light of day, I'm surprised I'm not desperate to draw the curtains or go and grab the quilt from my bedroom. When he touches me, his fingers drawing lines all over my body, it's like my nerve endings are exposed and I want to laugh and cry at the same time. Then, suddenly, I grab his wrists.

'Wait. I want to tell you something.'

He looks concerned. 'What is it? Have I done something wrong? Do you want me to stop?'

'No, it's not you. It's just . . .' I roll on to my back, pick my T-shirt up off the floor and lay it over me. 'I want to tell you what I did. Why I'm in anger management.'

Jake grabs a cushion and covers himself too, looking both anxious and intrigued about what I'm going to say. 'OK.'

'But do you promise if I tell you, you won't think any less of me?'

It's a stupid thing to ask. How can he know what he'll think of me when he has no idea what I'm going to tell him? But I'm suddenly terrified I'm about to lose him.

'Of course. I promise. What is it?' He looks confused, and I feel bad, like I'm pausing his favourite film at the best bit.

'I glassed someone.'

Jake is unable to hide the shock on his face but doesn't say anything.

'I used to work in a pub. One night, this guy wouldn't stop sleazing over me. I went out the back for a smoke but then suddenly noticed someone walking down the alleyway. It was him. I told him to leave me alone but he wouldn't. He kept trying to kiss me, to touch me. I did tell him to stop.'

I suddenly feel the need to excuse what I did, to make it sound better. Was he going to rape me? I don't know. But he shouldn't have laid a hand on me without my permission, should he? Just because I'd let him buy me a few drinks? I didn't ask for that.

'So what did you do?'

I feel the shame running through my veins so, as usual, I cover it with rage. 'I smashed him round the head with a beer bottle and then cut his neck with it.'

I can tell by the look in Jake's eyes that he's wondering who the hell he's ended up in bed with, who the hell has been looking after his child. 'Was he OK?'

It hurts, like he's more concerned about that arsehole than about me.

'Luckily, I didn't hit any veins. He was shaken up but no injuries a bandage couldn't fix.'

Jake reaches down for his boxers and I feel the disappointment deep in my stomach. 'Why are you telling me this now?'

Because I want you to want me despite all the shitty things I've done.

'I don't know. I just thought you might want to know before . . . well, before we, you know.'

Jake looks at his watch and suddenly starts grabbing the rest of his clothes. 'Shit. It's three o'clock. I've got to get Alfie.'

He dresses quickly and then puts on his shoes.

'Shall I come and get him with you?'

Jake looks me up and down. 'No, don't worry. It might confuse him after this morning. I'm really sorry but I'd better run or I'll be late. I'll see you in the morning though, yeah? If you're feeling up to working tomorrow, that is?'

Jake calling it 'work' hurts, like he still just sees me as Alfie's nanny. 'I'll be fine. Sorry about today.'

Jake gives me a brief smile, then heads for the door.

'Jake, you don't hate me, do you?'

He shakes his head. 'Of course not.'

But his eyes say something very different. And I'm left feeling exposed and ashamed, and, as usual, rejected.

* * *

It's 8 p.m. Jake hasn't called. I was stupid to think he was going to be different. That revealing the real me wouldn't scare him off like it has every other man in my life. Rapidly working my way through the third bottle of wine I bought last night, I feel sick. I know I should eat, but when I checked the fridge, all that was in there was a tub of Chinese chicken noodles – some twisted joke from the universe. I don't want to eat Chinese without my nan. I'm not sure I'll ever be able to eat it again.

I grab a packet of cheese-and-onion crisps and manage one or two before clipping the top and putting them back in the cupboard. I try to watch TV but my eyes just flick around the screen.

Then the phone rings, Jakes name emblazoned on the screen. I'm not sure if I want to speak to him or not, but I can't help wondering what he's going to say. I take a deep breath and answer it.

'Hey, it's me. Jake.'

'I know. Your name appears on the screen. It's this newfangled contraption called a mobile phone.'

'Just blame my advanced age. I'm not down with you kids.'

I take another sip of my wine. 'How was Alfie when you picked him up?'

'He wanted you.'

I picture Alfie's little face and realize that I desperately want to see him too.

'I'm sorry I said you shouldn't come and pick him up,' Jake continues.

'It's fine.'

'It's not fine. The truth is when you told me about what happened, I just felt really odd. I can't explain it. I felt . . .'

I know exactly how he felt. It's what I feel every time I think about it.

'Disgusted?'

'No. No, not at all. I felt furious.'

'Furious? Why?'

'I don't know. That there are men out there who think they can do exactly as they please. That I wasn't there to protect you. That you were forced into anger management and made to feel like it was all your fault. I'm so sorry for everything you've been through, Em.'

A definite feeling of relief washes over me and yet it's like a switch has been flipped inside of me, and I can't bring myself to let him back in.

'Well, thanks for calling.'

'I've messed everything up again, haven't I?'

I shrug, even though he can't see me.

'I should never have left you on your own,' he continues. 'I should've taken you with me. You were so brave to tell me everything you did.'

I feel like I'm going to start crying and I'm determined not to. 'Honestly, Jake, it's fine.'

I hear him let out a long breath. 'I really care about you. I think perhaps it shocked me to realize how much. Will you come and stay here tonight? No funny business. Just so you've got some company.'

309

'It's OK. I'll probably just fall asleep in front of some trash TV.'

'I thought you might say that. That you're fine, even though you're not.'

There's a knock on my door, at first a gentle tap, but then more insistent.

'Look, there's someone at the door. I'll see you in the morning, OK?'

'OK, see you soon.'

I put the phone down. When I open the door, there's an overweight man standing there, reading from a notepad.

'Emily Davies?'

'Yes.'

'There's a taxi waiting downstairs for you.'

'I didn't book a taxi.'

'Yeah, he said you'd say that. It's from Jake, apparently, to take you to Leckhampton Road. You happy with that?'

I picture Jake's face, wondering how I'm going to take his surprise. He's interfering, but oddly I find I don't mind as much as I would have expected to. Perhaps it's because the thought of spending the night by myself is too much to bear. Or maybe it's just nice to have someone who cares enough to force the issue.

'Give me two seconds.'

As I throw some clothes and my washbag into a ruck-sack, my phone buzzes. It's a text from Jake.

> I hope you don't think I'm
> being too pushy. I just really
> don't want you to be alone
> tonight x

I text back.

> This doesn't mean you're
> forgiven, you know? x

* * *

On the day of the funeral, I try on six outfits, rejecting each one and throwing them on to my bed one after the other. Nothing feels right. I wish I hadn't shaved my head again. I imagine Nan looking down and tutting at me. Just that image is enough to push me over the edge and I sit on my bed in my underwear and sob. There's a knock on my door and I quickly pull on a hoody, wipe my eyes and go to answer it.

It's Jake, with a bunch of flowers in his hand. 'As I was walking up to your door, I suddenly thought it might not be the done thing, bringing someone flowers on the day of their loved one's funeral, but I hope you like them.'

He holds them out and I take them from him. 'They're beautiful, thank you. But you didn't have to drive them all the way here on your lunch break. Have you got time for a quick coffee?'

Jake walks past me into the flat and starts taking off his shoes. 'I took the afternoon off. What are they going to do, sack me? Good luck finding someone else willing to take on my classes.'

'You took the afternoon off to come with me?'

It still feels strange, having a man do something thoughtful for me. In the back of my mind, there's a niggling voice that says: *What's the catch?*

'Of course.'

'Thank you. But you didn't have to. I would've been OK going on my own.'

'I know. But I didn't want you to.'

We stand there for a moment and I'm not sure if I should give him a hug, but instead I go through to the kitchen, Jake following behind, and I put the kettle on. Since the whole 'nearly having sex' thing, it's been quite awkward between Jake and me. He's been very sweet, checking that I'm OK about Nan, but he hasn't mentioned what happened (although there've been a few times I thought he was about to) and there's no way I'm going to be the one to bring it up. So I've just reverted to being Alfie's nanny, except now when I'm near Jake, it's like I can physically feel the tension, like our skin is coated with static electricity, and I have to force myself not to touch him.

I rummage around on the top of the boiler unit for something to put the flowers in and manage to find my only vase. Well, it's actually a giant beer mug I got from a charity shop, but it'll do the job. I've never had much use for a vase. I fill it with water, tear the paper off the bouquet and begin arranging the flowers. When I glance up, Jake's staring at me and I feel his eyes wander down to my bare legs, then back to my face.

And I'm not sure whether it's the look in his eyes, the murky shadow of our mortality or the fact he turned up on my doorstep when I most needed him without me having to ask, but something comes over me and I march towards him and kiss him. At first he stands there motionless, but then he kisses me back and starts running his hands under my hoody, first up to my shoulders and then down until he reaches the base of my back.

We move towards the lounge like we're tied together with rope, trying to remove our clothes as we go, but my hoody gets stuck on my head and Jake nearly trips over the trousers he's attempting to kick off. Giggling, we finally manage to get naked and I push Jake on to the sofa and climb on top of him. The rest is a blur, but unlike the other day, there's no pausing, no reserve, there's no way I'm going to do or say anything that puts a stop to it. I never want it to end.

When it does, and I'm lying on Jake's chest while he massages my shoulder, our sweat sticking us to the leather sofa, it feels like I'm floating, levitating. And it hits me that I'm in love with him. There's no hiding from it any more.

'That was amazing,' he says, running his hand over my scalp. 'I didn't expect any of this. To feel like this.'

I want to tell him that I didn't expect it either, that I feel it too, but something locks up inside me even though I don't want it to, and I sit up and kiss him quickly on the lips. 'Right, I suppose we better get dressed.'

He looks a little affronted but he follows me into my bedroom and helps me to pick out something to wear. In the end, I go for black jeans but with a bright jumper. Nan wouldn't want me looking all morose.

At the church, we sit in a pew near the back and Jake takes my hand in his. In a way I find it comforting, but part of me wishes I'd come alone. I'm not sure I'm ready to share something like this with him, which seems crazy considering we just had sex, but somehow this feels more intimate.

It's a reasonable turnout. Not tons of people but enough

for the church not to feel empty. I look around at some of the faces and wonder which ones are distantly related to me. Not that it matters. The only person that I would class as family is the one in the box at the front.

Nan's best friend from the retirement flats, Mary, reads the eulogy. She starts off with the key facts: date and place of birth, school attended. I find out a few things about Nan I didn't know, like she used to swim for the county and that she worked for a while as a veterinary assistant. It's funny to learn things about someone when they're no longer here. To listen to a person's life summarized in the space of a few minutes. It makes everything feel so futile.

'She was a loving mother to her only child, Justin. He had his troubles, bless his soul, but she loved him with all her heart. She always talked about him. How she wished he'd taken a different path in life, but how she was proud of his kindness, his good heart. And she was so grateful to him for giving her her granddaughter.' Mary looks directly at me. 'She loved you so much, Emily. You brought her so much joy. I think if she hadn't met you, she never would've survived losing your dad.'

I force a smile, then, unable to cope with any more eye contact, I look at the floor. It feels weird to be the important person in someone's life. I still remember the eulogy at Tina's funeral as if it were yesterday. Her three children huddled at the pulpit, her eldest daughter doing the speaking. I wasn't even mentioned by name, just lumped under the umbrella of 'her many foster children'. I've never hated my mum as much as I did at that moment. One time, when Tina and I were having a heart-to-heart, she told me she would've adopted me if Mum hadn't come back. I can't think about it too much, how different life would've been.

Mary brings a handkerchief to her eyes and dabs underneath them. 'She was a wonderful woman and a true friend. Rest in peace, Edith. The world will be that bit darker without you in it.'

Then she climbs down from the pulpit and returns to her seat. When the coffin is wheeled through the curtain, I release my hand from Jake's. I can feel him looking at me questioningly, but I continue to stare straight ahead. I can't stay connected to him for this bit.

Afterwards, we wander through the churchyard until we reach my dad's grave. I want to keep walking but something makes me stop.

'Give me a minute.'

'Sure.'

Jake takes a seat on a nearby bench and I walk over. I've never understood why people talk aloud to a grave. It's not like anyone's listening. But I want to stand here. Just for a moment. Before I leave, I run my hand across Dad's headstone, as cold and dead as he is, and then walk back to Jake.

'You OK?'

I nod. 'Can we go and get Alfie, please?'

'Of course.'

We head back to the car in silence. Once we're both inside, I lean over and kiss him on the cheek, a meagre attempt to show him my gratitude.

'Thank you. If you weren't here, I'd probably be lying in a ditch somewhere, off my tits.'

Jake grips my hand, lifts it to his mouth and kisses it. 'Any time.'

Jake

Emily and I sit on the hard plastic chairs and I feel more nervous than if I had a life-changing job interview. We're about five rows back. We've watched the Christmas show. Alfie was a roast potato. Luckily, he doesn't seem aware that's a terrible part. I mean, seriously, how much more insignificant does it get? Of course George had the leading role. The perfect kid with the dickhead dad I nearly beat the shit out of in the playground. I had to resist the urge to heckle when he got one of his lines wrong.

Mr Frampton gets up on stage and starts thanking all the children – those with 'proper' parts he thanks individually – then he praises the teachers and support staff, and my heart sinks. Alfie's convinced they're going to show his stop-motion film but it seems like they're wrapping things up.

But then Alfie's teacher gets up on stage. 'And this year we've got something a little different. A very special film made by a very talented boy in my class, Alfie Edwards.'

I catch a glimpse of Alfie, hidden between rows of other children, and can see that he is grinning from ear to ear.

'So here it is. I'm sure you'll all enjoy it. It's called *Superhero Christmas*.'

'*Superhero Lego Christmas*,' Alfie shouts out and the audience laughs.

'Sorry, I stand corrected. *Superhero Lego Christmas.* Tom, can you press play?'

A prepubescent kid sitting at the laptop fiddles around for a few seconds and then Alfie's film is playing on the big projector at the front of the hall. It looks terrible. Hands keep flashing into view, the timing of the sound effects is just off, the transition between each photo is jerky and it's hard to follow what's happening. For a moment, I feel embarrassed, but then I look at Alfie, staring up at the screen in wonder, and I can't help but feel proud. I turn to Emily – her eyes watering like she's standing face-first into the wind.

The film finishes and it's silent for what feels like ages and then a stilted and very gentle applause fills the room. Emily surveys the audience as if she can't believe what she is seeing and then, suddenly, she stands up, holds her hands above her head and claps them ferociously.

'Woo hoo!'

I pull on the hem of her top to get her to sit down, but she just looks at me and laughs, cheering more loudly. The whole room turns to look at her, including Alfie, who has never looked happier. I stand up so he can see me too and he sticks both thumbs in the air.

Mr Frampton looks over at us with an awkward expression and we sit down, giggling.

'Well, thank you, Alfie. That was wonderful. And thanks again to all of Key Stage One for a fabulous Nativity.'

The audience erupts in rapturous applause. The sort of applause they should've given my son and his terrible, barely watchable, wonderful film.

As we walk home, Alfie's full of it. 'Did you hear them

clapping, Daddy? Everybody loved it. I told you they were going to show my film, didn't I?'

'You did, little man. It was brilliant.'

'Everybody cheered, didn't they? That means it was really good, doesn't it?'

'Yes, Alfie, it does.'

'I was a good roast potato too, wasn't I? Did you see when George ate me?'

'You were amazing,' Emily says. 'We loved every minute.'

I look over at her and smile, hoping to tell her with my eyes that I'm so glad we met her, and hoping to read in hers exactly what it is she's feeling about me, but she just smiles back and looks away. In true Emily fashion, she's been keeping her cards pretty close to her chest. So many times I've been tempted to ask her to define what's happening between us but, as much as I'd love to know where her head's at, I'm scared it'll push her away, or that I'll discover that she's not feeling what I'm feeling.

When we arrive home, I reach into my pocket for my house keys. 'Right, who wants hot chocolate?'

'Me,' Emily and Alfie say in unison and then they both laugh.

'Come on, then.'

I put the key in the lock and open the door.

My heart flips as Jemma emerges from the lounge. She locks eyes with me and I feel stuck to the spot, and then she turns her attention to Alfie.

'Hey, baby, come and give Mummy a cuddle.' She bends down and holds out her arms.

Alfie doesn't move straight away, but then he ambles into Jemma's arms. 'Mummy, you're back. They just showed my Christmas film at the school show like I told you they would. Everyone clapped.'

Jemma's eyes are dewy. 'Sounds amazing, baby. I'm sorry I missed it.' Then she looks Emily up and down before standing and holding out her hand in a strangely formal gesture. 'You must be Emily?'

Emily shakes Jemma's hand, her eyes lowered like a child who's been sent to the head teacher. 'I'll leave you guys to it. Welcome home, Jemma.'

I know that I should tell her that she doesn't have to rush off, but I'm so shocked I can't find the words to say anything.

'But what about hot chocolate?' Alfie says.

'It's OK, buddy. You enjoy yours. I'll see you soon.'

When Alfie rushes towards Emily and clings on to her thigh, Jemma looks like she's been slapped; she turns to me for reassurance, but I have none to give her.

Emily hugs Alfie back, but only loosely, as if she's trying to present a professional front, then she turns and walks out the door.

* * *

Once Alfie is asleep, I pour Jemma a glass of wine and she downs it as if it's water and she's just been for a run. It's unusual for her. She rarely drinks and, on the odd occasion she does, one glass usually lasts her the night. But she seems nervous, on edge, her hand shaking slightly against her glass. I open a beer and sit beside her at the breakfast bar. We've not really said anything to each other yet, other than in conversation with Alfie, and I feel strangely anxious being alone with her, like there's a huge can of worms in front of us just waiting to burst open if either of us says the wrong thing.

'Alfie seems very fond of Emily. She seemed OK, a bit awkward and offhand, but OK. I was a bit surprised by the skinhead.'

I allow her this dig. It pisses me off, but I can imagine it would've really hurt to see the way Alfie ran to Emily and held her.

'Yeah, she takes a while to warm up, but she's good with Alfie.' *And me. She's good with me.* 'So what are you doing here, Jem?'

'I wanted to surprise you. I thought you'd be happy to see me. I guess I was wrong.'

The truth is I don't know how I feel about seeing her. She looks as beautiful as ever. A little weary perhaps, but still beautiful. But I immediately feel irritated by her. Not by anything in particular that she does or says. It's more like she's walked into the house, a house that was starting to feel happy, and brought back all the old tension and resentment. Sitting here with her in the kitchen feels like a step backwards.

'That's not really fair. You can't expect to turn up at the door and for me to jump up and down with joy. I mean, is it a visit? Are you back for good?'

Jemma reaches out and grabs my hand. It feels odd, foreign – the temperature, the texture of her skin – it's different to Emily's. 'I want to come home. If you'll have me?'

I pull my hand away. It feels like she's been gone for so long, so much has happened and I haven't the first idea how to explain to her everything she's missed.

'I'm sorry, Jake,' Jemma continues. 'I know I've hurt you. But I just needed some headspace.'

How nice it must have been to have that luxury. What I wouldn't give for the time to make sense of everything.

'And now?'

'Now I want to be with you and Alfie. To be a family again.'

She makes it sound so simple, and yet it feels anything but.

'And what makes you think it's going to be any different this time? We weren't exactly happy, were we?'

Jemma pulls a hairband off her wrist and ties her hair into a ponytail. 'I know that. But I had time to think while I was away. I did some soul-searching, as they say. And I wonder if I had a form of postnatal depression that never went away. I just didn't feel like me. I felt permanently sad, and guilty, and resentful. And I thought it was your fault. Or even Alfie's.' As she says his name, her voice cracks. 'I still feel terrible for thinking like that, but I'm starting to accept it was beyond my control. I'm so sorry that I left you, but in a way I'm glad I did, because I think that's what it took to shift it. To see things more clearly.'

My anger is suddenly replaced by guilt. I hate the thought that she was struggling so badly and I didn't spot it. I didn't help her, I just made it worse.

'I wish you could've told me. I just felt like you didn't want to be around us. That you'd rather be at work, doing exciting projects, socializing with your colleagues . . . anything but being with us.'

Jemma runs her finger around the top of her wine

glass, her eyes following the movement. 'Work was the only place I didn't feel like a failure.'

I nod, understanding exactly how she felt, and it's a while before I manage to speak. 'But I didn't have anywhere, Jem. I always felt like a failure. Every single day.'

Jemma shuffles her chair towards me and pushes my hair off my forehead in an act that, oddly, makes me long for my mum. The intensely comforting feeling of being unconditionally loved.

'I'm so sorry, Jake. You're a wonderful dad. I should've told you that more. I was just bitter because you were so close to Alfie and I know that wasn't fair because I chose to work full-time. I don't regret that. I love my job. But I still hated missing out on so much. His first steps, his first words . . . I was jealous that you got to experience all that with him and I missed it all.'

I know how hard it must be for her to admit all of this. If only we'd had this conversation months ago, years ago, even. Instead of tearing each other apart, we could've helped to build each other up. But I can't help feeling that it's too late, that the scar tissue has already formed, that we can never go back to how we were.

Jemma grasps my hands in her own. 'Look, Jake, I'll do whatever it takes to make it work. I've spoken to Adam and he's agreed for me to reduce my hours and do some work from home so I can take Alfie to school and pick him up. It'll mean less money, but if you're working as well, that should easily make up for it. We'll start taking more holidays again. And my parents have said they'll have Alfie once a month so we can go out for dinner, have some "us" time.'

'Seriously? Your parents looking after Alfie?'

When she sees I'm joking, her whole body seems to relax, muscle by muscle, and I know she thinks it's that straightforward. That she's won me back.

'I love you, Jake. I know we're still going to argue sometimes and I know things with Alfie are never going to be easy, but we'll find a way to be happy again.'

She stands up, wraps her arms around my neck and kisses me. The familiar taste of her lemon lip salve hurtles me back through the years of our marriage. The way we slowly merged into each other before we started to repel. At first, I don't kiss her back, but then I allow myself to relax into it, because a huge part of me wants to believe her, a huge part of me wants to believe we can start again, like covering the stains and cracks on a wall with a fresh coat of paint. And as I'm kissing her, somehow it feels simultaneously totally wrong and like coming home. But afterwards, as she rests her head on my chest and my hands fall on to the small of her back, it's like they no longer fit, I can't get comfortable, and my stomach's churned up with guilt, the horrible feeling that I'm cheating on Emily, even though I'm not sure if she actually wants a commitment from me. I'm glad when Jemma releases me.

Then there's this surreal moment when she starts putting away the glasses on the draining board and I stack the dishwasher and it's like she never left, except she doesn't tell me I've put the bowls in the wrong place even though I know she notices, because her eyes linger on me doing it for a split second before she looks away.

'So what shall we do now?' Jemma says, laughing awkwardly. 'Do you want to watch a film?'

It's like a first date, both of us frantically trying to work out what the other one is thinking so we know the right move to make.

'OK. I'll be in in a minute.'

As I grab myself another beer, a photograph on the noticeboard catches my eye. It's the one from the ride at Legoland, with all of us looking like we've had facelifts. I unpin it, find my workbag and slip it in there. It'd break Jemma's heart to see it and, right now, it's too confusing for me to look at too.

When I go through to the lounge, Jemma has found a film we'd been intending to watch before she left. She doesn't seem to get that it's weird, that it only serves to highlight the fact she went away.

'Is this one OK?'

'Sure, it's fine.'

I sit at the other end of the sofa but, once the film starts, Jemma gradually moves towards me until her head is resting on my shoulder and her hand is on my leg. I feel stuck, like any movement might give her the impression that all is now mended between us. As her thumb moves up and down on my thigh, I long for the film to end.

'You OK?' Jemma tilts her head to make eye contact with me and I realize I must have been staring into the middle distance.

'Yeah, I'm fine. Actually, I'm really tired. I'm going to go to bed.'

'I'll come with you.'

'No, you stay and watch the end. I'll see you in the morning.'

It's clear from Jemma's face that I've upset her, but

being so close to her is like being in a lift that suddenly grinds to a halt. I'm struggling to catch my breath.

As soon as I'm on my own, I text Emily. I write, delete and rewrite it over a dozen times. Then, finally, I press send.

> Jemma would like to take Alfie
> to school this week. I hope
> that's OK? I'll still pay you, of
> course, and I'll call you to sort
> out next week x

It's not what I want to say and I regret it as soon as I've sent it.

When her reply arrives, it's like a punch in the stomach.

> No problem.

* * *

'I like having you home, Mummy,' Alfie announces after he's finished gobbling his breakfast.

'Oh, thank you, baby.' Jemma looks like she might cry. 'I like being home too.'

She kisses his cheek, then he climbs down off the stool. 'When is Emily getting here?'

'Well, I'm going to take you to school now.'

'Will Emily pick me up?'

'No, I'm going to do that too. Isn't that great?'

Alfie doesn't look like he thinks it's great. 'But when will I see Emily, then?'

Jemma tries and fails to hide the hurt on her face. 'Well, I don't know. I . . .'

I put my hand on Alfie's shoulder. 'I'll call her. We'll sort something out, OK?'

Jemma glances over at me and I can tell it's not the answer she wanted me to give, but I can't just remove Emily from Alfie's life. And although I can't tell Jemma, I'm not ready to completely remove her from mine either, at least not without knowing if she wants me to.

'OK, as long as I can see her really soon. I'm going to go and beat the timer getting ready. It's got orange sand in, Mummy, my favourite colour. Emily got it for me.'

Jemma gives a forced smile and Alfie runs upstairs, leaving us to listen to the dripping tap, the whir of the dishwasher, the sizzling pan – the current state of our relationship, lingering, unresolved, swirling through the atmosphere between us.

'Here you are.' Jemma places the full English breakfast she's cooked for me down on the worktop and I pull up a stool and tuck in.

'Thank you. It's delicious.'

'Well, you can't go and face all those teenagers hungry, can you?'

I smile. 'I suppose not.'

Jemma picks up Alfie's cereal bowl and puts it in the sink. 'Oh, I was wondering, do you want to go for dinner tonight? My parents are available. Or we could go at the weekend, if you think you'll be too tired?'

Although I appreciate her making the effort, it feels like she's trying too hard, piling on the pressure. I already know what the 'right' thing to do is. Mum's voice is always there: *Be loyal.* I don't need Jemma being the perfect wife to remind me that we made our vows, that she's the mother of my child. That you don't give up on that unless there's literally no possible way of salvaging it.

And yet, right now, my head is so full of someone who isn't my wife that it feels like it might actually explode, just burst open in front of Jemma, exposing its guilt-ridden contents. And doing the right thing feels so much harder than I ever thought it would.

'Let's do it at the weekend. Sounds nice.'

Emily

I think he's called Simon. I can't quite remember. It might be Steve. I know it was one of those names that make you picture someone with no discernible features. If someone says the name River, or Gabriel, it immediately conjures up an image of an artist or a musician – scruffy hair, a mysterious vibe. Simon, Steve – whoever it is that's snoring beside me, his mouth open, a small trail of dribble slithering down his chin – he's as nondescript as the name I can't remember. He's neither fat nor thin. Not ugly but not particularly handsome. He seemed nice enough after a skinful.

Careful not to wake him, I wriggle out from under the duvet, pick my clothes up off the floor and put them back on. My mouth tastes of copper coins so I go into the kitchen to get myself a glass of water. I open the cupboard and am greeted by a white coffee mug with the letters UNT printed on it in large black font and a black handle forming the C. Well, if the shoe fits. I fill it with water, take a few large gulps and leave it on his worktop to welcome him when he gets up.

On the bus to Gardner's Lane, there's a young mum with her two little boys, probably about two and six. She's sitting next to the youngest, while the older boy stands beside them, flying across the aisle every time the bus driver brakes. She taps the screen of her phone while the youngest chews on his shoe, which he has removed from his foot, and the eldest tries talking to her about a film he's watched. I want to throw something at her and shout, 'Listen! Because one of these days, and it'll come sooner than you think, he won't be there every day, you won't be the person he wants to share everything with, and the hole he leaves will feel like a cavern.' But I know she wouldn't get it.

I pass a Spar on the short walk to the community centre so I pop in and buy a bottle of vodka. The guy serving can't even be bothered to say the price out loud, so deep does his misery seem to run; instead he just points to the numbers on the screen of the till. I can't really blame him, stuck in this dingy little shop serving misfits like me all day long. I thank him – not that he acknowledges it – and leave, stuffing the alcohol into my shoulder bag.

In the toilets of the community centre, I open the bottle and slug away merrily. I know that by the time I walk back out, Jake will be sitting in the circle telling the group how wonderful it is that his wife's come home and how they're going to be better parents to Alfie and I can't listen to that shit sober. It's been four days. He hasn't called. He sent a couple of texts, one on the day Jemma came home to basically tell me I was out of a job. And one the following day that simply said *Are you OK?* I didn't reply and there's been nothing since. Not that I expected there to be. She's his wife. Alfie's mum. And just to add insult to injury, she's even more stunningly beautiful in the flesh than in the photos dotted around their house. How could little old me compete with that? I manage nearly a third of the bottle, then it starts rising back up into my throat like bubbles in a lava lamp so I replace the cap and put it into my bag.

When I walk into the circle, Jake looks up in acknowledgement so I stare at the floor. I sit by Sharon. Even enduring her is better than being near to him. As I sit down, she smiles at me, but it's the kind of smile you give someone you really can't stand, a short sharp twitch of the cheeks. I mirror her and then turn away so there's no chance of us being trapped in a polite conversation that neither of us wants to have.

It's not long before Sam taps his stupid triangle and the group members bow their heads. I stay looking up. Sam glances at me and, if I'm not mistaken, he looks scared. Like he can see he's got a potential bomb in the room that could explode at any time.

Sheltered inside my hazy vodka bubble, sitting in the anger management session feels surreal, like I'm watching myself through a screen.

'Right, let's make a quick declaration to our partners, then.'

Keeping her hands in her lap, Sharon mumbles, 'I promise to listen without judgement and to be honest to myself and to you.'

I snort. 'What a load of crap.' All eyes, loaded with unease, turn to me. Jake's face is filled to the top with pity and I can't stand it. I don't want him feeling sorry for me. 'I mean, seriously, you all judged me the day I walked in with my skinhead. And, come off it, none of us are really being honest. We say what we think you want to hear, Sam; maybe we even manage to convince ourselves it's what we really feel. But the truth is we are who we are and sitting around drinking shit coffee and imagining our happy place is not going to change that.'

Sharon shakes her head so violently it looks like it might topple off. 'So we're all just doomed, then? No point trying to change anything?'

I shrug. 'Looks that way to me.'

She sits on her hands like she's scared what they might do. 'Well, you can't speak for everyone, OK? Some of us here have changed and we *are* being honest and this group is really helping us, so keep your negativity to yourself.'

Sam raises his hands. 'Everyone has a voice here, Sharon. We don't all have to agree with each other but we do have to allow each other a voice. Maybe this is you finally being honest, Emily. Maybe now you will make the progress you feel you haven't made so far.'

I raise my eyes to the ceiling and exhale loudly. I've had to listen to this psycho mumbo jumbo my whole life. I can talk until I'm blue in the face but it doesn't change anything.

Sam turns back to the group. 'So, as it's our penultimate session, we're going to talk about rebuilding any damage that may have occurred as a result of your anger. It might be damage to a relationship with a loved one, it could be difficulties in the workplace, or it might even be damage that your anger has caused within you – maybe it sends you off on a path of self-destruction or you feel guilty all the time.'

I'm not stupid. I know you're talking to me.

'Whatever the damage is, I want you to talk with your partner about ways you could fix it. Off you go.'

I cross my arms and look at Sharon. 'Well, it's clear I've

learnt bugger all, so why don't you share your new-found wisdom with me?'

Sharon's heels scrape the floor as she adjusts her position in her chair. 'Fine. OK. For what it's worth, even though you're going to think it's a load of bullshit, I realized that my anger messed up my relationship with my daughter. I felt guilty for not being the best mum in the world. And instead of facing up to that, I blamed her. But she's right. I probably did give her trust issues. In fact, a lot of the things she blames me for probably are my fault.'

When the veneer of self-righteousness leaves Sharon's face, what's left is something decidedly fragile.

'So I'm going to tell her that,' Sharon continues. 'And I just hope she forgives me. Because if she doesn't, then I guess you're right, what's the point?' Sharon's hands shake as she pulls at her lip. 'So come on, tell me it's all pointless, that the damage has been done.'

I shake my head, picturing Mum's face. 'Tell your daughter what you just told me. I can't say whether she'll forgive you or not, but either way, it won't be pointless.'

Sharon draws back her head and examines my features closely, as if she's not sure who it is she's talking to. 'Thanks.'

Sam taps his triangle and the conversations going on around the room peter out. 'Anyone want to share?'

Bill slowly raises his hand. 'Actually, I've got something to say if you all don't mind listening to an old bugger like me for a few minutes?'

There is a collective murmur of support.

'We'd love to listen to you, Bill,' Sam says.

'Well, first, I just want to say I'm sorry that you don't feel the group has helped you, Emily. But you've helped me.'

I smile awkwardly, feeling strangely emotional and yet unsure how anything I've said could have had a positive impact on anyone.

'Something you said a few weeks ago really struck a chord with me and I've been thinking about it a lot since. You said I was just blaming other people and you were right. I thought I was angry because the neighbours put their bins in the wrong place or didn't stick to the rules about not hanging their washing in the front garden. But really it had nothing to do with that.' He wrings his wrinkled hands. 'I was angry at Else, for leaving before me. That wasn't the plan. She was younger than me. I was supposed to go first. I was angry at God for taking her. But I'm trying to put things right. I even took round cakes for all the neighbours the other day. I bet they thought they were poisoned.'

Bill laughs and I look around at a room of waterlogged eyes, trying my best to retain some composure.

'I've never baked cakes before. Can you believe that? I'm eighty-two and I've never baked a cake. But things were different when we were young. Men didn't do that sort of thing. Else did everything for me. I don't think I even realized how much she did until she'd gone. So they probably weren't the most delicious cakes you've ever tasted but it felt like a step in the right direction.'

'Thank you for sharing, Bill,' Sam says. 'It sounds like a wonderful way to repair the damage to me.'

I know if I don't escape I'm going to burst into loud embarrassing tears so I sneak out of the room and go back into the toilets, sitting in one of the cubicles with my bag on my lap and the bottle in my hand. The burn of vodka on my lips is a welcome comfort, but my head's starting to spin so much I'm not sure how much longer I can keep it held upright. After a few more swigs, I go to the sink, splash some water on my face and steady myself to go back in.

When I rejoin the circle, Sam is just finishing off. 'It's our last session next week so if anyone wants to bring some food – crisps, dips, cakes, that sort of thing – we'll have a little "last supper", for want of a better phrase.'

There's some discussion amongst the group about what they might bring and then people start gathering their things, stacking chairs and filtering out. As I pick up my bag, I feel a hand land on my shoulder. I look up and, despite myself, am disappointed to see Sam's face.

'Stay here for a minute. Let me make you a coffee.'

I move away from his touch, more aggressively than I mean to. He sits down on the chair beside me.

'I'm fine. I don't need babysitting.'

'I know you don't. But I don't think a coffee would hurt.'

I know he's only trying to be nice but the last thing I need is someone mothering me.

'Now if you were offering me something stronger, that *would* be appreciated, but a coffee's really not going to do it for me. So, if you don't mind, I'm just going to go home.'

'OK, but only if you let me drive you. At least let me do that.'

I sit forward and put my bag on my shoulder. 'Seriously, I'm fine.'

When I stand up, my legs nearly give way. I steady myself using one of the towers of chairs and it screeches across the floor, me sliding with it.

'I'm driving you home.'

Sam packs up his things. I feel so light-headed that I'm not sure I'll make it to the bus so I give in and stagger with Sam to his car. Getting in, I bash my head on the door frame. It stings to shit but I pretend it doesn't bother me.

We don't talk on the drive home. My eyes keep closing and I think maybe I even drift off a couple of times, but I'm not entirely sure. When Sam pulls up outside my flat, he turns off the engine and puts his hand on mine.

'Please take care of yourself, OK, Em?'

I have no idea why, but I lean across the handbrake and kiss him. He pulls away, gently manoeuvring me back into my seat.

'Em, you're drunk. Let's talk next week, yeah?'

I snigger, trying to disguise the fact I feel like an idiot. 'Your loss. I would've been an easy lay.'

'Em.'

Somehow, I manage to open the car door and stumble out and into my flat. I collapse on the sofa, drink some more of the vodka from my bag and eventually pass out.

Alfie

Mummy came home so Emily doesn't look after me any more. Mrs Young gave me a big smile when she saw Mummy dropping me off at school and said, 'Isn't it wonderful your mummy is home?' and I nodded. I didn't want to tell her that I was feeling really sad in my tummy because then she'd think that I was mean and that I don't love Mummy and I do. But in the morning when I show Mummy that I beat the timer, she says, 'Well done,' but she has a sad face, and it's supposed to be happy, like Emily's was. Emily always picked me up and spun me around so my legs stuck out in the air like a windmill. I don't know why Mummy isn't happy I beat the timer.

I want to show Emily my plan for my new film. I've drawn all the pictures and made a list of everything we need. It's going to have Scuba Batman in it, and Holiday Joker. I got them both the other day. I think Emily would like them, especially Holiday Joker, because he has a rubber ring and an ice lolly so he looks really funny. In my film, they're going to go to the beach and play chase the waves and Batman can live in a sand Batcave like the one we built when we went together. I'm going to make one with all my yellow Lego. I think Emily would like that. I hope she can help me make it. I keep asking Daddy when she can come over and he keeps saying,

'Soon,' but soon never seems to come so I don't think it's soon at all. I tried to make a magic spell to make Emily appear, but it didn't work so I'm not sure I've got the right ingredients yet.

Jake

When I arrive at Emily's flat, she's in joggers and a T-shirt and there are three empty packets of Wotsits on her coffee table.

'Healthy tea tonight?'

'Almost as good as that roast you cooked me.'

She sits down and puts her feet up on the coffee table, her arms crossed like armour.

'You didn't reply to my text.'

Emily shrugs. 'I didn't have anything to say.'

'I just wanted to know that you were OK.'

'Of course I'm OK. Why wouldn't I be?'

It's the Emily I met all those weeks ago at anger management, and I know she's going to make this as hard for me as she possibly can. I can't blame her. But I could really do with some of the 'other' Emily right now.

'Good. Well, I'm glad you're all right.'

Emily takes a sip of her drink. I'm guessing from the glaze on her eyes, like a thin layer of icing, that it's not just Diet Coke. 'Is there anything else, Jake? I'm just about to go out.'

I suspect it's a lie, and it hurts that I've caused her to shut down when she was just beginning to open up to me.

'Look, there's no easy way to say this, but Jemma's decided to permanently reduce her hours so she can do the school run. I'll help you find another job. I'm sure there'll be someone at Jemma's work who needs a nanny and I'll ask around at school.'

Emily nods, but she keeps her face like stone.

'Of course I'll pay you until we sort out something else for you,' I continue, insultingly matter of fact. I don't know what to say. I don't know how to make it any better. 'I'll write you a great reference. I'm good at lying.'

I'm trying to lighten the mood but she doesn't laugh, and another flurry falls on my already compacted layer of guilt.

'What makes you think I want a job as a nanny?'

'I thought you loved looking after Alfie, that's all.'

At the mention of Alfie, her eyes start to fill with tears and I can see how hard she's trying to keep them at bay. 'I do. Because I love Alfie, not because I love being a nanny.'

I wish that I could wrap my arms around her, but I know she'd push me away if I got anywhere near her.

'Sorry, I was just trying to help. I'll pay you until you find whatever it is you want to do.'

Emily smirks. 'So Jemma's back for good, is she?'

'She says she wants to try to make it work.'

Emily downs the last of her drink. 'If only she could've realized that without buggering off to Paris. Would've saved us all a lot of hassle.'

The words come before I can stop them. 'I'm sorry that getting to know Alfie and me has been such a hassle.'

It's totally unfair, I know. I'm an arsehole. I just feel so angry. At Jemma, for coming home before Emily and I had a chance to figure out what this thing between us really is. At Emily, for not giving me something, any-thing, to hold on to. Even though I'm not sure what I'd do with it if she did.

Emily stands up and puts her glass on the side. She's so close to me that I want to pull her in to me and kiss her. I want to rip her clothes off and make love to her right here on her living-room floor.

'Well, I'm glad Alfie's got his mum back. He deserves that. He deserves a proper family.'

The thing is, she's right, but that doesn't make it any easier to give up on what we'd started.

'I still want you to see Alfie. We can meet up at the park and stuff.'

Emily nods but she won't look me in the eye.

'And I still want to see you too. I want us to be friends.'
Tell me you want more. Tell me it's not enough.

'Friends. Perfect.' Emily moves towards the door and holds it open.

'Bye then, Jake.'

But I don't want to go. There's so much left to say. 'You know, this thing with us, do you think that it could've become –'

Emily cuts me off. 'We helped each other through a tricky time, Jake. That's all it was. Don't worry, I was never looking for a relationship.'

I suppose I should be relieved. She's taking the decision out of my hands. But I'm not. In fact, I feel exceptionally sad.

'Good. I'm glad we're both on the same page. See you soon.'

I walk out and, as I do, I know there's no going back.

This is our goodbye. And it makes me realize how much I wish it wasn't.

* * *

I always hate taking Alfie to birthday parties. First, there is the obsession about the party bag (will there be one? What will it have in it? When will I get it?) that starts as soon as he's received the invitation and intensifies three-fold by the time we are getting ready to leave the house on the day of the party. Second is having to waste my hard-earned cash on a bit of plastic tat for some kid I don't even know, and third is the inevitable meltdown when the mixture of excitement and anticipation all gets too much for Alfie.

Today's party is at the climbing centre. I have to admit it's an awesome venue. I wish places like this had existed for kids when I was little. There's a boulder room, a proper climbing wall, where the kids get strapped into a harness and have to race against the clock to get to the top, and a digiwall, where the grips light up and you have to chase them. It's a harsh reminder of the fact I didn't even let Alfie have a party, let alone one as cool as this.

Most of the children are chasing around the room, ignoring the activities on offer and whacking each other with balloons. Alfie, however, is playing the chase-the-lights game for the umpteenth time. He's completely focused, oblivious to the other children beating the crap out of each other. He's the sort of kid who I'm sure will, one day, cure cancer. I just hope he has fun along the way.

Another boy comes over to the digiwall and I brace myself for it to kick off. He darts towards the glowing grip but Alfie barges him out the way with his shoulder and smacks the light with his hand. As it goes out, the boy looks at him, confusion dashing across his face, then they both return their focus to the wall.

I walk over to Alfie and whisper in his ear, 'Work as a team, yeah? This boy's going to help you get an even higher score.'

The boy hurtles towards the next light and subconsciously I try to stop his progress, like some kind of mind-bender, but it doesn't work and it feels like everything's happening in slow motion, as the boy's palm meets with the plastic seconds before Alfie's.

In a fit of rage, Alfie throws himself on to the padded matting and pounds it with his fists. 'No, I want to do it on my own!'

The other boy surveys him for a second, like a rare creature he's not encountered before, then continues with the game, stepping over Alfie when necessary to get to the lights. After a few moments, the music begins its countdown to the end of the game (as if we needed the tension cranking up any more) and Alfie looks up at the wall. I can see the conflict all over his face, as he's torn between racing towards the lights to get a better score or continuing to make his stand against what he sees as a great injustice. He starts to get up but then the music comes to its dramatic finale and Alfie crashes his head back on to the mat, erupting into tears.

I feel the eyes of the other parents burning a hole in my shirt and then Ben's mum comes out of the party room, where she's been setting up the food.

'Is everything OK? Did Tom hurt him or something?'

'No. Tom's fine. Alfie's just very competitive about the game and was trying to beat his score.'

Ben's mum smiles, but I can tell she thinks Alfie is being a spoilt brat. It's what I would've thought before I met Emily. She kneels down beside him and I pray that he doesn't lash out at her.

'Parties are a time for sharing,' she says in a patronizing tone.

Alfie turns away from her and lies on his side. She gives me a look that says 'tut, tut, tut' and I know she expects me to castigate Alfie for being rude. Usually I would. Usually I'd pick him up, take him over to the side of the room and bollock him, delivering the ultimate punishment that he's no longer allowed his party bag. But today, I think about what I've read and imagine what Emily would do if she were here, and I pick Alfie up and carry him to the sofa, where I sit down with him cradled in my arms.

'Look, little man, I know you wanted to finish your game and beat your score. I know sometimes it's rubbish when other people want to join in something and you don't want them to. I get why you're angry and if Tom had been my little boy, I'd have told him to wait until you'd finished, but he's not, so I can't. Now let's not let it ruin the rest of the party because there's so much fun stuff here. It's your turn on the big wall with the harness next.'

I expect Alfie to argue, to squirm out of my arms, to tell me he hates me, but he doesn't. He puts his arms around my neck and hugs me back, letting his head rest on my shoulder. And I know it's a drop in the ocean. I know, within minutes probably, he'll be arguing with me about something else, but right at this moment it feels like a breakthrough. Right at this moment, I feel the deepest love for my little boy that makes me physically ache.

* * *

There are three other kids with Alfie in the auto-belay room: Tom, the boy he had the conflict with earlier, Ben, the birthday boy, whose mum gives me a cursory smile from across the room, and bloody George.

The young girl that works at the climbing centre puts harnesses on the boys and I'm already hoping that George can't climb for shit and that Alfie races up the wall and puts him to shame. I know, in reality, that will never happen, but it's a nice image to sit with for a minute.

As soon as the boys are attached to the wall, George confidently traverses the various grips and makes his way up. Tom starts crying and chickens out and I'm secretly glad, as it takes the pressure off Alfie. And Ben has a go but keeps losing his grip, quickly deciding that swinging around in the harness is actually much more fun than climbing anyway.

Alfie looks up to the top of the wall and then over at me. 'I'm going to get to the top, Daddy.'

I give him a thumbs up, but my heart sinks, as I know there's no way my clumsy little boy is going to manage to get even halfway, let alone to the top. Once the instructor has clipped him to the wall, Alfie starts his ascent and then his foot slips, followed by his hands, and he ends up swinging around on the rope so that he's facing the opposite way. I know there's another meltdown on the horizon and I wish Ben's mum wasn't here, as I know that, in her eyes, my parenting is going to come up short, yet again.

I twist Alfie round, helping him back on to the wall.

'Don't worry. Just try again. It doesn't matter if you get to the top or not.'

Alfie furrows his brow. 'But I want to get to the top. Like George is. Look.'

Alfie points at George, who is looking down on us, his head nearly touching the ceiling. It feels so apt, him all the way up there like some kind of miniature Spider-Man and us standing beneath, staring up at him in wonder.

'Then you go to the top, little man. I believe in you.' As I say it, I know it's a lie and I feel guilty for having absolutely no faith in my son's ability.

Then something incredible happens.

Alfie starts mounting the wall like Indiana Jones. Every now and again, his shoe slips, but he grips on with his hands and tries again to find his footing, succeeding and pushing himself upwards. In no time at all, he's at the top, slamming the button to stop the timer and looking down at me with a smile as wide as the Cheshire cat's.

Before I realize what I'm doing, I'm fist-pumping the air and whooping. All the other adults in the room look at me as if I'm crazy, but I don't care. Alfie bounces his way down to the ground, repeatedly smashing himself against the wall, and I run over and give him a huge hug.

'That was amazing!'

'See, I told you I could do it.'

'You did. And you were right. You didn't give up. You kept going.'

Alfie looks at me like he's questioning my intelligence. 'It's called perseverance, Daddy.'

I laugh. 'That it is.' I ruffle his hair. 'I'm so proud of you, little man.'

As I say it, the look on Alfie's face makes me want to cry. He looks exactly how I felt the day I won the Year Six drawing competition at school. I'd spent hours copying the front cover of one of my comics, erasing and trying again multiple times until I got Spider-Man's mask just right. I hadn't shown Mum or told her about the competition. Then, at the school fete, there it was on a board in the hall with a first-place rosette attached to the corner. Mum held my face in her hands and told me it was the most amazing picture she'd ever seen, then marched me over to the cake stall and bought a whole chocolate gateau to celebrate. I'm guessing my face at that point in time was just like Alfie's is now. And it makes me realize that I don't tell him enough how proud I am of him.

'How about on the way home we go and buy a DVD and popcorn and you can stay up late for film night?'

'Yeah, yeah!' Alfie jumps up and down, making the metal clasp on his harness clank loudly. 'Can we have ice cream too? Please, Daddy, it is a treat night?'

So typical of Alfie to try to negotiate better terms. 'We'll see.'

'So that's a yes?'

'Go on, then. Now get to the top of that wall again before the session finishes.'

There are times as a parent when you feel like you're winning. When you experience a sudden realization that the love you feel for your child is the most intense thing you will ever feel. Like you're right bang in the focal point of your life and everything else has been or will be slightly blurred in comparison. And you will yourself to treasure it, to cling on to this time for dear life and savour it. And then they won't go to bed and they spill your pint and they argue with every fricking thing you say and you forget this feeling. You wish the hours away until they're asleep and you finally get 'you' back, if only for a short while. But right at this moment, I'm riding high on being-a-parent euphoria and it feels great.

* * *

The following day, Jemma calls to say she has an important meeting that she can't get out of, so I sneak out of work early and pick Alfie up from school. When we get home, he runs straight up to his room. I make myself a coffee and then head up. He's sitting on his floor with my camera around his neck, trying to line up a row of figures, but they keep toppling over.

'How's it going, little man?'

Alfie pushes all the figures over. 'I can't do it. They won't stand up.'

'How about we get a base plate to put them on?'

Alfie walks around his room like he's looking for something and then slumps on his bed. 'I don't want to. It's rubbish.'

I sit down beside him and put my arm around his shoulder. 'Come on. This isn't like you. Do you want me to help you?'

Alfie hangs his head. 'Can Emily take me to school tomorrow?'

'Remember we talked about this, Alfie? Mummy takes you to school and picks you up now.'

'But you picked me up today.'

'That was because Mummy had to work late. But normally she does it now, doesn't she?'

'But can't Emily just do it once? Just tomorrow? So Mummy can do some more work?'

I rub Alfie's back. 'Do you want to call her?'

'Who?'

'Emily, silly.'

Alfie can barely contain his excitement and I feel guilty that needing to stifle my feelings for Emily has prevented him from seeing her. 'Can we?'

'Let me just get my phone.'

As I listen to the dial tone, a mixture of nerves and excitement bubble in my chest. I'm not sure Emily will answer, and even if she does, I'll probably crash into a wall of negativity, but I'm desperate to hear her voice, to know she's OK. It seems to ring forever but, eventually, she picks up.

'What is it, Jake?' she says in an exasperated tone.

'Alfie wanted to call you. He misses you.'

Her voice changes in an instant. 'Of course. Put him on the phone.'

Alfie hasn't quite got the hang of having a conversation on the telephone yet. He keeps moving the phone to his mouth when he wants to speak and then misses what Emily has said, but with me regularly putting the phone back to his ear, they just about manage to communicate. Alfie tells her all about the climbing party and his idea for a new film that he wants to create. His face is so animated and he has so much to say to her . . . it stings.

After he's told her everything he can think of to tell her, he hands back the phone. 'Emily says she has something to say to you.'

I take it, feeling an anxious anticipation at what she might say. 'Everything OK?'

'Look, I'm not sure if you'll be interested or not, but I found this private paediatrician online. Lots of the parents on the PDA Society website said they'd had more luck with him than with their normal doctor. Obviously it'll cost, but I thought I'd just let you know..I can send you the details, if you want. But it's up to you.'

'Yeah, that'd be great. Thank you. Send them over and I'll get in touch with him.'

'No problem. I just want the best for Alfie.'

She sounds so distant I want to reach through the phone and pull her towards me.

'I know you do.'

'Anyway, I've got to go. Give Alfie a kiss from me.'

'Of course. And, Em?'

'What?'

'Do you want to meet us in the park after school one day this week? I could get away early and bring him straight out. Whichever day suits you?'

It just comes out and then Alfie's jumping up and down and I know I can't go back on it.

Emily doesn't respond straight away, then she says, 'OK. Thursday?'

'Perfect, I'll see you about four.'

I'm not sure what Jemma's going to think, or if I can get away with not telling her at all, but I know by Alfie's face that it's the right thing to do. And I can't pretend it's entirely selfless – I'm desperate to see Emily too.

Emily

'I've missed you oodles and oodles, you know?'

Alfie sits next to me on the park bench and plays with the Velcro on his shoes. 'Are you going to start taking me to school and picking me up again?'

'No, buddy. You have Mummy to do that now. That's good, isn't it?'

Alfie doesn't say anything at first, just keeps pulling the strap off his shoes and then re-securing it.

'I'm allowed a snack after school now, like you let me. It doesn't have to be a fruit bar. I can have a Kit-Kat.'

I smile. 'Awesome.'

'And Mummy lets me use the timer in the morning. I beat it every time.'

The compression starts somewhere in my tummy and then spreads up through my chest to my throat.

'You're super-speedy.'

'Like the Flash.'

'Just like the Flash.' I put my arm around Alfie's shoulders. He doesn't lean into me but he doesn't pull away. 'How's the new film going?'

Alfie sits up, suddenly animated. 'It's awesome. I got Clayface the other day, so he's in it now. Can you come and see it?'

'How about you send me it?'

'OK, I'll get Daddy to send it the second we get home. Shall I go and tell him now?'

'It's OK; you can tell him in a minute.'

'I'll just run and tell him now.'

I know better than to argue. Alfie runs over to Jake, who is circling the field beside the playground. After a few minutes, he runs back and gives me a thumbs up.

'He says that's fine.' He climbs back on to the bench.

'Great.'

I stroke his soft blond hair. I want to stroke his hair every night and watch him slowly falling asleep, asking questions until the second he drops off.

'This might not make a lot of sense, Alfie, but I want to thank you. Becoming your friend has made me very happy. It's like before I met you, everything seemed a bit cloudy, and then you made the sun come out.'

Alfie looks up at the sky. 'But it's cloudy today.'

'I know. That wasn't a very good explanation, was it? I mean . . . I was quite sad before. Then you made me happy, like the sun makes me happy. Because it makes everything bright and more colourful and warm.'

Alfie wrinkles his forehead, then he props his hands on his waist and smiles. 'Best bugs.'

'Huh?'

Alfie's intense brown eyes peer up at me from underneath his fringe. 'We're best bugs, aren't we?'

I suddenly realize what he means and it hits me like standing in the middle of oncoming traffic on the motorway. 'Oh, best buds. Yeah, of course we are. Always, Alfie.'

Alfie wraps his arms around my waist and rests his

head on my chest, and I use the back of my finger to wipe away the tears escaping from the corners of my eyes.

After a minute or so, Jake wanders over. He's wearing his navy peacoat and his hair keeps blowing into his eyes. It looks like he hasn't shaved for a week or so and I wish it made him look worse, but it doesn't. In fact, he looks lovelier than ever.

'Can Daddy have a quick chat with Emily now, little man? You could go and show us how awesome you are on the monkey bars?'

Alfie sits up and the cold bites into my side where his body was keeping me warm. 'As long as you both watch me the whole time. I can do the whole thing now, Emily.'

'Wow, that's amazing. Go and show me.'

It hurts. The thought of all the ways he's changing that I'm missing. He runs off, turning back every few steps to check we are watching. Each time he looks, I wave.

Jake sits beside me but keeps his eyes on Alfie. 'So have you found a new job yet?'

'No. But I don't need you to pay me. I've got enough money to keep me going for a while and then I'll find something.'

'Well, I'm not sure if you'd be interested or not, but I mentioned to this family at Jemma's work that you are a really great photographer and they'd like you to do some family shots for them.' Jake takes a piece of paper out of his pocket and hands it to me. 'Here are their contact details. They've got loads of money and a lot of important friends so, who knows, maybe it could be the start of something for you.'

I feel at once grateful and patronized. 'Thank you. You didn't need to do that for me.'

'It's the least I could do.'

We sit in silence for a minute or so. There's so much I want him to say, but I know that he won't.

'Oh, and thanks so much for the details of that consultant. We've been emailing back and forth and he actually gets it. It's amazing. We're taking Alfie to meet him in a couple of weeks so maybe, this time, we'll get some answers.'

'I'm really glad it went well.'

'It's all thanks to you.'

I love you.

'Happy to help.'

Jake nods slowly. 'Those cast-iron walls are firmly back in place, I see.'

I wish they were. I wish I'd never let them down.

I take my gloves out of my pocket and pull them on. 'I better get back.' I stand up and put my rucksack on my shoulders. 'I'm just going to go and say goodbye to Alfie.'

I go to turn away but Jake grips on to my hand. 'Come on, Em, give me something. Don't just go.'

I wriggle my hand free. 'What do you want from me, Jake? Do you want me to say you're forgiven? You are. I forgive you.'

Jake shakes his head.

'Do you want me to say I'm happy? That you and Alfie meant nothing to me? Would that make you feel better? Or do you want me to say I'm heartbroken and pining for you? Is that what you want? Tell me what you want me to say and I'll say it.'

'Well, are you? Are you heartbroken? I never know what you're feeling.'

His words feel like needles trying to penetrate my skin, but I can't let them. I won't let them.

'You have a beautiful family, Jake. Go home.'

I leave him sitting on the bench, his head in his hands, and go to say goodbye to Alfie.

* * *

When I arrive home, I take the piece of paper Jake gave me out of my pocket and start to draft an email. I don't expect anything to come of it, but like Alfie always tells me, if you don't try, you won't succeed.

I go to the kitchen and collect the various half-drunk or full bottles of alcohol. Collecting them together, I can't believe how many there are. I tip them down the sink, lamenting the wasted money as the liquid gurgles down the drain. It's a powerful concoction. I expect it will do wonders for the grimy pipes that emit the smell of rotten eggs every time I run the tap.

The cigarettes take a battering too. I chop them into tiny pieces over the kitchen bin, knowing that if I just cut them in half I'll find myself rooting through there later, pulling out the ends with the filter on and smoking them.

With the flat cleansed, I open my box of prints and start to put them in chronological order. I only spent a couple of months with Alfie, but it feels so much longer, like the first photographs from in the park the day it was raining were taken a lifetime ago. It doesn't even feel like it was me who took them.

It's funny how a single choice can have such a knock-on effect on the rest of your life. Like a row of dominoes. I don't think you can ever get back to the very first push that set everything in motion, but I know if I hadn't attacked that guy then my life would've taken a very different path. I still regret what I did. I still wake up drenched with sweat sometimes, the image of his bleeding neck glued to my eyelids and the terrifying feeling of not being in control pulsing through me, but it seems sometimes beautiful things can come out of even the ugliest of actions.

I stick the photos, in order, into the album I've bought. As I get to one of Alfie hung upside down from the monkey bars – his fingers made into glasses and his tongue sticking out – I giggle. Then there's one of Jake and Alfie when neither of them knew I was looking. Jake's telling Alfie a story about Captain America and, in typical Alfie fashion, unable to sit still, he has his legs twisted into a strange shape up against the wall, but his hand is resting just lightly on top of Jake's and his face is fixed in fascination as he hangs on Jake's every word. There's Alfie completely absorbed making one of his Lego films, Alfie proudly holding up his box of conkers, Alfie and Jake in matching Spider-Man costumes, Alfie tirelessly working on his sand Batcave until every bit of it was exactly as he had envisaged.

When I get to the one of Alfie holding his map at Legoland, pointing to the ride he insisted we go to next, Jake standing behind him trying his best not to look exasperated, I start sticking them in at speed, barely looking at them until I get to the last photo. I debate whether or not to include it, but in the end decide to. I close the album and wrap it, first in Christmas wrapping paper, then in brown paper. I write a note to Jake, stick it in an envelope and attach it to the front of the parcel. Before I can change my mind, I walk into town and take it to the post office.

* * *

I get to the pub early the following evening and order a Diet Coke, then sit at a table in the corner, near the open fire. Even with the heat coming from the flames, I can't stop shivering. When the door slams, I look up to see Mum, wearing a long white puffer jacket that makes her look like the Michelin man. Her permed hair is dragged back into a ponytail, a few strands escaping around her face, and instead of her usual brightly coloured make-up, she's wearing subtle nude shades. Her skin is dull and her cheeks gaunt, but there's no denying she's beautiful.

She looks around the room, all twitchy like a mouse, and I stand up to go and put her out of her misery, but then she notices me and hurries over. When we hug, I can feel her bones through her clothes, like if I held her any tighter she might snap. She slips her coat off and puts it next to mine.

'Nice top,' I say, sitting down.

Mum runs her hands down her black sparkly T-shirt, her face glowing at the compliment. 'Oh, thank you, love. Primarni's finest. Three ninety-nine. Can you believe it? I don't know how they manage the prices in there. I'm glad you like it. I bought it especially for today.'

Sometimes I envy how completely lacking in pride she is. Other times I feel sorry for her.

'Do you want a drink?'

'It's OK, love, I'll go and get one.'

I stand up. 'It's fine. I'll get it. What do you want?'

'A lemonade would be great. Thanks, love.'

I go to the bar to get Mum a drink, trying to formulate in my head what it is I want to say, and then anxiously return to the table.

Mum takes the glass from me. 'Thanks for this. And thanks for asking me to meet you. It made my day to get your text. Well, it made my year, to be honest.'

I nod, touched by her appreciation, but finding it hard to squash the resentment that resides permanently in my stomach.

'Look, I invited you here because I want to ask you some stuff. I want to hear things from your side.'

Mum's eyes anxiously survey the room. 'What is it, love?' She fidgets in her seat.

'I wanted to talk to you about when I was little. When you . . .'

I can feel Mum's leg jigging under the table.

'Mum, are you OK? Are you listening to me?'

'Of course I am.' But she doesn't look like she is. She looks distracted, her eyes repeatedly glancing over at the door.

'I want to talk to you about . . .'

Just before his name leaves my mouth, I see him coming into the pub. His hair's now densely peppered with grey and his face seems to have sagged, like all his features have fallen further down his face. He's still as fat; his beer belly hangs disgustingly over his corduroy trousers, which are being held below his hips by a brown leather belt.

My heart starts racing and I can't help it, as much as I hate to admit it, I feel scared. A huge part of me wants to sprint out the door, but I won't run away from him. He's not winning this time.

I look at Mum, unable to stop the tears forming in my eyes. 'Why would you bring him here?'

Mum reaches out and tries to grab my hand, but I pull it away. 'He wants to see you. To apologize. He just wants to help put things right between us.'

I can see in Mum's eyes that she really thinks this is going to make things better. I bet she begged and begged Shane to apologize until he reluctantly agreed just to shut her up. But she doesn't get it. It's not just him I hate for what he did.

When Shane arrives at the table, he looks me directly in the eye and smiles. It's the same obnoxious arrogant smile he's always given me and I know he hasn't changed one bit.

'All right, Em?' he says as he sits down next to Mum. He leans across to kiss me on the cheek but I swiftly move my head away. 'Well, nice to see you too.'

Shane puts his arm around Mum and kisses her on the lips, and she looks at him like he's a bloody newborn. All sappy-eyed. I want to slap her round the face. She nudges Shane in the side with her elbow.

'All right, all right, let me just get a beer first, will you?' He gestures to the waitress and she comes over. 'A pint of Stella, if you don't mind, gorgeous.' He flashes her his most charming smile and I realize I would feel no remorse if I killed him barehanded.

The waitress goes to get his beer and he turns his attention to me. 'Look, I am sorry I used to be a grumpy bastard and shout at you and shit. I was drinking too much, you know? I know it wasn't great. I wasn't as good to your mum as I should've been, I'll accept that, but I am now, aren't I, sweetheart?'

Mum nods repeatedly. 'He is. He really is, love. He really looks after me.'

The waitress comes over and puts Shane's beer on the table. He winks at her. The same stupid wink he used to give me when he sat across the dinner table from me or when he was sat on the opposite sofa with Mum. Like he was trying to make me complicit. Trying to make this our secret. But it wasn't my fucking secret.

'I'm really happy for you both.' I spit the words out, then grab my stuff and stand up. 'Take care, Mum.'

Mum clings on to my wrist. 'Please don't go yet. Let's just talk about it. Please, love.'

'Come on, Em,' Shane says. 'It was all just a laugh. There wasn't any malice in it.'

I sit back down, look directly at Shane and speak in a low voice. 'Turning around in the shower to see you staring at me and wanking off wasn't very fucking funny.'

As the words leave my mouth, it's like jumping into the sea, the waves washing over me and cleansing my skin.

Shane grabs my arm. 'Em, that's enough. You're talking bollocks.'

I yank my arm away from him. 'Don't you dare fucking touch me. You do not get to touch me any more, do you understand?'

'Look, you want to make stuff up about me, go ahead. I don't care if you don't like me. But you owe your mum some respect. None of this is her fault.'

I contemplate throwing my glass at his head. 'You

seriously think you can play the noble protector? You're a joke. You want to play happy families, go ahead, but leave me the fuck out of it. I'll tell you what's her fault. Choosing you. That's her fault. She could've stopped you. She could've told you to get the fuck out of our house. But she didn't.'

Shane sighs and shakes his head. When I look over at Mum, she has tears streaming down her face.

I look her right in the eyes and suddenly everything feels so much clearer. 'And you lied about Dad, didn't you? He didn't hit you.'

She looks down at her hands and I know that I'm right.

I turn my attention to Shane. Just looking at his vile face makes me sick. 'You wanted to keep him away from me because he would've killed you if he'd found out. So you gave her the bruises and then said it was him. He wanted to be my dad, didn't he?'

At this point I look back at Mum, but she won't meet my eyes.

Shane swipes his hand out in front of him. 'Oh, give it a rest, Em. That useless bastard didn't give a shit about you. You're lucky I stepped in and took you on. You should be thanking me.'

Mum's eyes are so fucking sad that somewhere beneath the rage I can't help but pity her. I want her to stand up, to scream at Shane to get away from her daughter. I want her to finally choose me. But as Shane puts his arm around her and she takes his hand in hers, I know that she never will. And that this will be the last time I ever see her.

'I do love you, Mum. I always will. Even after everything. But you will never accept what you did, so I can't ever forgive you.'

I walk to the door. I can hear Mum crying and calling my name but I don't turn around. The cold air hits my face and the tears feel warm as they slip down my cheeks. It's like jumping out of a plane. Now I've taken the leap, there's no looking back.

* * *

'Firstly, I want to say sorry for my little outburst the other week. I'm not sure half a bottle of vodka on an empty stomach really agreed with me. I wouldn't advise it, by the way.'

I'm relieved when everyone smiles.

'So, as it's the last session, I thought it was about time I tell you all why I'm here.'

They look like a circle of rabbits, ears pricked up in anticipation.

'I should've told you all earlier, but the truth is I was scared. And ashamed. I kept trying to tell myself that he deserved it, that me being sent here was this great injustice, but I think, deep down, I just felt guilty.'

I pause and Sam catches my eye. 'No one's going to think any less of you, Em. You're safe here.'

I chew my lip. 'I used to work in a pub. This guy was trying it on with me all night. Then I went out the back for a smoke and he followed me. He started trying to touch me and I told him to leave me alone but he didn't. He wouldn't stop.' I shake my head, unable to tell them exactly what I did. 'Anyway, the kid who washes the dishes came out and said I looked like I was about to kill him. In the end, it was my word against his and they concluded that I had an anger problem I needed to work on. So they sent me here.'

'No wonder you were angry about coming here,' Bill says, visibly incensed. 'They should've given you a pat on the back and a well done for what you did.'

I can't help it. I feel my eyes pricking with tears. 'Thank you, Bill. I'm starting to accept that it wasn't my fault. I didn't deserve it. But I did take it too far. And I *was* angry. They were right about that bit. You see, the thing is . . .'

I pause, and Sam and Jake both look at me as if they're wondering how much more I'm going to say. I'm not even sure myself.

Then the words start falling from my mouth. 'When I was about ten, my mum met this guy called Shane. He . . .'

Why is it so hard to say the word? But I need to. I need to be rid of it.

'He abused me.' I hear sharp intakes of breath but I don't look up. 'The first time it happened, I'd had a really bad nightmare. I still remember it now. Someone had cut off my head and I had to push it around this maze in a shopping trolley.' I smile at the absurdity of it, but then feel my face fall because I know what's coming next. 'I climbed into bed with Mum and Shane. I was in the middle. I'm not sure if I'd drifted off to sleep or not, but the next thing I knew, Shane had his hands down my pants.' I clench my teeth. 'So when that guy outside the pub started touching me, I just flipped. It's not an excuse, but it's what happened.'

I look up to see Sharon's eyes full of tears. She gives me a supportive smile and a subtle thumbs up.

'The thing that hurts the most is that my mum knew about it and she did nothing. This one Christmas, she was taking a photograph of us. She made us stand in front of

362

the tree. Shane put his arm around me and I tried to squirm away from him but he pulled me in tight. Then he started touching my breast, right in front of her. I slipped out from under his arm and ran upstairs. Mum never came up. She never even mentioned it. In fact, if anything, she seemed angry with me. Anyway, because of this group, I decided to confront her. But she wouldn't accept it. She stood by him. I guess he just means more to her than I do.'

'I'm sorry it didn't work out how you wanted it to, Em,' Sam says, after a long silence. 'But I hope coming here has had some positives.'

'It has. No offence, but I don't think the calming mantras and the breathing techniques are really going to work for me.'

Sam smiles.

'But I'm glad I came here. It's been good to listen to you all. I don't think I'm exactly fixed yet, but I hope I'm getting there. Thank you all for putting up with me and for being part of my journey.'

I offer a half-smile and sit back down. Sharon starts the clapping, and then they all join in, until the room is filled with rapturous applause and yelps of support. I can see Jake clapping out the corner of my eye, but I can't bring myself to look at his face.

*   *   *

'Em, hold on a minute, will you?' Sam says.

'Yeah, course. Not in trouble, am I?'

Sam smiles, then shakes his head. 'Actually, it's a good thing. Well, I hope it's a good thing. Now I sound arrogant. Sorry, this isn't going quite as I planned.'

'It's fine. What is it?'

'I was wondering if you would like to go for a drink with me?'

'Wow, that's a bit unexpected.'

'I'm sorry. Am I completely out of line?'

'No, not at all. I'm just surprised. Especially after my excruciatingly embarrassing behaviour in your car last week.'

'You don't have to be embarrassed. I just didn't want to take advantage of you being drunk. I wanted you to decide while sober if you wanted to go out with me.'

'Thank you.'

'So, do you? Want to go out with me, that is?'

I don't know what to say. 'See, the thing is, Sam . . .'

'You don't see me in that way? It's fine, you don't need to explain. I just thought I'd ask on the off-chance.'

'It's not you. You're lovely. I'm just not in any place to start anything new at the moment. It wouldn't be fair on you.'

Sam nods. 'I understand. You're still in love with Jake.'

I'm stunned that he's noticed. 'No, of course not. Why do you say that?'

'I've been in this job a long time, Em. You learn to read people pretty well. I just hoped I was mistaken on this occasion, but seriously, it's fine. I shouldn't have asked.'

'No, it's not that. Jake's back with his wife. This isn't about Jake.'

'OK. Sorry. It's really none of my business, anyway. Look, I'll let you go. It was lovely meeting you, Emily. I hope things continue to improve for you.'

'Please don't think it's you, Sam. Trust me, you've had a lucky escape.'

Sam shakes his head. 'Don't do that. Don't put yourself down. Whoever ends up with you will be a really lucky guy.'

He's so wonderfully kind that part of me thinks sod it, just go for a drink with him. But I've spent my life jumping from one doomed relationship to another. I don't want to do it again, and especially not with Sam. He's too good for that.

'Thank you. And I can definitely say the same about you – except girl, of course. She'll be one lucky girl.'

'Thanks, Em. Take care.' Sam kisses me on the cheek, turns away and starts to tidy his paperwork. When I leave the community centre, I can't help scouring the pavements for Jake, although I'd have nothing to say to him. But he's gone and, walking down the busy street, I feel achingly alone.

Jake

When I get to my classroom, there's a parcel on my desk with an envelope attached to the front. At the bottom of the envelope, it reads: *Please open me first.* I recognize her handwriting immediately.

There's only a quarter of an hour before the students come in, so I put the parcel in my rucksack and write the date on the whiteboard. I start to finalize my slide show but I can't help myself. I shut my laptop, open my bag and pull the letter off the front of the parcel.

Dear Jake,

Thank you for the details for Jemma's friend. I've contacted her now, so hopefully something may come of it. Thanks for thinking of me.

This is your Christmas present, well, yours and Alfie's, really. Don't worry, I don't expect anything in return. I've been working on it for a while so I thought you might as well still have it. Don't open it until Christmas Day, though – it's bad luck!

I realized after seeing you and Alfie at the park that I can't meet up with you for a while. Please explain to Alfie that it's not because I don't want to see him. Maybe you could tell him I've gone away with work for a little bit?

I'm sure you know how much I miss him so you should realize how much I just need some space. It sounds like something Sam

would say at group, but I really need some time to get my head
straight before I can see you both again. I hope that makes sense.
Have a wonderful Christmas.

Bye, Emily xx

I could see it at anger management, the change in her. The way she was shelving her past, us included, and moving on with her life. I wanted to tell her how proud I was of her. For having the guts to stand up and say what she did. I should've told her. But there's no use thinking like that now, because it's done. I have to let her go. To allow her to find someone who makes her happy, someone without all the baggage and complications. And I have to give Jemma a proper chance. Emily's right. Not seeing each other makes perfect sense, but knowing that I can't just makes me want to see her more.

* * *

Alfie marches up and down the lounge, constantly glancing at the clock on the wall. He looks like he's taken some strange concoction of drugs. His eyes are bloodshot and underlined with dark crescents because of the extreme lack of sleep he's had over the past few days and his movements are jittery, frantic. I want to help him out, but Jemma has this stupid rule that we can't open any presents under the tree until her parents arrive. He's had his stocking, which he tore through in record time, and, according to Jemma, that should be enough to keep him going.

'Can I just open one?' He looks up at me, imploring me to free him from his internal misery.

'They'll be here in ten minutes, little man. Come on, let's go and play that cool card game you got in your stocking and then the time will whizz past and they'll be here.'

Alfie shakes his head. He's still pacing the room. It's making me dizzy. 'No. I want to be able to see the clock. I can't concentrate on the clock if I'm playing the game.'

'Looking at the clock's not going to make the time go any quicker, Alfie. Come on, I'll even let you have that special card you like. The one where you get to swap cards with me.'

Alfie knits his eyebrows. He's considering it. I'm on the verge of victory. Then he shakes his head, his feet start stomping and he crosses his arms. We're on the brink of all the presents being picked up and launched at the walls.

'The big hand's not moving, Daddy. Why is it not moving? Go and get me Joker clock.'

I feel myself bristle but I can see he's not in the headspace for pleases and thank yous right now.

I go upstairs and hunt for his Joker clock. I spot it on the floor by his bed and, as I pick it up, it changes to 11:01. I know there's no more containing the situation. I feel like a lone policeman standing against an angry mob of protestors. I don't fancy my odds. I take the clock downstairs and hand it to Alfie, bracing myself for his reaction.

'You promised they'd be here at eleven o'clock. You lied.'

Here come the tears, the dramatic fall to the ground, the kicking legs. I leave Alfie fitting on the floor and go into the kitchen. Jemma is sprinkling 'ho ho ho' confetti over the dining-room table. She's wearing a tight-fitting black dress and looks beautiful – every part the Stepford wife celebrating a perfect family Christmas. Except that drowning out the sound of the Christmas carol CD she has playing is the sound of our son screaming, while tears and snot are inevitably being wiped over his neatly pressed Christmas shirt with matching bow tie. She looks up at me as I walk in and smiles, as if she can't hear him.

'I'm going to let him open his presents. It's gone eleven. He can't wait any longer.'

'They'll be two minutes. Just tell him they'll be two minutes. Please, Jake.'

'No, I'm sorry, Jem, but it's just not fair on him. He's losing his mind in there.'

I don't wait for her to argue. I walk back through to the lounge and pick Alfie up. He struggles until I plonk him in front of the Christmas tree and hand him a present.

'Go ahead, little man. Time to open your presents.'

His face is such a mixture of shock and delight, I can't help but smile. He doesn't wait for me to change my mind. Instead, he starts ripping off the wrapping paper.

'A book.' He can't hide the disappointment on his face, but he tries his best by painting on a big smile and it makes me love him that little bit more than I already did.

'Yeah, I think it's a mystery. You know you love solving mysteries.'

'Can I open another one?'

I laugh. 'Of course.' I point to a present under the tree. 'That one doesn't look very book-shaped.'

He takes the paper off to reveal a foam sword. His eyes sparkle and he starts swiping at me and saying 'ah-har' in his best pirate voice.

At this point I hear Jemma's parents coming in through

the front door, Jemma subserviently taking their coats and offering them elaborate drinks.

When they come into the living room, Wendy's eyes survey Alfie working his way through his pile of gifts, then she turns to glare at me. 'I thought you might at least wait until we arrived before you started opening presents.'

'I did tell them that,' Jemma calls from the kitchen.

'Actually, he did wait. He waited really well, even though he was desperate to get started, but you said you were coming at eleven o'clock, so when it got to eleven, he couldn't wait any longer.'

Wendy looks at her watch. 'It's only ten minutes, Jake. It's not a big deal to wait an extra ten minutes, surely?'

'See, the thing is, Wendy, for a child with autism, that extra ten minutes *is* a big deal. It's unbearable.'

Wendy lifts her chin and swats the air with her hand, as if autism is a bad smell she wants to waft away. 'Well, next time we'll make sure we get here exactly on time.'

'Or perhaps we could just ignore the arbitrary Christmas law and allow the poor kid to open his presents whenever he wants to. That'd save a lot of stress for everyone involved,' I say, handing Alfie another present.

Jemma walks in holding a tray of drinks and I can tell from her eyes that she's overheard everything and is pleading with me to play nice, but I'm done trying to impress her parents. I'll never be good enough for Jemma in their eyes, but I realize now that they're not good enough for Alfie in mine.

The rest of the present opening goes pretty smoothly, as Jemma and I had ensured we got all of the things Alfie has been obsessing about since the end of the summer holidays.

Jemma's parents present me with a bag of gifts carefully chosen to highlight each one of my inadequacies – a smart shirt and tie, a drill, a set of kitchen knives and the last one, the real killer, a voucher for Toni & Guy. My hair is my thing. It's supposed to look untamed. That's the style.

I force a smile and offer over-the-top thanks for the shit gifts. There's an hour or so of relative calm. When I say relative calm, that does include being shot every few minutes with the Nerf gun Alfie has been badgering me about every day for the past six weeks, but he's happy and he's not having a tantrum or demanding stuff of me, so all is well (other than the fact I have to listen to Jemma's parents wittering on about their amazing house renovations and their latest holiday to Antigua, where they had private waiter service).

After a fairly brutal attack on me, Alfie turns the gun on Richard. It's a great shot. Hits him right in the chest. As the foam bullet falls to Richard's lap, he looks at it like a golden pixie has just tumbled from the sky.

Jemma comes over to Alfie and grasps his shoulders. 'No, Alfie. You do not shoot Grandpa; do you understand?' Then she looks at me and seems to remind herself to be more gentle. 'You might hurt him, mightn't you?'

Richard picks up the bullet and hands it back to Alfie. 'Now I'm sure you didn't really aim that at me, little chap, but just be careful from now on, hey? I don't want to have to take it off you now, do I?'

His passive aggressive tone makes me want to take Alfie's gun and shoot him at point-blank range. Alfie looks over to me as if to say 'shall I do it again, Dad?' and I have to force myself to be a responsible parent.

'Come on, little man. Just shoot it at me, OK? I can take it.'

I flex my muscles like Popeye and Alfie laughs. Jemma goes back to sit beside her mum and they coo over the jewellery they bought for each other.

'Why did you get that silly gun for him in the first place?' Wendy chimes in. 'It's not exactly going to help with his aggression.'

I hate how she talks like she knows the first thing about him. 'It wasn't us, Wendy. He got that in his stocking. It was from Santa, so it was out of our hands, I'm afraid.'

Wendy rolls her eyes at me. I can't help but take great pleasure in irritating her.

Alfie lingers in the corner for a moment, loading his gun. He looks a bit crazed, his blond hair sticking out at all angles, his eyes wired, the mixture of excitement and exhaustion finally taking its toll. Time to start damage control.

'How about I look after your gun for a minute and you go and get that special present you made for Mummy at school?'

Alfie's reluctant to hand over his gun but excited enough about his surprise to go with it. He runs upstairs and comes charging back in with the clay pot he has made, wrapped in tissue paper.

'Here you are, Mummy.' He knocks the present Wendy's just given Jemma out of her hands and replaces it with his.

'Hold on a minute, Alfie. I'm just opening Grandma's present first.' Jemma retrieves the extravagantly wrapped present off the floor and begins opening it.

'No, Mummy, do mine first. I made it all by myself.' Alfie puts his present back on top of Wendy's.

'Just wait a minute, darling. I'm really looking forward to opening it, but you just need to wait one minute, OK?'

Alfie barges in between Jemma and Wendy, knocking the sherry glass in Wendy's hand, and the deep-red liquid splashes up on to her pale floral blouse.

'Alfie, what have you done?' Wendy shrieks, then rushes to the bathroom, with Jemma following behind.

'Mummy, you haven't opened my present,' Alfie shouts, heading out the door after her.

Before he gets there, Richard grabs hold of his arm, tight enough to make Alfie wince, and then he pulls Alfie towards him so that their faces are nearly touching.

'Look here, son,' he says, his eyes locked intimidatingly on Alfie's. 'You need to go and apologize to your grandma right this second. Do you hear me?'

Alfie wriggles free and runs up to his room, thumping the wall as he goes.

I stand up. 'He's not your son. He's mine. And if you ever touch him again, I'll kill you.'

It's a little too much, I know, but I can't stand the guy at the best of times and I know how much his scolding will have upset Alfie. I race up to Alfie's room, but I can't get in.

'Alfie, it's Daddy. Let me in.'

Alfie hits the door hard, hopefully not with his head. 'I want to be on my own.'

'OK, but I know it was just an accident. You didn't mean to upset Grandma. I'm not cross with you.'

'Just go away.'

I know that he's feeling scared and confused and that

he just wants to shut the world out, but I suddenly think of something that might help. I go into my bedroom and pull out the box under my bed. It's my man box, full of old surf mags, cufflinks and watches that no longer work – a place I know Jemma will never look. I extract Emily's parcel and take it with me to Alfie's door.

'Emily sent us a present. Do you want to open it with me?'

There's a shuffle of things on the other side of the door and then it opens.

'Come on, little man. Let's sit on your bed and open this.'

We pull the cover up over our legs and I let Alfie rip off the brown paper. Underneath, there's a layer of Christmas wrapping paper.

Alfie laughs and starts tearing at it. 'It's like pass the parcel.'

I smile, but my heart feels heavy as I catch a glimpse of the leather album beneath the paper and realize what Emily's present is going to be. Alfie removes the last bit of wrapping paper and opens the photo album.

'Look, it's me! That was when we went to the park in the pouring rain. It was so fun. Look at the raindrop on my nose.'

Alfie points at the picture of him, standing at the top of the climbing frame, dripping wet, his face full of nothing but glee. Then he turns the pages, slowly at first but then more quickly, and my breathing feels laboured. The photos are beautiful. I knew Emily was talented, but these images are something else. And every one captures Alfie, just as he is. Whenever we try to take a photo of him, he hides or pulls a strange face. It's his attempt at a smile, but he can't quite connect his mouth and his brain so he

374

always ends up looking odd. But Emily's snapped him when he's not looking or when he's so full of joy that his face is full of it too. And there are photos of him and me too. And we're happy. We're really happy.

When I get to the last picture, it feels like being winded. It's a selfie of Emily and Alfie. He's got his arms around her neck and is peering over her shoulder and both of their eyes are watering from laughing so much.

'Look, it's Emily.' Alfie rubs his fingers across Emily's face. 'Can we call her, Daddy? Can we take her a present? I could make her one out of Lego.'

I desperately want to call her too, but I owe it to her to respect her wishes.

'She's had to go away for a little while, Alfie, and her phone doesn't work there, but she says she can't wait to see you when she gets back.'

Alfie looks wounded and continues to stare at the photograph of her.

'What are you both doing?' Jemma's voice startles me as she appears in the doorway.

Alfie scrambles out of bed and holds the album up to her. 'Look, Mummy, it's lots of photos of me. And Daddy. And there's one of Emily.'

Jemma nods slowly, as if realizing something very important.

'It's his Christmas present from Emily. I was just trying to calm him down for a while. It was all getting a bit much downstairs.'

Jemma sighs. 'Yeah, I'm sorry it got a little bit heated. I got the sherry off Mum's top. She's borrowed one of mine for now. It actually looks better on her than it does on me.' Jemma smiles. 'They're going to stay for Christmas lunch and then they're going to go so that we can have a bit of family time, just the three of us.'

I know that she's trying her best to put things right. In the past, she never would've apologized. In fact, somehow, she would've blamed me. And, usually, pleasing her parents would be the focal point of her day. There's no way she would've asked them to leave early.

'Sounds good.'

Alfie pulls Jemma down to sit on the bed and starts showing her all the photographs, talking in detail about each one. Jemma paints on her best enthusiastic expression, but her eyes just look sad.

'Wow, Alfie, look at all the fun things you did when I was away.'

Before they get to the end, I pull the album away. 'Come on, let's go downstairs. I'm starving and the food smells great.'

Jemma looks up at me and I wonder if she knows I'm trying to protect her.

'But I want to show Mummy all of them.'

'We will. But first, we need to get to the table before Grandma and Grandpa pull all the crackers without us.'

Alfie glances at the album in my hands and then looks out the door. 'Quick, they might have done them already.'

And then he's off. I put Emily's present on the bed and guide Jemma out of the room with me.

* * *

I'm lying on the bed reading the surf magazine Jemma got me for Christmas. I'm not sure why I do it to myself.

Pages and pages of waves I'll never get to enjoy and adventures I no longer have time to experience.

The bathroom door opens and I look up, expecting to see Jemma in her usual flannel pyjamas, hair tied back, make-up removed and moisturizer on. Instead, she's wearing a red lacy corset and a Santa hat.

'Merry Christmas, baby,' she says in her sexiest voice.

I know I'm supposed to be turned on, but I've never really been one for dressing up and it just feels too much. I'm not sure if I want to laugh or hide.

She crawls up the bed, pushing her chest out in front of her, takes my magazine off me and throws it to the floor. Then she puts her weight on my chest so that my head slides down the headboard and she straddles me.

'I told you I'd got you one more special present,' she says, kissing my neck.

To be honest, I was hoping for a surprise holiday to the Alps or at least the Fitbit I've been dropping hints about for weeks. This is very much unexpected. And not entirely desired. But then I look in her eyes and she looks so fragile, so desperate for me to reciprocate some of her affection, that I know that, unless I'm certain I want to say goodbye to my marriage for good, I can't make any more excuses.

I roll Jemma on to her side and kiss her. It's more of a peck than a kiss – it's over before it's begun. So I do it again, trying to get lost in the physical sensations, the feel of her hands on my body, her soft lips, her smooth skin.

Afterwards, I lie back on the bed and Jemma rests her head on my chest, neither of us daring to speak. Looking down at her body lying against mine, it occurs to me that

I know every part of her, every mole, the exact texture of her hair, the tempo of her resting heartbeat. We've been together so long, shared so much. Surely there's a return route to where we once were. How hard can it be to fall back in love with your wife?

Emily

I put the flowers I've bought on Nan's grave and a cactus on Dad's. I'm not sure why I went for a cactus. I picked up daisies first, but then I saw the prickly potted plant and it just seemed a bit more manly.

I never thought I would, but I like coming here. I still never say anything out loud, but occasionally in my head I'll have a little chat to them both. Tell them what I've been up to. And I always imagine my nan shouting down, 'WHY ARE YOU TALKING TO AN INANIMATE OBJECT, YOU PLONKER?' And it always makes me smile.

As I leave the graveyard and walk back down the lane to my car, I think I hear Alfie's voice. It's not unusual. I think I hear it a lot. But then I look into the field next to the churchyard and there he is, playing football. Jake's in goal and Jemma's running along beside Alfie.

'Pass the ball.'

Alfie ignores his mum, charges ahead and kicks the ball towards the goal. It sneaks past Jake's fingers and he falls to the ground theatrically, putting his hands on his head.

'Goal!' Alfie shouts and runs up to Jemma, jumping up and giving her a high five. Then he runs over and jumps on Jake, bouncing up and down on his tummy.

Jemma follows him over, pulls Alfie off and helps Jake up. Then she puts her arm around Jake's waist and kisses him on the cheek.

It's hard not to stay and watch, like when you drive past a car crash on a motorway, but I force myself to walk back to my car, with a stabbing pain in my chest and a sudden realization that I can't do this. Living here, it's like having Alfie and Jake in surround sound and three-sixty vision. I can't get over them like this. So, as soon as I get home, I open my laptop and google 'nice places to live as far away as possible from Gloucestershire'.

* * *

Alice walks into the bar wearing skinny jeans, a skintight body and killer heels.

'Wow, you look amazing!'

She does a twirl. 'It's very rare I get a pass for a proper night out. I'm going to make the most of it.'

'Well, you're certainly dressed to impress.'

She raises her hand and the barman struts over. 'A bottle of Prosecco, please. Two glasses.'

'Coming right up.' The barman pops the cork and pours us our drinks, putting the rest of the bottle in an ice-cooler.

'I was like a dairy cow earlier. Pumped enough of the good stuff to last Billy until he's sixteen, I reckon, so I can drink to my heart's content tonight.'

The barman looks terrified and we both laugh.

'So how's the business going?' Alice says, taking a large gulp of her drink. 'It looks like you're doing great. How many likes has your page got now?'

'Four hundred and eighty-seven, not that I keep checking or anything.'

'Well, the photos you've put on there are amazing, Em. You are so talented. I always told you that.'

'Thank you.'

Alice leans back, mock-startled. 'I'm sorry, did Emily Davies just accept a compliment without batting it back? You've changed.'

'Ha.'

'And the one about whom we should not talk? How are you feeling about him?'

I fiddle with my nails. 'I'm getting there.'

'Good. You're better off without him.'

'Yeah, I guess. Look, Al, I need to tell you something and you're not going to like it, but I promise I will still see you all the time and call.'

Alice's face fills with concern. 'What is it?'

'I'm moving to South Devon.'

'South Devon? Why the hell are you moving there? Please tell me you've met a gorgeous millionaire who's asked you to go and live with him in his seafront mansion because, if not, there is no way I'm letting you go.'

'Unfortunately not. I just need a fresh start.'

'This is Jake's fault, isn't it? I'm going to go to his house and cut off his penis.'

I smile. 'It's not his fault. I just realized that I've never been anywhere. You went off to uni. You had adventures. I've spent the past twenty-five years stuck in the same town, working the same crappy jobs. I'd like to live by the sea. Meet new people.'

'Thanks very much.'

'You know I'll never meet anyone like you.'

'Well, that's a given.' Alice reaches out and grasps my hand. 'Are you really sure about this?'

I nod, even though I'm still full of doubt.

'OK. If you think it'll make you happy, then I have to support your decision, but I can't say I'm not absolutely gutted.'

'I know. I don't want to leave you. But I think I need to do this. You'll have to put up with having me as a regular house guest, though.'

'That's cool. You can sleep in Billy's room. As long as you don't mind listening to me and Ben making wild frantic love in the room next to you.'

I slap Alice's arm. 'Don't be disgusting.'

Alice empties her glass. 'Well, I suppose we better make this a night to remember then. Come on, lady. Let's get those shots in.'

'We haven't finished this bottle of Prosecco yet.'

She looks at my almost-full glass. 'Drink up, then.'

I push my glass towards her. 'Actually, I'm taking a break from it for a while. I didn't want to worry you so I haven't said anything, but it was getting a bit out of hand.'

Alice looks alarmed. 'Why didn't you tell me? Shall I not drink either, then? I can give this to someone else, if you want?'

'No. I insist. You go ahead. I will not be happy unless you're passed out on the pavement by the end of the night.'

'Sure?'

I nod.

'OK then.' Alice starts on my glass and then, after drinking almost the whole thing, she puts it back on the bar. 'Right, keep an eye on this Prosecco for me, will you?' she asks the barman. 'We're going to have a dance.'

'Are we?'

'We are.' Alice takes my hand and pulls me on to the dance floor.

It's not really a dance floor, just a bit of space around the DJ deck, and it's still quite early so we're the only ones brave, or devoid of pride, enough to step on to it. The DJ's playing some terrible grime music and it's impossible to catch a beat so we just throw our arms in the air and pump them like we're holding glow sticks.

All of the trendy and sophisticated people sitting at the tables, having just popped in for a quick one after a day schmoozing clients in their important jobs, stare at us and whisper to each other, but we don't care, we just keep on dancing, or doing the thing we're doing that's not really dancing at all.

When we're hot, bothered and our feet are hurting us, we return to the bar. Alice tops up her glass of Prosecco and then calls the barman over. 'I'd like a Slippery Nipple, please. And don't worry, I'm not talking about mine this time.'

The barman looks decidedly uncomfortable, but pours Alice a shot. As he does so, two blokes saunter over, standing either side of us and sandwiching us in the middle.

'I'll get that for you in exchange for a kiss,' the bloke next to Alice says, putting his arm around her shoulder. He's clearly wasted and looks like he's using her to help hold himself up.

She puts her left hand in front of his face. 'I'm flattered, but I'm married.'

'That's not necessarily a problem.'

'Except it is, because we believe in this strange concept called monogamy. I'm not sure if you've heard of it, but it's actually pretty cool. You should give it a go some time.'

The guy smirks and returns to his table, leaving his friend alone to try his luck with me.

'How about you? I don't see a ring on your finger.'

'You're very observant.'

'It's hard not to study every part of you like you're a code I'm trying to crack.'

I can feel Alice giggling beside me and have to bite my lip. Then her phone starts ringing.

'It's Ben. I'll be back in a second.'

She goes outside to take the call and leaves me with Mr Smooth. 'So are you going to let me buy you a drink?'

I look at the stash of alcohol behind the bar, calling to me like a witch trying to put me under her spell. Then I return my eyes to his relatively handsome face, wondering what it would be like to wake up to it, rather than the glare of my empty pillow. And I immediately know that both things would ultimately make me feel worse, not better.

'I don't drink, but thank you. I hope you have a good night.'

He looks like I just told him I'm part of a religious cult, and hurries back to his friend. As I order a Diet Coke, Alice returns from outside.

'I'm so sorry, Em, but Billy will not sleep without me. Ben's been walking him around for the past three hours because he didn't want to ruin our night, but Billy just won't stop screaming. I'm going to have to go and save him.'

'No problem. I totally understand.'

'So do you want to share a taxi or are you staying out a bit longer?'

'I'll come home with you.'

Alice looks surprised. 'Good.'

While we wait for the taxi to arrive, we finish our drinks and then head back to the dance floor. The DJ's playing the R 'n' B part of his set so we gyrate and wind our bodies in the way the music encourages, giggling and holding each other's hands, and I wish for the thousandth time that I could take Alice with me.

In the taxi, she lies with her head in my lap, looking up at me. 'I feel sick.'

'I need a wee.'

'Remember the time we went for a wee at the back of that pub thinking we were hidden only to look up and see those builders in their van laughing at us? They got a right show, dirty buggers.'

I smile at the memory and play with one of Alice's curls. 'I miss Alfie.'

She touches my hand. 'I know you do.'

'And I know you think he's a prick, but I miss Jake too. I really do.'

'You'll meet someone better, Em, I promise.'

'I hope so. I wasn't even sure I wanted it, you know, the husband, the two-point-four children. But I think maybe I do.'

'You'll find it. Don't worry.'

I lean across to look out of the windscreen. 'Are we even going the right way? It seems to be taking a long time.'

The red numbers on the screen in the front already say thirteen pounds twenty.

'He probably thinks we're pissed and is taking advantage of the fact by driving us round in circles.'

'Well, he'll be sorry when I wee on his seat.'

Alice lifts up her head. 'Just don't get it on my hair, will you?'

The taxi driver clears his throat. 'Um, excuse me, but I am a reputable taxi driver and I would never take advantage of my passengers being in an inebriated state just to make more revenue. And please be aware that urinating on the upholstery carries a hundred-pound charge to cover cleaning costs.'

Alice and I both try to stifle our giggles but they come out as loud splutters.

'Do you think he swallowed a dictionary?'

The car pulls up outside my flat. 'Right, this is me. Hope Billy sleeps for you.'

Alice sits up and wraps her arms around me. 'Love you, Em. If you really feel that moving away is what you need, we'll make it work, OK? You'll still always be my best friend.'

'And you mine. Always.'

When I go into my flat, I take my box out of the wardrobe and pull out the one photo of Alfie that I kept, him holding out a Lego camera that he made me. The thought of never seeing him again makes me feel like I'm about to have a panic attack, like I might actually keel over from the pain. But I don't want to visit him once in a blue moon, to watch him slowly drifting away, caring that little bit less each time I see him. I want to be in the centre of it. I want the whole thing. Before meeting Alfie and Jake, it didn't even seem possible. That I too could have what everyone else seems to have, what Alice has. They opened my eyes and now I can't close them. I can't unsee. Who knows if I'll ever find it again, but I know I have to at least look.

Jake

'You're right. It's PDA. I mean, they don't officially diagnose that in this county, so on your report it'll say something like ASD with a demand avoidance profile, but you'll know what it means. I'll also mention the OCD stuff. At this age, it's sometimes hard to separate the anxiety-triggered behaviours associated with autism and the more distinct OCD symptoms, but ultimately it all comes down to the same thing – the need to control your environment – and quite often these conditions are co-morbid.'

Dr Ambusha looks at me like he's waiting for me to say something, but I don't know what to say. I look over at Jemma and she has tears in her eyes but her lips form a wide smile. She meets my eyes, grips my hand and then turns back to the doctor.

'Thank you so much. It's wonderful, isn't it, Jake? We're so happy, aren't we?'

I nod my head slightly but don't say anything. I don't feel happy. I really thought I would. When I pictured this moment, I thought my reaction would be just like Jemma's. But it's quite the opposite. I'm strangely devastated.

'It can be a lot to take in. I have to say I don't like slapping labels on children of Alfie's age, but I think ultimately it's all about giving you a greater understanding and enabling you to feel confident to adopt the suggested strategies. I'll give you the details of some support groups and also refer you to a specialist for the intrusive thoughts. Hopefully, Alfie, and you, will start to get the help you need.'

Jemma looks at me again. 'Thank you. We're so grateful, aren't we, Jake?' When I don't respond, she turns back to Dr Ambusha. 'We've waited such a long time for this. For so long we've been judged and dismissed and told we're just bad parents. So this is amazing, it really is. Thank you.'

Except it doesn't feel amazing. When I first read about PDA, I felt relieved. That there was a reason behind Alfie's behaviour. That I wasn't entirely to blame. In many ways it's been liberating – researching the symptoms to understand him better, adopting the strategies – but hearing the 'official' diagnosis, I suddenly realize I'd rather it *was* my fault.

I don't want my son to have to live with this for the rest of his life. I don't want the tiny challenges everyone has to face on a daily basis to be like mountains for him to climb. There are enough bloody mountains in this life as it is. Will Alfie ever get married? Have children? Will he ever find anyone who can understand him, who can see beyond his condition?

Jemma touches me on the shoulder and I realize she's already standing up and ready to go.

Dr Ambusha reaches across the table and shakes my hand. His handshake is so much stronger than mine and as I remove my hand, the fingers hurting, I see the photo on his desk. Him and his wife with their three boys. Three tall, strapping, perfect boys.

'You know, Mr Edwards,' he says, following my gaze, 'it might not always feel like it, but there are lots of positives

to this condition. Children with PDA are often very creative, imaginative, passionate, determined; they have a great
sense of humour. The key is discovering how to channel
these strengths to capture their interest, reduce anxiety
and promote positive engagement with others.'

I nod.

'Take care of yourselves. It's not easy doing what you're
doing.'

* * *

In the car, Jemma crosses her arms, turns her head to the
side and sighs loudly in a clear effort to show me she's
pissed off. I'm tempted to ignore it, but I give in.

'So what have I done to annoy you?'

Jemma makes a noise with her lips, like a horse – I'm
pretty sure it means 'are you seriously going to pretend
you don't know?' but I wait for her to clarify.

'Why did you act like such an idiot in there? He's the
first professional who has really listened, who's finally
given us what we've been waiting for all this time, and
you couldn't even say thank you.'

'I just didn't feel very thankful, Jem. I'm sorry that I'm
not jumping up and down in quite the same way you are but
I just don't think it's wonderful that our son is autistic.'

I deliberately use the exact term, not the acronym, not
the wishy-washy 'special needs'. Those all seem to mini-
mize it, to cover the condition in a soft veil.

'He's not typically autistic, Jake. He has pathological
demand avoidance. It's very different.'

I snort. 'If it makes you feel better to give it a different
name, do so, but he's on the spectrum, Jem.'

389

'But we knew that, didn't we? You're the one that told me about all the PDA stuff in the first place. I thought you'd accepted it.'

'So did I.'

'Look, try to see the positives. Finally, other people will recognize what we've been going through and can help us, instead of telling us what an awful job we're doing.'

I shake my head. 'You think we're suddenly going to get all this help, but they can't wave a magic wand and change him. He's always going to be like he is. It's never going to get any better.'

This is our life now. We will always have to prepare him in advance for every eventuality of everything we do, wc will havc to live our lives ruled by his obsessions, his need to control everything around him. I'll always feel suffocated and exasperated and now I'll also feel extreme guilt for feeling that way. Because he can't help it, and it must be even worse for him, living with that sort of anxiety.

Jemma reaches over and puts her hand on my thigh. 'It will get better, Jake. They can teach us techniques. They can work with him. I know they can't change him completely. Of course I wouldn't want them to. But I'm sure they can help to improve things. Come on, this is a good day. Try to be happy.'

Her hand feels too hot. I want to get out of the car. 'I'm sorry. You're right.'

Jemma moves her hand away and looks out of the window. 'I think we should invite Emily to dinner. To say thank you. Without her, we'd never have got the diagnosis.'

At the mention of Emily's name, I feel a flutter in my

chest. I definitely do not want to have dinner with Emily and my wife. It feels like a test that I'm not sure I can pass. But, God, do I want to see her.

'Well, um, I'm not sure . . .' How can I explain to Jemma that Emily doesn't want to see me? 'I'll ask her. See what she says. I'm sure Alfie would love to see her.'

Jemma fiddles with her seat belt and I already know what she's going to say next. 'Perhaps we should do it after Alfie's in bed. Then we can talk properly without him monopolizing Emily's time.'

'Sure.'

'Great. If you sort out which night suits her, I'll cook that duck in plum sauce that I do. She's not vegetarian, is she?'

'No. That sounds good. I'll give her a ring when we get home.'

Jemma studies me and it feels like she has Superman's X-ray vision and can see my rapidly beating heart straight through my skin.

* * *

I try on a selection of tops and then settle on my favourite short-sleeved navy Farah shirt. I run a small amount of some supposed wonder cream through my hair – apparently it styles, holds, nourishes and prevents your hair from falling out – then spray aftershave on to my neck and across my chest.

When I walk into the dining room, Jemma is setting the table using the 'special' tableware that we used to use for dinner parties but haven't got out for years. She is wearing her ridiculously expensive tight-fitting black-and-white dogtooth dress. I know it was ridiculously expensive because I remember sitting in bed with my laptop on my knee asking her why eight hundred pounds had mysteriously been taken out of our joint account. She'd gone red, giggled, taken a shiny carrier bag from the top of the wardrobe and taken it into the bathroom with her. A minute or so later, she'd emerged in the dress and, before I'd had time to give her a lecture about sensible spending, she'd hoicked it up and pounced on me. I can't help thinking her wearing it tonight is an intentional reminder of that occasion and possibly a thinly shrouded act of one-upmanship towards Emily.

'You look great.'

At the sound of my voice, Jemma turns around and there's such gratitude in her eyes that I wish there'd been more feeling behind what I said. I walk over to her and kiss her on the cheek.

'And the table looks amazing. The food smells delicious. You really didn't have to go to all this effort. It's only Emily. She won't . . .'

I'm about to say she won't care about any of this, that she's not interested in image or pretence, but I know that will make Jemma feel I'm saying she shouldn't care about any of this too.

'Emily won't expect it, but it's lovely,' I continue. 'I'm sure she'll appreciate the effort you've gone to. It's a really thoughtful gesture. Thank you.'

I hug her and then help her to finish laying the table.

By the time Emily arrives, I've worked my way through my first beer. She knocks on the door and Jemma almost leaps off the sofa.

'You stay there. I'll get it.'

I'm not sure why she's so desperate to get the door, but I'm more than happy to avoid an awkward conversation with Emily in the hallway.

'Welcome. Come on in. Can I take your jacket? Do you want a glass of wine?'

Jemma sounds like she's on a first date. I want to tell her to rein it in, not to sound so eager to please.

'Thank you. I'm driving, but a soft drink would be great.'

It feels weird to hear the sound of Emily's voice in our house again. It makes me realize how much I've missed it. I didn't think she was going to come. She didn't answer her phone at first and then when she did, she seemed desperate to hurry me off the line. When I told her Jemma wanted to make her dinner to thank her for all her help with Alfie, she went quiet and I thought she was using the time to fabricate an excuse, but then she agreed to come.

'Schloer?'

'Perfect. Thanks.'

They walk into the kitchen and I can just about hear snippets of conversation – about the weather, the food, how lovely the house is. I can imagine it's killing Emily, with her aversion to small talk.

When I join them, Emily is sitting at the breakfast bar with her back to me while Jemma puts the finishing touches to the meal. Emily's wearing skinny jeans and a grey turtlenecked jumper and it makes Jemma look like she's dressed for an interview.

'I was just about to call you. I'm plating up,' Jemma says.

Emily looks over her shoulder and, for a minute, it's like Jemma's not even in the room. 'All right, Jake?'

'Yeah, I'm OK. It's nice to see you.'

Before Emily has a chance to respond, Jemma takes off her oven gloves and strides through the middle of us carrying two plates of steaming food.

'Right, dinner's served.'

At the table, the three of us exchange uneasy glances, as if we are all waiting for someone else to be the first to talk. After a while, Jemma accepts the challenge.

'So what sort of things did you two get up to while I was away?'

'Uh, well, we didn't see each other much as you were working, weren't you, Jake?' Emily looks over at me and her eyes seem to be pleading with me to help her out.

'Ships that passed in the night.' I laugh awkwardly.

Jemma's eyes dart from me to Emily. 'I meant you and Alfie.'

Emily's face turns a telltale red. 'Oh, sorry. Of course. Well, as you know, with Alfie, it's all about the Lego really.'

Jemma nods, finishing her mouthful. 'Yep, he loves that Lego.'

'We started making these stop-motion films. It was just for fun, really – they're not exactly masterpieces – but he seemed to enjoy it.'

'Yeah, he's shown me all of them. About fifty times.' Jemma laughs but there's more than a hint of hostility in it. 'Like you say, they're not going to win any film awards, but he's proud of them.'

For a few minutes, none of us speak. It's so quiet I can hear myself chewing the duck. It's perfectly cooked, of course, and the sauce is as good as anything you'd get in a restaurant. It puts my roast to shame.

Jemma sets down her cutlery. 'So we invited you here to say thank you for helping us to get the diagnosis.'

Emily holds up her hands and shakes her head dismissively. 'You really don't have to thank me. I just happened to be watching the right programme at the right time.'

'And you managed to convince my stubborn husband here to consider it. That's no mean feat, I know. I'd been trying to tell him something wasn't right since Alfie was a baby.'

Emily shifts her weight in her seat and offers an awkward smile. 'He didn't listen to me either. I think I just planted the seed, but like Alfie, you're not going to be told what to think, are you, Jake?'

I can physically feel the animosity in the room building and I can't help feeling I'm the target.

'Mind you, you are quite impulsive, aren't you?' Jemma says. 'You tend to jump on new things, get all excited about them for a short time and then forget about them weeks later. Hopefully you won't do that with the PDA stuff though, of course.'

What Jemma's saying doesn't even make sense and I wonder what point she is trying to make. 'No, I don't.'

'You do. Like paddleboarding. I spent all that money on getting you the equipment and then you only went about twice.'

'I just never had any free time.'

'And *Breaking Bad*, remember how obsessed you were with it?' Jemma turns to Emily. 'Seriously, he was like Alfie, going on and on about it. We had to watch an episode a night without fail, didn't we, Jake? Then suddenly you just gave up on it.'

'The third season wasn't as good,' I say, exasperation making my voice louder than I intended.

Why is she being like this? I don't understand. But as soon as everyone has finished their food, I look for an out.

'I fancy going out to build a fire. If either of you want to join me, you're very welcome.'

The two women look at each other, waiting for the other to either accept or decline my offer first. Finally, Jemma shakes her head.

'I hate the cold. And let's face it, you're not the best at lighting fires. Do you want dessert, Emily? I'm afraid it's shop-bought, but it looks pretty good. Chocolate cheesecake?'

'Sounds great, thanks.'

'Jake?'

'I might save mine until later, I think. I'm stuffed.' I rub my stomach in the universal gesture of being full. 'You ladies enjoy.'

Then I'm out of there, terrified about what they're going to say to each other while I'm away but desperate to escape.

After about twenty minutes, Emily comes out to join me. She sits down on the bench opposite me by my meagre fire. Within a few minutes, her teeth begin to chatter, like those wind-up plastic mouths.

'I'm sorry, my fire's shit. I'm trying my best. Do you want to go back inside?'

Emily shakes her head. 'You need to stop putting that wet stuff on. It's just dampening it every time you start to get it going.'

'Well, I didn't know you were such a fire expert. Here you go.' I hand her my pile of kindling, twigs and newspapers.

'There's a lot you don't know about me.' She rolls the newspaper and places it carefully on the fire, followed by the kindling, tossing the damp twigs on to the decking. The fire starts to blaze.

'So what other delightful things was Jemma saying about me while I was out here?'

'Nothing. It's not all about you, you know?'

'I know. I just thought . . .' But then I see from Emily's face that she's teasing me.

'We were just talking about Alfie. The PDA. Nothing bad.'

I poke at the fire with a stick and it immediately starts to fade. 'You know, I'm scared I'm not getting things right with Alfie without you around. I keep thinking, *What would Emily do?* But I'm nowhere near as good as you are with him. He misses you. I mean, Jemma's trying. She really is. But he misses you like crazy.'

And so do I.

'I'm sure you're doing a fantastic job. I'm no expert. I guess I just tried to give him the benefit of the doubt whenever I could. But you know what you're doing.'

'I hope you're right.'

'I'm always right, remember?' And there it is. Her beautiful smile. 'Besides, the diagnosis should help. You should start getting the support you deserve.'

I nod and I can tell by Emily's face that she knows exactly what I'm feeling without me saying a thing.

'It's not a life sentence, you know? Yes, he'll always

have the condition and it will bring with it its challenges, but it also makes him amazing and driven and sensitive. He'll see the world a different way to other people, but it might just make it all the more beautiful.'

I love how she sees Alfie. I always want to see Alfie through her eyes.

'I'm not sure I'm the right person to be his dad. When we got the diagnosis, part of me was gutted for him, but I think a big part of me was also gutted for me. I'm a selfish arsehole, Em. He deserves someone like you.'

'Probably,' she teases. 'But he's stuck with you, so you best stop feeling sorry for yourself and see that you have an amazing child, diagnosis or no diagnosis. He's the best kid I've ever known.'

At this, her voice quivers and I quickly change the subject, because thinking about how much she misses Alfie makes me hate myself.

She puts another bit of kindling on the fire. 'By the way, just so you know, I'm moving.'

It feels like I'm on a free-falling rollercoaster. Despite the fact I don't see her any more, the thought of her moving away is intolerable.

'Where are you going?'

'South Devon. I need a change.'

'But . . . I don't want you to go.'

Emily sighs. 'I never see you, Jake. Why does it make any difference if I'm around the corner or a hundred-odd miles away?'

'Because I still want to see you. It wasn't my choice, remember?'

'Wasn't it?'

'I told you I still wanted to be friends, Em. I didn't want to cut you out of our lives.'

Emily runs her hand through her hair. She's let it grow again and, looking at her now, I can't believe it took me so long to realize how stunning she is.

'You don't get it, do you? The fact that you could just be friends makes me realize . . .' She shakes her head. 'Forget it. I'm going to go and say goodbye to Jemma. Tell Alfie that I miss him, will you? Actually, just let him forget me, if that's easier for him.'

She stands up to leave but I block her way. Not clear about my intentions, I lean my face towards hers so that the tips of our noses touch, like magnets. But then it's like she flips the magnet over as she takes a step back.

'Take care, Jake.'

'He can't forget you, Em. That's the problem.'

Emily gives me this look, like she can't find the words that she's searching for, then turns and walks back up the garden towards the house. Through the kitchen window, I catch a glimpse of Jemma watching us before she turns away.

* * *

'I think maybe it would be better if Emily doesn't come over again.'

I'm washing the dishes and don't turn around.

'I think it would be less disruptive for Alfie,' Jemma continues. 'Less confusing.'

I nod, knowing full well it has nothing to do with Alfie's needs. 'She's moving away, anyway.'

'Oh, right. Where?'

'South Devon, apparently. So you don't need to worry; we won't be seeing her again.'

As I say it, I feel a pressure behind my eyes and I'm glad that I'm not facing Jemma.

'Probably for the best. Anyway, why don't you leave the rest of that stuff until the morning? Shall we go up to bed and watch something?'

The thought of another night lying next to each other but barely touching, both trying to convince ourselves that it's going to get better but knowing deep down that it's not – I don't think I can stand it. I'm so sick of it all. Of hurting people. Of feeling guilty all the time.

I turn around, dry my hands on a tea towel and gesture for Jemma to come and sit beside me on the bar stools. She does, looking both nervous and weary, her eyes noticeably missing the twinkle they used to have when we first met.

'Are you happy, Jem? In this house? This marriage? Honestly?'

I know that she's not. That neither of us are. That the sad truth is we're not what each other needs any more.

'Of course I am . . .' Then she stops, sighs deeply and puts her head in her hands, her elbows propped up on the worktop. 'No. But I should be. I love you and Alfie so much. Why doesn't all this make me happy?'

When Jemma looks up, she has tears in her eyes and I move my stool closer to hers and put my arm around her shoulder.

'I don't know. But it's not like we haven't tried, is it?'

She slips out from under my arm and looks me straight in the eyes. 'Are you happy?'

I look down and shake my head, such a tiny movement saying something so huge.

'So what now?'

'I don't know.'

Considering the technical details of Jemma and I splitting up makes me feel sick. Whenever I've thought about it, it's just been this ethereal idea. I've not contemplated the nuts and bolts of it – the living arrangements, the money, the belongings. There's so much stuff to sort out when you've been married a long time. It's not like when breaking up just meant deleting a number off your mobile phone. And then, of course, there's Alfie.

'I'll move in with Mum and Dad until we can sort something more permanent,' Jemma says, suddenly sitting up tall like she's organizing particulars in a business meeting.

'I can move out. You stay here with Alfie.'

Jemma shakes her head. 'We both know he's better off with you.'

'You're a wonderful mum, Jem. Don't ever think otherwise.'

Jemma nods, but I can tell she's mentally pushing the words away, not allowing them to ruin the brave face she's putting on. 'I'm sorry, but I'd like to go back to work full-time. Lots of the women at work have nannies so I can get some recommendations.'

'Sure. We'll sort something out.'

'He can come and stay with me whenever he wants, but it's probably best to put something more concrete in place. Some kind of timetable.'

'OK.'

I just want the conversation over and done with. In fact, part of me wants to rewind it and just lie, because surely you can't end up regretting staying with the person you chose to spend your life with, but there's a huge, terrifying chance that you might regret leaving them.

'I'll go and start packing a bag. I'll talk to Alfie in the morning.'

'There's no rush, Jem. Stay here as long as you need.'

Jemma stands up. 'I think it's for the best.'

For a moment, she doesn't move, and I wonder if she wants me to beg her to stay, but I let her go. 'OK.'

* * *

On my way to our room, I take my nightly detour to check Alfie's OK. Peering through the gap in the doorway, I see Jemma lying next to him, her arm draped across his waist.

When she hears me, she looks up. 'Come and join me for a minute?'

I lie on the other side of Alfie, place my arm next to Jemma's, across Alfie's tummy, and watch how his eyelashes flutter as he sleeps.

'I don't want him to be from a broken home, Jem.'

'I know. Me neither.'

But even as I say it, I know that he is. It's been broken for a long time. Long before Jemma left for Paris, long before everything with Emily.

'We'll make sure he knows how much we love him, Jake. He'll have more love. Not less.'

I hope she's right. I hope we can put the pieces of our family back together, but just in a different way, like shards of clay made into a mosaic. It's not the way I pictured it but that doesn't mean it can't be beautiful.

* * *

'So what are you going to do about work?' Dad wraps his hands around his beer as we sit across from each other at a very small table at the local pub.

'I don't know. Jemma's talking about finding another nanny. They've offered me a permanent job at school when the maternity leave runs out, but I'm not sure whether or not to take it.'

'I think you should. I think work's been good for you.'

He's right. It has. But I still feel like I'm letting Alfie, and Mum, down if I go back permanently.

'I don't know. I always thought it was better for Alfie having me there, but watching Emily with him, I'm not sure I was ever very good at it anyway. I'm certainly no Mum.'

Dad waves his hand. 'Don't be so hard on yourself. You know, often I'd get home from work and your mum would be tearing her hair out. She'd give me a look like thunder, hand you straight over to me and go and lock herself in her bedroom for an hour before she could face coming out again. And you were pretty easy, as kids go.'

'Really? I don't remember that.'

'Of course you don't. You remember all the wonderful stuff she did with you, the fact she loved the bones of you. And that's just how Alfie will remember you.'

I just about manage to get the words out. 'Thanks, Dad.'

'Why can't that Emily do it again, anyway? Alfie loved having her looking after him. Every week when you were at your class, he'd go on and on about her.'

'She's moving away.'

'Oh.' There's something about Dad's expression that makes me think he's aware of more than he's letting on. 'Well, you'll find someone else to do it. Don't give up the job, Jake. You were there for the most important years of his life. It's not going to do him any harm.'

I take a sip of my beer, then put it back down on the table, feeling a huge weight pressing down on me that I need to remove. 'I feel like I've messed everything up, Dad. My child. My marriage. Alfie has enough to deal with without Jemma and me splitting up. I've failed everyone.'

'Of course you haven't. Some marriages end. It's not your fault. It's not Jemma's. It just didn't work out how you wanted it to.'

'But why not? I meant my vows when I made them. We promised we'd stand by each other. I'm sure you and Mum went through hard times, but you stuck at it.'

Dad finishes his pint, wiping the foam off his top lip with the back of his hand and shaking his head. 'I didn't stay with your mum because I'd made a promise to her, Jake. I stayed with her because she made me happy. She was my best friend. She was stubborn as a mule sometimes and, God, she'd argue black was white, but I was a better version of myself when I was with her.'

It's almost more than I can bear to look at him, the pain in his eyes is so intense, and I can't help thinking about Emily and how I've lost her and how it's all my fault and how I wish there was a way I could put it right.

Dad gathers his wallet and keys and unhooks his coat from the back of his chair, as if he feels he's revealed too much and needs to get away. 'Right, I suppose we should be getting back.'

I finish my pint, put the glass down and pick up my phone. 'You know, I wish every day that Alfie had got to meet her. He would've adored her.'

Dad stands up and puts on his coat. 'But you know neither of us would've got a look in then, don't you? She would've been so besotted with that boy.'

I smile, standing up and tucking in my chair, then Dad holds out his hand for me to shake.

Without considering how he might react, I bypass his hand and wrap my arms around him. At first, he's stiff; it's like hugging a mannequin, and I worry that it's a step too far, but then his arms tighten around me too and I'm so glad I took the plunge.

Emily

The flat looks all right in the pictures. When I called, they said it needed 'a bit of work', which I know is estate-agent code for 'it's a dump', but it looks spacious enough and it has a bit of outdoor space at the front where I could put a table and chairs. Plus it's ten minutes drive from the sea, so I have this romantic image of going for a run along the beach every morning, picturing myself as one of the women in *Big Little Lies*. The reality is, unlike them, I'll be running into the pelting rain day after day, but it's good to dream. With the photography business, I can work anywhere, and hopefully, if I can build my client base down there, I can say goodbye to the joys of servitude forever. It's for the best. The pros list far outweighs the cons.

I finish packing my case – my essentials, enough clothes to last me the week, my camera, a few DVDs and a book. The plan is to go down and spend a week in a B&B, check out the flat and get a flavour of what it's like to live there. Then, as long as I like it, I'll hand in my notice on my flat here.

I have one last straighten, pick up my things and head out. As soon as I step into the hallway, I notice the large envelope on the floor. It just says *Emily* on the front, no address. Unable to leave without finding out what's inside, I go back into my flat, sit on the sofa and open it. Inside is a memory stick. I retrieve my laptop from my bag and insert it. I see it's a movie file. I swallow hard and double click.

The backdrop is a picture of the Brooklyn Bridge. Jake's clearly drawn the outline and, from the rough pen strokes, I can see that Alfie has coloured it in. The Green Goblin enters the shot with Gwen Stacy attached to him with string. Then there's Alfie's voice in imitation bad guy: 'I've got you, Gwen Stacy. I'm never letting you go.' Then Jake, a high-pitched squeak: 'Spidey, Spidey, help me!' Spider-Man swings in from stage left and then he and the Green Goblin engage in a huge battle, Jake and Alfie's hands visible as they smash the plastic figures together again and again, Alfie giggling in the background.

Alfie puts Gwen Stacy in the Green Goblin's fist and then launches her so that it looks like she is being thrown from the bridge. In the next shot, suddenly Gwen Stacy is in Spider-Man's arms. Then the figures' faces are pushed together, accompanied by a loud and comical kiss sound effect, followed by tinned applause.

Without realizing it, I've started to smile. But then I notice the time in the corner of the screen. I've got to go. My appointment with the estate agent is in a few hours and I might hit traffic. I return my laptop to its case, slip the memory stick back into the envelope and stuff that in with the laptop. I pick up all my things and race to the car.

I head south on the motorway, speeding straight into the fast lane, the film going round and round in my head. What does it mean? Is it from Alfie? Or is Jake trying to tell me something? And if so, what? That he's sorry? That he wishes he hadn't hurt me?

I'm in no fit state to drive so I pull over at the services

and park up. Without thinking, I reach into the glove compartment for my half-drunk bottle of vodka and take a swig, shuddering at the taste. I'm not sure why I left it there when I detoxed the house. I'd like to say I forgot about it, but I didn't. I just couldn't bring myself to get rid of it. I think I always felt that I'd never really escape being a fuck-up. That I could play the part of someone clean-living and successful, but that ultimately, no matter how far or how fast I run, I'll always end up right back where I started. Maybe I was right?

I take my laptop out of my bag and retrieve the envelope. I need to watch the film again. I need to try to make sense of it. But as I put my hand in to pull out the memory stick, I feel another smaller envelope that I didn't notice before. I take it out, open it and inside there's two of Alfie's treasured Lego Minifigures stuck to a piece of paper. Next to Spider-Man, Jake's drawn an arrow and labelled it *Me*, and next to Gwen Stacy he's drawn an arrow and labelled it *You*. I can't help but smile. Then there's another piece of paper – a note in Jake's handwriting.

I wish I'd caught you.

As the words sink in, it's like every fibre of my being starts to break down, my body shaking violently with the force of the tears falling down my nose, into my mouth, off my chin. I catch a glimpse of myself in the rear-view mirror – my face a mixture of Mum and Dad, and even a bit of Nan around the eyes. It feels like there's so much darkness in my past, I'm not sure I can ever be free of it. Will this thing with Jake just turn black, like everything else? What if the things Jemma said were true? That Jake jumps into stuff without thinking. That, after the novelty wears off, he'll leave and break my heart again. I'm not sure I could cope with it. But then, isn't it broken anyway, sitting here alone, trying to pretend I'm not missing them, running to somewhere I know no one in the hope of finding something I might already have?

I pull the Gwen Stacy figure off the paper and rub my thumb across it, picturing Alfie putting it into the envelope, panicking about whether it would be safe, would I get it, would he eventually get it back. I re-read Jake's note, open the car door and pour the vodka out on to the tarmac. Once it's all gone, I throw the empty bottle on the passenger seat, start up the car and turn around. It's time to go home. Because, for the first time in my life, I think I might really have one.

Alfie

They say I have PDA and a little bit of OCD. I'm not sure why they have funny letter names instead of real names – they don't even spell anything. Maybe the person who came up with them wasn't very clever. I'm really clever. In my spelling test, I only got one wrong. I had to put it on the Marvellous Mistakes board. I don't really think it's marvellous but at school they say that's how you learn, and I *have* learnt my marvellous mistake word now so maybe they're right. It's t, r, e, a, s, u, r, e and it spells 'treasure'. The first time I put s, h because it sounds like there's a 'sh' in the middle. Tre-sh-ur. But I know now that it's not.

Emily says what the funny letter names mean is that I have a superhero brain so it works a bit differently to the other children's and that's why I get sad if people don't follow my rules or if they make me do things that I don't want to. And the OCD bully is the one that puts the horrible thoughts in my brain, like when my brain says I want to kill my friends or Mummy or Daddy. I used to think that I really thought those things and that I belonged in prison, but the OCD lady that I see after school on a Tuesday says it's just the OCD bully and I have to tell him to go away. Sometimes, she lets me pretend the cushion on the chair is the OCD bully and I'm allowed to punch him. I like it when she says I can do that. It's really fun.

After school, Mummy is picking me up because it's a Mummy weekend. That means I stay at Mummy's new house. The rest of the time I stay at my real home. I like Mummy's house because she has a huge fish tank with three fish and she lets me feed them, and I was allowed to name them. There's Zippy, because he's fast, Orange, because he's orange, and Fishy, because, well, because he's a fish, of course.

I prefer my real house, though, because all my stuff is there, like all my Lego models and my real bed and Daddy is there and Emily helps me make Lego films all the time. The film we are making at the moment is a Ninjago one. Daddy's annoyed that I've moved on from superheroes but I still like superheroes too; I just like ninjas better at the moment. Emily always laughs at Daddy when he gets grumpy and then he laughs too and then I laugh so we're all laughing. It's really funny.

If I could choose, I would have Daddy and Emily and Mummy living in my real house, but Daddy said that he and Mummy are happier when they don't live in the same house and just see each other as friends. I think he might be right because him and Mummy have happy faces more now and I still see Mummy lots because she comes over even when it's not a Mummy weekend and takes me to really fun places, like the park or the cinema or McDonald's, where you actually get a toy with your food.

Emily is taking me back to Legoland next weekend. Daddy kept saying, 'Do we have to go again?' and moaning that it's too expensive, but Emily said he could go surfing and she would take me as a special treat, so we booked it on the computer. She takes photos for her job now so she has a bit more money for things like that. Now that I've got the funny letter names, we get a special pass for Legoland that means I don't have to queue. It's awesome. Emily says it's because I'm super-special and unique, which means it's a good thing not being like other children. I wonder if Emily has PDA and OCD, because she's unique too and not like other grown-ups. She's not my nanny any more. She still takes me to school and picks me up and looks after me, but it's not her job now. She just does it because we're best bugs.

When I'm a grown-up, I'm still going to make Lego films, but I'm also going to be a magician. I know loads of tricks already, like making coins disappear and rabbits pop out of my hat. I can't fly just yet, but I will be able to soon. I just need to find the spell.

Acknowledgements

First and foremost, I have to thank my parents. Mum –
for filling my childhood with stories and creativity. I'm
convinced I wouldn't have become a writer if it weren't
for you. You are forever an inspiration. Dad – for being
the kind of dad who wanted to listen to love songs and
watch romcoms with me (and who wasn't embarrassed
to shed a tear at the end). You're the reason I write what I
write! I lucked out to have you both as my parents. You've
always been there for me, believed in me and been proud
of me, no matter what. A million thank yous would never
be enough but I hope you know that I am so grateful for
everything you have done and continue to do for me.

To the Curtis Brown Creative team – your belief in me is
the reason I finally finished this book after years of crip-
pling self-doubt. To my wonderful tutor, Lisa O'Donnell,
for constantly pushing me to be better and for helping me
to find my voice. To all my course members for your
insightful comments. Looking forward to seeing your books
being published in the near future.

To my first readers – my very close friends, Alice and
Vikki; my parents and my sister, Emily. Thank you for
putting up with this novel in its raw stages and for telling
me it was great when it really wasn't.

To my agent, Alice Lutyens, for 'getting' my story from
the outset, for your help shaping it into the book it is
today, for putting up with all of my neurotic emails and

always making me laugh at the end of it. I knew when I signed with you I'd be getting an amazing agent, but I didn't realize I'd also be gaining a friend.

To my editor, Tilda McDonald – for loving Emily, Jake and Alfie as much as I do, and for your intelligent and gentle approach to editing that somehow helps me to find the answers to questions I didn't even realize I needed to address, and for allowing me to achieve things I never thought possible. To Emma Horton for making the copy-edit process such a breeze (and teaching me about the correct use of the hyphen!) and to the rest of the team at Michael Joseph who have worked so hard to get this book to as many readers as possible.

To my husband, Carl – for not moaning (too much) when the house is a mess because I've been writing all day, and for always supporting me. I know I don't say it enough but I am so lucky to have found you.

To my eldest son, Jacob – for so many of Alfie's wonderful words. I never realized how hard, but also how utterly amazing, parenting could be until I had you. You constantly fascinate me and challenge me to be a better person. 'Best bugs' forever. And to my youngest son, Dylan – for filling every day with sunshine, cuddles and giggles. You see the world in such a beautiful way that it makes it all the more beautiful for me too. I hope seeing me following my dreams shows you both that you can achieve yours.

And last but not least, to you, the reader – for your support in reading my book. It is such a privilege to be able to share my words with you. I hope you enjoyed it!

**If you enjoyed *Saturdays at Noon*,
we'd love to hear from you!**

Leave a review online, or tweet @Rache1Marks
using #SaturdaysatNoon – and look out for
news of the next book from Rachel Marks,
coming soon . . .

He just wanted a decent book to read ...

Not too much to ask, is it? It was in 1935 when Allen Lane, Managing Director of Bodley Head Publishers, stood on a platform at Exeter railway station looking for something good to read on his journey back to London. His choice was limited to popular magazines and poor-quality paperbacks – the same choice faced every day by the vast majority of readers, few of whom could afford hardbacks. Lane's disappointment and subsequent anger at the range of books generally available led him to found a company – and change the world.

'We believed in the existence in this country of a vast reading public for intelligent books at a low price, and staked everything on it'
Sir Allen Lane, 1902–1970, founder of Penguin Books

The quality paperback had arrived – and not just in bookshops. Lane was adamant that his Penguins should appear in chain stores and tobacconists, and should cost no more than a packet of cigarettes.

Reading habits (and cigarette prices) have changed since 1935, but Penguin still believes in publishing the best books for everybody to enjoy. We still believe that good design costs no more than bad design, and we still believe that quality books published passionately and responsibly make the world a better place.

So wherever you see the little bird – whether it's on a piece of prize-winning literary fiction or a celebrity autobiography, political tour de force or historical masterpiece, a serial-killer thriller, reference book, world classic or a piece of pure escapism – you can bet that it represents the very best that the genre has to offer.

Whatever you like to read – trust Penguin.